The Missing Wife

By Sheila O'Flanagan

Suddenly Single
Far From Over
My Favourite Goodbye
He's Got To Go
Isobel's Wedding
Caroline's Sister
Too Good To Be True
Dreaming Of A Stranger
Destinations
Anyone But Him
How Will I Know?
Connections
Yours, Faithfully
Bad Behaviour
Someone Special
The Perfect Man
Stand By Me
A Season To Remember
All For You
Better Together
Things We Never Say
If You Were Me
My Mother's Secret
The Missing Wife

Sheila
O'Flanagan

The Missing Wife

First published in Great Britain in 2016
by HEADLINE REVIEW
An imprint of HEADLINE PUBLISHING GROUP

1

Cataloguing in Publication Data is available from the British Library

ISBN 978 1 4722 1076 0 (Hardback)
ISBN 978 1 4722 1077 7 (Trade paperback)

Typeset in ITC Galliard by Palimpsest Book Production Limited, Falkirk, Stirlingshire

Printed and bound in Great Britain by Clays Ltd St Ives plc

Headline's policy is to use papers that are natural, renewable and recyclable products and made from wood grown in well-managed forests and other controlled sources. The logging and manufacturing processes are expected to conform to the environmental regulations of the country of origin.

Acknowledgements

As always I have to thank Carole Blake, Marion Donaldson and Breda Purdue – my agent, my editor and the MD of Hachette Ireland – three strong women who have been with me for most of my publishing career and who have saved me from myself on more than one occasion.

Thanks also to Jane Selley, who copy-edits with such dedication and who somehow manages to refrain from writing pointed notes in the margins when I make the same stupid mistake over and over! And thanks to Team Hachette/Headline around the world for always being so supportive – with a special mention to Abbie and Fran for such amazing work on my behalf this year.

Special thanks to my translators and overseas publishers who bring a smile to my face when I see all of your wonderful editions of my books.

Merci beaucoup to Derí Molyneux and Séverine Lefeuvre for checking the French.

The inscription above the library at Thebes in ancient Egypt said it offered 'medicine for the soul', which is a wonderful description of the joy that books bring to us. Thank you to librarians and booksellers everywhere for the work they do in ensuring that we all have the right medicine!

Of course I can't thank you, my readers, enough for buying my books and for getting in touch with me on social media to talk about them. You are an amazing group of people and I'm lucky to have you all in my corner.

And finally, to Colm and to the rest of my family, thank you for being so supportive of all my book stuff. But thank you even more for the non-book stuff too!

Chapter 1

Standing in the line of passengers boarding the intercity coach, Imogen started to panic. A cold sweat dampened the back of her white cotton blouse and she froze on the spot, wedged behind a tall man in a brightly coloured Madiba shirt and an impatient Parisian woman who'd been checking her watch every five minutes for the past half an hour. The woman made a disapproving sound, indicating that she should get a move on, but Imogen stayed where she was, on the bottom step of the coach, clutching the handrail, unable to move.

'*S'il vous plaît*,' said the woman through clenched teeth.

'I'm sorry.' Imogen moved to one side. 'Go ahead.'

The woman pushed her way past, followed by the remainder of the passengers, while Imogen remained at the doorway, unsure of whether or not to board.

'Madame?' The driver looked at her enquiringly.

'Yes,' she said hesitantly. 'Yes. I'm . . . I'm getting on now.'

But she could hear his words in her head.

What on earth d'you think you're doing? You can't manage on your own. You'll make a mess of it. You always do.

She shut him out. He was wrong. She wasn't going to make a mess of it. Because she had a Plan.

Don't make a complete fool of yourself. It was his voice again as her hand tightened on the handrail.

She wouldn't make a fool of herself if she stuck to the Plan. It was foolproof. Hopefully. And she'd already successfully carried out the start of it. There was no need to doubt herself about the rest. Besides, she thought, it's too late to back out now.

It's never too late.

This time the words were her mother's, one of the many clichés she'd liked to use on a daily basis. But in this case, they were true. It wasn't too late. She could still walk away without too much collateral damage. Whatever problems that might arise from her actions could be fixed. She could find a way to explain them.

But going back and trying to make excuses wasn't why she was here now. It wasn't why she'd spent so long refining the Plan. Nevertheless, she had a choice. Go forward, or go back. She reminded herself that this was the chance she'd been waiting for. Her first opportunity to execute the Plan. How would she feel if she let it slip away?

She took a deep breath and began to climb the steps.

The coach was comfortable and air-conditioned, which was a pleasant relief after the unexpected humidity of the June day. The exhibition hall had been hot and crowded, and she'd spent a lot of time wishing she'd worn something lighter than the navy wool business suit Vince had told her was appropriate for her business trip to France. But whenever she'd broken out in a sweat that morning, she'd been unsure if it was because of the suit, or because she was worrying about what she was intending to do and the way she was going to do it.

She walked down the aisle of the coach. Having let so many people board ahead of her, her choice of seat was limited. She slid into the first one available, beside a long-legged young man with earbuds in his ears who was busy scrolling through playlists on his phone. A student, Imogen decided, as she glanced at his stubbled cheeks, logoed T-shirt and ripped jeans. She felt a pang of nostalgia for her own student years, even though she wouldn't have considered them to have been typical. Unlike many of her peers, she hadn't wanted to travel or have assorted life experiences. She'd wanted to put down roots. Her own roots in her own place instead of somewhere decided for her by someone else. That had been very important to her. Unfortunately.

She gave the young man a brief smile, but he was far too busy with his phone to notice.

The driver put the coach into gear and it moved slowly away from the station.

A few minutes later, they turned towards the Boulevard Périphérique and Imogen's phone buzzed.

She counted to ten before she looked at the text.

Are you at the airport? she read.

On the way now, she replied.

How long?

She looked at the facades of the buildings around her as the coach driver waited for the lights to turn red. They were mainly office blocks of glass and steel. They could have been anywhere in the world.

Twenty minutes.

Text me when you arrive.

OK.

Love you.

She hesitated before sending her reply. *Love you too :)*

She saw a sign for the airport as they moved forward again. The coach gathered speed, then turned in the opposite direction. She exhaled slowly. The student beside her was still absorbed in his music. Imogen stared out of the window. When the coach passed an exit marked 'Disneyland', she sent another text.

At airport, it said. *Phone battery about to die. Talk later.* This time she didn't add a smiley face.

She picked up her handbag from beneath the seat in front of her and opened it. Then she slid her engagement and wedding rings from her finger and dropped them into the bag. After that, she took a hair clip from a small bundle in one of the side pockets and used it to pop out the SIM card holder on the phone. She took the card from the cradle and held it between her teeth while she closed the phone again. As she bit down hard on it, she realised that the student had begun to watch her.

'You'll damage it,' he said in French as he removed one of the buds from his ears.

'I know,' she said in the same language once she'd taken the card from her mouth.

She balanced it between her thumb and forefinger and began to squeeze. After a while, the SIM card started to bend. She kept the pressure on until it had doubled over and the tiny metallic bands had cracked. The student shrugged. Imogen sat back in her seat and stared straight ahead.

* * *

Vince Naughton always had a plan. He liked to have his day scheduled and he hated being taken by surprise. Years earlier, at one of those corporate think-ins and staff bonding days, which he thought were a total waste of time, a colleague had called him controlling. Irritated by her snap assessment, Vince had said that he wasn't controlling but he did like to be in control, a comment that resulted in a round of applause from the group and left his colleague looking embarrassed. A few months later, Vince had been promoted and she'd left the company, which made him feel vindicated. It was good to know how things were supposed to pan out, he thought. And good to ensure that they did.

Which was why, when he turned into the car park at the hotel in Cork, he was within ten minutes of the arrival time he'd set himself – the ten minutes was to allow for the unexpected. Vince believed in allowing for the unexpected. It was why he was one of the company's better associates. He thought of every eventuality. Very few things ever surprised him. He planned for the worst and hoped for the best. It had served him well all his life.

He parked the car, checked in at reception and went to his room. He'd specified a first-floor room if possible, and he was pleased that the conference organisers had met his request, although the room itself overlooked the car park instead of the river, which he would have preferred. Nevertheless, everything else was fine: the Wi-Fi worked, there were tea- and coffee-making facilities, and the TV was a modern flat-screen on the wall.

He sat on the bed and sent a text.

Arrived on time. Room OK. Text me when you're home.

Then he left the phone on the bed and went into the bathroom to have a shower.

According to the bus timetable, the journey would take more than eleven hours. There were, of course, infinitely quicker ways to travel from Paris to the south-west of France than by road (although if she'd driven herself, Imogen knew she could easily have cut the time in half). A flight would have taken less than ninety minutes, but catching a flight meant having to give your name and credit card details, and she hadn't wanted to do that. The train would have been the best option of them all, given how superb the French rail system was, and would have had the added advantage of taking her exactly where she wanted to be. However, although she might have been able to buy a ticket without having to reserve it, she felt sure there were plenty of CCTV cameras throughout the marble concourse of the ultra-modern Montparnasse station, and she didn't want to be caught by any of them. She'd watched too many news reports with grainy images of unsuspecting people going about their daily business not to know that public places were hotbeds of CCTV surveillance. She realised that it was possible she'd been caught on camera buying the coach ticket too. But she didn't think so. Besides, nobody would have expected her to take a bus. That was why it was part of the Plan.

It began to rain as they arrived at their first stop, four hours into the journey. Imogen dodged the languid, heavy drops as she hurried into the service station and made her way to the ladies'. In the cubicle, she took the battery out of her phone and threw it into a red plastic bin. At their next stop, another four hours later, she disposed of the phone itself in a blue bin near the coach park. It was the first time in more than fifteen years that she hadn't had a mobile phone, and it was a strange sensation. Even though the phone had been useless without the SIM and then the battery, it had been a part of her. Now it was gone. She wanted to feel that everything it signified was gone too, but the truth was that she wasn't feeling anything at all. Other than apprehensive. Or maybe just scared.

When she got back on to the coach, the student was playing a game on his own mobile, his fingers tapping urgently at the screen. He looked up as Imogen settled herself in her seat and gave her a faint smile before turning back to the game.

She was pretty sure that she'd received more texts by now.

Are you home yet?

Where are you?

And then perhaps the voice message.

'Haven't you charged your damn phone? Ring me.'

But she wouldn't be ringing. That was part of the Plan too. And because she'd destroyed her phone, she had to stick to it.

She held her hands out in front of her. They were shaking.

The student finished playing his game and took the buds from his ears. He turned to Imogen and asked if he could get by her so that he could take his rucksack from the rack. She stood up while he got his bag and rummaged around in it. Then he slid back into his seat and she sat down again. He lowered the plastic tray in front of him and put a bottle of water and a triple-decker sandwich wrapped in cling film on it. He had other food too – a KitKat, a chocolate muffin and a couple of bananas. He offered one of the bananas to Imogen.

'No thank you.' They continued to speak in French.

'Are you sure?' he asked. '*Maman* packed all this for me. I like my food, but two bananas is one too many.'

'It's good of you to offer,' said Imogen. 'But I'm not hungry.'

'Fair enough.' He unwrapped the sandwich and took a large bite.

Imogen tried not to look at him. Without a phone or a magazine to distract her, it was hard to stare straight ahead.

'Do you mind me asking why you trashed your SIM card?' he asked when he'd finished the sandwich.

She hesitated before replying. 'I wanted to get away from it all.'

'You could've simply switched the phone off.'

'It's not the same.'

'A bit drastic nonetheless.' He grinned at her.

'But at least I know I can't be tempted by it,' she said.

He nodded and turned his attention to the muffin. It disappeared in two bites and he spoke again.

'Are you on holiday?' he asked.

'Um . . . sort of,' she said. 'I was working and now I have some time off.'

'Cool,' said the student. 'I've got summer work in a vineyard.'

'That'll be fun.' Imogen's plan hadn't included talking to anyone, because she hadn't anticipated casual conversation with random strangers. She wasn't used to it. Besides, she'd wanted to remain anonymous, forgettable. But it was an unexpectedly welcome distraction. Anyhow, the student was doing most of the talking. All she needed to do was nod a few times.

'What's your name?' he asked, during a pause.

'Imo . . . gen,' she mumbled.

'Nice to meet you, Jen,' he said, apparently unfazed by her hesitation over what was a simple question. 'I'm Henri.'

She didn't correct him.

He talked a lot. He was twenty years old and studying environmental sciences at Orléans University, and he was interested in winemaking and viniculture. The previous year he'd travelled to California to visit the vineyards there, which had been great, he said, but he was looking forward to Bayonne. Would she like to meet up for a coffee?

She couldn't remember the last time she'd smiled with genuine amusement, but she did now. Henri was at least ten years younger than her, but he was happily hitting on her. Which was sort of flattering, she supposed, if very French.

'I'm sorry,' she said. 'I won't be staying in Bayonne. I'm travelling further.'

'*Dommage*,' he said. 'It would have been nice to have coffee with you. But perhaps another time? Where are you from?'

'Provence.' She'd lived near Marseille when she was small.

'My family holidayed in Cannes once,' said Henri. 'But I don't remember very much of it.'

'It's a nice town,' Imogen said. 'Though very bling-bling.'

He laughed at the English words. And she smiled again.

It was midnight when they finally pulled into the terminus, near the train station in the Aquitaine city of Bayonne. It had stopped raining about an hour previously and the sky was completely clear. Imogen sat in her seat while everyone around her stood up. She'd felt herself relax talking to Henri, but suddenly her hands were shaking again. She'd been protected for the last eleven hours, cocooned from the rest of the world as the bus made its way through the country. Now she had to step outside and face it all once more. And she was having to do it on her own. There was nobody to organise her, to tell her what to do. Nobody to help with the Plan.

'Excuse me, Jen.' Henri, who'd fallen asleep a little while earlier, had been roused by the activity and was ready to get off.

'Yes. Sorry,' she said, standing up. 'Enjoy the vineyards.'

'Enjoy your break. If you come back to Bayonne, please call me.'

'No phone,' she reminded him.

'I'm at the Bernard Noble,' he said. 'Look me up.'

She knew she wouldn't.

She followed him off the bus and waved as he walked away, his rucksack on his back. She waited while the driver took the rest of the luggage from the storage area. Her silver-grey case was one of the last to be retrieved. She picked it up and looked around her. Beyond the car park, the surrounding buildings were typically French, their warm brick illuminated by street lights, wrought-iron balconies at their shuttered windows.

She'd memorised the location of the hostel where she hoped to stay, and so, after taking a moment to orientate herself, she crossed the road and walked down a narrow side street. At the corner, she could see the dark green canopy over the door, embossed with the name. She hesitated when she reached it. She'd never stayed in a hostel before. Not having done the student travel thing.

She pushed open the glass door, which was set into a brick surround. The interior of the building was clean and renovated, with a black and white tiled floor and exposed walls decorated with iron sculptures. A middle-aged woman was seated behind a small reception area, engrossed in a book. She didn't look up until Imogen stood in front of her and cleared her throat.

'Can I help you?'

'Um . . .'

You can't manage without me.

Imogen whirled around, convinced he was standing behind her. But there was no one there.

'*Mademoiselle?*'

You'll fail. You know you will.

'I . . . I'm looking for a room.'

She realised that she was waiting for the woman to ask her why she'd turned up so late at night. And why she was on her own instead of with him. And where she was planning to go. And what she planned to do. And . . .

'For how many nights?' The woman sounded bored.

'Just one.' Her voice was barely above a whisper. She cleared her throat and spoke a little louder as she repeated herself. 'Just one.'

The woman took an electronic key from the desk, coded it and handed it to her.

'*Premier étage, mademoiselle,*' she said.

Imogen wondered if it was fetching up at a hostel that had turned her from a *madame* to a *mademoiselle* again. She glanced at the bare finger on her left hand before starting up the stairs with her bag. She stopped outside the door of room 14. The card didn't work the first time.

You can't manage without me.

She dropped the key and it slithered along the corridor. It took her a while to pick it up because it kept sliding out of her grip. When she finally had it in her trembling fingers, she inserted it into the lock again the right way up. The light turned green and the door opened.

The room was better than she'd expected. The walls were painted pale cream, brightened by some framed floral prints. The single bed was surprisingly firm. There was a net curtain at the long window, which led out to a tiny balcony overlooking the street. The window also had a pair of green-painted shutters, which Imogen pulled closed. Apart from the bed, the only furniture was a tall, narrow wardrobe, with interior shelving. A full-length mirror was on the wall beside it. The en suite bathroom (the reason she'd picked the Hostel Auberge in the first place; whatever else, she wasn't going to share a bathroom) boasted a shower, toilet and hand basin. Two dark green towels hung on the rail beneath the sink. Though nothing was luxurious, it was impeccably clean.

It was also empty. She realised that she'd half expected to see him there, waiting for her. She sat down abruptly on the edge of the bed, a wave of relief washing over her. Her breath was coming in short gasps. She put her head between her knees, terrified that she was going to faint.

'I am a strong, capable woman,' she muttered to herself. 'I can look after myself.'

But she wasn't sure she believed it.

Chapter 2

He'd always told her that she was no good at planning, and that without him her life would be a chaotic mess. It was certainly true that she was the sort of person who hoped things would turn out for the best rather than ensuring they would by micro-managing every detail. But she'd micro-managed the Plan, which had been in the making for two years. Its main attribute was flexibility, so that she could take advantage of the first opportunity that presented itself. When it had, she'd been ready, because she'd gone over it a million times in her head before. But even as she'd packed her cabin bag – not caring that she had to leave so much behind – she hadn't really believed that she was actually doing it. She hadn't trusted herself to carry it out because she'd mislaid the part of her that made her own decisions and she wasn't sure if she'd be able to find it again.

Vince had dropped her at Dublin airport and told her to enjoy herself, even though he'd been unhappy about her going in the first place.

'I have to,' she told him when he remarked that it seemed a waste of her time. 'It's my job.'

'It wasn't your job last year,' he pointed out.

'Last year Conor hadn't broken his wrist,' she said. 'He could take photos and notes at the fair himself. It's different this time.'

'I don't see why it has to be you.'

'Because I'm his PA,' she reminded him.

'Surely that means you should be holding the fort for him back at the office?'

'I'll be doing that from Paris on the mobile.'

'I don't like you going without me,' he said. 'Especially not with a man who isn't your husband.'

'Don't be silly!' It was important to hide her anxiety, so she kept her tone light and cheery. 'I could hardly bring you with me, and nothing's going to happen between me and Conor. He's married, for heaven's sake!'

'And that shows how naive you are,' Vince said. 'Being married won't stop him from propositioning you in a warehouse.'

'We won't be in any warehouses,' she said. 'We'll be at the exhibition hall the whole time.'

'Or propositioning you in the hotel.'

'If he does – and I think that's highly unlikely – I'll remind him of his marital responsibilities,' said Imogen.

She knew that Vince wasn't satisfied. But there was nothing he could do about it. As she got out of the car, he asked her once again if she had her passport and her boarding card. 'You won't need much money,' he'd added. 'Everything will be on expenses.'

He got out and came around to the passenger side. 'Stay safe,' he said.

'Of course.'

'Call me if you need anything.'

'I won't need anything.'

'Well if you do, just call. It doesn't matter what time.'

'OK.'

'I love you.'

'I love you too.'

He kissed her.

When she glanced back after walking inside the terminal building, she could see him standing there, looking after her. But by the time she'd gone up the escalator to the departures area, he'd driven away.

She waited until she'd gone through security before finding a cash machine and withdrawing the maximum she could from their current account. Then she checked the balance on the other account. Her account. The one he didn't know about.

She'd made three transfers into it. Each of them was from the company she worked for, bonus payments from the head office in Paris. She'd managed to arrange with the Dublin accounts office to pay her bonuses separately. Annie Costigan, the company's accountant, had looked at her curiously.

'But we have your account details on file,' she said.

'That's our joint account,' Imogen explained. 'I want the bonus money to go to my personal account.'

'Why don't you get your salary paid to your personal account?' asked Annie. 'Then you could set up a transfer to the joint account . . .' Her voice trailed off as she saw the expression on Imogen's face.

'I'd rather have it this way,' Imogen said. 'Please, Annie.'

Annie hesitated, her fingers poised over her keyboard.

'Is everything all right at home, Imogen?' she asked.

'Of course it is.' Imogen spoke sharply. 'Absolutely. It's

just that . . . it's his birthday soon, and I want to surprise him with a gift. But I can't do that if he sees the information on the statement.'

'Oh.'

'And as for transferring my salary to my own account, I know I could do that, but we agreed to have a joint account for both our salaries so—'

'Fair enough,' said Annie. 'I'll set it up for you.'

'Thanks,' said Imogen.

She didn't get huge bonuses. PAs, even ones as dedicated as Conor said she was, never did. But it was enough to start her off. Enough to make the Plan more than just something to think about. Enough to carry it through. At least this far. She lay back on the bed and closed her eyes. Nearly there, she murmured. Nearly there.

At half past six the following morning, they snapped open again and she was wide awake. It took a moment for her to realise that she wasn't in Dublin. That she wasn't in Paris. That she really had done it. Adrenalin shot through her and she sat up, surprised to find that she was still wearing her navy suit. She didn't remember falling asleep in her clothes.

She opened the shutters, allowing a weak beam of morning light to filter through the net curtain. Then she got undressed, went into the bathroom and stood under the tepid shower, leaning to one side so that she didn't get her hair wet, because the Hostel Auberge didn't run to shower caps and it wasn't something she'd thought about. A hiccup in the Plan, she said to herself, but a minor one. She got out of the shower, dried herself with one of the thin green towels and walked back into the bedroom. She dressed in a plain T-shirt and faded jeans. Then she looked at herself in the mirror.

Her brown eyes were huge in her pale face. Her dark mocha hair had survived the shower and was curling gently under her ears. It was the hair that startled her the most. The day before, it had been long and luxuriant; the shining, tumbling tresses of a shampoo advertisement. Now it was a sleek bob, slightly shorter than shoulder length. Imogen hardly recognised herself. Which was a good thing, she told herself. Making herself unrecognisable was the reason she'd had it cut. Her Swarovski earrings – a twenty-first birthday present from her stepfather – were more visible with the new hairstyle. The tiny crystals glittered in the sunlight that was now beaming through the window.

She dabbed some tinted moisturiser on her face, which dealt with the pallor, then sprayed Nina Ricci perfume on her neck and wrists. After that, she folded her suit and put it in the suitcase. She thought about leaving it behind, but discounted the idea. Although it was unlikely, she might be remembered if she left clothes hanging in the wardrobe. Besides, if things worked out, she might need the suit for a job interview in the future. Having zipped up the case again, she put on her flat shoes and left the room.

It was a twenty-minute walk to the bus stop, but the next bus wasn't due for nearly an hour, so – in a random, unplanned moment – she sat down at a pavement café, which was already open and serving fragrant coffee and the hot, flaky croissants that tasted so different in France than anywhere else in the world. The coffee and croissants revived her, as did the summer sun, which was rising in the clear blue sky. In the distance, for the first time, Imogen saw the purple and green peaks of the Pyrenees.

She finished and paid for her breakfast and also bought a ticket for the bus. It was already at the stop when she arrived, and she hurried along the uneven pavement, worried in case she missed it. Even though there were other buses later in the day, it was important to stick to the Plan, to get it all exactly right. Getting everything right was her insurance policy. It proved that she could do it. It helped maintain the confidence that she struggled so hard to hold on to.

The other passengers were a mixture of old and young, commuters and other travellers. There were more students too, like Henri, laden down with rucksacks and engrossed in their mobile phones.

Imogen wondered what the messages on hers might be now.

What the hell is wrong with you? Why aren't you answering my texts?

Have you forgotten to charge your phone?

Tried ringing you. FFS, Imogen, you're hopeless!

*Gone to meeting. P**d off. Talk later.*

The journey on the bus, although not as comfortable as the coach, was still beautiful. Even the part through the streets of Bayonne before heading towards the coast was pretty. Imogen leaned her head against the window and gazed out at the deep blue of the Atlantic as the waves pounded the shore. Then the bus wended inland again, passing low rolling hills that reminded Imogen of Ireland before approaching the high mountains that were so very different. The houses were different too, resembling alpine chalets with their shallow sloping roofs and wide eaves. Imogen pictured them covered in snow. She'd lived in this area after they'd left Provence, but she didn't remember snow. She didn't remember as much as she'd like. She wondered if anything would be familiar when she arrived. But it didn't matter if it wasn't. She was looking to the future and leaving the past behind.

Nearly two hours after they'd set off, the bus finally entered the coastal town of Hendaye, nestling at the foot of the Pyrenees. At first glance, nothing seemed familiar there either, but it was a long time since Imogen had returned to the place she'd once called home. The truth was that her sense of home was fractured. She didn't know whether she should think of herself as Irish or English or French. She didn't know where she belonged. That was why roots had been so important to her.

Vince had made her feel as though she belonged with him, anchored and secure in Dublin. But she didn't feel that way any more. And that was why the reasons for leaving had finally outweighed the reasons for staying and she'd followed the Plan.

She'd chosen to come to the French Basque country because she'd been happy here and she'd always promised herself she'd return. But more importantly, she'd come because very few people actually knew that it had been part of her life. Whenever she talked about her time in France, she talked about Provence and Paris. She didn't mention Hendaye because people might ask why she and Carol had left, and that wasn't something she wanted to discuss. Provence and Paris were easier to explain. Besides, they were the places in France that most people knew.

The bus stopped near the train station. As she stepped on

to the pavement with her bag, Imogen told herself that Vince would have laughed at her train paranoia. In the warm sun of the Basque town, surrounded by chocolate-box scenery and houses, her fears of the past couple of days seemed totally unwarranted. Yet the coach and bus had been an important part of the Plan. And it had been comforting to follow it.

Chapter 3

Vince was more annoyed than worried that Imogen hadn't texted him the previous night as he'd asked her to. He'd checked the airline's app on his phone and discovered that her flight had been delayed and so hadn't arrived into Dublin until after midnight. He assumed she'd gone home, and, in the thoughtless fashion he'd tried so hard to cure her of, had stuck her mobile on the charger downstairs before heading straight to bed. He'd called her even though it was nearly 1 a.m. at that point, but it had gone straight to her voicemail. The message had annoyed him too: 'Hi, this is Imogen. I'm currently away at a business exhibition. Leave a message and I'll get back to you on my return.' It made her sound as though she was some high-flying executive instead of simply Conor Foley's dogsbody. And it wasn't as though washing machines and fridge freezers were very high-flying either. But he knew she liked to think of herself as an essential cog in the wheel of Chandon Leclerc, and she'd been excited about going to Paris even though he'd told her that business trips weren't all they were cracked up to be. He'd warned her that she'd be cooped up in the exhibition hall and wouldn't have time to visit her old haunts.

But she hadn't cared. She'd been fizzing with anticipation, though she'd calmed down quite a lot as the visit drew closer and had actually seemed nervous getting out of the car at the airport. Perhaps she'd learned her lesson, he thought, and wouldn't be looking to accompany her boss anywhere else in the future.

The same annoying voicemail had kicked in that morning when he phoned from the hotel in Cork before the 7 a.m. conference session. He hadn't bothered leaving a message, as she'd see his missed call. But she hadn't returned it. When he phoned her yet again on his way back to Dublin, he was diverted to her voicemail once more, although that wasn't entirely surprising, as the Chandon Leclerc offices and warehouse were in the middle of a mobile blackspot. Imogen often complained that it was bad business for them to be in a location where clients couldn't use their mobiles.

He tried again now as he turned on to the motorway and flicked the cruise control on his car to a steady 110 kph. The same irritating message played over the speakers and he cut it off in annoyance. She really is walking on thin ice, he thought. Pushing me to the limits of my patience. She's being thoughtless and inconsiderate. As usual.

Vince's grip tightened on the steering wheel. That's the problem with Imogen, he fumed. Thoughtless and inconsiderate. And no matter how hard I've tried to turn her into someone a little more sensible by introducing some rules and routines into our lives, she can always be relied upon to mess it up sooner or later.

She always apologised afterwards, he acknowledged to himself. She'd say she was doing her best. And then she'd try to persuade him that it wasn't thoughtlessness or a lack of consideration on her part but innate ditziness that made her do such stupid things.

He'd had warning of it, of course. He'd met her because of her combination of thoughtlessness and misplaced optimism; in a city centre pub, an unusual location for both of them as it turned out, neither of them being big drinkers or frequent pubgoers. Imogen had come inside to shelter from a heavy downpour. She'd hurried through the doors on the heels of others with the same idea, and stood there shaking raindrops from her gleaming dark hair.

'A bit damp out?' he'd remarked, and she'd looked at him in surprise.

'A bit damp?' he repeated as he folded the newspaper in his hand.

'Slightly.' She smiled. 'To tell you the truth – torrentially damp.'

'It was forecast,' he told her. 'Bright spells mixed with heavy showers. You should have brought an umbrella with you.'

She gave him a wry smile, which made two dimples appear in her cheeks.

'I never look at the weather forecast in Ireland – it's either sunny with a chance of rain, or rainy with outbreaks of sun.'

'In which case you definitely should bring an umbrella with you.'

'I'm an optimist.' This time her smile was bright. 'I like to think that I'm outdoors in the sunny intervals.'

'Hope over experience,' he said. 'Not the way I approach it.'

'Sometimes my optimism is misplaced,' she acknowledged.

'Plan for the worst, hope for the best,' he said, then asked her if he could get her a drink.

'Oh, no thanks. I'm only here until it blows over.'

'How about a coffee to warm you up?'

She hesitated.

'No ulterior motive,' he assured her. 'Just coffee.'

'I couldn't . . .'

'I'm getting one for myself.'

'I really don't . . .'

'It's only coffee. Cappuccino all right for you?' He ordered two from a passing lounge boy, then made space for her at the table by moving the folded newspaper.

'I don't often sit in pubs on my own doing the crossword,' he told her. 'But my central heating packed in and won't be fixed till tomorrow, so I thought being here this evening was a better option.'

'Sure is.'

The lounge boy put the coffees in front of them and Vince paid immediately.

'Vince Naughton,' he said to her.

'Imogen Weir.'

'Nice to meet you, Imogen.'

'You too. Thank you for the coffee.'

'You're welcome.'

She was very pretty, he thought. He liked the Mediterranean vibe she had going – slightly olive skin, dark eyes, dark hair, rosebud mouth.

'What d'you do, Imogen?' he asked.

'At the moment I'm between jobs,' she told him, her manner relaxing a little as she cupped her hands around the mug of coffee. 'I was doing some research work for a professor of European history, but my contract ended last month. I'm hoping to get something soon, but you know how it is at the moment, the economy is all over the place. Still, fingers crossed.'

'European history.' He sounded impressed. 'Are you an academic yourself?'

'God, no.' She shook her head. 'I'm – I'm nothing really. Like I said, I'm job-hunting. I was at an interview today.'

'For something exciting, I hope.'

'Not very,' she admitted. 'A distribution centre for a French manufacturing company looking for admin staff. Not exactly the glittering career I was hoping for, but needs must and all that.'

'You're right,' he said. 'Not very exciting. But you never know.'

'It'll help keep the wolf from the door at least,' she said. 'And what about you? What do you do?'

'I work in life insurance,' he said.

'Someone's got to,' she joked.

'Life insurance is very important,' he told her. 'People should look after their dependants.'

'You're right.' Her cheeks dimpled again and he wondered if she was laughing at him. But he didn't mind. Everyone laughed at life insurance. Until they needed it.

'Would you like another coffee?' he asked, as she drained her cup.

'No thanks. I think it's eased off a bit out there. I should get going.'

'Do you have far to go? Have you a car parked nearby, or are you getting public transport?'

'The bus,' she said. 'But the stop's just round the corner.'

'I listen to the weather forecast, so I have an umbrella. I'll walk you.'

'Oh, you don't have to do that.'

'I should get going myself. I don't want to spend all night in the pub.'

They left together. The rain was continuing to fall, but not as heavily as before. Vince put up the umbrella, which was stamped with the insurance company's logo. He held it over both their heads as they walked to the bus stop.

'Five minutes to the next one,' Imogen said as she looked at the information display.

'I'll wait with you.'

'It's very nice of you, but there's no need.'

'Don't want you getting soaked.'

They stood in silence beneath the umbrella, looking down the street in the direction from which the bus would come.

'Here it is,' said Imogen as it appeared in the distance.

'Do you have far to walk afterwards?'

'Not really. A few minutes, that's all.'

'Take the umbrella.'

'I can't possibly . . .'

'Please, Imogen. I'd like you to.'

'But then you'll be the one to get soaked.'

'Oh, I don't mind. You can return it to me sometime.'

'I . . .'

'I'd like to meet you for coffee again,' he said, taking his phone out of his pocket. 'Let's share numbers.'

'Well . . .'

'No strings, honestly. If it doesn't work out, no problem.'

She hesitated for a moment before giving him her number. He put it into his phone, then sent her a confirming text.

'I'll call you,' he promised as the bus arrived at the stop.

She climbed on board and he watched while she settled into a seat. As the bus pulled away, he waved at her. When she waved back, he smiled.

Chapter 4

As with her overnight stay in Bayonne, Imogen had used her phone before she'd left Paris to check out the budget accommodation possibilities, although she hadn't booked anything because she didn't want to leave any details of who she was on the internet. (More paranoia, she realised. Vince might be right about her after all.) Most of the really cheap places were a little out of town, but she needed to be closer to the centre of things so that she could try to organise herself with something more permanent. Or at least somewhere less temporary. She wasn't sure how long she'd be staying in Hendaye. The Plan was vague on that point.

She began to walk from the bus stop. The small hotel she'd chosen was in a residential part of the town, about fifteen minutes away. She hadn't realised when she'd picked it online that the street it was on was quite so steep, and she was breathless by the time she stopped outside. Once again she was gripped with the sudden fear that he'd outsmarted her and was waiting for her within. She wished now that she'd kept the phone and simply disabled the location services. At least that way she'd have seen any texts he'd sent. But would he have known she'd seen them? Would he be able to use them to trace her anyway? She never was certain on that point. She stood on the pavement indecisively as she watched people walking in and out of the hotel. After a few minutes, when she realised that some of them were looking at her curiously, she walked up the short pathway and went inside.

The Atlantique was a three-storey whitewashed building with the typical red-painted wooden shutters and balconies of the area. Inside, the walls were whitewashed too and the floor was terracotta. It was bigger and brighter than the Hostel Auberge, with a more relaxed atmosphere. Two black and white cats sashayed languidly across the reception area, where a friendly girl told Imogen that they could offer her a basic room for five days. Imogen said that five days would suit her perfectly and insisted on paying cash in advance, much to the bewilderment of the receptionist, who handled the banknotes as though she didn't quite know what they were. Once she'd checked Imogen in, she handed her an old-fashioned brass key to a room on the top floor.

The room was more spacious than the one in the Hostel Auberge, and overlooked a small swimming pool set in a garden full of flowering shrubs and trees. In the distance, over the ubiquitous terracotta rooftops, Imogen could make out the blue of the sea. There was no air-conditioning, but the breeze through the open windows was cool. She turned back into the room and began to unpack her bag. As she hung her navy suit in the wardrobe, she began to panic about her financial situation.

You can't seriously think you'll be able to find a job and somewhere to live in under a week.

She whirled around. It was as though he was standing right behind her.

For God's sake, Imogen, it's about time you came to your senses. You're being incredibly silly.

Maybe she was. She sat down abruptly in the old leather armchair in the corner of the room. Everything she'd done until now, she'd done in a kind of controlled frenzy. The Plan had been something to focus on. Now she was here and suddenly it all seemed impossibly ridiculous. He'd laugh at her if he knew.

Running away doesn't solve anything.

This time it was her mother's voice again. Imogen remembered when she'd said those words to her. Not here, in Hendaye, but in Ireland after they'd left. She'd been feeling miserable in the grey dampness of the Irish winter and had had a row with everyone before stalking up to her room, declaring that she was leaving them all for ever.

She'd been nine years old.

She'd got as far as packing half a dozen T-shirts and a pair of pink trousers in her Barbie case when Carol came into the room.

'Where are you going?' she asked.

'Hendaye,' replied Imogen.

'Why?'

'Because I hate it here.'

'Do you really?'

'Yes. It's different. Everyone's different. They're mean to me.'

'Agnes and Berthe aren't mean to you.'

'No, they're lovely. But everyone else. At school.'

'You'll make friends, don't worry,' said Carol.

'I hate them all,' said Imogen. 'I want to go home.'

'Sweetheart, this *is* home.'

'No it's not,' she said. 'Home's at the Villa Martine.'

'The Villa Martine wasn't our home.' Carol put her arms around her and hugged her. 'You know quite well it belonged to Monsieur and Madame Delissandes.'

'But we were living there by ourselves for a long time!' cried Imogen. 'And then you had the indiscretion and ruined everything.'

Now Imogen remembered the pained expression that had crossed her mother's face at her words, and she winced. She'd been cruel in the way that children can be cruel, not caring about Carol's feelings, only that she herself hated everything about her new life in a place she didn't want to be.

I was a horrible child, she thought, as she drew her knees up to her chest and rested her head on them. The only person I thought about was myself. It's no wonder it all turned out the way it did. And maybe it's because I'm still horrible that things are the way they are now.

She stayed nestled in the leather chair for about fifteen minutes, her arms wrapped around her legs as she rocked gently backwards and forwards. She'd made a mistake. She knew she had. She couldn't carry on without him. She needed him. He loved her and she loved him. They were a perfect couple. Everyone said so. If something had gone wrong, it was her fault. Like twenty-odd years ago when she'd said the wrong thing at the wrong time. If she'd kept her mouth shut back then, everything might have turned out differently.

She lifted her head again and reached for her bag. Then she remembered that the phone wasn't in her bag and that she couldn't call him, couldn't ask him to come and get her. Instead, she took out the piece of paper and read it.

The most difficult thing is the decision to act, she read. *The rest is merely tenacity.*

It was a quote from the American aviator Amelia Earhart. In addition to her store of clichés, Carol had a trove of inspirational quotes she used on a daily basis. That one was Imogen's favourite. She'd written it on the hotel stationery in Paris before she'd checked out, because she'd known that at some point she'd panic like she was panicking now and that sooner or later she'd lose confidence in herself. She stared at the words for another minute, then took a deep breath and stood up again. She'd already acted. Now all she had to do was be tenacious. To stick with the Plan.

She went into the bathroom, splashed some water on her face, redid her minimal make-up and then brushed her hair, still getting used to the shorter style. After that, she went downstairs again and looked around her.

'Do you need any information about the area?' The receptionist was bright and cheerful.

Imogen had been about to say no, she could manage, when she realised that a map would be useful, because despite the past, she didn't really know the town.

'Here you go.' The receptionist handed one to her. 'This is where we are. And here's the town centre. There's a tourist information office here . . .' She circled a point on the map. 'And if there's anything I can do to help, just ask.'

'You're very kind, thank you,' said Imogen.

She took the map and went outside. She was feeling calmer

now, her anxiety levels of earlier receding, and she looked around her carefully.

She didn't recognise any of the nearby streets, but she hadn't expected to. When she'd lived here, she hadn't ventured much beyond the Villa Martine and its immediate vicinity. All she remembered about the house was that it had been in one of the most spectacular locations in the town, perched on a hillside facing over the beach and the sea. She wasn't sure exactly where that was, but she was confident that she could find the general area. There were things she could remember clearly, like the bridge over the railway line that she loved to peer over, and a big camping park further along the road. She'd checked them on Google Maps while she was in Paris, and she was sure that she'd found the right location. But although she'd spent a lot of time looking at various street views, she couldn't locate the Villa Martine.

The house wasn't the reason she'd come to Hendaye. But she wanted to see it all the same. She wanted to remind herself that when they'd lived there, she'd been the Imogen who ran along the beach in her bare feet with her hair blowing in the wind. The Imogen who was swept into her mother's arms when she could run no further and twirled in the air as she shrieked with laughter. She wanted to reconnect with the young girl who'd been full of confidence, who'd had total belief in herself and the world around her.

Perhaps, even with the Plan, it was too tall an order.

She walked towards the bay, where hundreds of sailboats bobbed on waves that sparkled beneath the clear blue sky, and was overcome by a sense of déjà vu, of having been on this exact spot looking at the exact same boats before. It was entirely possible, she supposed. Did she recall it, or was she just imagining someone pointing at the land on the other side of the water and telling her that it belonged to Spain and not France, and was a completely different country, with a completely different language.

'But still Basque country,' she recalled someone else saying. Had it been Madame? Or Monsieur Delissandes himself? She knew he had Basque heritage, and that was why the family stayed there every summer. The house had been . . . She frowned as she tried to remember. His family home passed on from his grandparents? Or a great-aunt? Something like that at any rate. There had been lots of talk about it during various summers. But she couldn't recall the actual conversations.

As she gazed across the water, more long-buried memories began to emerge, even though she couldn't be sure if they were real or not. She thought she remembered sailing in one of the boats. She and Oliver and Charles wearing bright orange life jackets and leaning over the side while Carol watched them anxiously and Monsieur Delissandes adjusted the sails. Had that happened? She was almost sure it had.

But she was absolutely certain that they'd raced along the wide expanse of beach in front of her. She definitely remembered doing her best to keep up with the Delissandes boys, which was impossible because they were older than her as well as being stronger. Carol had suggested a race where Imogen would have a head start, but she refused. She'd wanted to beat them on equal terms. But she never had. She'd always lost, while Oliver was usually the winner, although occasionally he slowed down at the end and allowed Charles to pass him. Those times Charles would raise his arms over his head and jump around in excitement while Oliver watched him with an amused expression. Imogen sometimes wondered whether Oliver would have allowed her to win if she'd managed to get in front of Charles. Somehow she doubted it. There was a rivalry between them that was different to the one he had with his younger brother.

There were a lot of tourists on the beach. She watched as men drove spikes into the sand for the beach umbrellas, while children whooped their way into the sea. It was like any holiday resort in the world. But she'd *lived* here. No matter how jumbled and unreliable her memories, she'd been a part of it for almost five years, and she hadn't wanted to leave.

She walked along the Boulevard de la Mer, dividing her attention between the sea and the houses on the other side of the road. It wasn't as though she expected to spot the Villa Martine among them. But she was alert to the possibility.

'Oh for heaven's sake!' She surprised herself by speaking the words out loud. 'It doesn't matter whether you ever see it again or not. You came here to move on. And that's what you're going to do. Right now!'

She deliberately turned away from the beach and back into the town. She wandered through the streets, pausing outside a variety of shops, looking at the summer offerings, deliberately blocking out the memories that tried to surface. Her stomach grumbled, and she sat at a pavement café and ate a tuna salad, the sun warm on her back and a soft breeze whispering across her neck.

A new start, she said to herself. I've done it lots of times before. I can do it again. I've already made the decision. And I definitely know how to be tenacious.

Chapter 5

It was late in the afternoon when Vince arrived home, but he'd made good time, which pleased him.

He parked in the driveway, then took his overnight bag out of the boot of the Toyota and unlocked the front door. The house was quiet and deserted. He went upstairs. Everything was still and undisturbed. Even the tie he'd rejected before leaving for Cork was where he'd left it, on the chair beside the bed.

He frowned. Imogen always hung up his discarded clothes. She knew he liked everything in its place. Why hadn't she done what she usually did and put the tie away? Why hadn't she answered his phone calls and texts? What the hell was going on?

He put his bag beside the bed and opened the curtains. It was one of his rules to leave the curtains half closed when they were out of the house, and Imogen followed it faithfully. Yet although everything was exactly where it should be, Vince was beginning to feel more and more uneasy. He was uncomfortably aware of the silence around him, and would have preferred to see a sign of Imogen's more disorderly habits to reassure himself that she'd been here.

He told himself that he was being stupid. She'd come home very late, fallen into bed, got up and gone to work. She hadn't had time to either disarrange things or put his tie where it should be. Although, he thought, hanging up the tie should have been second nature to her. Perhaps she'd planned to do it before he got home. Silly, but, knowing Imogen, entirely possible.

He went back into the bedroom and looked in the laundry basket. There was a white blouse as well as some of her underwear in it, but he wasn't sure if it had been there previously or not. He opened the drawer in the dresser where she kept her blouses. They were arranged in neat piles of blue and white, the colours he preferred her to wear to work. There were too many and they were too alike to know if any were missing. A thought struck him, and he looked under the bed. He frowned at the dust beneath it. And then again because her travel bag wasn't there. He felt his jaw tighten.

He walked down the stairs and into the kitchen. The red mug he'd used for his coffee the day before was still on the draining board. His jaw tightened even more. Another rule was to put things back in the cupboard as soon as they'd dried. She should have done that at least.

He took out his phone and called her.

'Hi, this is Imogen. I'm currently away at a business exhibition. Leave a message and I'll get back to you on my return.'

He took a deep breath and replaced the phone in his pocket. Why hadn't she called him? Why hadn't she put away the things that needed putting away? What the hell was she doing?

The missing bag was a worry. Did it mean she hadn't come

home at all? Or was it that she hadn't wanted to spend the night on her own and, despite the lateness of the hour, had gone to her friend Shona's instead? Vince felt his shoulders relax. It was the most likely answer. She'd done that once or twice before when he was away. A girls' night in, she called it. Dedicated to wine-drinking, make-up-sharing and gossiping. He didn't exactly approve, but he couldn't object when he was away himself.

He dialled Shona's number.

'Hi, this is Shona. Leave a message blah blah blah.'

'It's Vince,' he said. 'Did Imogen stay with you last night? Call me.'

He waited, but there was no immediate response. Shona worked as a gym instructor, so she probably didn't even know she had a message yet.

He picked up the phone and dialled again.

'Welcome to Chandon Leclerc. This is Imogen. I'm not at my desk at the moment, but please leave a message and I'll return your call.'

Vince jabbed at the disconnect button and dialled a different number.

'Welcome to Chandon Leclerc. Please choose from one of the following options.'

When the automated voice stopped at option five, the chance to speak to a real person, Vince selected it.

'Hello, this is Janice. How may I help you?'

'Hello, Janice.' Vince had never spoken to her before. He tried to keep his voice steady, even though he was already irate over yet another voicemail from Imogen and the automated phone system. 'This is Vince Naughton. I'd like to speak to Imogen, please.'

'Imogen?'

'Imogen Naughton. My wife. Conor Foley's PA.'

'Oh, right. Hold on a moment.'

The line went silent. Vince wondered if the stupid receptionist had cut him off. He tapped his fingers on the table, feeling the anger bubble up inside him, although it was tempered by concern. When she answered, he'd let some of the anger show. She deserved to know how much she'd upset him. There was a sudden series of clicks and the phone was answered again.

'Welcome to Chandon Leclerc. This is Imogen. I'm not at my desk at the moment, but please leave a message and I'll return your call.'

'For fuck's sake!' Vince roared at the phone. The stupid girl had simply put the call through to Imogen's desk and her voicemail had picked it up. It was no wonder the company was in trouble. (Which, according to Imogen, it was. That was part of the reason Conor had been eager to go to the exhibition. To see and be seen. To align the Irish distributor to the French owner.)

He debated for a moment before leaving the house and getting into his car again.

He was going to fetch his wife and bring her home.

Chapter 6

On her walk back to the Hotel Atlantique, Imogen bought herself an ice cream. She couldn't remember the last time she'd walked along a street with an ice cream cone in her hand. Maybe it was the last time she was here. Carol might have bought one for her from the very same shop and she could have walked the same pavement more than twenty years before. Although that was unlikely. The shop had been bright and new, while her memories were vague, impressions of colours and sounds, light and shade. And of people lifting her and talking to her and kissing her on the cheek and telling her that she was *très, très jolie*.

But the memory of arriving at the Villa Martine was still razor sharp. She couldn't recall Denis Delissandes collecting her and Carol from the airport, or getting into his car (although the smell of sweet tobacco would ever afterwards bring the image of a dark green Renault Espace to her mind), but she very clearly remembered pulling up outside the gates and Monsieur Delissandes using a remote control to open them. Carol had squeezed her hand at that point and Imogen had squirmed away from her, eager to watch the gates opening as if by magic.

The car had moved forward and then stopped almost at once because a football bounced off the windscreen, and Monsieur Delissandes slammed on the brakes and got out, leaving Imogen and her mother sitting in the back seat staring at each other.

'Are you out of your minds!' they heard him yell. 'Get into the house this instant. And wait for me there.'

He got back into the car and, without another word, drove it up to the house, where he cut the engine and got out again. He opened the door for Carol, and Imogen scrambled out with her.

'I'm sorry,' Monsieur Delissandes said. 'This isn't the best welcome to our home. The boys know they shouldn't be playing football in that part of the garden. I'll deal with them later.'

Imogen had exchanged an anxious look with her mother, wondering how the boys, whoever they were, were going to be dealt with. Carol had winked at her in return and squeezed her hand again. Then the front door of the house had opened and Lucie Delissandes had come out to greet them. Imogen's first impression of her was of an angel, because she was blond-haired and blue-eyed, and was wearing a long white dress trimmed with broderie anglaise, which floated around her legs in the gentle breeze. She was also barefoot, her toenails painted a brilliant gold.

She kissed her husband on both cheeks and spoke quietly and rapidly to him. Neither Carol nor Imogen could hear what she was saying, but Denis Delissandes snorted and stomped into the house. Then Lucie stretched out her hand to Carol, kissed her in the same fashion as her husband, and after that hunkered down on her knees in front of Imogen.

'You're the prettiest girl I've ever seen,' she said. 'And it is so lovely to have a pretty girl in a house full of men. Come in, come in. You're both very welcome.'

At the time, Imogen hadn't really understood their role in the Delissandes household. She'd thought it was the same as at the Maison Lavande in Provence. There, they'd lived with Carol's sister-in-law Agnes, Agnes's partner Berthe, and Berthe's widowed mother, who ran the place as a small guest house. They were part of the family and were treated very much that way, although only Berthe called her mother *Maman*; everyone else, including Imogen, addressed her as Madame Fournier, because she had a certain presence that seemed to demand it.

All of them worked together to keep the guest house running smoothly. As a baby, Imogen's job was to charm their visitors, and she'd apparently been very good at it. Whenever she'd crawl or toddle into a room, they'd invariably smile at her and tell her what a good girl she was, and how pretty. She allowed them to pat her on the head, or lift her on to their laps, or brush her silky brown hair, because they liked it, and even then, she knew that it was important to keep the guests happy.

She sometimes wondered how her life would have turned out if she and Carol had stayed in Provence. Carol often talked about the sun-kissed days and warm evenings, the faint scent of lavender and lemons, and the house filled with laughter. But things changed: at seventy-two years old, Madame Fournier met a man she wanted to marry and decided to sell the guest house. Although Agnes and Berthe had considered buying it, a job offer for Agnes in New York at almost the same time was too good to turn down, and so she and Berthe left for the States together. They'd suggested that Carol and Imogen might like to come too, but it would have been almost impossible for Carol to get a work visa, and besides, she was uneasy about raising her daughter in New York. It was Madame Fournier who found her the housekeeper's job in the Delissandes' holiday home in Hendaye, seven hundred kilometres away.

There had been tears at their departure, but Imogen didn't remember them. She didn't remember the flight to Biarritz. No matter how hard she tried, her first clear memory was of the gates of the Villa Martine opening and of Denis Delissandes yelling at his sons.

The sudden sound of a mobile ringtone startled her so much that she jumped and instinctively put her hand into her bag, before remembering that her phone was in its component parts and scattered around France. At the same time, a man walking out of a doorway took his own phone from his jacket pocket and started talking. Imogen pinched her nose with her fingers as her heartbeat slowed down again.

How did I let it get to this? she asked herself as she leaned against a wall for support. How did I become the kind of person who jumps at the slightest thing? And will being here really turn me back into the Imogen I was before?

The hotel reception area was busy with new arrivals when she returned. She skirted around them and walked out into the garden, where a few sunbeds and garden chairs were dotted around the small swimming pool. A teenage girl in the skimpiest of skimpy bikinis was tapping at her iPad as she lay on one of the sunbeds, while a small boy splashed happily in the pool under the watchful eye of his parents. The partly watchful eye, Imogen noted, because both of them were scrolling on their smartphones. I'm completely divorced from the modern world without my phone, she thought. I wonder, will I be able to last?

She sat at one of the tables and stretched her long legs out in front of her. She was hot and tired after her tour of the town, and her feet were aching. She wished she'd thought to pack a swimsuit. But if Vince had seen it, he'd have asked questions about a business trip that also included swimwear. She could have lied and said it was for the hotel swimming pool (if indeed it had one), but then he would have freaked out at a trip that allowed her time for swimming. He probably would have checked to see if the hotel had a pool too, and if it hadn't . . . She shuddered. I can buy a swimsuit, she told herself as she watched the boy diving into the pool, then hauling himself out and diving in again. I can do whatever I want. That's why I left, isn't it?

'Joel, can't you read the sign?' The woman spoke to him in English.

'I don't need to read it,' he said. 'It's a picture.'

'It's a picture that says no diving,' his mother pointed out. 'So stop it.'

'Nobody minds,' said Joel.

'You don't know that,' said his mother. 'And whether they mind or not is irrelevant. You're not supposed to be doing it.'

Joel heaved an enormous sigh and began running around the garden, his arms outstretched as though he was an aeroplane. An aeroplane that, not watching where it was going, tripped over a garden hose and landed spreadeagled in Imogen's lap.

'Oh!' she exclaimed.

'Joel!' his mother cried out. 'For heaven's sake!'

She jumped up from her sunbed and hurried over to where Imogen had steadied him.

'I'm so sorry,' she said, noticing that his wet body had effectively soaked Imogen's dress. 'Joel, you're a total menace. Apologise.' She looked at Imogen. 'Um . . . Madame, um . . . *je regrette . . . mon fils* . . . we're both sorry.' She gave a helpless shrug.

'It's OK,' said Imogen. 'I speak English.'

'Oh good.' The woman beamed at her. 'I'd hoped you might. It's awful, isn't it, how we English expect everyone to understand us. Especially in a place like this which is a little less touristy, you know?'

Imogen nodded.

'Are you actually English then?' the woman asked.

'Irish.'

'It's just I heard you talking French at reception earlier and I thought . . . you speak it very well.'

'Thank you,' said Imogen.

'Anyhow.' The woman caught her son by the arm. 'Joel, say you're sorry to the lady for falling all over her.'

'Sorry,' muttered Joel.

'Now get back in the pool, and no more diving.' His mother turned back to Imogen. 'He's a good kid really, but you know how it is when they're on holiday. Look, can I buy you a drink? To apologise.'

'There's absolutely no need,' said Imogen. 'He ran into me, that's all. He didn't hurt me.'

'I'm getting one for myself,' said the woman. 'So I might as well get one for you too.'

'A glass of water would be nice,' said Imogen.

'Oh, have something stronger,' said the woman. 'The house wine here is lovely.'

'I . . .'

Vince didn't approve of her drinking wine, certainly not in the afternoon, without food. He used to say it depressed her, and as a consequence depressed him. But Vince wasn't here.

'OK then,' she said.

'White?'

'Sure.'

The woman walked into the hotel bar and returned a few minutes later with three glasses and a bottle in a cooler.

'It's cheaper this way,' she said as she filled the glasses. She brought one over to her husband, who had abandoned his phone and was reading a Jack Reacher novel. Then she came back to the table and raised a glass to Imogen.

'Cheers,' she said.

'Cheers,' said Imogen.

'I'm Samantha,' the woman told her. 'That's my husband Gerry, and you've met Joel.' She glanced at the pool. Her son was doing lengths now with an enthusiastic, if ungainly, overarm stroke.

'Imogen.'

'Nice to meet you, Imogen. Are you here for long?'

First a conversation with the student on the bus. Now a woman in a hotel garden. Neither of them part of the Plan. But she couldn't ignore people. That would have the effect of making her more memorable. The Woman Who Wouldn't Speak. The wine drinking wasn't part of the Plan either, of course, but she couldn't be The Woman Who Wouldn't Drink Wine in France either.

'I'm not certain,' she said. 'I have a few options, but I haven't decided yet.'

'As soon as Joel was born, most of my options took to the hills.' Samantha grinned. 'I wouldn't be without him, of course, but he can be utterly exhausting. Do you have children of your own? Are you here with family?'

Imogen shook her head. 'I'm by myself.'

'In that case, you must come to dinner with us one night,' said Samantha.

'Oh, I couldn't . . .'

'Don't say you can't impose or something like that. We'd love the company. It's nice having romantic dinners for two, or family dinners for three, but it would be fun to eat with another adult, and there's a chic restaurant near the seafront we'd like to try.'

It was ages since Imogen had been in a restaurant, chic or otherwise. Vince always said . . . She pushed Vince and his ideas out of her mind. She wasn't going to think about him every time she did something different. She couldn't let herself. Otherwise what was the point of the Plan?

'We'll talk before then,' Samantha said when Imogen told her that it would be nice to meet up. 'I suppose I'd better go and supervise my son more closely. Would you like another drop of this?' She held up the wine bottle.

'No thanks.' Imogen shook her head. 'But I appreciate it.'

She drained her glass, then made her way back into the hotel, feeling light-headed from the alcohol. She went up to her room and lay on her bed.

The Plan's flexibility was being tested, she acknowledged as she gazed at the ceiling fan turning lazily above her. She hadn't counted on interaction with other people. But it was impossible to avoid them.

All the same, she knew she needed to keep contact with strangers to a minimum. She was acutely aware of the dangers of social media, where no matter how good your privacy settings, posts could end up being seen by the most unexpected of people. She didn't want that to happen. She wanted to stay invisible.

She'd deactivated her own Facebook page while she was in Paris, not that she'd had many friends on it to start with. But it had been a liberating step to take. If only everything could be that easy, she thought, she wouldn't have needed a Plan at all.

Would Vince have tried to send her a Facebook message? Or would he have sent an email? Her email account was still active, so if he had, it wouldn't have bounced back to him. She wondered if he'd figured the situation out by now, and if he intended to do anything about it. He'd once told her, when she'd asked him about previous girlfriends, that when a relationship was over, it was over. He wasn't in touch with any of them. He didn't want to be. Yet she knew this was different. She wasn't a girlfriend. She was his wife. So she'd allowed for him to try to find her. Not because she wanted him to. Not because she wanted to go back. Simply because she couldn't imagine him letting her go.

Chapter 7

It was almost six o'clock by the time Vince arrived at the industrial estate where Chandon Leclerc had its distribution centre and offices. He knew that it closed to the public at five, but it was usually an hour later before Imogen left.

He parked the Toyota in a vacant space directly outside the door to the building and took out his phone. This was his wife's last chance to answer before he went in to get her. And before he completely lost his temper about her thoughtlessness. But she was right about the poor mobile signal, because even as he scrolled to her name, the final bar showing signal strength disappeared and a no service message replaced it. He got out of the car, slammed the door and walked inside the building. The small reception area was empty except for a tired-looking potted plant. Beside it was an intercom to speak to anyone in the office. Vince pressed it, and a few moments later a crackling voice asked him what he wanted.

'It's Vince Naughton,' he said. 'I'm here to collect Imogen.'

'Hold on.'

Vince paced the grey carpet for a couple of minutes. When there was no further sound from the intercom and when nobody came to meet him, he tried to open the door that led to the office area. It was locked. He banged on it in frustration and then buzzed the intercom again.

'I'm sorry,' said the voice when he repeated his request. 'She seems to have gone home. We close at five, you know.'

'She was in today, wasn't she?' asked Vince.

'I presume so,' said the voice. 'I'm not sure if I saw her or not, to be honest.'

'I want to talk to Conor Foley,' said Vince.

'I'm sorry, he's busy right now.'

'I need to talk to him.'

'Like I said, he's busy.'

'Listen to me.' Vince's voice was hard and uncompromising. 'I want to talk to Conor Foley and I want to talk to him now. And if you don't let me, I'll put my fist through the door down here, which I'm sure will cause trouble for you.'

'What?'

'Get me the goddam managing director!' yelled Vince.

There was silence from the intercom. A couple of minutes later, a tall man with greying hair opened the double doors that led to both the office and the warehouse of Chandon Leclerc. His right wrist was in a plaster cast.

'Vince,' he said.

'Conor.' Vince held out his hand and the other man touched it briefly with his fingers.

'Why don't we go to my office,' said Conor.

'I'm here to pick up Imogen,' Vince said. 'I'm angry that after a long day yesterday, she's putting in another long one today. She should have time off, you know that.'

'My office,' said Conor.

Vince followed him up the stairs to the administration area that overlooked the warehouse. He looked around for Imogen but didn't see her. He felt himself tense up. Conor ushered him into a compact office. He sat behind a desk covered in brochures and paperwork and motioned Vince to sit opposite him.

'I thought it was better to speak to you privately,' he said.

'Why?'

'There's obviously an issue here,' Conor said. 'I'm sorry to tell you, Vince, but Imogen doesn't work here any more.'

'What the hell are you talking about? Did something happen in Paris? Did you fire her? Where is she?'

'I don't know. She didn't come in to work today.'

'Why?'

'Well . . .' Conor shuffled the papers on his desk and picked up a single sheet. 'The truth is that she's resigned.'

'She's . . . Give me that.' Vince grabbed the paper from him and looked at it.

Dear Conor, he read. *This is to let you know that I am resigning from Chandon Leclerc with immediate effect and am taking the annual leave due to me in lieu of notice. I apologise for the inconvenience. I have left all of the necessary notes from our visit to the exhibition in the green folder. Thank you for your support over the past years. Yours sincerely, Imogen Naughton.*

'What the . . .' Vince looked up from the letter.

'She put it in my briefcase yesterday,' said Conor. 'Along with a variety of papers from the exhibition. I didn't see it until a short time ago. And I'm guessing . . .' he looked sympathetically at Vince, 'I'm guessing she didn't say anything to you about it either.'

'No she bloody well didn't.' Vince's voice was shaking with anger. 'But I'm sure she said something more than this to you. You must know where she is. It's probably all to do with you anyhow. Isn't it?'

'I don't know what you're talking about,' said Conor. 'I was completely taken aback to see this.'

'You were, were you? Or is it all part of a plan?'

'A plan?'

'You and Imogen,' said Vince. 'Don't think I haven't noticed how you look at her. You fancy my wife, don't you? And you took her to Paris. So what have you done with her now?'

'Vince, I assure you my relationship with Imogen has only ever been professional.'

'Yeah, right.'

'Honest to God.' Conor was looking uneasily at Vince, whose face was red and who was balling his fists on the desk. 'We went to the exhibition. It was hard work. When we finished, Imogen left to catch the flight to Dublin and I went to get the Eurostar to London.'

'London? Why?'

'Because I had a meeting there first thing this morning and it made sense to get the train. I arrived back in Dublin at lunchtime and haven't seen Imogen since she left the hall yesterday.'

Vince didn't know whether to believe him or not.

'I'm a happily married man, Vince,' said Conor. 'I have two kids. I wasn't having an affair with Imogen.'

'I'd expect you to say that.'

'It's true.'

'Where is she?' asked Vince again.

'I really don't know,' replied Conor. 'She seemed fine in Paris. A little anxious, but we'd all been anxious about the exhibition. I didn't know she was planning to leave the company. We'll miss her.'

Vince read Imogen's resignation letter again.

'I'm sorry if there's some issue between the two of you,' said Conor. 'Obviously she didn't tell you anything about . . . well . . .' His voice trailed off.

'She's my wife and you allowed her to disappear in a foreign country.' Vince banged his clenched fist on the desk.

'Not disappear,' said Conor. 'She clearly made some kind of decision to . . . to . . .'

'She texted me from the airport.' Vince took out his phone and showed the message to the other man.

Conor read it, then looked at him sympathetically. 'She must have changed her mind about coming back to Ireland.'

'She wouldn't do that.'

'Doesn't she have family in France?' asked Conor. 'Maybe she decided to visit them on the spur of the moment.'

'And resign her job at the same time?'

'I don't know what was going on in her head,' said Conor. 'As I said, she seemed perfectly fine to me.'

'Imogen is a very fragile person,' said Vince. 'You had a duty of care to her and you allowed her to disappear.'

'Imogen made a decision of her own,' said Conor. 'It had nothing to do with me.'

'She's been under huge pressure!' cried Vince. 'This stupid company. All your restructuring. People being made redundant. You must have said something to her to make her do this.'

'Of course I didn't,' said Conor. 'The company has had

trading difficulties, but we're still profitable. Imogen was a valued member of our team and treated as such. She wasn't under any pressure.'

'But she left,' said Vince. 'While you were responsible for her. You didn't make sure that she got on the plane. You didn't make sure she got home. You didn't keep an eye on her.'

'We were away on a business trip,' said Conor. 'And I wasn't responsible for her. She's a grown woman.'

'So basically my wife has disappeared and you don't give a shit.'

'She hasn't disappeared,' said Conor.

'She hasn't come home!' cried Vince. 'Which is disappearing in my book.'

'I'm sure she'll be in touch,' said Conor. 'This wasn't an unplanned event, otherwise she wouldn't have written the letter.'

Vince studied it again. 'How do I know she wrote it?' he demanded. 'How do I know it wasn't you? That something terrible hasn't happened to her and you're trying to concoct an alibi?'

'For heaven's sake!' exclaimed Conor. 'Why on earth . . . Look, Vince, you'll have to leave. I'm sorry there's some issue between you and Imogen that kept her from telling you she planned to leave her job. And that she'd made a decision not to come back to Ireland. But it's not my fault and I can't help you with it.'

'She's having a breakdown!' Vince cried. 'And you didn't even see it.'

'If she was having a breakdown – which I doubt – then you're the one who should have seen it,' said Conor. 'You're her husband. I'm just her employer.'

'So you're not going to do anything about it?'

'It's none of my business,' said Conor.

'A missing woman is none of your business?'

'If she really is missing and there's anything I can do to help, I will,' said Conor. 'If you feel you have to go to the gardai, I have no problem speaking to them. But all I can say is that she behaved perfectly normally all the time we were in Paris, and if I'd known she was thinking of . . . well, running away or whatever, I'd have tried to persuade her otherwise. She's . . . she was a good employee and a very nice person. She got on well with everyone.'

Vince said nothing.

'Is there anywhere else she might have gone?' asked Conor. 'We've been talking as though she didn't return from France, but perhaps she has family she went to see here in Ireland?'

Vince shook his head.

'Anywhere?'

'She's not really in touch with her family,' said Vince.

'But she must have someone.'

'She has stepfamily in England and a couple of dotty aunts in the States. I can't imagine she'd go to them.'

'Nevertheless, they're the people you should ask.'

Vince gritted his teeth.

'I'm sure she'll come home,' said Conor. 'She probably just needs a few days alone. I can understand that. We all do sometimes.'

Vince got up and walked to the door. He opened it and turned to Conor.

'I hope you can sleep at night,' he said, and slammed it behind him.

* * *

Shona Egan had always thought that the decor of Imogen's kitchen betrayed her French origins. To Shona it was quintessentially Gallic, with its distressed off-white cupboards and blue gingham accessories, as well as the pots of fresh herbs growing on the window ledge. There was a continental air about it, Shona would insist as she and Imogen drank coffee together at the wooden table, and there was no point in Imogen pretending otherwise.

'You like to think you still live there,' Shona told her one day. But Imogen shook her head and said that she was happy in Dublin and happy with her life.

'So you should be,' Shona said. 'I'd be happy if I'd landed a hunk like Vince Naughton too.'

And Imogen had laughed and agreed with her and said that Vince was the man of her dreams.

In which case, thought Shona, as she sat across the table from him now, why the hell had Imogen walked out without a word? What on earth had got into her? Vince treated her like a princess. They had a perfect marriage, everybody knew that.

She'd called around to the house after she'd returned Vince's call and he'd told her that Imogen hadn't come home.

'She can't have walked out on you without a word,' she said. 'She loves you.'

'And I love her,' said Vince. 'But clearly something's wrong. You know how fragile she is.'

Shona didn't think that Imogen was fragile, but it was true that her friend sometimes lost the plot about something entirely forgettable. You love being a drama queen, she had told her once. You like black moods and shrugging your shoulders and doing your French thing, even though your parents were Irish through and through. Imogen had admitted that she could be a little melodramatic, but only when life was really, really unbearable, which made Shona look at her intently and ask if everything was OK. Imogen had replied that it was now, that Shona always knew how to put things into perspective. That she was lucky to have a friend like her.

'And you're lucky to have a husband like Vince,' said Shona.

'Indeed I am.' Imogen nodded. 'I couldn't be luckier.'

If there had been something wrong, thought Shona now, why hadn't Imogen confided in her?

'Did you guys have a row?' she asked Vince.

'We never row,' he replied.

'She wouldn't leave without saying anything.' Shona picked up her phone and looked at it. There had been no messages or emails from her friend.

'That's why I'm so worried,' said Vince. 'I promise you, Shona, we didn't have a fight. There's nothing for us to fight about.'

'What do the police say?'

Vince thought back to his hour at the garda station, where he'd gone directly after his encounter with Conor Foley. A female officer had questioned him about Imogen, specifically about whether his wife had accessed their bank accounts since her departure. Vince hadn't even thought about that. When he logged into the mobile app and saw that she had withdrawn cash on the day she'd left for France, and again while she'd been in Paris, his face had darkened.

'Coupled with the resignation letter, it does point towards a specific decision by your wife.' The garda's voice had been full of sympathy. 'Did you argue about anything before she left?'

Vince had said the same to her as he'd said to Shona. That they never rowed. That they had a perfect marriage. That he loved Imogen and she loved him.

The garda asked him if Imogen was on medication or if he had any reason to think that her life was in danger, and he'd been honest with her and said no to the medication but that her life could easily be in danger because she was the sort of person who couldn't cope on her own. The garda asked why that was, and he'd replied that she needed him, and then the garda had looked at him with a curious expression in her eyes and asked why it was he thought she couldn't cope when she was apparently holding down the sort of job that required her to go to Paris with her boss.

'That's the point!' he'd cried. 'The job is very basic really, anyone could do it. The reason she went to Paris was because her boss had injured his wrist and needed some help. She's not some kind of high-flying businesswoman. She's an ordinary person and she needs me to look after her.'

'Of course, we'll make enquiries,' the garda said. 'But going missing isn't a crime, even though it's very distressing for everyone left behind. If it's any comfort to you, Mr Naughton, nearly eight thousand people are reported missing every year, and most of them come home. I'm sure your wife will be in touch very soon. Sometimes people need a bit of space, that's all.'

'. . . and so,' he told Shona, 'she said they'd make enquiries, but they're definitely not taking it seriously.'

'Maybe they're right,' she said. 'Maybe she'll be home tomorrow.'

'Oh great.' He looked at her in disgust. 'Now *you're* on their side.'

'No I'm not!' cried Shona. 'I completely understand how worried you are. But taking the money, sending the letter – it does sound like she planned it, doesn't it? Could she have decided to revisit her home in France?'

'She would have said something to me first,' said Vince. 'I can't believe she planned anything. She's crap at planning, you know that.'

'What if the idea just came to her?'

'On the way to the bloody airport!' Vince snorted.

'She could have decided at the last minute and . . .' Shona's voice trailed off. She knew that Imogen's disappearance wasn't the result of a sudden impulse. Her friend had known what she was doing.

'What I'm thinking,' said Vince, his voice taut, 'is that there might be someone in France.'

'A man, you mean?' Shona's eyes widened. 'Oh Vince, I really don't think so. She never seemed anything but totally devoted to you.'

'That's what I thought too,' said Vince. 'But . . .'

'I'm sure there's no one.' Shona's voice was firm, although she wasn't sure of anything any more. After all, she never would have expected Imogen to run away in the first place. So perhaps there *was* someone she was running to. In which case, as soon as she heard anything at all from her friend, she'd give her a piece of her mind. She wasn't going to be judgemental about Imogen's relationships, but she sure as hell was regarding how she'd gone about things.

'I find it hard to imagine there was anyone either,' said Vince. 'Besides, we'd been trying for a baby.'

'Oh.' Shona was surprised. Imogen had never said anything to her about starting a family. Not that she had to, of course, but they talked about things like that, and, if anything, her friend had seemed against the idea. In fact she'd said a number of times that she didn't think she'd ever have kids. Too much responsibility, she'd said. To easy to fuck them up, like it says in the poem. Shona hadn't been able to help wondering if Imogen was thinking of her own experiences, for all that she rarely talked about them.

'The thing is,' said Vince, 'she thought she might be pregnant, but she wasn't. That could be what's upset her.'

'Oh Lord. Did you say this to the gardai?'

Vince nodded. 'But again, they were sort of dismissive.'

'Aren't they going to do anything at all?'

'They said they'd make some investigations. I don't know what that really means.'

'We'd do better to investigate ourselves,' said Shona. 'And the most likely people she would have gone to if she was feeling upset would be her family.'

'*I'm* her family,' said Vince. 'That's the thing, Shona. We're a team, Imogen and me. There *is* no one else.'

'Her stepfather? Maybe she didn't get on a flight at all. She could have taken the train to London and gone to see him.'

'Her boss caught the Eurostar. She wasn't with him.'

'There's more than one train,' Shona pointed out.

'I don't have any contact details for her stepfather,' said Vince. 'I'm not entirely sure where he lives.'

'I expect you'll find something somewhere. Do you have an address book?'

'Does anyone these days? I have contacts on my phone. So does Imogen.'

'Did she back it up on to her computer? You might be able to find it that way.'

'I don't know.'

'Or Facebook?' suggested Shona.

'That's a thought.' Vince took out his phone and accessed the app. After a moment, he looked up at Shona and frowned. 'It's not there,' he said. 'Her account is gone.'

Shona took out her own phone and started tapping. 'You're right. Jeez, Vince, she must have deactivated it.'

'She's deranged!' he cried. 'She deserves to be locked up! I don't know what the hell . . .' He stopped as he saw the look on Shona's face. 'I'm sorry,' he said. 'I'm stressed.'

'I understand,' said Shona. 'All this, and the baby stuff too – it must be doing your head in.'

'I'll keep looking,' he said, suddenly calm again. 'There must be details of other friends, other people . . .'

'I'll ask at the gym,' said Shona. 'She may have said something to someone there. But I'm her best friend. It's me she should have confided in.'

'I'll email her.' Vince opened his email and began to type rapidly. 'All I want is for her to be OK,' he said when he'd sent it. 'Whatever's happened. Whatever's the matter. We can fix it.'

'Oh Vince.' Shona got up and stood behind him. She put her arms around his shoulders and gave him a hug. 'I'm sure it'll sort itself out. She'll be in touch soon.'

'I hope so,' he said. 'I really do.'

Shona picked up her bag and walked out of the house. How could Imogen have done this to Vince? she asked herself as she got into her car. No matter what was wrong, he deserved more than this. And so did she. She was supposed to be Imogen's best friend. But Imogen clearly had other ideas. And Shona was beginning to think that she knew her a lot less well than she'd originally thought.

Chapter 8

Tired from travelling, but more than that, exhausted from the stress of the last few days, Imogen went to bed early. She hadn't expected to sleep very well, but she fell into oblivion within a few minutes of her head hitting the pillow and didn't wake until the rising sun flooded the bedroom with warm light. She stepped on to the narrow balcony and gazed out over the deserted hotel garden and tranquil pool. The serenity of the scene was instantly calming and she felt herself relax a little. It would have been lovely to go for a swim in that pool, she thought, the lack of a swimsuit niggling at her again. She shook her head. If a swimsuit was the only thing she had to worry about, she was doing all right.

It wasn't, though. There was still Vince. She wondered what he was doing and how he was taking it. He would have called Chandon Leclerc by now and learned about her resignation from the company. He'd have called Shona too. Imogen felt bad about having kept the Plan a secret from the woman who was supposed to be her friend, but she couldn't have trusted Shona to keep silent. She knew Shona. She'd have wanted to help, and Imogen had needed to do this on her own.

She looked at her watch. She had to make a phone call. But not yet. Right now, she wanted to stay out of touch, in her own bubble. No internet, no mobile phone. Totally alone and uncontactable. Answering to nobody but herself. There was an intense freedom in it. A freedom too in not having to listen to him saying how much he worried about her. He'd made her feel afraid, even though she used to consider herself fearless.

But she didn't feel afraid today. She felt good. Anxious. But good.

She showered, dressed and went downstairs. There was one free table in the small breakfast room and Imogen sat at it. A young waitress asked if she'd like coffee; when Imogen said yes, she told her that she'd bring it shortly and invited her to help herself to the buffet in the meantime.

In Imogen's view, nobody did breakfast better than the French. She loaded her plate with ham and cheese, as well as some freshly baked bread, which she slathered with a pat of dewy butter. Then, while she waited for her coffee to arrive, she took a local paper from the bundle on the side table and began to flick through it. As she'd hoped, it was mainly filled with ads for rental property. She studied them carefully, uncomfortably aware that the start of summer probably wasn't the best time to be looking for a cheap rental. Property owners were looking to get profitable short-term holidaymakers rather than people who wanted to commit at a lower price for a few months. It would have been better to initiate the Plan during the winter. But there hadn't been any opportunities in the winter. The exhibition had been her first chance, and she'd jumped at it. So despite the season, she'd go looking for a rental property, and she'd also see what job opportunities were out there. There were plenty of bars and restaurants in Hendaye where she might have a chance of something temporary. And she did have some experience – she'd waitressed in her student years, after all.

She was conscious of a tremor of excitement running through her. A sense that for the first time in a long time she was taking control of her own destiny. Followed by a shudder of fear that she wasn't up to it, that she'd fall flat on her face and then . . . and then what? she asked herself. I haven't made a fall-back plan. Because there's nothing and nobody to fall back on.

She looked up as Samantha and her family came into the breakfast room. Samantha stopped to recommend the restaurant where she and Gerry had eaten the night before, while Joel pulled the petals off the pretty pink daisy in the small flower-holder on the table.

'We're driving to Hondarribia, just across the border, after breakfast,' said Samantha. 'Everyone says it's gorgeous. Would you like to join us?'

Another invitation. But this time she had a genuine excuse to turn it down.

'I've plans for today,' she said. 'I'm sorry.'

'We might see you back here later, in that case,' said Samantha. 'What about joining us for a drink?'

'That'd be lovely,' Imogen said.

She meant it.

She gathered up her things and left the hotel. She'd seen an advertisement for an estate agency in the paper that looked interesting, but as she approached the coast, she stopped outside a different agency, attracted by a photograph in the window. She looked at it closely, but it wasn't, as she'd first thought, the Villa Martine. This house was bigger and grander, although like the Villa Martine it was bordered by trees and with a view to the sea. The house was for sale and the price was high. Once again, Imogen wondered if the Delissandes had sold their home.

She was about to move on, but stopped again as she caught sight of the sign on the agency's wall proclaiming that Bastarache Immobilier provided a complete range of property services as well as financial advice. I could probably do with financial advice, Imogen thought. And maybe a lot of other advice too. But not right now. Right now, it's all about getting somewhere to live. And as Bastarache Immobilier had apartments to rent, she supposed it would do no harm to check it out.

She pushed open the door and stepped inside.

There was nobody behind the desk, and so she looked at more photos of houses while she waited. She was so engrossed in reading a description of an apartment overlooking the sea that she didn't notice the tall, dark-haired man coming into the office.

'I'm sorry,' he said in English at her startled exclamation as she realised he was behind her. 'I was on the phone.' He held up his mobile, which started to buzz. 'Sorry,' he repeated as he rejected the call. 'Can I help you?'

'Yes,' she said, also in English. 'I'm interested in renting an apartment.'

'I'm sure I can help you with that. What are you looking for?'

'I won't be your best client,' she told him. 'I want something small, just for me. Not too expensive. And for about three months.'

His phone rang again, and this time he held up his hand to her and answered it. She listened while someone ranted at him from the other end and he made placating comments in French about getting someone soon and doing his best and being with a client right now.

'So,' he said, reverting to English when he'd finished. 'A single apartment for the summer at a good price. That'll be difficult, to be honest. I certainly don't have anything near the sea.'

'I don't mind,' she said.

'Most people want a sea view.'

'The view doesn't matter to me.'

'Normally it does,' he said. 'If you're flexible, that will make things easier. But it's difficult to find something for three months.'

'I can be flexible about the time, too,' she said.

He shot her an inquisitive glance, but when she didn't say anything else, he returned to scrolling through the computer screen. 'Will you need a guest bedroom?' he asked.

'No.' Her response was so quick and so emphatic he looked startled.

'Sorry,' she said. 'I'm here for some peace and quiet. No guests. So even a studio would be fine.'

'Ah, the get-away-from-it-all.' He nodded. 'Are you a writer looking for inspiration? Or an artist here to paint our beautiful countryside?'

She smiled. 'Nothing as exciting as that.'

He didn't say anything else but continued his search,

tutting from time to time as he clicked on the images in front of him. Eventually he sat back and sighed.

'I have one suitable proposal for you,' he said. 'Normally apartments in this building are rented out to students or young people on adventure holidays. But it is what you're looking for, and at a good price.'

Imogen winced. A student let wasn't exactly what she'd had in mind, but she couldn't afford to be picky. So she said it sounded fine and asked if she could see it.

'If you like, we can go now,' he said. 'Where are you parked?'

'I don't have a car,' she said.

'It's a short drive,' he told her. 'I'll take you.'

He selected a bunch of keys from the drawer in his desk and then led her out of the office and across the road to where a small silver Citroën was parked.

'*Alors*,' he said. 'Let's go.'

He drove along the Boulevard de la Mer before turning inland again. For a moment the road seemed vaguely familiar, but then the estate agent took a sharp turn and continued on until he stopped at yet another whitewashed house with red shutters and balconies. It wasn't a figment of my imagination, Imogen thought, when all I could remember of Hendaye was red and white.

She got out of the car and followed him to the building.

'I'm sorry,' he said as they walked up the pathway together. 'I didn't introduce myself earlier. René Bastarache.'

'Imogen Weir.' It was good to use her own name again.

'Well, Madame Weir,' he said, 'I hope this is what you're looking for.' He opened the main door. 'This was a family house that has been converted into six apartments. As I already told you, they're usually rented to students and younger people because it's such simple accommodation.'

Imogen followed him inside. The hallway was mainly taken up by the wide stairway, but was also cluttered thanks to the bicycles against the walls.

'Residents are supposed to leave their bikes outside,' said René. He started up the stairs and she followed him.

'*Et voilà*,' he said, opening the first door they came to.

Imogen had braced herself for the worst, so she was pleasantly surprised to find herself in a bright, sunny room. The furnishing was basic and the small galley kitchen even more so, but there was a separate bedroom along with the tiniest bathroom she'd ever seen. The bedroom had a very small window high up in the wall, and the conversion meant that the bathroom's natural light was limited to a skylight in the ceiling. There was nothing especially quirky or beautiful about the apartment, and the balcony was only wide enough to hold a few potted plants, but it was clean and liveable in. She couldn't help comparing it to her home in Dublin, with its blue and white kitchen, spacious living room and well-tended garden. It should have been hard to leave all that behind. She felt the throb of her pulse at the base of her throat.

'As you can see, there is also a small garden with a communal pool,' added René as she gazed out of the window without speaking.

'How much?' She turned to him, her voice cracking on the question, which she had to ask again.

The amount that René mentioned made her gasp.

'For pity's sake, this isn't Paris,' she said in French.

'You speak French?' He looked at her in astonishment.

'Yes,' she said.

'And it sounds like the French of France, too! Why didn't you say before?'

'Your English was so good,' she made a face at him, 'I didn't see the point.'

'But you are not French, are you?'

'I . . .' She was going to tell him that she'd lived here, in Hendaye, but she remembered the Plan and told him that she'd lived in Provence when she was very small.

'Ah, Provence,' he said dismissively.

'It may not be the Pays Basque, but it's still France,' she said.

He grinned. '*C'est vrai.* Anyway, let me see what I can do for you on the price.'

He took out his phone, dialled a number and started talking quickly and urgently.

Imogen caught enough of the rapid-fire conversation to realise that he was asking for a discount for a long-term rental for a charming woman from Provence – yes, Provence, but what can you do? – who wanted to enjoy the delights of Hendaye for a few months. The conversation continued fast and furious for a while, but eventually he ended the call and told her that he had obtained a discount of thirty euros on the monthly price, which he thought was fair and generous. Because, he said, this might not be Paris, but it was infinitely superior to Paris. Did Paris have the sea? Or mountains? Or the people?

Imogen couldn't help laughing as she said that she'd be delighted to take the apartment for three months at that price.

'When would you like to move in?' asked René as they went back to the car.

'I'm staying at the Atlantique,' she replied. 'I've booked till next week, but if I can leave sooner, I will.'

'The apartment will be ready for you on Monday,' he said. 'I have to arrange for it to be cleaned, but we are a little short-staffed at the moment so I cannot do it today.'

'It seemed perfectly OK to me.'

'We always clean our properties before they are let,' René said. 'It's in the paperwork. Now, come back to the office with me and we can organise it.'

Imogen struggled to shut out the voice in her head telling her that she was paying far too much for an unsuitable apartment in a poor location, as she filled in the forms and then signed them, somewhat cautiously, as Imogen Weir. It was five years since she'd used her maiden name, even though it was still on her passport and driver's licence. Vince had wanted her to change everything immediately after they'd married, but when he realised that was as expensive as getting new ones, he told her to wait until the renewal date. A total rip-off, he'd said. We're not giving the government money for nothing. She'd been surprised at his sudden stinginess back then. Now she was grateful for it.

'All that remains, Madame Weir, is for you to pay the first month's rental in advance,' said René. 'Do you wish to do that by credit card or debit card?'

'Cash,' she said as she opened her bag.

He looked startled. 'We do not have the facility to take cash.'

'There's a problem with my card at the moment,' she told him, although the truth was that she didn't yet want to use the one from her new bank account. 'I thought that as cash might be an inconvenience for you, I could pay you the full amount in advance.'

'That is not our normal procedure,' he said.

'I realise that.' Imogen nodded. 'I'm not a money launderer or anything if that's what you're afraid of.'

René sighed. 'I suppose as it's only for three months . . .'

Imogen took an envelope from her bag and opened it, then began counting out the euros in front of him. 'You have a copy of my passport,' she said when she'd finished. 'I'm not going anywhere.'

'It's not safe to walk around with that much cash in your bag,' he told her.

'I know.' She smiled at him. 'But now that I've given most of it to you, I don't have to worry.'

René smiled in return.

'Monday,' he said. 'Any time after nine o'clock I will have the keys for you.'

'Thank you,' she said. 'I look forward to it.'

'*A bientôt*, Madame Weir.' He extended his hand and she shook it.

'*Au revoir*,' she said.

She felt exhilarated as she walked back to the Hotel Atlantique. In the last few days, she'd left home, travelled through France on her own, found places to stay and now somewhere to live. And she'd done it by herself, despite the constant nagging in her head. She wasn't hopeless. She wasn't useless. She was perfectly capable of living her life on her own. Without rules. Or routines. Or Vince.

She started to sing beneath her breath. The song that

Berthe used to sing to her when she was very small. The one to put her to sleep.

'*Sur le Pont d'Avignon, l'on y danse, l'on y danse. Sur le Pont d'Avignon, l'on y danse tous en rond.*'

Chapter 9

Vince had forgotten to buy milk on his way home from work and so there wasn't any for the cup of coffee he'd just made himself. He swore loudly and threw the black coffee down the sink, then walked out of the house and down the road. The pub was about fifteen minutes away on foot, and he spent every one of them in a hot rage. At the bar he ordered a pint – coffee wasn't going to cut it for him any more. He also asked for a toasted ham and cheese sandwich, even though Friday evenings were supposed to be takeaway nights. He hated that Imogen had disrupted his entire week. No football training yesterday because he'd been at the garda station. No takeaway tonight. The shift in his routine was nearly as unsettling as her inexplicable disappearance.

He sat in one of the corner booths, where nobody could disturb him, and checked his phone. Obviously there had been no calls from Imogen, but there was nothing from Shona either. Vince had encouraged Imogen's friendship with Shona, but he sometimes worried that they were too close. He didn't want Imogen depending on someone other than him for emotional support. He didn't think she confided too much in Shona, but he couldn't be certain that she didn't know something about what was going on. However, if she didn't, he couldn't believe that Imogen wouldn't get in touch with her. Women might walk out on men, but not on other women. The important thing was that if and when Imogen did make contact, Shona would tell him about it. He hoped she was convinced enough of Imogen's mental fragility to discount whatever story his wife spun her about her reasons for running away.

He wanted to know the reasons himself. Because from where he was sitting, he couldn't see any. He was a perfect husband. He was good to his wife. He'd been unswervingly faithful to her. He remembered her birthday and their anniversary, and sometimes he came home with flowers for no reason at all. She was lucky to have him and she'd no right to walk out with no explanation.

He realised that he was clenching his fist again and he relaxed it. He wasn't a violent man. He'd never lifted a finger in anger towards Imogen, not even when her thoughtlessness was at its most annoying. He despised men who were violent in their own homes. They disgusted him. On the very rare occasions when he and Imogen quarrelled, he would use the force of his arguments, not his fist, to prove his points. Not that they quarrelled much. They agreed on most things. He had no idea what it was that had made her resign her job and not come home. If she was trying to punish him for something, she should have told him what was upsetting her, and if he really had made some silly mistake, he'd have apologised. But if (more likely in his opinion) she'd simply got into a dark mood about something, he'd have talked her out of it, because he knew how to do that.

He picked up his phone again and checked the Find My

Friends app for the hundredth time. Imogen's location was still unavailable. He grunted as he recalled her texts telling him that she was on the way to the airport. She'd lied to him. Quite brazenly. It was as though she didn't care any more. Didn't it bother her that when they found out, the neighbours would think she was crazy? It sure as hell bothered him. Even more, it bothered him that they would be asking each other if it was his fault she'd done this insane thing. Yet he'd no reason to blame himself. He'd always put her first. Always. He opened his email. Still nothing from her. He thought for a moment and then sent another, tossing the phone to the table when he'd finished.

He sipped his pint and his anger abated a little. Then he thought about his wife's situation. The money she'd taken from the current account wouldn't last very long. And without money, she was going to have to come home. The question was, how would he play it when she did? Would he be forgiving or furious? Would he have to come up with some new rules for her behaviour? He rather thought he would.

He switched to the Facebook app. Her account was still deactivated, of course. Then he had another thought. He went back to the email log-in page and this time logged on as Imogen. She didn't know that he knew her username and password, but he'd found them out ages ago, and every so often he checked her emails. He liked to keep an eye on her, to see what she might be up to. The last message in her inbox was the one he'd just sent. It was still unread. She hadn't read the previous one either.

He felt the anger bubble up within him again. He wasn't worried about her any more. But nobody could blame him for being angry. He had every right to be bloody furious! He did love her, though, he reminded himself. He would always love her. She knew that. She knew she belonged with him.

And always would.

Shona Egan was having a fruit smoothie in the gym's café and thinking about Imogen. It was clear to her that her friend had deliberately vanished, and she was both hurt and worried by the fact that Imogen hadn't said anything to her about it. In fact she hadn't had the slightest idea of what was going through Imogen's head, and that disturbed her. They'd known each other since their college days and become friends after Imogen had joined the gym before she'd got married (in order, she'd said, to look good in her white dress). Shona had believed they were close. She'd shared some of her innermost secrets with Imogen: stories of her break-ups and make-ups; her preferences in bed – and things like the fact that her previous boyfriend had liked her dressing up as a librarian and saying 'Quiet, please' whenever he cried out. Imogen had asked what exactly dressing up as a librarian meant, because Tess Harte, who lived on their estate, worked in the local library and usually wore jeans and a T-shirt to work. Shona had admitted that Jeff had liked the whole grey cardigan and glasses look, and that he probably had some serious issues but it had been fun at the time. They'd had a light-hearted and fun discussion on the lengths women went to to keep men happy. Imogen had certainly given no indication that she was anything other than ecstatically happy with Vince. Shona had told her on more than one occasion how lucky she was to have him, and Imogen had nodded and said that he was definitely the sort of man other women dreamed of.

So why, Shona wondered, had Imogen upped and left without a word to anyone? Even though she could be a bit quirky from time to time, she was usually dependable. And the quirkiness Shona had always put down to the fact that Imogen had spent her early years in France, which had given her a slightly different way of looking at things. It was also probably partly because Imogen's family was such a fractured mess. Shona knew that after a rather eclectic upbringing, her friend craved love and stability, and she'd thought that was what she had with Vince. As well as a man who seemed to be totally devoted to her. A little too much, Shona thought sometimes, because when she and Imogen were out together, Vince would usually text at some point to check that everything was OK and ask if they needed a lift home. Still, she thought, at least he cared, which was more than a lot of men. And it was always nice to be picked up after a night in the pub, even if they could have made it home themselves.

Was it the baby thing? she wondered. Perhaps, despite what Vince had said, there had been a disagreement between them about it. Maybe Imogen was feeling pressured into getting pregnant. Shona felt sure that she would have talked about her plans, because they did sometimes have deep discussions about biological clocks and freezing eggs and the whole fertility issue. As far as Shona could remember, Imogen's view was that she was far too flaky to bring a baby into the world right now. Shona had told her there wasn't a woman on the planet who didn't have her flaky moments, and the two of them had clinked their wine glasses in agreement.

Could it possibly be another man? Shona couldn't believe that was something Imogen would have kept from her, but clearly her friend had hidden depths. Vince had said that it was nothing to do with her boss (Shona could have told him that!), but what if Imogen had become romantically entangled with someone else at the company where she worked? Someone in France? Someone she'd met while she was at the exhibition and run off with in a mad frenzy of lust and passion? Although, knowing Imogen, that was highly unlikely. Then again, her disappearing was highly unlikely too.

Nevertheless, why keep it all a secret? Imogen must have known that Shona wouldn't have been judgemental. Shocked, yes. But they were friends. Shona would have talked it through with her, helped her make the right decision. And if the right decision was running away with a lover, she still wouldn't have judged her, much as she would have sympathised with Vince.

Her phone rang and she grabbed it straight away, hoping it would be her friend, although she didn't recognise the number.

'Hello,' she said cautiously.

'Hello. Am I speaking with Shona Egan?'

'Yes,' said Shona.

'My name is Ellie. I'm from the Missing Family Foundation,' said the caller.

Shona felt her heart beat faster.

'Yes?'

'I have a message for you from Imogen Weir, also known as Imogen Naughton.'

The first thought that went through Shona's head was that Imogen was using her maiden name again.

'Imogen is safe and well,' said Ellie. 'She's decided to make a new life for herself. She doesn't want anyone looking for her.'

A new life! Shona was dumbstruck. Why on earth would Imogen need a new life? What was wrong with the one she already had?

'You could be anyone,' she told the caller. 'You could be her kidnapper, for all I know.' In fact, Shona thought, Imogen being kidnapped sounded far more likely than Imogen running away to make a new life.

Ellie acknowledged Shona's concerns. She gave her a website address to check out and told her to call her back when she was ready. Shona hung up and immediately looked up the website. She was shocked to see so many missing people on it, although many cases went back a long way. She dialled the number on the site and asked to speak to Ellie.

'Hello again,' said Ellie.

'You need to tell me something that nobody but Imogen would know,' said Shona.

'After your Pilates class last week, you shared a bar of chocolate,' said Ellie. 'Imogen didn't finish hers, and she put the last three squares into the side pocket of your kit bag when you weren't looking.'

Shona hung up. She went to her pink and white kit bag and opened the side pocket.

The three squares of chocolate were squashed and melted.

Chapter 10

On Monday morning, Imogen arrived at the estate agency a few minutes before it opened. While she waited for René to show up, she studied the photos of the houses for sale. With their whitewashed walls, terracotta roofs and wooden balconies, they were very different to the house she and Vince had bought in Dublin. They'd both agreed that Bellwood Park was a bargain: a three-bedroomed home reduced in price for a quick sale on a small housing development around a green area. Vince had said they'd be mad not to buy, and so they'd gone to the bank and put themselves through the tortuous mortgage application procedure, made a little easier by the fact that Vince was very well paid, and that Imogen's mother had left her enough money for a sizeable deposit. A month after the bank had cleared them for the loan, they'd moved in.

It had been an exciting time. Imogen couldn't wait to turn the suburban house into a warm, welcoming home, although in the end, it was only in the kitchen that she felt she'd truly succeeded. Even though it took some time before the morning sun reached the room, it was always bright and cheerful thanks to the light décor, which had been inspired by the kitchens of both the Maison Lavande and the Villa Martine. They'd been warm and welcoming places, filled with the enticing scents of herbs and flowers. Imogen always had flowers in the kitchen, and grew her own herbs on the window ledge. Vince's view was that the whole thing was a bit flouncy, but Imogen stood firm. It wasn't flouncy, it was evocative, she insisted. He'd laughed at that and told her that times had changed and kitchens should be sleek and modern.

'However, I'll live with it because I can compromise,' he said.

'So can I.'

Her compromise was a minimalist living room with a black leather suite and a sixty-inch wall-mounted TV. It was very stylish, she agreed. But she'd never felt truly comfortable there. She sighed. Vince had probably never felt comfortable in the kitchen, either.

'*Bonjour*, Madame Weir.' René arrived, a beaming smile on his face, and dragged her thoughts away from Dublin. '*Ça va?*'

'*Très bien*,' she replied. 'Another glorious day.'

'But of course.' He smiled again. 'We are in summer. Although,' he added, 'there is some rain forecast from the Atlantic tomorrow.'

'Oh no.'

'But by then you will be happily in your new home, I hope.'

'I hope so too.'

'I have the keys,' said René. 'We will go and inspect the property together, OK?'

She nodded and got into the car with him. I'm going to be living on my own again, she thought. I was good at living on my own. I liked it.

A short time later, they stopped outside the apartment.

'If you have visitors, or if you hire a car, you may park in space number six,' René told her as they got out.

'Thanks,' said Imogen. She followed him into the building and up the stairs.

'Oh for goodness' sake!' exclaimed René when he'd unlocked the door and stepped into the apartment. 'It has not been cleaned. I thought . . .' He took out his phone and punched numbers on the keypad. Then he started talking heatedly to whoever had answered. Meanwhile Imogen went over to the windows and opened them.

The apartment overlooked a small garden, where a variety of flowering shrubs partially obscured a kidney-shaped swimming pool. I'm going to be living in an apartment with its own pool, she told herself. I'm lucky. Really lucky.

'. . . paying for a cleaning service,' she heard René say as she stepped back in from the narrow balcony. 'It is embarrassing and inefficient. No. No. Yes. No.' He finished the call.

Imogen turned to him.

'I am very sorry,' said René. 'We have had a problem these last few weeks with cleaning staff. You'd think jobs were growing on trees. They keep leaving.'

'Could it be you're not paying enough?' asked Imogen.

'I agree that it is not the best-paid job,' said René. 'But we pay the legal wage. I'm sorry,' he repeated. 'I will get someone here to clean this for you as soon as possible.'

'Don't worry about it,' said Imogen. 'It's fine the way it is, and it won't take me long to go over it.'

'But—'

'I'll do it myself, honestly. It doesn't matter . . .' Her voice trailed away as a thought occurred to her.

'I appreciate your consideration, Madame Weir,' said René. 'Nevertheless—'

'Nevertheless, I have a question,' she said slowly. 'I know it may seem strange to you, but . . . but . . .' She couldn't ask. He'd think she was crazy. But did it matter?

She cleared her throat and spoke rapidly before she could change her mind. 'Monsieur Bastarache, you said you were in need of cleaners. Would you employ me?'

'You!' He stared at her in astonishment. 'I really do not think—'

'I'm here for the entire summer,' she said. 'I need a job.'

'But you are a client. And you have paid already for the apartment.'

'The thing is,' she said, 'I'm making some changes in my life. I need to work. I'll happily clean apartments or holiday houses if you think I'm suitable.'

'I do not think you are a cleaner.' René looked at her sceptically.

'I'm perfectly able to clean, and clean well,' she said.

'But you have not worked as a cleaner before?'

'Actually,' said Imogen, thinking of the Villa Martine, 'I have. It was a long time ago, but I assure you I know how to clean a house.'

His expression remained dubious.

'You could give me a trial,' she suggested. 'A week. If it doesn't work out, there are no hard feelings.'

'You are a member of the European Union?' asked René.

'I'm Irish,' replied Imogen, 'so of course I am.'

'You would work for the minimum wage? And not a fixed contract?'

'That's OK. I'm not here for a fixed time. But I'll give you plenty of notice before I go,' said Imogen.

'This is . . . unusual,' said René.

'Not really,' said Imogen. 'I'm sure you regularly have people doing part-time cleaning work for you.'

'Well yes, but—'

'It would be great for me,' said Imogen.

'Some days would be very long,' said René.

'I don't mind hard work.'

'Let me think about this,' said René. 'I will call you.'

'I don't have a phone,' said Imogen. 'But I can get one.'

'You will need a phone,' he said. 'It is an essential part of working. I need to be able to contact you.'

'I'll buy one now and come back to you with the number,' Imogen told him.

'All right.' René was still doubtful. 'I will think about it further. I cannot be definite in my answer yet. OK?'

'OK,' said Imogen and shut the windows.

Although she'd intended to get the most basic pay-as-you-go phone possible, she ended up with an inexpensive smartphone. There might be times, she acknowledged to the sales assistant, when she'd need to access the internet. Besides, it wasn't linked to any of her old phones or contracts, and nobody would have the number unless she gave it to them. Weirdly (and a bit worryingly, she thought), she felt more settled with a phone again, even though it had been cathartic to throw the Irish one away and she'd felt more and more free every time a piece of it ended up in a service station bin. Having a new phone made her feel connected with the world around her, which on balance was probably a good thing.

She returned to the estate agency and gave the number to René, who assured her that he'd call her later. Deciding that she was on a good-luck roll, she decided to have a celebratory coffee at one of the seafront cafés before going home. She repeated it to herself a few times. A coffee before going home. A coffee before going home. And each time it seemed a little more worth celebrating, even if a cup of coffee was hardly pushing the boat out. Carol had always enjoyed celebrating good news, but over the years, Imogen had become more circumspect. Things that had appeared promising at first had often turned out not to be quite what she'd expected. She'd learned to be more moderate in her celebrations. But the demitasse of coffee and the chocolate square that the waitress brought her were rich with luxurious flavours and seemed to Imogen to be a perfect celebration of the success of the Plan so far. She sipped the coffee and gazed towards the sea.

The wide expanse of beach was a rainbow of coloured sun umbrellas, and the sea was full of people, many of whom appeared to have hired kayaks and were paddling furiously across the water. She suddenly remembered walking down from the Villa Martine with Carol and the Delissandes boys. Her mum had been carrying a picnic basket and a beach umbrella and the children had all brought an assortment of beach toys. They'd been singing 'Alouette', another French rhyme, each one chiming in with their part as required, before the previous person had finished. And afterwards Carol had taught them 'Row, Row, Row Your Boat', which was the same sort of song. They'd sung it lustily as they tramped along the road. Had that been the day Oliver had pushed her into a hole he'd dug on the beach so that she'd wailed that she'd broken her ankle? (It was actually only a sprain and was better before nightfall, but Lucie Delissandes had fussed over her and made her a hot chocolate drink to help with the healing process.) Or had it been the day they'd buried Charles in the sand and run away telling him that he'd drown when the tide came in? Poor Charles had screamed and shouted after them as they'd laughed as his terror. So it wasn't always sweetness and light back then, she reminded herself. And I could be quite horrible when I chose.

Her memories were difficult to pin down, and yet they were still there, like faded photos in an old-fashioned album. But today they were clearer than ever before. And even if some of them were less than perfect, they were all of easier times.

Maybe everything seems easier looking back, she thought as she finished her coffee. Maybe it's simpler to think that the past was lovely and straightforward when I know perfectly well that it wasn't. Because nothing ever is. And perhaps Vince is right about me. Perhaps I specialise in fooling myself. Perhaps I'm doing it now.

It wouldn't be the first time.

She went back to the hotel. She hadn't checked out, as she'd already paid for six nights and she reckoned she might as well have the flexibility of the room. She climbed the stairs and looked at the clothes hanging in the wardrobe. A meagre selection, she thought, and none of them really suitable for the summer. She packed them into her bag, along with her toiletries, and went downstairs again.

'You're leaving now?' The receptionist was aghast. 'There is a problem?'

'No, no,' said Imogen. She explained about the apartment.

'You will be staying here the whole summer?' This time the woman was surprised.

'Yes.'

'How nice for you,' she said with a smile. 'I'm sorry, it's probably too late to get a visitor for your room. I cannot refund you.'

'I understand.' Imogen nodded, although she reminded herself that she couldn't carry on behaving as though she had an unlimited source of income when she was living on the edge as far as money was concerned. She'd never really been broke before. She wasn't sure she knew how to manage it.

The sudden shrill tone of the phone in her bag beside her made her jump, her heart beating so quickly that she thought it might explode. There was only one person with her number, she thought as she took it out. And that person wasn't Vince Naughton, so there was no need to get into a flap. But her 'hello' was tentative, and at the other end of the line, René Bastarache had to ask if it was Imogen who was speaking.

'Yes, yes, it's me,' she said.

'Well look, I've chatted with Angelique, my partner, and she says to go ahead and give you a trial. So if you come to the office tomorrow morning, you can start.'

'Fantastic,' said Imogen. 'Thank you so much, René. I mean, Monsieur Bastarache.'

'Too late to call me that now,' he said. 'You can stick to René. *A bientôt.*'

'*A bientôt,*' she said, and waited for her heartbeat to slow down again.

She was about to wheel her bag out of the hotel and start the walk to the apartment when Samantha, Gerry and Joel came into the reception area.

'You're not going!' Samantha looked shocked. 'We haven't had our night out together yet.'

Imogen explained that she was leaving because she'd rented an apartment for a few weeks.

'What a brilliant thing to do!' cried Samantha. 'And how lucky you are to be able to do it! But were you planning to walk there now? With your case and everything? Don't even think about it. Gerry will drive you.'

'It's not that far,' protested Imogen. 'Fifteen minutes at the most.'

'You don't want to have to walk dragging a case behind you,' Samantha said. 'It'll only take a couple of minutes in the car. And you must come out with us tonight. You have to celebrate.'

'You know, I really don't want to intrude on your holiday.'

'You're not intruding. And if I were you, staying for the whole summer, I'd be celebrating like there was no tomorrow.'

Imogen smiled at Samantha's enthusiasm.

'At least have a drink with me before you go,' said Samantha. 'Gerry will put your bag in the car.'

'I . . .'

But Gerry had already picked it up and was walking towards the car with it. Imogen shrugged and followed Samantha into the hotel garden, where they sat at a table in the shade. Joel peeled off his T-shirt and shorts.

'No diving!' cried Samantha, but her words were lost as he jumped into the pool. 'Kids,' she said to Imogen. 'You love them, but they spend their lives tormenting you.'

'I can imagine.' Imogen asked where they'd spent the morning.

'Kayaking,' said Samantha. 'There was an event on at the beach. Great fun.'

Imogen nodded. 'I was down there earlier and saw lots of people on the water.'

'You should give it a try if you haven't already. It's really enjoyable. They had a kids' section today, which Joel loved.'

'He's pretty fearless, isn't he?' Imogen glanced at the pool, where Joel continued to ignore the signs about diving into the water.

'You know what they're like at that age.'

Imogen remembered her mother saying the same thing to Lucie Delissandes when Charles came home with an egg-sized bump on his forehead. He'd been freewheeling his bike down the lane near the house, hit a stone in the road and shot over the handlebars. Lucie had been distraught at the sight of her son's injury. Carol had been remarkably unfazed.

Or had it been Oliver who'd come off the bike? wondered Imogen. She wished things were clearer in her head. But it had all happened such a long time ago, it was surprising she remembered anything at all.

Gerry came out to the garden and asked Imogen if she wanted to leave for the apartment now or if she was planning to stay at the hotel for a little longer.

'I think it's time for me to go.' Imogen stood up. So did Samantha.

'What do you think about that dinner tonight, Imogen?' she said. 'It would be nice to celebrate your decision to stay on for a while. I'll book the restaurant I mentioned before and we can meet here at seven thirty.'

'If you're sure I won't be in the way,' said Imogen.

'Of course not,' said Gerry. 'We love meeting people on holiday.'

'In that case it would be great, thank you.' Imogen gave Samantha a quick hug before following Gerry out to his car.

'You're very kind to give me a lift,' she told him as she got in. 'I could have walked, honestly.'

'I'm sure you could,' said Gerry. 'But there's no need. OK, which way?'

She directed him to the apartment building.

'Nice,' he said when they arrived. 'Looks like a big house really.'

'It used to be,' she explained.

'Would you like me to pick you up this evening?' asked Gerry. 'The restaurant is within walking distance of the hotel, but it'll be a bit further for you.'

'Oh, please don't worry,' said Imogen. 'I'm happy to walk.'

'If you're sure.' Gerry gave her directions, then got out of the car and took her bag from the boot.

'Thank you so much again,' said Imogen. 'I'll see you both later.'

She pulled her case up the flagstone pathway and opened the door to the building. At the top of the stairs, she took a deep breath before unlocking the apartment.

Home, she thought as she stepped inside and looked around. This is my home, at least for the next three months. I can arrange the furniture whatever way I like. I can come and go as I please. I can read whatever books I want to. I can cook anything I want to cook, drink anything I want to drink. I can go to bed at eleven or twelve or one – it doesn't matter. I'm here. I'm home. And I make the decisions. She felt intoxicated by the sense of freedom.

She opened the shutters on the windows and stepped on to the narrow balcony. A man was doing energetic circuits of the pool while a couple sat on a pair of sun loungers, chatting intently. Imogen watched them for a moment and was about to turn back into the apartment when she heard footsteps on the balcony next door. She felt herself tense up until she saw a young woman, her blond hair in plaits, leaning over the wooden rail as she drank a bottle of water.

'Hi,' said the woman, looking straight at Imogen.

'Hello.'

'English?'

'I speak English,' said Imogen.

The young woman beamed at her. 'I'm Nellie. I'm here on holiday with my sister.'

Imogen couldn't remember how long it was since she'd spoken to so many complete strangers. There was a certain intoxication in that too.

'Imogen,' she said, as an almost identical blonde appeared beside the first.

'Becky.' The second blonde introduced herself. 'We're twins, though you might have guessed that! Australian. Cycling around Europe.'

'All of Europe?' asked Imogen.

'We started off in Croatia,' said Nellie. 'Then we came through Austria and Germany to Italy before getting a ferry to Barcelona.'

'Wow.' Imogen looked at them in awe. 'That's amazing. You must be super-fit.'

Nellie laughed. 'We didn't cycle all the time. Some of it was by coach.'

'It's still impressive,' said Imogen.

'And you?' asked Becky.

'Oh, I'm staying here for a few weeks.'

'In that case, we'll see you around. We could have drinks together some evening.'

'That would be great,' said Imogen, thinking that it was years since she'd had so many invitations to drinks. 'I'll see you around.'

She went back inside the apartment. Maybe that's what I should have done, she thought. Got on a bike and kept going. But despite the fitness classes with Shona, she didn't think she'd have the legs for Europe by bike.

She unpacked her bag and hung her clothes up again. She knew she'd have to spend some of her cash on more stuff. But given that it was the summer, she hoped she'd get by with some cheap shorts and T-shirts. Despite the flurry of drinks invitations, it wasn't like she'd be socialising that often, so there was no need for skirts or dresses or high-heeled shoes. She thought of her shoe collection in Dublin. Vince had encouraged her to buy heels. Until then, she'd mainly stuck to wedges and ankle boots. And to be fair to Vince, she'd grown to like the heels too. But apart from the court shoes she'd worn to the exhibition, she'd left them all behind.

She spent such a long time luxuriating in the solitude of her apartment that she squeaked in dismay when she eventually looked at her watch and realised how late it was. She thought about phoning the Hotel Atlantique and asking them to tell

Gerry and Samantha that she couldn't make dinner after all. Being honest with herself, she didn't really want to go. She'd just been unable to say no. And yet she felt it was important to do something normal and ordinary. She dithered over the choice of staying in or going out, changing her mind multiple times before telling herself that she'd made a commitment and that Gerry had been decent in driving her to the apartment and it would be very rude not to turn up.

She arrived five minutes late, hot and slightly breathless, with the beginning of a blister on her toe because she'd worn the court shoes and they weren't really designed for hurrying. She knew that in her navy suit skirt and a plain white T-shirt she didn't look remotely holidayish, even with the multicoloured bead necklace and matching bracelet that had been a Christmas present from Shona the previous year, but it was the best she could do. She hadn't bothered with any make-up other than the tinted lip salve she always wore.

Samantha, in an elegant floral dress and cherry-red espadrilles, linked arms with her as they began to walk to the restaurant.

'Where's Joel?' asked Imogen.

'We have a child-minder for him this evening,' Samantha said. 'The hotel organised it. She's a local girl and highly recommended.'

'He's OK with being left on his own?'

'They're having a room-service dinner.' Gerry, a few paces behind, joined the conversation. 'He loves room service. It's his favourite thing. And afterwards he's going to watch some Disney on his iPad.'

'Are you sure you're all right about leaving him? Because we can go back to the hotel if—'

'Are you out of your mind?' Samantha interrupted her. 'This is only our second night out without him in four months, and I have to tell you it's a total pleasure to eat out without a hyperactive six-year-old in tow.'

'I feel like I might be in the way,' Imogen said.

'Meeting people is half the fun of holidays,' Gerry said. 'It's great to have you along.'

Vince wouldn't have agreed with him, she knew. Although he liked talking to people at poolside bars during the day, he never accepted invitations to join other holidaymakers for dinner. He said it was a waste of precious holiday time to spend it with people you didn't know and weren't likely to meet again. Imogen knew that he had a point, even though there had been times when his abrupt turning-down of invitations embarrassed her.

'Here we are.' Gerry indicated the restaurant, which was brightly lit with coloured fairy lights strung around the windows. 'We've been looking forward to coming here. It's got some great reviews on TripAdvisor.'

A waiter greeted them and settled them at a table near the window, where they began to study the menu. Although Imogen's choices were mainly influenced by price, she liked being able to try dishes she normally didn't have the opportunity to eat, and happily ordered a main course of txangurro, which the waiter told her was a type of crab.

'So how long do you plan to stay here?' asked Gerry.

'A few months,' she replied, and then wished she hadn't. It wasn't as though they'd ever meet Vince, she knew, but she was supposed to be keeping a low profile and not talking about herself. It would have been better to stay non-committal about her plans.

But being non-committal was difficult because Samantha kept peppering her with questions about herself until Gerry told his wife that Imogen wasn't getting any time to eat.

'Sorry.' Samantha grinned. 'I can't help it. I'm a reporter.'

'Reporter?' exclaimed Imogen, dropping her fork on to her plate.

'More of a blogger, to be honest,' admitted Samantha. 'I blog about sports and the local sports centre, but a few of my pieces were picked up and I've been asked by a couple of papers to do some stuff for them from time to time, which is very exciting. So I feel entitled to call myself a reporter too.'

'Nothing as glam as that for me,' said Imogen, her heart rate returning to normal as she picked up her fork again. 'I'm an admin person, that's all.'

'Smile!' Samantha picked up her phone and took a photo of Imogen and Gerry as the waiter cleared their table at the end of the meal. 'You're on your holidays!'

'Oh God, I hate photos,' said Imogen. 'Please don't keep it!'

'It's lovely.' Samantha showed it to her. 'D'you want me to forward it to you?'

Imogen shook her head. 'I'm not a photo person.'

'I used not to be,' Samantha said. 'But when I started up the blog, I got a lot more into it. And of course people love seeing themselves online.'

'Not me,' said Imogen.

'I agree with you completely,' said Gerry. 'I hate having my photo taken. But Sam has a talent for it. She took some great pictures at the kayaking earlier. Especially of me managing to capsize, which was totally embarrassing.'

Samantha gave him a teasing smile. Gerry signalled for the bill and waved away Imogen's efforts to pay for her share.

'You can buy us a nightcap in the bar down the road,' he told her.

So even though Imogen was already fuzzy from two glasses of wine and the shot of brandy that had been brought at the end of the meal, she accompanied them to the bar. She and Samantha sat at an outside table while Gerry got into conversation with one of the people they'd met kayaking earlier.

'Is everything OK with you?' asked Samantha after they'd clinked their glasses of Baileys and toasted holiday fun.

'Why wouldn't it be?' asked Imogen.

'It's only . . . well I don't want to offend you, but for someone who's about to take the summer off, you seem to be a little distracted,' said Samantha.

'Oh, I'm not taking it off completely,' said Imogen. 'I'm going to work for a while.'

'Really!' Samantha's eyes widened. 'What will you do?'

Another mistake, thought Imogen. She shouldn't have said anything about working in France. Perhaps it was the alcohol that was causing her to be so careless. In an effort to retrieve the situation, and remembering Henri, the student she'd met on the bus, she told Samantha that she planned to spend some time at a vineyard.

'That sounds so romantic.'

'I'm sure it's more backbreaking than anything else,' said Imogen, feeling guilty about lying to her.

'You'll have to keep in touch with us,' Samantha said. 'Here's my card. It's got all my details on it.'

'Thank you.' Imogen put it in her bag.

'Same again?' asked Samantha as she drained her glass.

'I might just go for water this time,' said Imogen.

'Oh, live a little.' Samantha winked at her. 'You're only young once.' She waved at her husband. 'Bring the cocktail menu, Gerry,' she called. 'We're just getting going over here!'

Chapter 11

The following morning Imogen woke up with the first hangover she'd had in years. Whenever she went out with Vince, she limited herself to a single glass of wine. But she'd drunk more the night before than in the previous six months put together. She wasn't entirely sure it had been worth it, but it had definitely been fun.

She got up and fished in her handbag for a couple of paracetamol tablets, taking them with the remains of the litre bottle of water she'd bought the previous day. I hope it's not a bad omen, she thought as she showered and dressed, to have got blotto on the day before I start a new job! Vince would be right to despair of me if that was the case.

Her headache had disappeared by the time she arrived at the agency an hour later, although she was conscious that she was feeling a certain tension about the job. Which she decided was utterly ridiculous. After all, she told herself as she watched René park in the space outside the building, I have a university degree, I've translated important technical documents, I've negotiated with trade suppliers on behalf of Conor Foley – I can't be worried about being a cleaner.

And yet she was.

The light rain that René had forecast began to fall as he stepped out of his car, a massive bundle of keys in his hands.

'Ah, *bon*, you're here already,' he said. His eyes narrowed. 'Are you OK?'

'Yes, of course.'

'You look a bit pale. I don't want you fainting on the job.'

'I won't.'

'And you're absolutely sure about doing it?'

'Absolutely,' she said.

'Follow me.'

He raised the shutters and unlocked the glass door. They both went inside the office, where he switched on the lights and started up his computer. Then he printed out a document and handed it to her.

'This is your schedule for today. They are all apartments to start you off. It looks like a lot, but they should take you no more than half an hour each, as they are holiday lets and all you need to do is dust, sweep and mop. You will bring this sheet back to me, signed by you, at the end of the day, along with the keys to the properties.'

'OK,' said Imogen. She looked at the addresses and then at René. 'I'll need a proper map. The one I have only shows the main streets.'

'Google,' he said. 'On your phone. With driving directions to each one.'

'I don't have a car,' she reminded him.

'I didn't think of that.' He frowned. 'Without a car you will be doing a great deal of walking back and forwards and lose a lot of time. And you will get wet today too,' he added as he looked out of the window at the darkening sky.

'I don't mind walking,' said Imogen, fearful that he'd

change his mind. 'I walk quickly, I don't stroll. As for the rain, I'm used to it. I'm Irish, after all.'

'Walking is not efficient,' said René. 'Wait a moment.'

He disappeared through a door and a few minutes later returned pushing an old-fashioned ladies' bicycle. It was painted in pastel pink, with yellow and white flower decals stuck to the frame. There was a cane basket attached to the handlebars.

'It belonged to my wife,' said René. 'When she left me, she left the bike. So you can have it while you are working for us.'

'It's like a prop from a romantic movie,' said Imogen. 'I feel as though I should be wearing a floaty dress and a cashmere cardigan instead of this.' She glanced down at the rain jacket she'd put on over a T-shirt and leggings that morning, and made a face. She didn't know what had possessed her to include a rain jacket in her packing, but she was glad she had.

'Hmm, well it didn't help the romance in our relationship,' said René. 'The most important thing is it will get you where you need to go. Also . . .' He reached beneath the desk and took out a telescopic umbrella. 'This might come in handy.'

'Cleaning products?' Imogen looked at him questioningly.

'There are some things in the back,' said René. 'Take what you need.'

Imogen propped the bike against a wall and went through the door, which led to a storage area. She selected a bottle of disinfectant and a couple of cleaning sprays, as well as a few cloths, hoping that every apartment already had a mop and bucket and a brush.

She put the cleaning fluids and cloths in the basket and set off, glad that she'd paid the extra for the smartphone so that she could use Google Maps as René had suggested to guide her. It took her nearly twenty minutes to reach her first location, although she reckoned she could shave at least five off that in future, especially if it wasn't raining. She slid from the bike and pushed it up the narrow pathway that led to the unexpectedly modern block.

She tapped on the door of the apartment, but there was no reply. She put the key in the lock and let herself in. Then she grimaced.

A pile of breakfast dishes had been left on the kitchen table, and the draining board was covered in used cups and glasses. In the two bedrooms, the unmade beds were a tangle of sheets, while the used towels had been abandoned on the bathroom floor. It had been a long time since she'd seen anything so messy. Vince didn't allow mess. He didn't like disorder. Dishes never went unwashed. Beds never went unmade. Everything in Bellwood Park had a place, and it was her job to know exactly where that place was.

She took a deep breath. She'd left Bellwood Park precisely because of that. She should be glad to find disorder everywhere, although she had to admit that she was a tidy person at heart – and that was probably Carol's legacy.

The other apartments on the list were less work, but she was behind schedule by the time she finished and worried that René would have left before she got back to the agency. However, when she freewheeled down the hill and stopped outside the building, she saw that the halogen lights over the photos in the window were still on and he was sitting behind his desk.

'Will I have to bring the page and keys back to you every evening?' she asked as she handed him the signed sheet. 'Because there may be days when I won't be finished before you close.'

'We don't close until eight p.m. in the summer,' he told her. 'You've plenty of time. But if you're delayed for any reason, you can post the keys and the paper into the box on the wall, where they'll be secure.'

She nodded.

'Are you happy with what you did today?' he asked.

'Yes. Although I'm a bit tired,' she admitted. 'It's been a while since I had so much running around to do.'

'Are you sure this is for you?'

'Absolutely,' she said.

He looked at her doubtfully.

'It truly isn't a problem,' she assured him. 'I've done cleaning work before.'

'You said that, but . . .'

'My mother was a housekeeper.'

It wasn't quite the same thing, Imogen knew. But Carol had been good at keeping the Villa Martine spick and span. Until the day of the indiscretion, Lucie Delissandes had always said that she was the best housekeeper in the world and that she wanted to keep her for ever. She'd said that she'd never find anyone as good as Carol again. Imogen wondered if eventually she had.

'Ah, I understand,' said René. 'It's in the family. *D'accord*. I will see you tomorrow at the same time.'

'See you then.' She left the bicycle propped up against the wall, but René called after her.

'You can take it with you,' he said. 'It's not exactly what I use for getting around town.'

'Thank you.'

'You're welcome.'

She got on the bike and started pedalling again. When she arrived back at her own apartment, the first thing she did was turn on the shower. She hoped the warm water would help her aching muscles. She couldn't remember the last time she'd worked so hard.

After a few days, she began to find a rhythm. Although the houses and apartments she was given were different every day, she was getting more familiar with the town, and was quicker at travelling between each destination. She'd also streamlined her dust, sweep and mop routine and found it satisfying to see order come from the chaos that often awaited her. Nevertheless, on the day that she realised she'd arranged a selection of towels in colour-coordinated piles in the airing cupboard, she immediately took them out and replaced them in a random rainbow display. Enjoying her job was one thing. Being as obsessive as Vince was something else.

As the cleaning took up most of her day, she didn't have much time for anything else, but she found a couple of hours to buy some summer tops and skirts, as well as doing some food shopping and filling her small fridge with juices, vegetables and cold meats. She also detoured into the small wine shop on the corner of her street and bought herself a couple of bottles of local Muscadelle.

She'd moved the furniture in the apartment so that the

small table was beside the window, and she sat at it with her salad and wine, allowing her aching body to relax. In addition to Becky and Nellie, with whom she usually exchanged a few cheery words every day, she'd started to recognise other occupants of the building, although she was aware that most of them were short-stay holidaymakers. It was a pity, she thought, that despite the convenience factor, René hadn't yet offered her the chance of cleaning the apartments in her own building.

She was beginning to disassociate herself from her Dublin self, with the Imogen who'd been married to Vince, the Imogen who'd burned her bridges with her family and who'd allowed most of her friends to slide out of her life. She was also beginning to feel the shreds of her lost confidence returning. She'd forgotten how to be confident in Dublin. She blamed herself for that. She should have known what was happening. She wasn't a stupid person. And yet she'd allowed herself to do some very stupid things. She didn't know why. She didn't understand it. She didn't think anyone else would understand it either.

Without wanting to, she thought about Vince. She wondered what he was doing now, whether he'd set about finding out where she was. The reason she'd rung the Missing Family Foundation was so that he couldn't mobilise some kind of official force to track her. But she was quite sure he'd think of other ways, if that was what he wanted. It was hard to know how he would take it. Would he try to find her, or pretend that she'd never even existed? The thing is, she thought, he's better off without me. He must know that really. But she knew that wasn't the point. And that sooner or later she was going to have to find out.

She took a deep breath, then picked up the phone in front of her. She opened the browser, and hesitated. Then, for the first time since she'd left Ireland, she logged in to her email account.

Imogen's emails were normally mostly from the gym advising her of new classes, Amazon recommending new reads, and a beauty site from which she'd once bought a moisturiser bombarding her with the latest products designed to deal with every beauty crisis she could possibly think of. But today the first one she saw was from Vince.

From: Vinnock@carlisledirect.com
To: Imozhen@gmail.com
Subject: WTF????
What the hell do you think you're playing at? I got home and there was no sign of you and I was worried sick. I tried calling and calling. In the end I went to your office and GUESS WHAT, Imogen, you'd resigned. Your boss told me – I'm sure he was laughing his head off looking at me. The poor sap husband who's the last to know that his wife has run away – with another man, Imogen? Is that it? Is that what you've done? Because if it is, I will come and find him and tear him limb from limb. What has happened to you? You're clearly not right in the head.

I love you and forgive you.
Vince

The second email was shorter.

From: Vinnock@carlisledirect.com
To: Imozhen@gmail.com
Subject: I Am Very Worried
Imogen, I realise that you have problems. I understand that. I know that you're not yourself. Come home. We can sort it out.

I love you and forgive you.

Vince

The third had no subject.

From: Vinnock@carlisledirect.com
To: Imozhen@gmail.com
You rang a **ing missing persons helpline but you didn't ring me!!! Is Shona involved in this, Imogen? Is she? What the hell is going on? You need help. You know you do.

I love you and forgive you.

Vince

There were emails from Shona, too.

From: Blondie@moonshine.com
To: Imozhen@gmail.com
Subject: Where Are You?
Imogen! Where are you? What's happened?? Vince is going mental. He's terribly worried. So am I. Are you all right? Are you upset about anything? He went to the police and they said there was nothing they could do, but he's going back to them and I think he's right

because you might have chucked your job and whatever but you can't possibly be all right. Why would you do this? Why? You have a perfect life. You've always said so. I know things might have been a bit rocky lately because Vince told me about you trying for a baby with no luck so far. I'm so so sorry. Maybe IVF could help? Oh Imogen, I'm hoping that you're alive and OK and that I'm not sending an email you're never going to read!!! Please please call me. Whatever's happened we can work it out. If you're upset about something else we can fix it. I know we can. Vince is devastated. Totally. And so am I. I'm really really worried. Why didn't you tell me what you were going to do? I'd have helped. Or something.

Call me.

Love

Shona xxxxxxx

And then:

From: Blondie@moonshine.com
To: Imozhen@gmail.com
Subject: Missing Person??!!??
OMG, what's happening? Got a call from a woman from a missing persons helpline. She said you'd phoned and told her to tell me you were OK and that you were starting a new life. A new life??? What does that mean? Why won't you call me? I can't believe you're doing this to me. Or to Vince. He's beside himself with worry. Beside himself! Look, whatever's the problem, you can tell me and we'll work it out. Even if it has something

to do with Vince. *Especially* if it has. **ck him if so. We're girls. We're mates. We'll stick together. Call me. Please. Talk to me. We can fix this.

Shona xxxxx

Imogen nibbled at her nail as she read the messages again and again. She could feel Vince's rage radiating from the screen. She supposed he was also angry that she'd given Shona's name as a contact to the Missing Family people and not his. She hadn't wanted them to talk to him. Just in case he'd wheedled some additional information from them. Not that there was anything to wheedle, but still – she didn't trust him and she didn't trust herself.

And as for his comments to Shona about a baby . . . She might have guessed he'd try that again. He liked suggesting to people that she wanted to get pregnant, or that she might even *be* pregnant, even though she knew he didn't want a baby because that way he would no longer have her undivided attention. And she didn't want one either because a child would have made things worse, as well as linking her to him for ever.

She exhaled slowly. She felt bad about not having confided in Shona, but the thing was, somewhere along the line, her friend had become Vince's friend too. They'd occasionally send each other jokey texts, usually about dogs, because Shona had a gorgeous boxer and Vince had owned one as a kid. The boxer connection was one of the reasons why Shona was the only one of Imogen's friends that Vince approved of. Her former college friends had been weeded out, although Imogen hadn't really noticed it happening at the time. But later, after she'd come up with the Plan, she had been afraid that Vince had got inside Shona's head in the same way he'd managed to get inside hers. Because that was what he did. He was fun and charming and great to be with and you couldn't help agreeing with him over one thing and then another, until one day . . . Imogen's teeth snapped over her nail and bit right through it. Until one day you were the person he decided he wanted you to be and you wished you'd never met him. And the only way of breaking free was running away.

Chapter 12

Vince had been utterly furious when Shona told him about Imogen's call to the Missing Family Foundation.

'She phoned complete strangers to say she was OK? And they called you and not me? What the fuck!' he raged.

'I'm sorry,' she said miserably.

'I'm going to call them myself!' Vince jabbed the disconnect button and phoned the number she'd given him. When he got through, he asked to speak to Ellie.

A softly spoken woman came on the line and listened to him as he demanded to know where Imogen was.

'I'm really sorry, Mr Naughton,' she said, 'but I can't tell you that.'

'You bloody well can!' cried Vince. 'She's my wife and I'm entitled to know.'

'Our service is completely confidential,' said Ellie. 'But in any case I don't know where she is; that's not a question I asked her.'

'Why the hell didn't you?'

'All we're concerned with is passing on a message from a loved one,' said Ellie. 'To put your mind at rest about their safety.'

'My mind isn't at rest,' said Vince. 'It's about as far from at rest as it's possible to be. Did she say at least whether she was in Ireland or not?'

'No,' said Ellie.

'Why does everyone think it's OK to keep information from me?' asked Vince. 'I'm her husband, for God's sake!'

'I'm sure Imogen will come back when she's ready,' said Ellie. 'People often do. She could simply need her own space for a while.'

Vince snorted and ended the call.

He decided to go back to the garda station and demand they look into her disappearance. Sinead Canavan, the same female garda he'd spoken to when he'd first reported Imogen missing, came to talk to him again. The police were already aware that Imogen had been in touch with the Missing Family Foundation, so Sinead pointed out that as his wife was obviously alive and well, there was nothing the gardai could do.

'It doesn't matter that she's mentally unstable?' asked Vince. 'That doesn't worry you in the slightest?'

'I asked you about her mental state before and you told me she wasn't under medical care,' Sinead reminded him.

'Well, no. She's not officially bonkers,' said Vince.

The garda raised an eyebrow.

'She's . . . well, she needs me,' he said. 'She can't cope without me. She's hopeless on her own. Utterly hopeless.'

'Yet she's made contact and has assured people she's well. She resigned voluntarily from her job. She's withdrawn money from the bank account. I'm sorry, Mr Naughton, but there's nothing more we can do.'

'How do you know her resignation was voluntary?' demanded Vince. 'She might have been pressurised into it.'

'By whom?'

'I don't know!' he cried. 'The people who blackmailed her into taking money out of our account in the first place? Someone connected with the company she works for? A criminal gang? It's your job to work that out.'

'I do sympathise with your very understandable distress,' said Sinead. 'But we followed up on your original report by contacting her ex-employer. Our investigations don't lead us to think a crime has been committed.'

'Every bloody day I see notices and news about people who are missing. You put up photos of old ladies and kids, but for my wife, nothing at all?' Vince was furious.

'Mr Naughton, as I already told you, people sometimes just need a break. It's upsetting, I know, but this seems to be one of those cases. We're not concerned for Imogen's safety because she's let people know that she's OK. That's why we're not actively looking for her.'

'Do you already know where she is?' demanded Vince.

The garda shook her head. 'I'm sure she'll get in touch with you when she's ready. Please don't worry.'

'Don't worry! Don't worry!' he cried. 'How can you sit there on your lardy arse and tell me not to worry when anything could have happened to my wife?'

Sinead ignored his insult and spoke calmly. 'We've done all we can at this point. If you have further reason to believe that Mrs Naughton is at risk, or if you have additional information to give us, we'll be happy to help you. But in the meantime, there's nothing I can do.'

Vince stared wordlessly at her before storming out of the station. He got into his car and revved the engine, angry with the police and even angrier with Imogen. How dare she do this to him? How dare she?

When he got home, he sat in front of the laptop, willing her to send him a message so that he could respond to her straight away. He was certain that if he could talk to her, even by text or email, he'd be able to put a stop to this nonsense. But there was nothing, and his anger ratcheted up another notch.

He was still angry when he called to see Shona the following day.

She invited him in and made coffee while he raged about the intransigence of the missing persons woman and the incompetence of the gardai.

'Nobody will look for her,' he said. 'I'm going to have to try to find her myself.'

'How?' she asked.

'You suggested social media. I know she's deactivated it, but her Facebook page would still be there. I could try hacking into it. D'you know her password?'

'Of course I don't! What I meant by using social media was you putting out something on your own page,' Shona said. 'Or setting up a page saying she was missing and asking for help in tracing her. Although I'm not convinced about that now that she's been in touch. Putting something up might scare her off. Make her feel under more pressure.'

'I'm fed up with everyone talking about the pressure she's under,' said Vince. 'What about me? What about the pressure *I'm* under?'

Shona said nothing.

'I know. I know. She's upset.' He sighed. 'It gets her off the hook for everything. Anyway, on the Facebook thing, what I was thinking is that she could be in contact with someone she knows. And they might send her a message. And I can intercept it.'

'She won't be expecting a message if she deactivated her account.'

'True, but—'

'But even then you shouldn't even dream of doing that,' said Shona firmly. 'Besides, the gardai are probably right. She might need a bit of time to herself, especially if she's upset about the pregnancy. The most important thing is that she's OK, otherwise she wouldn't have rung that Missing Family place. At least she did that.'

'Big deal,' he said. 'Telling some stranger she's alive but not her own damned husband.'

'I emailed her and didn't get a reply either,' Shona reminded him. 'You're not the only one she's avoiding.'

'If she does get in touch with you, let me know straight away.' Vince didn't say that he'd already accessed Imogen's email account and seen Shona's messages.

'Yes.' There was a certain reticence in her voice and Vince heard it.

'She's not well, Shona. She needs help.'

'Or time.'

'Anyone who disappears from home needs help,' said Vince. 'And although you might think that it's me she's run away from and not be prepared to help, I can assure you that I've only got her best interests at heart.'

'Oh Vince, I know that.' Shona's tone was heartfelt. 'Of course I'll help you in any way I can.'

He gave her a wan smile. 'I'll keep looking to see if I can find anything at home that'll point me in the right direction,' he said. 'You'd think that the digital age would make things easier, but it doesn't, exactly because Imogen kept everything on her phone and she didn't back it up. I'm still hoping to unearth a phone number for her aunts in the States. I reckon they're the people she's most likely to get in touch with.'

'Agnes and Berthe?'

'Berthe, given that Agnes is away with the birds now,' said Vince.

'Don't worry them too much,' advised Shona. 'Don't say she's missing. Just that she's gone off for a few days and you'd like to know if she's gone to them.'

'I need to find her for her own good,' said Vince. 'And I'll persuade Berthe of that.'

'If I hear anything, I'll tell you,' Shona told him. 'I promise.'

'Thanks.' Vince stood up and gave her a hug. 'You're a proper friend to her. She never appreciated you.'

Shona's eyes welled with tears. And yet she also couldn't help feeling a stab of guilt. Because surely if she'd been the friend that Vince said she was, Imogen would have been able to confide in her. Or at least call her and not that Missing Family crowd. Why hadn't she trusted her? What was she afraid of? And what had gone so wrong in her marriage that she believed she had no choice other than to disappear without a trace?

Despite Shona's reservations, Vince tried to reactivate Imogen's Facebook account when he got home, but failed utterly in his attempt. Then he had the idea of searching for members of her stepfamily on the site. To his immense satisfaction, he eventually found the profile of a Cheyenne Scott who lived in London but who also listed Dublin and Birmingham as previous places where she'd lived. The profile picture was of a daisy, which wasn't much help, but when he checked her photos, he saw one of Cheyenne and Imogen at Cheyenne's wedding. He punched the air with his fist and then sent a message to her explaining that Imogen was missing and that he was doing his best to trace her. He ended by leaving his mobile number and asking her to call him. He also sent her a friend request, because he knew the message might otherwise end up in her spam folder.

He picked up the phone and called Shona. Her voice, when she answered, was sleepy, and Vince glanced at his watch, surprised to see it was nearly midnight.

'I'm sorry if I've disturbed you,' he said.

'Has she been in touch?' asked Shona.

'No, but I found Cheyenne and I've sent a message to her.'

'Well done you! Has she any clue about where Imogen is?'

'She hasn't replied yet, but hopefully she will soon and we can resolve this without any more fuss. Maybe that stupid woman at the gardai was right too. It is a family thing. She's gone off for a few days and Cheyenne might know where.'

'Vince, you have to be understanding whatever Imogen's done,' said Shona.

'I'll never understand it.' Vince sounded suddenly grim. 'But I'll forgive her, because I always do.'

'Jeepers, does she do that much that needs your continual forgiveness?'

'I always forgive her, no matter whether it's something big or small, because I love her.'

'Oh Vince.'

'I love her,' he repeated. 'I don't want anything to happen to her.'

'For the first time since this all happened, I'm beginning to think that it'll be OK,' said Shona. 'I really am.'

'I bloody well hope you're right,' said Vince.

Shona was wide awake after Vince's call. She wanted to do the right thing for Imogen and for Vince. As far as she was concerned, Imogen had the right to leave, but she'd gone about it the wrong way. All she'd managed to do was worry everyone, especially her husband.

But surely she didn't intend to walk away from her home and hide from everyone she knew for ever? Shona knew that Imogen didn't have a lot of money, so how would she live? She didn't want to read a story in the papers about an Irishwoman who'd ended up in the gutters of Paris. Or anywhere else for that matter. But Imogen wasn't stupid. Sure, she depended on Vince for lots of things, but she wouldn't have disappeared without some kind of plan. How long had she been planning for? How many times had she sat opposite Shona laughing and chatting while inside her head she was thinking about running away? Perhaps she'd had a job lined up to go to. Perhaps it would all work out fine for her.

Or perhaps it wouldn't.

I'm still her friend, thought Shona, as she picked up her phone. I still care about her even if she doesn't give a damn about me.

She decided to send both a text and an email.

Please call me, she typed. *I'm glad you're all right but I need to know what's going on.*

Then she turned out the light. But it was a long time before she fell asleep.

Chapter 13

At the start of her second week working for René Bastarache, and the third since she'd left home, Imogen glanced at her list of cleaning jobs and then at René himself. Her usual array of holiday apartments had been replaced by three houses headed *Permanent Residences.* But it was the name and address of the third house that caused her to look at René questioningly.

He'd clearly been expecting a reaction from her, because he smiled and said that they had decided she was too good a cleaner to waste on the holiday lets. They were moving her to the permanent homes instead.

'People who live here all year round?' she asked.

'But of course. That is what permanent means,' he replied. And then he shrugged. 'At least, almost all year. Sometimes they are families who live in Paris or Nantes or somewhere but have a home here for the entire summer. They are not properties rented out to clients. On that list . . .' he glanced at his own copy, 'the first belongs to the Landrys. They live here all the time and are very good customers of ours, because they also own an apartment that we rent on their behalf, so we want your best work for them. It will take you between two and a half to three hours for that house. For the other two, they are holiday visitors who spend the entire summer and most of their other vacations here.'

'And have they arrived yet?' she asked.

'The Blanchards at Le Petit Nuage are here, yes,' he said. 'The family at the Villa Martine were here for a week and have gone back to Paris, but they expect to return soon, so they asked that the house be cleaned as soon as possible. There will be laundry too, Imogen. You will bring the towels and sheets here and we will have them done. When they're here for the summer, they do it themselves. Madame likes the sheets to be dried in the open air when possible.'

If it was the Delissandes, Imogen knew that already. She remembered Lucie Delissandes telling Carol that the sun infused the sheets with light and the fresh air gave them a clean scent. She recalled her mother pegging sheets on the line and then smiling as they billowed out like white sails in the breeze. She wanted to ask René if the family still owned the house, but she knew the question would freak him out. But what if it had been Lucie and Denis who'd spent the previous week there? She could have bumped into them in the town. The thought made her go hot and cold. Would she have recognised them? Would they have recognised her? They'd be in their late fifties or early sixties by now, but she felt sure that she would have known them straight away. They, however, couldn't possibly have recognised her. She looked at the sheet of paper again. How on earth would they feel about the daughter of their ex-housekeeper being their cleaner now? What sort of weirdness was that?

Imogen didn't believe in fate. Her mother had once told

her that discovering she was pregnant after the road accident that had killed her parents and her husband had been fate, but Imogen had frowned at the comment and said that if Carol was trying to say that something good had come out of the crash that had obliterated her family, she was being very generous towards fate.

'But you're the best thing that ever happened to me,' Carol protested.

'I would've been born anyway,' Imogen pointed out. 'Wouldn't it have been better if Dad had been alive when it happened?'

Carol had struggled to answer her question. But then Carol had always struggled to answer her questions, Imogen thought as she got on her bike and began to pedal to her first job. At least until she went down the road of using inspirational quotes and clichés to make her points. In trying to make sense of what had happened to her family, Carol had allowed herself to get caught up in a New Age way of thinking, egged on, Imogen remembered, by Lucie Delissandes, who sometimes treated her mother like a project to be worked on, and was forever exchanging motivational sayings with her, as well as insisting on hanging crystal angels and dreamcatchers in the room that she and Imogen shared. Not that the inspirational stuff had done any good in the end. And as for the bloody dreamcatchers, thought Imogen, freewheeling down a short hill, they hadn't caught the dreams that left her mother crying out as she relived the accident. And they hadn't caught the indiscretion before it started either.

She stopped outside the first house, La Lumière, and rang the bell. Time to get to work, she told herself, and stop thinking about things in the past that had nothing whatsoever to do with the present. Or, as the quote from the Buddha that her mum had once had framed over her bed said: *Do not dwell in the past, do not dream of the future, concentrate the mind on the present moment.* Except it was hard not to dwell on the past right now. Because if it wasn't for things that had happened years ago, her future, and therefore the present moment, might have been very, very different.

Nevertheless, it was the present that required her time now, and she resolved to be the best cleaner that had ever worked for René Bastarache. The future could, at least temporarily, look after itself.

It was infinitely more satisfying to clean the homes of people who lived in them than the holiday lets. The owners took proper care of their things and Imogen did too, enjoying the shine of the furniture after she'd polished it and taking pleasure in putting everything back in its proper place. Although to be fair, neither of the first two houses was very untidy.

As she cycled along a road that tugged at the edges of her memory, she wondered what the Villa Martine would be like. She also wondered how accurate her memories of it really were.

She knew that there was a turn coming up even before Google Maps told her, because she'd seen the sign for the campsite near the house and she remembered the name: Jazkiel. When she'd seen it as a child, she'd thought it had something to do with jazz music and had expected to see a band playing at the gates. Fortunately she hadn't said that to anyone, particularly Oliver and Charles, who would have laughed at her. They used to laugh at her anyway because of her accent, although she always had the last laugh there because they were supposed to be speaking English, and every time they pronounced her name Imo-zhen, she would snort and say that they hadn't got a clue. Although they rarely called her Imogen. They'd been the ones to christen her Genie. Which they still pronounced in their very French way as Zhee-nie.

And so the present has finally brought me here, she said to herself as she stopped outside the front gates of the Villa Martine. After all the times I've wanted to come, after my silly childish thoughts about how to make things right, I've arrived by accident rather than design. I wonder would Mum think it was fate after all?

She looked at the chrome name plate set into the wall. It was new. So were the gates. When she'd arrived that first day, sitting beside Carol in Denis Delissandes' car, they'd been white-painted metal with the house name stuck on in gold lettering. Now the gates were stained wood, modern and new, and instead of opening inwards as they had before, Imogen could see that they were on a track, so that they would glide to one side. There was a wooden pedestrian gate beside them, along with a keypad. She pressed the bell on the keypad in case anyone was still there, but nobody answered, so she tapped in the code that René had given her. A quiet click told her that the gate had opened. She pushed it gently and walked through.

She didn't know what she remembered and what she didn't. The gravel driveway might have been gravel back then too, but the stone path that led from the pedestrian gate to the front door was unfamiliar. She was sure that the garden was neater – there were flower beds and decorative stone areas that couldn't have been there in the days when Oliver and Charles played football. But the house itself was the same: white-painted like so many of the houses in the area, with the traditional alpine-style shallow sloping roof and red-shuttered windows. The shutters were all tightly closed.

She walked up the steps to the front door and put the key in the lock. She opened it, and then swiped the tag in front of the alarm pad, relieved when the insistent beeping stopped. She took a deep breath. She was inside the house she'd lived in for nearly five years. The house she'd believed was her home, no matter how stupid that belief had been.

Zhee-nie. Zhee-nie! Where are you? The words echoed around the empty hallway. *We're going to the beach! Get your things. Zhee-nie! Depêche-toi!!*

Overwhelmed by the voices in her head, Imogen sank slowly on to the bottom stair and put her head between her knees, suddenly afraid that she was about to faint.

Come here, Genie. Let me do your hair.

Madame – as Imogen had always called Lucie Delissandes – loved to arrange her luxurious long hair, brushing it, plaiting it and putting it up in intricate styles that looked pretty but lasted for about ten minutes, because then she'd run outside to play with the boys and it always ended up falling around her face in wayward curls.

Genie, what on earth are you doing? Get upstairs this instant and under that shower.

Her mother approved of her playing with the boys, but not the fact that she invariably ended up filthy after their games of football or chasing or pirates . . .

She raised her head and looked around her again. Despite the clarity of the voices, the house was very definitely deserted. She realised that a tear was rolling down her face and she fished a tissue from her bag. Silly to be nostalgic, she thought, as she wiped it away. Silly to suddenly feel as though she belonged here again. She didn't. She'd changed. Everything had changed. Everything always did.

And that's a good thing, she told herself as she stood up. I've learned that. And I'm changing too, because I've taken back control of my life and control of my future. Now I have to get on with it.

All the same, as she began to walk along the still familiar hallway towards the kitchen, the memories continued to wash over her. And yet, she realised as she opened the shutters and allowed the bright sunlight to flood the house, they weren't entirely accurate. The kitchen, which had been updated with modern units, seemed smaller than she remembered. So did the living room beyond it. The rustic brick fireplace had been replaced by a sleek gas unit behind tempered glass, and the heavy mahogany furniture had given way to pieces that had clearly come from IKEA.

She left the living room and made her way upstairs to the bedroom where she'd once slept. Originally it had been a large room, but the Delissandes had divided it into two, one part for her mother and the other for her. Now it had been restored to the single bigger room it had been before and was dominated by a king-sized bed. The free-standing units Imogen remembered had been replaced by expensive fitted ones. Even though she could clearly recall being here with Carol, it was now something quite firmly in her past. Running her finger along the surface of the dressing table to check for dust, she realised that the Villa Martine wasn't some shrine to the way things had once been. It was a lived-in house that had aged with her. It was a house where old memories had faded and new ones had taken their place. And, she thought, it was a house that she was here to clean, not to wander around like a lost ghost. Nor was there a need to apologise for the past. Everyone had moved on. As people always did.

You've wasted enough time blubbering like a fool, she told herself sternly, and you've work to do. The first part of which was to get the laundry together. She took a deep breath as she opened the door to the master bedroom. It too was furnished in a modern style, but she didn't know if it always had been, or if the units were new, as she'd never been in it before. The sheets were in a pile on top of the mattress, along with some blue and white striped towels. She gathered them up and brought them downstairs. Without even thinking about it, she turned towards the utility room, where she knew the washing machine was housed, before remembering that she was supposed to bring the laundry back to René. She took a folded black refuse sack from her bag and piled the sheets and towels inside. Then she opened the door that led to the garden. The clothes line was still there, a selection of colourful pegs attached to it. It was a long time since Imogen had dried clothes on a washing line. She used the dryer in Bellwood Park. Vince hated seeing clothes hung up in the garden. He said it was offensive to have his shirts and shorts out there for everyone to see. But Imogen loved drying things in the fresh air. Once again she recalled the white sheets rising and falling in the offshore breeze while she and Oliver and Charles pretended they were the sails of a pirate ship and chased each other around them. She inhaled deeply. The sheets had always smelled faintly of the lavender washing powder that Lucie liked to buy. But today the only scent was from the vivid pink oleander bush that grew beside the wall.

She was late returning to the estate agency with the keys to the properties and the washing from the Villa Martine, and René's eyes narrowed as she walked into the office.

'Are you all right?' he asked.

'You're always asking me that. Why shouldn't I be?'

'You look peaky,' he said. 'And you're behind schedule.'

'Big houses take a lot of time,' she told him.

'I want you to do a good job,' he said. 'But you don't have to be forensic about it.'

'I wasn't. It takes time opening and closing shutters and making sure everything is secure. Also . . .' she grinned, 'it took me longer to cycle back because there was more dirty linen than usual and it was hard to see over the top of the basket.'

René took the bag from her.

'Are they returning soon?' she asked as he slipped a 'Villa Martine' tag on it.

'I don't know,' he replied. 'They usually phone beforehand. They're here for a lot of the summer.'

Once again, Imogen wanted to ask if it was the Delissandes. But René spoke before she had the chance to formulate the question.

'Did you reset the alarms?'

'Of course.'

'I'm putting a lot of faith in you,' said René. 'These are people's homes.'

A knot of worry wound itself around her stomach. Had he done a background check on her? Had he discovered something to concern him?

'I know they are.' She spoke calmly. 'I'm very conscious of that.'

He seemed to relax. 'Normally the person who does the cleaning for permanent or semi-permanent clients is the longest-serving member of the team,' he said. 'But Viktoria was the one to leave, and getting someone to do her work has been difficult.'

'Thank you for your confidence in me,' Imogen said.

'I didn't have that much at the start,' admitted René. 'And you haven't been with us very long. However, Angelique is impressed.'

'She is? But I haven't even met her.'

'She inspects the work after you've finished,' René said. 'Not every time, you understand. But for some of the properties. The apartments are always pristine when you've done them. Today she called to the Blanchards after you'd left. They told her you were the most thorough cleaner they'd ever had.'

'If a job's worth doing, it's worth doing well,' she said in English.

'Huh?'

'I think in France you say, "*Ça vaut la peine si c'est bien fait*".'

'Ah.' He nodded. 'In any event, we're happy with your work.'

'That's good to hear.'

'And yet . . .'

She looked at him enquiringly.

'Nothing,' said René. 'Nothing at all. I'll see you tomorrow.'

'See you then,' said Imogen.

She left the office and went to the seafront café for the after-work coffee that had become a ritual for her. The waitress, Céline, a slender woman of around her own age who wore her fair hair in a carefully disordered topknot, greeted her warmly and asked after her day.

'Strangely satisfying,' replied Imogen. 'I never thought I'd like cleaning houses, but I do.'

'Would you be interested in adding mine to your list?' asked Céline.

Imogen was a little surprised at the request. Céline saw the flicker of doubt in her eyes and grinned.

'I don't have time for it because I work such long hours in the café,' she said. 'I am the proprietor. I'm here all of the summer, for twelve hours a day, which is why my poor house is neglected so much. And I feel bad for it.'

'Oh, I see.'

'What do you think?' Céline gave her a hopeful look. 'I can probably pay you a little more than they do at the agency.'

'Well . . .'

'Take a moment to consider it while I make your coffee,' said Céline, and she turned back towards the building, picking up cups as she went.

Imogen sat at the café table and thought about the offer. Three weeks ago, working for Chandon Leclerc, she would have been the one paying for a cleaner (if Vince had allowed it, which he didn't; he said he didn't want strangers in their home, something Imogen understood even if she didn't agree with). Today, she was welcoming the idea of work she would happily have allowed someone else to do for her – and for a fraction of the money she would have paid, too. And yet she was enjoying being a cleaner. She liked the exhausted sleep it brought because it meant that she didn't spend her nights tossing and turning and worrying about what Vince might be up to. She liked doing something physical for a change. More important than anything else, however, was that she needed any work that came her way. Even though she was living as simply as possible, she couldn't afford to turn down any paying job.

'*Une noisette et une tarte au citron.*' Céline placed the small cup with its half-and-half of espresso and hot milk and the individual lemon tart in front of her.

'I didn't ask for a pastry,' said Imogen.

'On the house.' Céline's sea-blue eyes twinkled at her. 'While you think.'

'You're bribing me with cake?' asked Imogen with a smile.

'If it works. I really could do with some help.' Céline sat opposite her, allowing the student who also worked in the café to look after the other customers. 'Because you see, when I'm not here, I also help out in my father's restaurant. Everyone must work hard in the summer; it's when we make most of our money. I don't have time for my poor little house.'

'Oh, which restaurant?'

'It's called Le Bleu,' Céline replied. 'It's—'

'I know it!' exclaimed Imogen, recalling that that was the name of the one she'd visited with Samantha and Gerry. 'I had dinner there a while ago with some friends.'

'In that case perhaps you don't need a job with me,' said Céline. 'It's not cheap.'

Imogen grinned. 'It was a one-off. And very good.'

'Of course it was good,' said Céline. 'My father trained under Albert Roux. But he has continued to update his cooking. Now he does more Basque style.'

'I need to improve my own cooking skills,' said Imogen. 'I'm afraid my style is very plain.'

'Plain food cooked well is excellent,' Céline remarked as she watched Imogen eat the cake. 'Anyway, what d'you think about the cleaning?'

'You're sure you want someone?'

'Of course I want someone. I'm crying out for help,' said Céline. 'Besides, René says you're the best cleaner they've ever had.'

'René does? You know him?' Imogen looked at her in surprise.

'Yes, I know him,' said Céline. 'I used to be married to him.'

'You're joking!'

'Why would I joke?'

'You . . . and René.' Imogen wiped some crumbs from the corner of her mouth. 'I didn't realise . . . That's a coincidence.'

'We were at school together,' said Céline. 'And we live in a relatively small town. It's not such a surprise.'

'You look far too young to have been at school with René!'

Céline smiled. '*Merci pour le compliment.* He was a few years ahead of me. My childhood sweetheart. You should never marry your childhood sweetheart, it's bound to end in disappointment.'

'I didn't have one, so I don't have to worry about that ever happening,' said Imogen. 'In spite of René being your ex, you get on well with him?'

'Well enough.' Céline shrugged. 'It's better that way in a town where you are both in business, don't you think?'

'I guess so.'

'And so we are all hard workers,' said Céline. 'René with his houses, me with my café, my father with his restaurant and you . . . you with your cleaning, which you get to on my bicycle.' Her voice bubbled with merriment.

'Oh God, I forgot the bike must be yours! Is there a problem?'

'Of course not,' said Céline. 'I bought it when I was going through my fitness craze. It lasted about three weeks. That was one of the reasons René and I weren't good together. I get these enthusiasms and then they disappear. He found it very frustrating.'

'The bike is very convenient,' said Imogen. 'Plus I think I've lost weight with all the cycling.'

'In that case maybe I should take it back. You do not need to lose weight, Imogen.'

'Neither do you,' she said. 'You've got a great figure.'

'Only in the summer, when I'm busy,' said Céline, although Imogen doubted that.

'I used to go to a gym,' Imogen said. 'But I gave that up. It's nice to exercise again.'

'What did you do before you came to France?' Céline put the question casually. 'You weren't always a cleaner, were you?'

'Did René get you to ask me that?'

'No. Why?'

'He was surprised when I said I would clean houses,' said Imogen. 'But I was brought up . . . well, my mother was a housekeeper. I know a lot about cleaning.'

'Ah. I'm sure you must have some great stories about looking after other people,' said Céline. 'Perhaps you can tell me sometime.'

'Perhaps.'

'*Eh bien*. To our business – could you clean for me this Saturday?'

'Yes, I think so.'

René had so far only given Imogen cleaning work during the week. She told Céline that she'd be able to give her a definite time as soon as she knew her schedule.

'I open the café at nine on Saturdays,' said Céline. 'If you could come at eight thirty, that would be great.'

'No problem.' Imogen took out her purse to pay for her coffee.

'No, no!' protested Céline. 'Everything on the house today.'

'Oh, but—'

'Absolutely.' Céline's tone was firm.

'In that case, thank you very much.'

'You're welcome. And I look forward to seeing you tomorrow as usual.'

Imogen took her time cycling home, enjoying the slight breeze on her back as she made her way through the twisting streets of the town and feeling happy at her encounter with Céline. Like René, Céline would be an employer, not a friend. But there was a warmth about her that made Imogen feel like a valued person. Also, it was nice to know someone other than René, even if Céline was his ex-wife and Imogen was using her bicycle to get around!

When she got home, she took a plate from the cupboard and the ingredients for a mixed salad from the fridge. She also poured herself a glass of white wine and sat at the table beside the window. Something had happened to her today, she thought as she gazed out over the garden. Not only at the Villa Martine and with Céline. It was more than that. It was reliving memories and then putting them aside. It was talking to someone without a sense of guilt. It was feeling as though she were beginning to belong somewhere again. Feeling free.

And feeling confident. True, she'd been confident in her work at Chandon Leclerc, but whenever she pointed out to Vince that she had a good job and did it well, he'd tell her that looking after Conor Foley wasn't exactly rocket science. That she wasn't exactly in charge of anything. For all the fancy names they give people these days, he'd said, you're nothing more than a secretary.

She felt a tightness in her chest and took a sip of the chilled wine. She'd eventually realised that Vince said the things he said to undermine her. She came to believe that he didn't actually do it to make her feel bad, but to make him feel better in himself. Regardless of the title he held in the life assurance company, he was a salesman. A very good salesman, who frequently outsold his colleagues, but he wasn't content with that. He wanted to be on the senior management team. He'd gone for promotion three times during his marriage to Imogen, but each time someone else had been appointed instead. He blamed the company executives for not appreciating his abilities. He was scathing about them whenever he spoke to Imogen about them, saying that they were idiots who didn't recognise talent, that they were afraid to promote him because he'd rattle their cages.

'There isn't a policy I can't dissect,' he said one evening. 'I should be sitting around the board table instead of the muppets who're already there. They're afraid I'll show them up.'

She hadn't replied. Nothing she could have said would have been the right thing.

She finished the wine and poured herself another glass. Then, feeling fortified, she opened her internet browser and checked her emails again. There was one from Shona asking her to call her. She grimaced and exited the program. She tapped her fingers on the side of the phone for a couple of moments, then, for the first time since she'd bought it, she used it as an actual phone and dialled a number.

'Hello.'

The accent was American, but a trace of French remained.

'Hello, Berthe,' she said. 'It's me, Imogen.'

'Imogen! It's been such a long time. How are you?' Berthe's voice was full of joy.

'I'm very well, thank you. I have things to talk to you about, but first of all, how's Agnes?'

There was a moment's silence, and then a sigh.

'Some days she remembers me. Some days she doesn't. It's hard, Imogen. Very hard.'

'It must be. I'm sorry.'

'I always thought I'd have to look after her one day,' admitted Berthe. 'She's older than me after all. But the older you get, the harder it is to see any age as being old or needing help.'

'She's seventy-four this year, isn't she?'

'Yes,' said Berthe. 'Not that old at all. Especially not to someone who's sixty-seven.'

'Sixty-seven is young,' said Imogen.

Berthe laughed. 'It is to me, for sure.'

'I miss hearing from Agnes,' said Imogen. 'She was always so funny.'

'Alzheimer's is cruel,' Berthe said. 'When I see Agnes now, I think of your mother.'

'My mother? Why?'

'Her decision,' said Berthe. 'To turn off your father's life support. She sat there every day and she knew he wasn't there any more, but he was still breathing, and when someone's breathing, there's always hope. But Carol knew it was a false hope and she made a very brave choice even though it alienated her from your father's parents. With me, every time I see Agnes, I think that maybe this time she'll remember me and remember you and remember everything. But her memories are like scraps of paper on the wind, and my hoping she'll recover is like hoping they'll land on the ground and become a novel.'

Imogen was silent.

'I'm sorry,' Berthe said. 'You rang and you wanted to talk and all I've done is say depressing things. What's new with you? Is everything OK?'

'Actually, my life is a little complicated right now,' Imogen told her.

'In what way?'

Imogen hesitated. She hadn't confided in Berthe about the deterioration of her relationship with Vince because she didn't want to worry her and because she was embarrassed about having to admit that she'd made a terrible mistake. Especially as Berthe and Agnes had both fallen for him at the wedding, telling her that he was a real gentleman. She didn't want to go into the gory details now either. She took a deep breath.

'I've left Vince,' she said.

'Oh, Imogen. Why? What happened?'

'He wasn't the man I thought,' replied Imogen.

'This is a mutual thing?'

'No.' Imogen started to explain, giving Berthe a heavily edited version of events. When she'd finished speaking, there was silence at the end of the line.

'But . . . but *chérie*, why would you simply walk out? Why did you not get yourself a good divorce lawyer and make sure—'

'It wasn't that simple,' Imogen interrupted her. 'He . . . he might not have let me go.'

'He could hardly have stopped you.'

'I know it sounds crazy, Berthe, but I was kind of afraid he would.'

There was a long silence before Berthe spoke again.

'You mean he would have hurt you?' Her voice was like steel.

'No, no. Vince has never hurt me,' Imogen assured her. 'He's not like that. Absolutely not. No, it's . . . well, he has ways of making me do things without me wanting to.'

'How?'

'I can't explain. I think I'm going to do one thing, and suddenly after talking to him I'm doing something else, and I absolutely one hundred per cent needed to leave him so I came up with a plan.'

This time Berthe's silence was so long that Imogen thought they might have been cut off.

'Are you there?' she asked.

'Yes, yes. I'm thinking. You should have called me before now, sweetheart. If there were problems, I might have been able to help.'

'I don't think so. Not with this. It was better that I walked out without saying anything.'

'What about all your things? Your friends?'

'I had very few things. And fewer friends.'

'Because of him?'

'Oh, Berthe.' Imogen sighed. 'I lost myself and all my friends with him, and I had to get away because if I'd stayed I would have folded. And if I'd told him I wanted a divorce . . . well, somehow it would never have happened.'

'I can't believe you didn't say anything to me.' Berthe's hurt sounded in her voice. 'I know we haven't talked very much over the last while, Imogen, but I thought it was because you were too busy to bother.'

'Not at all!' she exclaimed. 'But Vince . . . he didn't like me talking to people from my past.'

'I'm not a person from your past,' protested Berthe. 'I'm your family.'

'He didn't think you were,' said Imogen. 'He didn't think anyone was. Except him, of course.'

'You should have found a way to talk to me. I might have been able to help.'

'I didn't know what to say. Besides, what could you do, Berthe? You're on the other side of the Atlantic and you have enough to worry about.'

'You definitely should have called me before you left.'

'I didn't know if I had the nerve to go through with it.'

'Do you want to come here, to Palm Springs? To stay with me?'

'Thank you, but no,' Imogen said. 'I'm not cut out for the States.'

'Of course you are. Anyone could be.'

'I wanted to come to France,' said Imogen. 'It seemed right, that's all.'

'Where are you?' Berthe's voice was suddenly sharp. 'Provence?'

'Hendaye.'

'There's no magic potion in Hendaye,' she said. 'And if you think . . . if you're planning on finding people you used to know—'

'Don't worry,' Imogen interrupted her. 'The only plan I had was to get here. It was a place I knew, that's all. I thought I'd feel safe here. And I do.'

She didn't say anything about cleaning the Villa Martine. She didn't want Berthe thinking that she'd somehow made that happen when it had been nothing more than a weird coincidence. And when it didn't matter in the grand scheme of things.

'I understand.' Berthe's voice softened. 'All the same, what if he comes looking for you?'

'I expect him to try, but he won't find me,' said Imogen. 'The reason I'm ringing you is in case he gets in touch to ask if you know where I am. He hasn't, has he?'

'Not yet.'

'I tried to get rid of any possible phone numbers or emails for everyone who knows me,' said Imogen.

'Are you sure there's nothing more to this?' asked Berthe. 'Because you're frightening me a little with this talk. He's not dangerous, is he?'

'Honestly, no,' replied Imogen. 'But he's dogged. If he wants to talk to you and there's a way, he'll find it. I wanted to keep you out of it so that you'd be able to say you didn't know anything. But I started thinking that if he did call and got you talking, you might mention Hendaye. Which would give him a place to start looking.'

'I'm getting more and more worried about you,' said Berthe. 'Please come to me. Please be safe.'

'I'm safe where I am,' Imogen said. 'Besides, Berthe, he's never laid a finger on me. I promise you. There's no need to worry.'

'He doesn't have to touch you to hurt you.'

'That's why I left.'

Berthe sighed. 'You think you will be able to support yourself in France?'

'I landed a job five days after arriving here.'

'That's impressive, considering that everything I read about France these days says the country is in terminal decline.' Berthe's tone was admiring. 'What sort of job?'

'Cleaning houses,' said Imogen. 'It's not much, but it's a start.'

'I suppose you have a lifetime's experience,' said Berthe.

'Who'd have thought?' For the first time there was humour in Imogen's voice. Nevertheless, she still stayed silent about the Villa Martine.

'Who indeed?' said Berthe. 'Have you made any longer-term plans?'

'Not yet. To be honest, I don't know if I'll stay here or go back to Ireland. But at the moment, I need to be in France.'

'I wish I could be with you.'

'It's fine. I'm fine,' Imogen assured her. 'Don't worry about me. I didn't ring so that you'd worry. But in case he calls – or in case a girl called Shona Egan does – please don't say anything.'

'Shona? A friend of his?'

'A friend of mine,' said Imogen. 'But he'd make her talk. I know he would.'

'I won't say a word,' said Berthe. 'I promise.'

'Thank you. I have to go, Berthe. I'm running out of credit. Tell Agnes I love her.'

'I tell her that every day.'

Imogen felt the tears prickle her eyes.

'I love you too,' she said.

'I know,' said Berthe, and ended the call.

Afterwards, Imogen sat in the chair and stared unseeingly out of the window. It had been good to talk to someone close to her again, even if it had been difficult to make the call in the first place. Partly because she felt so guilty about not having spoken to Berthe in months. But Berthe was never judgemental. Agnes hadn't been either. They'd always been the most supportive people in Imogen's life. It was a pity they'd decided to stay in the States. If they'd returned to France after that first year, Carol might have moved back in with them. They might even have bought the Maison Lavande. And then perhaps all their lives would have turned out very differently.

Chapter 14

Carol Weir had never planned on living in France. On the day of the horror crash that wiped out her family, she'd been expecting to buy a house near her parents' home with her husband Ray. Her picture of the life she was going to lead was one where she and Ray started a family and where she popped in to see her mum on a daily basis to share recipes and tips on cooking and homemaking. There was nothing more she wanted or needed.

The accident happened on a cold, frosty morning on their way to the new housing development about twenty minutes from her family home. Carol and Ray were chatting happily with her parents about the house they were about to see when David O'Connell's car hit a patch of black ice, skidded off the road and plunged into a field.

Afterwards, the doctors said that David, Maria and Ray had been very unlucky. Carol's parents had been killed outright when the car had slammed into a large boulder. Ray had been hit by a rusted metal bar that came through the rear passenger window, and suffered traumatic brain injuries. The hardest thing for Carol was to accept that her husband would never recover from those injuries. For more than a month she sat beside him in the hospital, willing him to open his eyes. When she finally told the doctors to switch off his life support, she felt as though she were the one condemning him to death. His parents, Betty and George, had never been able to forgive her, even though they knew that she was doing the right thing.

She hadn't known she was pregnant at the time. She didn't realise it for another month, until the day Ray's only sibling, his sister Agnes, came to see her. Carol had spent the time since Ray's funeral in a fog of grief and misery, unable to believe that everything she'd ever wanted had been snatched away from her in the blink of an eye. That particular week she'd felt even more lethargic than usual and had thrown up after her late morning breakfast of cornflakes and toast. That wasn't unusual, because since the accident she'd felt like throwing up every time she ate. Later in the day, a sudden sharp pain in her back made her think of the time of the month and she began to calculate dates. She didn't give the possibility of being pregnant serious consideration, but it niggled at the back of her mind, and so eventually she went to the bathroom and took out the pregnancy testing kit she'd bought a few months earlier. Back then she'd hoped that she might be carrying Ray's baby, but even as she'd been reading the instructions she'd felt a tugging pain in her stomach and had doubled over with the cramps that told her she very definitely wasn't. She'd returned the test to the bathroom shelf, where it had remained unused and unneeded.

Afterwards, she hadn't been able to believe the result. She was sitting on the sofa, trying unsuccessfully to come to terms with both the news and the mixed emotions that it generated in her, when she saw Agnes walking up the garden path and heard the ring of the doorbell. She didn't answer it at first. But then Agnes pressed the bell again and Carol thought it would be easier to open the door and tell her to go away than to have her come back another time. She didn't know why Agnes was here. The first time she'd met her had been at the funeral. Agnes hadn't come to their wedding because she and her girlfriend, Berthe, had been in the States at the time.

Carol didn't know much about Agnes and Berthe's relationship. Openly gay couples were a relative rarity at the time, and she didn't know any others. Ray himself had been unconcerned, saying that his older sister's choices were hers to make. Mr and Mrs Weir, however, were hostile and refused to accept that Berthe was anything other than their daughter's platonic friend. In fact the only time Carol recalled hearing them even speak about the pair was to say that they moved in legal circles. There was a grudging respect in Betty's voice when she said this – afterwards Ray told her that his mother would have preferred to be able to say that her daughter was married with kids.

Agnes was a solicitor, while Berthe worked in the legal department of the European Commission, and she was currently on a short-term secondment to Brussels.

'Which means I'm here on my own at the moment,' Agnes told Carol as she walked into the untidy living room. 'And I thought it would be a good idea to drop by and see how you were doing.'

Carol shrugged and said she was fine, and Agnes continued to talk to her and offer whatever support she could. Carol listened without really taking anything in, because she was still consumed by the fact that she was pregnant with Ray's child. Despite the test, she didn't entirely believe it was true.

She blurted it out when the older woman came into the living room with the tea she'd made for both of them. Agnes nearly dropped the tray.

'You're kidding me.' She stared at Carol in utter disbelief. 'It's not possible.'

'We were trying for a baby,' Carol said. 'We were disappointed when I didn't get pregnant before. And now he'll never see the baby.'

She burst into tears and Agnes put her arms around her to comfort her.

Agnes told her that her parents would be pleased at the news, and that they might even want her to stay with them in Donegal for a while, but Betty and George Weir weren't in the slightest bit interested in their daughter-in-law's pregnancy.

'They didn't want to know,' Carol told her a few days later when Agnes called around after work again. 'Betty said it was too late now and put the phone down.'

'I'm sure she'll come round eventually,' said Agnes.

'It doesn't matter.' Carol wondered if Betty's lack of interest was because neither she nor her husband really liked her. On the few occasions she and Ray had visited them, they'd been rather stand-offish, although she'd done her best to be outgoing and friendly herself. Now she didn't have the strength to care. She was torn between joy about being pregnant and grief over the loss of her husband and parents. She couldn't take on the burden of worrying about her parents-in-law. Throughout her pregnancy she felt guilty any time she was happy, and equally guilty any time she succumbed to tears. Which, she reckoned, was more than enough emotion to be going on with.

Slowly, however, her periods of grief were outweighed by her periods of happiness. Agnes was hugely supportive, as was Berthe when she returned from her secondment. The three women got on well together, and when Imogen was born, a smiling, beautiful and healthy baby, they were all joyful. Carol didn't care that Betty and George didn't call or send a card. The love and affection she received from Agnes and Berthe was more than enough for her.

The suggestion came when Imogen was six months old. Lilian Fournier, Berthe's mother, had been running the family guest house on her own for years, but had recently fallen and broken her arm. Berthe had gone to Provence to help her, and on her return to Ireland had put the proposal to Agnes and Carol. Lilian, at sixty-eight, was a fit woman, but the fall had shaken her and she'd talked about getting help at the guest house. Berthe had enjoyed her month in Provence and wondered if it wouldn't be good for all of them to go there for a while to help her mother out. Carol had been both excited and terrified by the prospect. Her experience of travelling abroad was limited to a couple of holidays with Ray on the Costa del Sol, while three years of studying French at school hadn't progressed her knowledge from a very basic level. Moving to another country would be a challenge.

'I can get leave of absence of up to five years,' Berthe told them. 'I doubt we'd stay that long, but wouldn't it be nice to take a bit of time out to live at a slower pace for a while? We've talked about it before . . .' she turned to Agnes, 'but we've always said the time wasn't right. And I do realise that we might not be the sort of people who seriously want to slow down or enjoy a quieter life, but isn't this an opportunity to find out?'

Agnes agreed. And so she handed in her notice at the law firm where she worked, Berthe applied for her leave of absence, and Carol got a passport for baby Imogen. Three weeks after Berthe had first suggested it, they'd moved to Provence.

Carol was enchanted by the Maison Lavande. It was a two-storey house set in pretty gardens close to the sea. It had twelve guest rooms and a separate wing for the family. Lilian Fournier was delighted to have other people in the family wing – she'd been living on her own there since her much older husband had died ten years earlier. She immediately fell in love with Imogen and took it upon herself to speak to her only in French.

'So that she doesn't have a terrible accent like her mother,' she told Berthe, who laughed and pointed out that other French people would recognise Imogen's Provençal accent anyway. To which Lilian had snorted and said that she should be proud to be from the south of France, and that there was no better place in the whole world to live.

After the horror of the crash that had wiped out her family, Provence helped Carol's soul to heal. Even though she still carried an ache in her heart, being at the Maison Lavande meant that she no longer sat at home in a pair of tracksuit bottoms and an old top, staring out of the window for hours at a time. Instead, while Agnes looked after the accounts and Berthe concentrated on marketing the guest house, she transformed herself into a chic, efficient housekeeper for whom Madame Fournier had immense affection and respect.

Carol would have been happy to stay at the Maison Lavande for ever, but when Lilian decided to get married, she knew that it would be impossible. She listened to everyone's plans with trepidation. She didn't want to go to the States with Agnes and Berthe, but nor did she wish to return to Ireland. Yet although her French was now fluent (despite some remaining Irish inflections), she lacked the confidence to go looking for another job. When Lilian told her about the possibility of becoming the Delissandes' housekeeper, she'd been uncertain, but after talking to Lucie on the phone, she decided that it was the right thing to do. After all, she thought, I don't have any ties keeping me here. And Lucie had sounded lovely on the phone, saying that she would be delighted to see her and Imogen, who could have the job of talking English to her sons.

And so they left Provence and moved to Aquitaine, where Carol's nervousness disappeared almost at once thanks to the warm welcome she and Imogen received from Lucie Delissandes. She loved working for the family and she cared for the Villa Martine as though it were her own home. She adapted quickly to the routine of that first summer, when Denis Delissandes lived and worked in Paris during the week and spent the weekends with his family in Hendaye. She did the housework in the mornings, while Lucie played with the children in the garden or took them to the beach. In the afternoons, she looked after the children while Lucie worked. Lucie was an editor at a small French publishing house specialising in literary novels, and when she shut herself away with an author's manuscript and her red pen, nobody was allowed to disturb her. She gave Carol some proof copies of books she'd worked on, but Carol – who enjoyed Jilly Cooper and Judith Krantz – found them hard going and usually abandoned them after a dozen pages.

Over time, as her relationship with Lucie blurred slightly from being employee and employer to a kind of friendship, Carol learned that Denis's family had aristocratic links going back for hundreds of years. They'd always been involved in both politics and business, and although Denis stuck to business himself – he was a director of a private bank – he and Lucie were often invited to exclusive dinners and events in Paris. Lucie confessed that the dinners bored her to tears, but she put up with them for Denis's sake.

'We're a partnership,' she told Carol. 'I have the cultural career that gives him certain credentials. He has the financial career that brings in the money.'

'But you love each other too, don't you?' asked Carol.

'It's hard not to love Denis.' Lucie smiled. 'He looks at you with those enormous eyes of his and you are gone in an instant. Love at first sight!'

Carol told Lucie that her relationship with Ray had been love at first sight too. Then Lucie, who knew her story from Madame Fournier, gave her a hug and told her that she and Imogen were to consider themselves part of the Delissandes family now. For as long as Carol looked after them, they would look after her and her daughter. She gave Carol the glass angels and the dreamcatchers for her room and told her she never needed to worry again.

When the Delissandes packed up and returned to Paris at

the end of the summer, they left Carol and Imogen behind at the Villa Martine to take care of it until they returned at mid-term. Carol couldn't believe her luck. She and Imogen would be living on their own for weeks in a five-bedroomed home in one of the best locations in town. As far as she was concerned, this wasn't a job, it was a gift.

Imogen was happy too, if a little lonely when everyone had gone. Carol enrolled her in the local school, which helped, but most nights the two of them were alone in the house together. Imogen would sometimes ask if she couldn't have some brothers and sisters to make it a bit more interesting, and Carol replied that they needed a daddy for that but unfortunately there wasn't anyone available. When Imogen suggested Denis Delissandes, Carol shook her head and told her that Monsieur belonged to Madame.

'What about you?' Imogen asked her. 'Does anyone belong to you?'

'Only my little girl.' Carol put her arms around her and hugged her. 'You'll be mine for ever. And I'm yours too.'

The family returned for the October mid-term, when the weather was glorious – not as hot as the summer, but still warm and pleasant. Lucie was pleased at how well Carol was keeping the house, and Imogen was glad to see the boys again, even if they quarrelled the whole time.

She rowed particularly with Oliver, who'd become very bossy and told her that he wasn't going to let her correct his English any more because she was a silly little girl who didn't know anything. She got her revenge on him by emptying a box of ants into his bed, which led to him screaming when he hopped into it and then running out of the room shouting for his mother to kill them. Lucie had blamed Charles, who protested his innocence, and it wasn't until she told him that he would have no supper for a week that Imogen admitted to being the culprit. Charles had roared with laughter. Oliver had been furious. But it put an end to him teasing her. Afterwards, he treated her with a good deal more respect and listened whenever she tried to explain why he was using an English word incorrectly.

Christmas was special. Lucie had told Carol where to find everything, and so, when she arrived with the boys in the middle of December, the house was already decorated with glass baubles, garlands and wreaths, the floors polished and the gas fire burning.

'*C'est magnifique*,' declared Oliver as he looked at the tree in the corner of the room.

And it was. Everything about those years in Hendaye was magnificent. And Carol wanted to make sure it stayed that way.

She kept in regular contact with Berthe and Agnes. Both of them were doing well in the States and had no immediate plans to return. However, they came back to France every year for holidays, and after seeing Madame Fournier, they would meet up with Carol and Imogen again.

'I'm so glad it's all worked out for you, Carol,' said Agnes on their second visit. 'Although obviously you can't live at the Villa Martine for ever.'

'I don't see why not,' said Carol. 'It's perfect.'

'But you'll want to find someone,' said Berthe. 'Have a home of your own.'

'I'm happy,' repeated Carol. 'This is my home. Imogen's too.'

The two women exchanged glances.

'It's the Delissandes' home and you're an employee,' Agnes reminded her. 'They could let you go at any time.'

'Lucie treats us as part of the family,' said Carol. 'Besides, I'm the best housekeeper in the world. They'd never be able to replace me. She said so.'

'And Imogen?' asked Berthe.

'She loves it here,' Carol told her. 'She gets on great with the boys and is doing well at school. Her teachers say that she's smart and outgoing.'

'A legacy from the Maison Lavande,' remarked Agnes. 'There isn't anyone Imogen doesn't get on with.'

'I know.' Carol nodded. 'I wish Ray could have seen her. But . . .' she took a deep breath, 'hopefully he's looking down and keeping an eye on us. He must be. I've been luckier than I ever expected.'

'I still think you need someone of your own,' said Berthe.

'No I don't.' Carol shook her head. 'Everything's perfect the way it is. I don't need anyone at all.'

Because Lucie could work from home, she had more flexibility in her schedule than Denis, and would sometimes come to the house with the children for long weekends without her husband. But occasionally Denis himself would arrive with some of his sailing buddies or, in the winter, with friends who wanted to ski. There was no skiing near the town, but Denis and his friends would stay overnight at the Villa Martine before driving to one of the resorts a couple of hours away. Carol always found those visits overwhelming – she was unaccustomed to being around groups of men, and Denis's friends were alpha males: confident, self-important and competitive.

It was being competitive within a couple of hours of arriving at the ski resort that caused Denis to fall on one of the trips, breaking a bone in his foot, which meant that another member of the group, an Englishman named Simon Thorpe, drove him back to the house after the doctors at the hospital had put his foot into a walking boot.

'I wouldn't mind, but it was on one of the easier runs,' said Denis as he eased himself into an armchair and took the glass of whisky that Carol offered him. 'I'm such an idiot.'

'I'm sure it could happen to anyone,' Carol said.

'I messed up the trip.' Denis took an appreciative sip of the whisky and then looked at Simon. 'Sorry, *mon ami*.'

'No problem,' said Simon. 'I'll stay here and keep you company.'

'No, no.' Denis shook his head. 'I insist. You must go back and enjoy yourself.'

'If you're sure . . .'

'Why wouldn't I be?' asked Denis. 'I have Carol to look after me.'

He smiled at her, and at Imogen, who'd been examining the boot with interest.

'I wouldn't mind her looking after me,' said Simon, and Carol blushed, murmured something about seeing to the ironing and left the room, telling Imogen to leave Monsieur Delissandes in peace and help her.

'She's pretty in an unsophisticated sort of way,' Denis remarked when she'd closed the door behind her. 'And an excellent *gouvernante*.'

'And have you . . .'

Denis grinned. 'No.'

'You're losing your touch,' said Simon.

'Perhaps.' Denis grinned again, then told Simon about Carol's history. Simon grimaced.

'That must have been rough.'

'I'm sure. However, she's moved on with her life and I'm glad she came here. She can cook as well as clean.'

'And you're sure you never even . . .'

'No,' repeated Denis.

'Would you mind if I had a crack at her?'

Denis looked at him in surprise. 'You? With my house-keeper?'

'It's been a while since Rachel,' said Simon. 'I need a bit of practice.'

'Well, I suppose you deserve something for having to bring me back here,' said Denis. 'Be my guest.'

Carol was utterly astonished when Simon came into the kitchen and asked her if she'd like to go out to dinner with him.

'But I thought you were keeping Monsieur company,' she said.

'He wants to rest,' Simon told her. 'He's going to bed.'

'I'd better help him . . .'

'It's OK,' said Simon. 'I already did.'

Carol had heard the sounds of people moving about but she'd assumed it was Denis using the bathroom.

'But his supper . . .'

'I poured him another whisky,' said Simon. 'I think that's taking care of his dietary needs.'

'He should have something more than that!'

'He's fine,' said Simon. 'He asked me to take you out for a bite to eat.'

'I beg your pardon?' Carol stared at him.

'Dinner,' repeated Simon. 'He asked me to take you out.'

'I'm sorry,' said Carol. 'I can't do that.'

'It's your boss's order.'

'I hardly think so,' she said. 'Thank you for the invitation – if that's what it is – but I've got things to do and they don't include going out with you.'

'Oh come on.' Simon couldn't believe she'd turned him down. 'You must get fed up here on your own with a kid. This is your chance to live a little.'

'I'm living perfectly well, thank you,' she said. 'Now if you don't mind, I'm busy.'

'Doing what?'

'Actually,' she said as she opened the door of the range cooker that had been in the house for years, 'I'm preparing dinner.'

'But Denis has gone to bed.'

'It's a casserole. It'll keep.'

'Smells great.' Simon's tone changed from bantering to sincere.

'Thank you.'

'Do you do everything here?' he asked. 'Cook, clean, look after all of them?'

'There's not much looking after as far as they're concerned,' said Carol. 'They're away more often than they're here.'

'It must be weird,' he said.

'Weird? How?'

'It's not your house.'

'It's no different to renting.' Carol lifted the Le Creuset pot on to a worktop and peered inside.

'I suppose not. Yet . . . well, you have the run of the place when they're not here, but when they are, you're banished to the kitchen.'

'Hardly banished,' she said drily. 'I'm happy here, Mr Thorpe, and I don't want to change a thing.'

'Simon,' he said. 'My name is Simon.'

'I know. But I prefer Mr Thorpe.'

'I'm not your employer,' he pointed out. 'You don't have to be as formal with me as you are with Denis. Which is kind of cute, by the way.'

She said nothing.

'OK, OK. You're the staff and you don't fraternise with friends of the family. But given that you won't come out to dinner with me, is there any chance I can have some of that casserole? I'm famished.'

'Of course,' she said as she put the pot back into the oven. 'It will be ready in a little while. Anything for a friend of the family.'

She had dinner with him in the end – the casserole at the kitchen table later that evening. She checked first on Denis Delissandes, who was asleep in his room, the empty whisky tumbler on the mahogany locker beside his bed. Carol tiptoed in and retrieved the glass, replacing it with a small bottle of Vichy water before closing the door gently and going downstairs again. Imogen was at the table, talking to Simon.

'You should be doing your homework,' Carol told her.

'I've finished,' she said. 'I was being sociable by talking to Monsieur's friend. Do you know that Simon's mum has a huge house?'

'No, I didn't know that.'

'And that he's met the Queen of England.'

Carol raised an eyebrow as she looked at Simon.

'She visited our company when we opened new offices,' he explained.

'Is it time for dinner yet?' asked Imogen. 'I'm starving, and so is Simon.'

Carol served up the casserole with crusty bread. She took a bottle of wine from the store, reckoning that Monsieur Delissandes would rather she opened a good bottle for a friend rather than serving the cheaper stuff she usually bought for herself, although the amount she poured into her own glass was small.

Simon ate the casserole and drank the wine, keeping up a stream of conversation and anecdotes that had both Carol and Imogen laughing. When the meal was finally finished, Carol sent Imogen to bed.

'There's a TV in the living room,' she told Simon. 'I think you can get the BBC on it.'

'I'd rather stay here with you,' he said.

'You're wasting your time.' Carol shook her head. 'I'm not available.'

'Why?'

'Been there, done that,' said Carol.

'And left with the daughter.'

'Imogen is the most important person in my life,' said Carol.

'I'm sure she is. And Denis told me about your husband – that must have been terrible for you.'

'Yes.' She kept her voice steady. 'It was.'

'But you can't stay out of the game for ever.'

'That's where you're wrong,' said Carol.

* * *

She was relieved when Simon left the following day. She'd never met anybody like him before, so sure of himself and his attractiveness to women. And he *was* attractive, there was no question about that. But Carol wasn't going to let a fleeting dalliance with Simon Thorpe mess things up for her. And she knew that was all he wanted, so it was easy to resist.

Nevertheless, she also missed him. Much as she hadn't been looking for it, having a man showing interest in her made her think differently for the first time in a long time. Made her think about things other than the most effective washing power, or the quickest way to clean porcelain tiles, or the best furniture polish. As she stood in front of the full-length mirror in her bedroom, she wondered what it would have been like if she'd said yes to dinner and yes to whatever else he might have suggested. She felt a fluttering sensation in the pit of her stomach and closed her eyes. She'd forgotten that feeling. The feeling of desire. Of wanting to be with someone. The way she'd felt with Ray.

The following day, she brought Denis Delissandes to the local hospital for his appointment there, although there was nothing more they could do for him other than give him physiotherapy exercises and confirm that it would take about four weeks for the bone to heal.

'I hope it doesn't hurt like this for four weeks,' said Denis as he eased himself into the car. 'I can't believe how bloody painful it is.'

'You should take the tablets they gave you,' said Carol.

'I will,' Denis assured her.

'What are you going to do about getting back to Paris?' she asked.

'I'll stick to the schedule of flying back with the boys next week. The doctor says it will be fine because I'm not in a cast. I'll just have to take the boot off.'

'You don't want to go back sooner?'

'It's easier to go back with the others,' said Denis. 'They can manoeuvre me on and off the plane like an unwieldy hippo.'

'Madame doesn't want to come here and bring you home?' Carol never called Lucie by her first name in front of her husband.

'Madame is probably very happy to have the house to herself.' Denis chuckled.

'But she's not by herself,' said Carol. 'The boys . . .'

'Oliver and Charles are staying with my sister,' said Denis. 'Lucie made her plans when she knew I'd be away, and she won't want to change them.'

'So you're stuck here for another four days.'

'You mean you're stuck with me for another four days.'

'I don't mean that at all!'

'No?' Denis gave her a sideways smile. 'It doesn't mess up your day to have one member of the family in the house?'

'Of course not.'

'And yet you must have a routine of your own when we're not here,' said Denis.

'Naturally,' she said. 'But I'm always happy when you arrive.'

'You know, Simon was right about you,' said Denis as they stopped at the gates to the house and Carol pressed the remote. 'You're an interesting character. You're worth getting to know.'

'Not a bit of it.' But she blushed as she brought the car to a halt outside the house.

* * *

She made sure that Denis was comfortably settled in a chair in front of the TV, then got on with her household chores, sticking to her plan to clean the room that Imogen called the library, as one wall was entirely covered in bookshelves. The shelves were divided into a dozen sections, with the books arranged in a method devised by Lucie that Carol didn't quite grasp. She used a small stepladder to reach the highest shelf of the first section, take down the books, dust them and the shelf and replace them. It was painstaking and tiring work, but every so often she stopped to flick through one of the heavy volumes and read a few pages. She didn't find them any more riveting than the books Lucie had given her, and was sliding one back on to the shelf when she was startled by a sound behind her.

'You scared me,' she told Denis Delissandes. 'I didn't hear you come in.'

'Which is odd given that I'm thudding around the place in this bloody boot,' he said. 'You were engrossed.'

'Not engrossed,' she said. 'Trying to figure it out. And I'm sorry, I shouldn't be reading your books.'

'Read all you want,' he said. 'That's what they're for.'

'Nevertheless . . .'

'Nevertheless, if you can understand half of what Gilbert Giraud is saying, you're a better person than me.' Denis made a face. 'Lucie made me read that last year. I think I managed ten pages before deciding that I was a total philistine. I'm impressed that you were so into it.'

'I wasn't,' confessed Carol. 'I was thinking that it's one thing being able to read the papers, but something entirely different when it comes to great literature.'

'Great literature?' Denis made a face. 'Have you ever met Gilbert Giraud?'

'No,' replied Carol. 'How would I?'

'Lucky you,' said Denis. 'The biggest bore I've ever come across. And so full of himself. "I use language to make people think, to question what they know about it. If a reader doesn't have to use the dictionary at least once when reading my novels, I have failed." Poseur.'

Carol laughed.

'Me, I prefer *les romans de gare*,' said Denis. 'In English I think they are called airport novels – exciting and thrilling. By authors like Robert Ludlum or Michael Crichton. At least things happen in those books. That one you just put back is nothing but the author sitting in his garden talking to a bluebell.' He clicked his fingers dismissively.

'But he's very successful,' protested Carol. 'Lucie told me he won an award.'

'Probably for novels that people buy but never read,' said Denis.

Carol laughed again.

'Are you going to spend all day among the dusty books?' asked Denis.

'I'm only a third of the way through cleaning,' Carol told him.

'Oh for heaven's sake, leave it and talk to me instead,' said Denis. 'I'm bored.'

Carol looked at the pile of books on the floor and shrugged. There was at least another couple of hours' work there, but she wanted to be finished in time to make the evening meal and before Imogen got home from school. She said this to Denis.

'Will the roof fall in if you don't finish?' he asked.

'No.'

'Will demons swoop from hell to scoop you up for abandoning it?'

'No.' She chuckled.

'Well then. Come and have coffee with me in the kitchen.'

'Well . . . OK.'

She walked to the door where he was standing.

'Wait,' he said.

'What?'

He reached out and ran his finger across her cheek. She recoiled in shock.

'Dust,' he told her, holding up his finger.

'Oh.'

She moved past him and into the kitchen, where she looked at her reflection in the wall mirror. He was right; her forehead was also streaked with a dark line of dust. She rubbed it away and then re-tied her hair in the short ponytail she always wore it in while working.

'*Très jolie*,' said Denis as he took the cafetière from a kitchen cupboard and began to ladle coffee into it. 'You are a pretty woman, Carol.'

'It's my job to do that.' She was embarrassed by the compliment.

'You're not a servant in this house,' said Denis. 'I can make coffee.'

'But—'

'Sit, woman! I've done nothing useful all day. Let me make it.'

Carol sat. She watched as Denis poured water into the cafetière and took two cups from the cupboard and placed them on the table. Then he looked at her, a rueful expression on his face.

'Do we have biscuits?'

'I'll get—'

'Just tell me where they are.'

'The cupboard to the left,' she said.

Denis found a packet of almond tuiles and shook some on to a plate. Then he sat at the table and slowly depressed the plunger on the cafetière.

Carol couldn't remember the last time someone had made her a cup of coffee. Or indeed told her to sit down while they did something for her. It was nice to be taken care of for a change. She allowed Denis to fill her wide coffee cup, then took one of the biscuits.

'So,' said Denis, taking a biscuit himself, 'what's it like here when we're away?'

He was a different man to the slightly remote figure who'd picked her up at Biarritz airport and had hardly spoken on the drive to the house, the man who enjoyed physical pursuits like sailing and skiing but who wasn't interested in talking. Not that she ever had much need to talk to him. Most of her interaction was with his wife. But she was talking to him now, telling him about the accident, and about her move to France, some of which he already knew from Lucie, although in a sketchy way.

'I admire you,' he said. 'You're a strong woman.'

'Not really,' said Carol.

'You recovered from a horrible event. You started a new life in a new country. *Formidable.*'

She smiled.

'But you don't have time for fun,' he said. 'You've talked

about the things you do around the house, about looking after Imogen – nothing about yourself.'

'I don't have time for myself.'

'You must find time,' said Denis. 'That's very important.'

'What's important is me tidying these things away.' Carol stood up and took the cups from the table, stacking them in the dishwasher.

When she turned around again, Denis was standing behind her. He'd taken the boot from his foot.

'It's time for you to live again, Carol,' he said.

'I . . .'

He pushed a strand of hair from her face and rubbed the spot on her cheek from where he'd previously wiped away the streak of dust.

'Monsieur Delissandes . . .'

'Relax,' he said, and kissed her.

She hadn't intended to become Denis Delissandes' lover. And yet that was what happened. In the four days they were alone together in the Villa Martine, they made love more times than Carol could count. And it *was* making love, she said to herself each night when she'd slipped back into her own room in the early hours of the morning so that Imogen wouldn't know she'd been missing. It was making love because it was so wonderful and so spectacular and because Denis said he loved her. And she loved him too, even though she knew it couldn't possibly last.

Of course she felt guilty about Lucie. She thought of Lucie as a friend. But Denis was dismissive when she said this on the night before he returned to Paris.

'You're friendly but she's not your friend,' he told her.

'You're not betraying her. Lucie is a sensible person. She knows that a marriage is different to an *affaire*.'

'So this is an affair?' said Carol.

'If that is the word you like to use.' Denis pulled her close to him. 'You and I – we're good together, Carol.'

'Better than you and Lucie?'

He looked at her in the darkness. 'In some ways. Which makes it more than a simple *affaire*, of course.'

'You're not planning on leaving her, are you?'

'You wouldn't want me to do that.'

It was silly to have hoped, even for a moment, that he might.

'Of course I wouldn't.' She rested her head against his chest.

'Good,' he said. 'We don't need to ruin what we have.'

It was only when she'd tiptoed back to her bedroom that she wondered what on earth that really was.

Chapter 15

Back in Dublin, Vince was convinced he should have made a bigger fuss about Imogen's departure. He shouldn't have allowed Shona (and the gardai and the Missing Family people) to persuade him that all his wife needed was time. He should have called the national newspapers and turned it into a big story, which would have forced the police to do something about it, instead of persuading him that she'd walked out on him without a word.

The neighbours were beginning to ask questions. Sadie Harris next door had remarked that she hadn't seen Imogen in ages and wondered aloud if she was away. Vince muttered something about her having work commitments in France, and Sadie said that it was great to see her doing so well, wasn't it, and that she hoped Vince was coping all right on his own. He'd been in two minds then about what he should say, wondering if he should exploit Sadie's good nature and say that he was doing terribly on his own, which might have led to her asking him next door for dinner; or if he should come out with it and say that Imogen had left him without a word and maybe trigger even greater sympathy.

In the end, though, he knew that he would never tell anyone that she'd walked out on him. Besides, she hadn't gone for ever. She'd be home soon, guilty and remorseful at having caused him pain, because she couldn't live without him and she was always remorseful when she'd done something stupid. This, however, was far and away the stupidest thing she'd ever done, and the fact that she'd planned it was driving him insane. He thought he knew her, and he couldn't believe that he hadn't had the slightest idea what she'd been up to. How long had she spent planning? he asked himself as he opened his laptop. How often had she sat in the living room beside him, thinking about leaving him? How often had she pretended to be listening to him when in fact she was thinking about running away? And had she really kept it a secret from everyone she knew? Surely she would've told someone, even if that person wasn't Shona Egan.

He logged into Imogen's email account again. He liked being able to access it even though it seemed that she wasn't bothering herself. He was hopeful that at some point an email would arrive for her with information that could be useful to him. He skimmed through the ones he'd sent her and pursed his lips. He'd been both angry and annoyed when he'd written them, and in re-reading them he could see those emotions coming through. Maybe that was why she hadn't replied to him. She knew she'd done wrong, she could sense how angry he was and she didn't know how to respond. Perhaps it would be better to take a different approach.

He closed her account, opened his own and composed another message.

From: Vinnock@carlisledirect.com
To: Imozhen@gmail.com
Subject: I Miss You
Imogen, I realise that you've gone through a difficult time. It's taken me a while because I couldn't understand how you could do this to me and I have to confess that I was very, very angry with you. But I realise you must be extremely distressed to have done this awful thing. All I want is for us to sort out whatever's wrong between us. I can come to you if you're not ready to come home yet. I love you and I miss you so please reply to me as soon as possible.

Vince xx

He sent the email without bothering to read through it again, then sat in thoughtful silence before opening his browser and typing *private detectives* into the search bar. Given the attitude of the police, and the fact that he hadn't yet heard anything from Cheyenne Scott, he'd been thinking that hiring an investigator of his own might be another way forward. After his initial astonishment that there seemed to be so many agencies to choose from, he was equally surprised to realise that many of them dealt with missing persons enquiries, and that people leaving home seemed to be a common occurrence. What was it about running away? he wondered. Why were people so weak and foolish? He studied the sites in detail before ringing one of the agencies and outlining his problem.

The PI was matter-of-fact about it and gave him a run-through of potential costs that made Vince gasp. He told him he'd get back to him and rang the next name on the list. And another after that.

They all charged per day, plus expenses. And the general consensus was that the search would have to start in Paris – a trip he'd have to pay for. Money for old rope, he thought angrily as he totted up the costs, and his anger with Imogen flared again.

He rang Shona.

As always, her first question was had he heard anything.

'No.' He told her about the private investigators.

'So are you going to hire one?'

'None of the ones I've talked to,' he said. 'They charge a fortune and they're talking about going to France and the UK and even the States, all of which would be part of their bill. They must think I'm a right mug!'

'I'm sure they don't. They have to cover all the bases.'

'Even if I had the cash to splash around, I'm not shelling it out for them to jolly themselves around Europe in the height of summer,' said Vince.

'What will you do in that case?'

'I'm going to go to France myself. Someone must have seen her and someone must know where she is. I'm going to find her, put an end to this nonsense and bring her back home.'

'Vince, I've been thinking a lot about this,' said Shona, her voice urgent. 'Maybe you should accept the fact that she's left.'

'Accept it!' he cried. 'You've got to be kidding me. Have you forgotten that Imogen isn't a well woman?'

'There's nothing wrong with her,' said Shona. 'There isn't, Vince. OK, so she's a bit upset, but—'

'A bit upset! A bit upset means not talking to someone for a few days. It doesn't mean disappearing without a trace.'

'The thing is, it's not without a trace, is it?' said Shona.

'She's said she doesn't want to come home. Perhaps . . . perhaps you should take her at her word.'

'You were perfectly prepared for the gardai to look for her.' Vince's voice was cool.

'When I thought that she'd properly gone missing,' said Shona. 'When I thought something awful might have happened to her. But she's doing her own thing, Vince. Of course I'm not happy that she snuck off without telling anyone, but it was her choice.'

'Her choice!' He snorted. 'She had no right to make that choice.'

'It wasn't a fair one,' agreed Shona. 'All the same—'

'I thought you understood,' said Vince. 'But you're as bad as her.'

'I don't want you to make things worse,' said Shona.

'How much worse could they be?'

'If you leave her to her own devices, she might come back of her own accord.'

She might, agreed Vince. But what Imogen might or might not do wasn't good enough for him. He wasn't the sort of person who sat around waiting for things to happen. He would make them happen himself.

And he would bring her home.

It was nearly eight o'clock in the evening when his mobile rang. The number was blocked, and his first thought was that Imogen had finally decided to call him. He felt a renewed surge of anger towards her and took a deep breath to calm himself before answering. But it wasn't his wife; it was her stepsister Cheyenne, who was getting back to him after their Facebook connection.

'I've only just seen your message,' she said. 'What d'you mean, Imogen is missing?'

'Exactly what I said.' Vince was terse. 'She's disappeared without a trace.'

'Oh my God,' said Cheyenne. 'When? Have you told the police?'

'They don't want to know.' He explained why they thought Imogen had left of her own accord.

'They're probably right,' said Cheyenne, a note of relief in her voice.

'It doesn't mean they shouldn't look for her,' said Vince. 'She could be in a distressed state.'

'Why? What did you do?'

'Me?' he said. 'I did nothing at all. This is all down to Imogen herself. Anyway, I thought you might have an idea of where she would have gone to.'

'How on earth would I know? And why would I tell you if I did? If she's left you, she's left you. End of.'

'She hasn't left me,' said Vince. 'She's gone AWOL, that's all. And I can't believe you're happy she's disappeared off the face of the earth.'

'Wherever she's gone, she's deliberately not told you, Vince, which is entirely up to her. Anyhow, she's pretty capable, for all you like to portray her as a helpless stick without you.'

'All I want is for her to be OK,' Vince said. 'And as a missing person—'

'She's not missing.' Cheyenne interrupted him. 'She's walked out on you.'

'I think you'll find that missing is the appropriate word for someone who hasn't been seen for nearly three weeks.'

'Because she doesn't want to be,' said Cheyenne.

'Look, I know you never really liked me, but all I want is for Imogen to be happy. The truth is that she's been a bit edgy because we've been trying for a baby and it hasn't been working out and she blames herself.'

'Really?' There was a note of scepticism in Cheyenne's voice.

'Yes, really. That's why I'm worried about her. She's fragile.'

'No she's not,' retorted Cheyenne. 'She's as tough as old boots. Always has been.'

'That's what you think. You and your father, who never loved her.'

'Don't give me that shit, Vince.'

'It's the truth.'

'It might be your truth, but it's not mine. Or Dad's. And it used not to be Imogen's either.'

'So if you have any idea where she is,' continued Vince as though Cheyenne hadn't spoken, 'as her husband who loves her, I'd like to know.'

'I haven't a clue,' said Cheyenne shortly.

'She has to be in touch with someone. Nobody walks out of a home with nothing more than a change of clothes.'

'Has she any money?' asked Cheyenne.

'She took some from our account.'

'Which proves she had a plan,' Cheyenne said.

'She never plans,' said Vince. 'She's erratic. You must know that already.'

'She's not erratic,' said Cheyenne. 'She can be a bit flighty sometimes, I admit, but she was always pretty together when we were a family. I'll agree that she changed after meeting you.'

'For the better.'

'In your opinion.'

'Look, are you going to help me find her or not?'

'I'm sure if she wants to talk to you she'll get in touch.'

'Has she been in touch with you?'

'No.'

'You must have some idea where she might be. You lived with her for a long time. I think she's still in France – where exactly did she live when she was there?'

'I don't know,' said Cheyenne.

'You don't know or you won't tell me?' Vince was getting more and more annoyed.

'I don't know, and if I did, I wouldn't tell you unless Imogen gave me permission first. As I haven't spoken to her, she can't do that and I can't help you.'

'You're such a bitch, Cheyenne. She was right about you.'

'She called me a bitch?'

'Can you give me your father's phone number?' Vince didn't answer her. 'Maybe he'll be more understanding.'

'I'm perfectly understanding the situation, which is that she walked out and left you, and that she doesn't want to talk to you,' said Cheyenne. 'That doesn't take much deduction.'

'I hope you'll be happy when her broken and battered body is found at the bottom of a ravine in that case,' said Vince. 'Which could easily happen. And you might be able to stop it. Just because you dislike me doesn't mean you shouldn't help find someone who's stressed.'

Cheyenne was silent.

'So I'm asking you again, where the fuck is she?'

'I really don't know.' Cheyenne's tone was less belligerent. 'Honestly, Vince. She hasn't been in touch with me in months.'

'What about your father?'

'He and Paula are on holiday right now,' said Cheyenne. 'On a cruise.'

'I'm sure he can take a call.'

'You know how it is on those ships,' said Cheyenne. 'Costs a fortune to make and receive calls. Dad wouldn't even bother to switch his phone on; he hates it at the best of times. Look, I'll send him a message for you. That's the best I can do.'

'Give me his number and I'll leave a message myself,' said Vince.

'I don't know it off the top of my head,' said Cheyenne. 'Nobody remembers people's mobile numbers.'

'Send it to me.'

'I'll look it up,' said Cheyenne. 'Meantime, I'm sure Imogen is fine. Maybe she'll come back to you when she's had a bit of time to herself.'

'Everyone keeps saying that. But I'm worried about her.'

Cheyenne sighed. 'I'll message Dad, and I'll pass on your number.'

'And send his to me,' Vince reminded her.

'Sure,' said Cheyenne.

Then she hung up.

Chapter 16

Imogen arrived at Céline's house, a compact single-storey home set in a small garden, at exactly eight thirty on Saturday morning. The sun was high enough that the orange and pink hibiscus flowers at the gate had opened, and their delicate scent flooded the air. Imogen closed her eyes and inhaled deeply. She was lucky, she said to herself. Lucky to be here. Lucky to have found a job. Lucky to be rebuilding her life. She'd come up with a plan that had worked, and everything was going to be all right.

She rang the bell and Céline opened the door, greeting her with a smile and thanks for being on time.

'It's not big,' she said as she waved her arm around to embrace her home. 'And it's not filthy. But it's very, very messy. I'm sorry.'

Imogen looked at the piles of cookery books, newspapers and foodie magazines, the heaps of unironed clothes, and the selection of cups upturned on the drainer.

'Don't worry,' she said. 'I've seen a lot worse.'

'Here's the money.' Céline handed her some euro notes, and Imogen's eyes widened. Céline was paying her nearly double what she earned at the agency.

'They pay close to minimum wage,' she said. 'I told you I'd pay you more.'

'All the same . . .'

'Take it,' said Céline. 'If you're terrible, I won't ask you again.'

'Thank you.'

'The cleaning stuff is in here.' Céline opened a door that led to a small utility area. 'Hopefully there's everything you need.'

'It's fine,' said Imogen.

'In that case, *au revoir*. I'll see you at the café, either this weekend or next week.'

'See you,' said Imogen.

As soon as Céline left, she set to work, methodically drying things and putting them away, finding places for the magazines and books. Her mother used to listen to music when she was working, but Imogen enjoyed the silence and immersing herself in her thoughts. Which were not as tense and fraught as before. She was less tense in herself too, not jumping at every random sound and less likely to regard everyone she met as a possible threat to her security.

Perhaps it was always easier to learn from your mistakes in another place, she thought as she began to polish Céline's rosewood dining table. Perhaps that was why Carol had fled to Ireland after hers.

Imogen hadn't suspected that there had been a change in her mother's relationship with Denis Delissandes after his accident. Neither had Lucie, at least until the following Easter, when the entire family returned for the holiday.

Denis had visited twice since his ill-fated skiing trip. He was supposed to be sailing on both occasions, but he spent more time in Carol's bedroom than on board the *Lobster Bisque*, and although Carol's feelings of guilt grew greater with every minute, she was wildly in love with him and her emotions blinded her judgement. She knew it was hopeless and she knew it was reckless, but she couldn't help herself.

It was Imogen who gave her away, innocently remarking one day that Lucie might be able to fix Carol's feet for her with one of her special lotions, because Denis hadn't had much luck so far. Lucie had asked her what she was talking about and Imogen said that Denis had spent a lot of time rubbing them on his last visit, but that as he had to keep doing it, his rubbing clearly wasn't working.

Lucie told Imogen that she would indeed try to help Carol, and then suggested that she go out to play while she talked to her mother. Imogen ignored the raised voices in the kitchen, but what she couldn't ignore was Carol coming into the garden half an hour later and telling Imogen to get her things as they were leaving.

'Will we be back in time for me to play football with Oliver?' asked Imogen as she scrambled to her feet.

'No,' said Carol. 'We won't be back at all.'

Imogen stared at her. 'But . . . but we're supposed to be camping in the garden tonight,' she said.

'I'm sorry,' said Carol.

'Where are we going? We can't just leave. What about Madame? What about Monsieur? What about—'

'Please be quiet, Imogen,' said Carol. 'We're leaving and that's that.'

'But we can't go without . . . What about school? I have to find out if I got a star for my project. And we're doing a—'

'Enough, Imogen.' Carol held up her hand. 'We need to get organised.'

The next few hours were a blur. All Imogen knew was that bags were packed and suddenly she and her mother were on a bus to Biarritz without her having had the chance to say goodbye to anyone. She was distraught.

'Oliver and Charles will think I don't like them any more,' she wailed. 'They'll say I was afraid of camping outside. They'll call me a scaredy-cat. It's not fair. You said that Villa Martine was our home. You said it was where we lived.'

'I was wrong.'

'I hate you,' said Imogen.

'I'm not that fond of myself right now,' Carol said. 'But you have to remember that the Villa Martine is Madame and Monsieur's home, not ours.'

'Even if it isn't our home, why do we have to leave?' Imogen rubbed her eyes with the back of her hand. 'Madame said we were her family. We can't just go away.'

'Yes we can,' said Carol. 'I'm sorry, Imogen. It's because I made a mistake.'

'What sort of mistake?'

'A big one.'

'Did you burn Madame's dress when you were ironing?'

'No.'

'Did you forget to take the washing out of the machine?'

'No.'

'Did you break Madame's favourite blue bowl?'

'No.'

Imogen searched her mind for other mistakes her mother might have made, but she couldn't think of any.

'You always say that everyone makes mistakes. And that we forgive each other.'

'Yes, I do.'

'So won't Madame forgive you?'

'Not this time.'

'How can we go back if they don't forgive you?'

'We're not going back,' said Carol. 'Not ever.'

Imogen burst into tears again, while Carol leaned her head against the bus window and stared blankly at the countryside.

Staying in a hotel for the first time as a guest didn't cheer Imogen up. Nor did the novelty of the flight to Dublin. She was still upset and cranky when she and Carol arrived at Agnes's house. Agnes and Berthe had returned to Ireland from New York six months previously, and now they wrapped their arms around the pair of them.

'Thank you for looking after me,' said Carol as Agnes kissed her on the cheek. 'For taking me in. Again. I can't believe how badly I've messed everything up.'

'It was foolish,' said Berthe. 'But everyone does foolish things. And I bet it wasn't his first indiscretion.'

'Probably not,' admitted Carol. 'I should have known better.'

'What's an indiscretion?' asked Imogen.

'It's a kind of mistake,' said Berthe. 'Doing something you shouldn't.'

'Mum said she made a big mistake and that was why we left,' said Imogen. 'But . . .' she looked at Berthe, a puzzled expression on her face, 'someone else must have had an indiscretion too. Because you said "his indiscretion". And Mum is "her".'

Carol and Berthe exchanged looks.

'It's not fair if Mum is taking the blame for someone else's mistake.' Imogen spoke rapidly. 'It's like when I put the ants in Oliver's bed. I had to admit to it in the end because Charles was getting the blame and Madame would have punished him instead of me. So maybe if whoever did the indiscretion admits to it—'

'Imogen, *I* was the one who made the mistake,' said Carol. 'Nobody else. I'm to blame. So let's have no more talk about this.'

'But Berthe said—'

'Stop it for now, Imogen.' Agnes intervened. 'Go on upstairs. Your room is the first door on the right.'

Imogen stomped up the stairs. Carol, after a helpless look at Agnes and Berthe, followed her.

'What did you do that you shouldn't have?' Imogen asked when Carol walked into the room.

'I was silly,' said Carol. 'Really silly.'

'You call me silly sometimes,' said Imogen. 'And I'm always doing things I shouldn't. But you don't send me away.'

'This was different.'

'But you said sorry, didn't you?'

'Sometimes sorry isn't enough.'

'You always told me it was.'

'Usually it is,' conceded Carol. 'But not this time.'

Imogen stared at her. 'So is the other person who made the indiscretion sorry too?'

'Give me a break,' said Carol. 'Stop asking questions.'

'You always said that asking questions is good.' Imogen was fractious. 'Now you won't let me. You're mean, Mum.'

'I know.' Carol slammed a drawer closed. 'I'm a mean mother and a mean woman and I don't know how anyone puts up with me.'

Imogen was shocked into silence. Her mother had never spoken to her like that before.

'You're not mean,' she said eventually, wrapping her arms around Carol. 'I'm sorry I said that. You're good. And if you said sorry and Madame didn't listen to you, then she's the one who's mean.'

Carol hugged her.

'You can't blame Madame,' she said. 'She was always very good to us, Imogen. One day we'll go back and apologise again. You and me both. And you can say sorry to Oliver and Charles for not being able to go camping with them.'

'OK.' Imogen sniffed. 'And we can say sorry to Monsieur too.'

Carol didn't answer. She just hugged Imogen tighter.

Although everyone agreed that she was a very adaptable child, Imogen struggled with being back in Ireland. It wasn't only that she'd been uprooted; it was having to start all over again. Finding a new school. Making new friends. Learning new ways of doing things. It was a lot of effort and sometimes she felt tired of having to be the one to make it. Agnes and Berthe continually told her how lovely it was to have her living with them again, but Imogen, who'd almost forgotten her time at the Maison Lavande, couldn't remember what it had been like before. She missed the Villa Martine, she missed Lucie and Oliver and Charles – and to a lesser extent Denis.

She missed being able to walk to the beach. She missed everything. And she wanted to go back.

She kept asking her mother if 'one day' had come yet and if it was time to go back and say sorry and fix everything, but Carol kept saying no. She asked if they could go back to Hendaye anyway, even if they couldn't live at the Villa Martine. After all, she said, I was doing better at school there than here. Carol told her that she'd get into the swing of things soon enough because she was a clever girl, and clever girls did well no matter where they lived.

She decided to run away in September. It had been a tough day at her new school where some of the girls had teased her about her accent, laughing at her pronunciation of 'hall' as 'all'. Imogen was perfectly capable of pronouncing the 'h' but sometimes, when she spoke quickly, she forgot. Karen Connolly, one of the ringleaders, had made a big joke of it which had left Imogen feeling humiliated. Then, when she got home, Carol had picked on her for not tidying her room. Agnes had taken her mother's side in the ensuing argument, and Imogen decided that she'd had enough.

She hated Ireland, she said to herself as she started stuffing clothes into her case. She'd go back to France without Carol and say sorry to Lucie herself. Then everything could go back to the way it was before.

'Running away doesn't solve anything,' Carol said when she'd looked into Imogen's room and seen her putting clothes into her small case.

'You did.' Imogen looked at her directly. 'You ran away from the Villa Martine.'

'No I didn't,' said Carol. 'Madame asked me to leave.'

'She didn't mean it,' said Imogen. 'She often told Monsieur

to leave! I remember, don't you? She would say to him to get out of her office and out of her house.'

'She didn't mean for him to leave for ever,' said Carol. 'Just while she was working.'

'She probably didn't mean for us to leave for ever either,' said Imogen. 'That's why I'm going back.'

'People can't go back either,' said Carol. 'You can never go back.'

'Of course I can,' said Imogen. 'Monsieur always came back. And Berthe and Agnes came back to Ireland.'

'That's not what . . .' Carol sighed. She knew it had been hard for her daughter, and she felt guilty once again for her reckless stupidity with Denis Delissandes. 'It's complicated.'

'Why do grown-ups always say things are complicated?' demanded Imogen. 'It's not complicated at all.'

'Believe me, Imogen, it is.'

'So you won't let me go?'

'You're too young to go by yourself,' said Carol. 'I told you we'd go back together one day. Besides, Agnes and Berthe are being lovely to us right now and we have to count our blessings.'

Carol's favourite cliché wasn't what Imogen wanted to hear. But it was clear that she wasn't going to be permitted to run away. So she gave in and unpacked her bag again, allowing Carol to fold her crumpled clothes and put them away neatly.

Soon I'll be old enough to go back on my own, she told herself. I'll explain it all to Monsieur and Madame. They'll understand. I know they will. And everything will be OK again.

But then Carol met Kevin, and from Imogen's point of view, things went from bad to worse.

* * *

Kevin Sutton was a project engineer on a city regeneration scheme. He and Carol met a year after her return to Ireland, while they were both attending a parent–teacher evening at Imogen's school. Kevin's daughter Cheyenne was in the same year as her, although not the same class. By that time Imogen had settled into her life in Dublin and there was no more talk of running away or returning to France. There was no more talk of France in the house at all. By tacit consent it had become a taboo subject, and Imogen put it to the furthest recesses of her mind. Agnes and Berthe – who were planning to go back to the States the following year – encouraged the relationship between Carol and Kevin, especially because they thought it would be good for Imogen to make friends with a girl of her own age. Although she had a knack of getting on well with adults, she still didn't seem to have made a close friend at school, but she was dismissive of her aunts' championing of both Kevin and Cheyenne.

'You like him?' she asked one evening when Carol had gone out with him, leaving her with Agnes and Berthe. 'But he's fat.'

'Don't be pass-remarkable,' said Agnes. 'Anyway, he's not fat. He's well built.'

'Pah!' Imogen wrinkled her nose in a very Gallic way. 'I say fat.'

Berthe grinned. 'But your *maman* loves him.'

'Does she?' Imogen made a face. 'I was hoping it was another indiscretion.'

Agnes and Berthe exchanged glances.

'A what?' asked Agnes.

'An indiscretion. You told me about it before, Berthe. It's doing something you shouldn't. I looked it up afterwards.

It's a mistake about sex. Mum had an indiscretion in France with Monsieur Delissandes and I thought perhaps she was having one with Kevin too.'

'O . . . K . . .' Berthe said.

'It makes sense,' said Imogen. 'You shouldn't have sex with someone who's not your husband. Everyone knows that's wrong. It's an *affaire* and it's nearly always a massive mistake. That explains why Madame was so annoyed with Mum, doesn't it? She was probably afraid that Mum and Monsieur Delissandes would run away together, even though Mum says that running away doesn't solve anything.'

'I see,' said Agnes.

'And so that's why we left. Mum had an indiscretion and Madame decided to forgive Monsieur because he was her family and she loved him and didn't want to divorce him, but she couldn't forgive Mum because we weren't family, even though I thought we sort of were. So I think you have to be careful with indiscretions. It doesn't matter so much if Mum has one with Kevin, because his wife died, same as Dad. But I still think he's a mistake for her.'

Agnes and Berthe exchanged glances.

'Mum didn't say sorry properly to Madame,' added Imogen. 'We left in such a hurry she couldn't possibly have. She rushed out without thinking really. But she said that one day we'd go back and apologise together. I think Madame will forgive her then.'

'I'm sure she's forgiven her by now,' said Berthe.

'But if she had, we'd go back.'

'Imogen.' Agnes spoke gently. 'You can't go back. You live here now, in Ireland.'

'Oh, why does everyone always say that!' cried Imogen.

'I go back to school, don't I? Why can't I go back to the Villa Martine?'

'It's different,' said Berthe.

'Because of the indiscretion?'

'No,' she said. 'Because things change, Imogen. They never stay the same.'

'I wish they did.' Imogen's lip trembled. 'It would be much nicer that way.'

Chapter 17

It was good to have the money from Céline in her purse, but Imogen knew that she was going to have to withdraw some cash from her bank account soon. Nevertheless, she didn't want to take out money in Hendaye. She knew she was being silly in thinking that Vince could track her, because realistically there was no way he could have found out about her secret account, much less accessed information about it, yet she'd got this far by being ultra-cautious and she wanted to keep it that way. So on Sunday morning she decided to cycle across the bridge to the small Spanish town of Irun on the opposite side of the river to find a bank machine. That way, she reckoned, if Vince somehow had managed to find out about it, he'd be sent on a wild goose chase around the Spanish Basque country instead of concentrating on France.

She smiled to herself as she hopped on to the pink bicycle and freewheeled down the road feeling happier than she'd done in ages. She waved at Madame Lefeuvre, from the boulangerie where she bought fresh bread daily, and then turned towards the Bidassoa river, which formed the border between France and Spain. According to Google Maps, the border actually ran through the middle of it, so halfway across, she stopped and took a selfie of herself with one foot in France and the other in Spain. She would have liked to send it to Shona, because she knew her friend would smile at it, but for now she contented herself with saving it to her camera roll before getting on the bike again. Once on the Spanish side of the river, she could see that the road signs were subtly different and that the language had changed too.

Irun lacked the coastal scenery of Hendaye, but Imogen wasn't interested in scenery. The most important thing from her point of view was that after a few minutes she saw a bank with a cashpoint outside it. She dismounted from the bike and leaned it against the wall while she inserted her card. When the screen flashed up with 'Welcome Ms Weir', she heaved a sigh of relief.

Once she'd taken some money out, she looked around her. There was a small café on the corner, and for the novelty value of having a coffee in a country she'd been able to cycle to in under twenty minutes, she sat at one of the outside tables and ordered an Americano. At the table beside her, a young couple were chatting animatedly to each other. Hearing their Spanish conversation made Imogen feel even further away from Vince than before. She felt her shoulders relax and she exhaled with the sheer pleasure of sitting in the sun.

'Imogen? Is that you?'

She whirled around in the seat, her heart pounding. For a moment she hadn't been sure what language the question had been asked in, but then she realised it was French and that the speaker couldn't be Vince.

'René,' she said as she saw him.

'What on earth are you doing here?' He pulled out a chair and sat down without being invited.

'I decided to do some exploring,' she said. 'What about you?'

'There's a wonderful open-all-hours deli around the corner that does the best chorizo in the world – you can't get it anywhere else. I drive over from time to time to pick some up. It adds great flavour to my cooking.'

'I didn't realise you were a cook,' said Imogen.

'I was married to a chef's daughter,' René reminded her. 'What did you expect?'

'Maybe that you'd rebel by eating nothing but McDonald's.'

He laughed, then looked at her enquiringly.

'I believe you're working for Céline now.'

'That's OK, isn't it?' she asked. 'It doesn't interfere with what I do for the agency.'

'Hey, if you want to earn more money, who am I to stop you. I was simply surprised when she told me.'

'She told you herself?'

'But of course. Like you, I get my coffee from her café. I always have.'

'You don't find it awkward seeing her all the time?' asked Imogen.

'Not at all,' replied René. 'We were in love once. We're not any more. We're happier apart than together. *C'est la vie.*'

'If only it was always that simple,' said Imogen.

'I've been fortunate,' agreed René. 'We had a good marriage, at least for a time. And an easy divorce. How about you?' he asked. 'It has not been simple for you?'

'I think I made it complicated for myself,' she replied.

'Ah well, we learn from our mistakes,' said René. 'There is someone in your life now? Or not?'

'Absolutely not,' she said. 'I don't have time for anyone.'

'It's only English or American people who say that,' René told her. 'Everyone should have time for another person.'

'Maybe in the future.' Imogen shook the unopened sachet of sugar on the side of her saucer.

'You're too busy being a cleaner to have a lover?'

'That's not what I meant.'

'Because it seems to me, Imogen Weir, that it would be good for you to have someone. Someone to help you, to support you – and, of course, to love you.'

'I don't need help or support or love.'

'Everyone needs love. And most of us need some help and support as well.'

'Love doesn't always work out the way it should,' remarked Imogen.

'And what way is that?'

'Happy. It doesn't work out happy.'

René said nothing. Imogen tore the top off the sachet and tipped a tiny amount of sugar into her coffee.

'I'm sorry,' he said. 'I think I've overstepped the mark.'

'A little.'

'It's just that I don't like to see you sitting alone at a table in a pavement café.'

'I'm perfectly happy,' said Imogen. 'Besides, I'm not alone. You're with me.'

He smiled. 'I keep thinking that you're a . . . a fragile figure, Imogen. But you're not, are you?'

Vince frequently called her fragile. And for a time that might have been true. But she wasn't fragile now.

'I can look after myself,' she told René.

'Yes, you can.' He nodded in agreement. 'Have you plans for the rest of the day?'

'Not really,' she said. 'Cycle home, sit by the window, read a book.'

'And in the evening?'

'I bought some fresh fish yesterday,' she said. 'I'm going to cook it and eat it with a salad and a glass of Sancerre.'

'All alone again?'

'Yes.'

'Perhaps you would like not to eat by yourself?' suggested René. 'Perhaps you would like to eat with me? I'm not looking for love, you understand. But if we don't eat together, we will both be alone this evening.'

'I'm sorry,' said Imogen. 'I bought fish for one.'

René grinned. 'I didn't make myself clear. I thought you might like to forget about the solitary fish in your fridge for tonight and eat out with me instead.'

'Thank you for the invitation, but you're my boss,' she told him. 'It's horribly inappropriate.'

'Bastarache Immobilier is hardly a global enterprise,' he remarked. 'It's not like we need a list of things that are appropriate or not.'

'Nevertheless, I'm your employee and I don't think you should be taking me to dinner.'

'Why not?'

'You might discover things about me you don't like,' she said. 'They might affect your judgement of me and make it more difficult for me to work for you.'

'Unless I find out that you're secretly a serial murderer who uses our cleaning products as a means to conceal her nefarious activities, nothing you say will alter my judgement of you.'

'I'm not sure it would do your reputation any good to be seen out with one of your cleaners,' said Imogen.

'It will do my reputation no harm at all to be seen out with a beautiful woman,' René said.

Imogen laughed. 'You're such a charmer.'

'Why wouldn't I try to charm an attractive woman into having dinner with me?' René shrugged.

'It's very nice of you,' said Imogen. 'But I can't.'

'Am I not charming enough? Do you not find me attractive as a dinner companion? Am I less interesting than a dead fish?' He looked at her with mock outrage.

'You're very attractive,' she assured him.

'Well then.'

'René, I . . .'

'I'm not trying to get you into bed with me,' said René. 'Well, maybe I'm thinking about it for the future. Why wouldn't I? But for tonight, dinner will be enough.'

'For heaven's sake, René.' She couldn't help laughing again. 'You don't have to be so blunt about it.'

'Of course I do,' he said. 'You're an *Anglaise*, you have repressed notions.'

'I'm an *Irlandaise*,' she reminded him. 'And I'm not repressed. Just not ready to hop into bed with someone I work for.'

'But you might be one day?'

'Aargh!' She shook her head. 'Please stop talking about going to bed with me.'

'Oh all right.' René sighed. 'But the dinner offer still stands.'

'Better not,' said Imogen.

'You've successfully blown away my chances of sleeping with you,' said René. 'But eating with you – why do you reject that too?'

'Because I feel it's a prelude to seducing me anyway,' said Imogen.

'Absolutely not,' he told her. 'If you say no, you mean no. And if you don't want dinner, that's not a problem, but please don't say no because you think you'd owe me something afterwards. You don't belong to me, Imogen.'

Imogen looked into her half-empty coffee cup and said nothing.

'Imogen?'

She could hear his voice but she couldn't look up.

She'd felt secure every time her mother had said it. But now Vince's voice was in her head saying the exact same words.

You belong to me.

And they chilled her.

'*Chérie*, are you all right?' René put his hand over hers and jerked her back to reality.

'Yes, yes, I'm sorry.' She blinked a couple of times and moved slightly so their hands were no longer touching. 'I go off into a world of my own occasionally.'

'There's nothing bothering you?'

She shook her head. 'Everything's fine.'

'Are you sure?'

'Absolutely.' She glanced at her watch. 'I should get going.'

'Do you want a lift home?'

'Not at all,' she replied. 'I have the bike with me, after all. Céline's bike,' she added. 'She says she doesn't mind, but to be honest, I find it slightly weird knowing that I'm getting around on your ex-wife's bicycle.'

'There's nothing weird about it,' said René. 'Better that it's being used, no?'

'I love the way the French can compartmentalise things,'

she said. 'She's your ex, it's over, the bike doesn't mean anything any more.'

'Why should it?' He looked genuinely astonished. 'It's only a piece of machinery.'

'True. And I couldn't do my job without it. But it's still a bit, oh, I don't know – *comme un cheveu sur la soupe.*'

René chuckled. 'It doesn't matter whose bicycle it was. Besides, Céline and I never made love on it or anything. It's a means of getting around, that's all.'

'Making love on a bike sounds painful.' Imogen's eyes twinkled.

'You'd be surprised,' said René.

She smiled. It was a long time since she'd had fun and banter in a conversation with a man. It was a long time, she realised, since she'd had a conversation in which she wasn't subliminally afraid that she'd say the wrong thing and provoke a rage.

I should have left him sooner, she thought. I should have known what was happening to me. I should have seen it. I'm such a fool.

'And now I really do have to go,' she told René. 'I'll see you on Monday.'

'OK.' He stood up as she did and gave her a farewell kiss on the cheek. 'Take care.'

'You too.'

She hopped on to the bike and cycled back across the bridge into France. When she arrived at the apartment building, she hurried up the stairs, warm from her exertions. She changed into the inexpensive swimsuit that she'd finally got around to buying and went out to the pool. There was nobody around and she managed six lengths before flipping on to her back and floating beneath the clear blue sky.

You belong to me. The words came back to her again. Strong and insistent. And she let the memories take hold.

Chapter 18

Somewhat surprisingly, it was the memory of Carol that came to her first. They were alone in the house together, and it was such a rarity that Imogen realised Agnes and Berthe had deliberately gone out so that her mother could talk in private. Carol sat down beside her and told her that she and Kevin wanted to get married.

'Do you love him?' Imogen asked.

'Yes,' replied Carol.

'More than Monsieur Delissandes?'

'I didn't love Monsieur Delissandes.' Carol's cheeks reddened. 'At least, I thought I did, but he wasn't mine to love. It was a dreadful mistake, Imogen, and I'm sorry for all the trouble I caused.'

'Why did you have the indiscretion with him if you knew he wasn't yours?'

Carol sighed. 'I wanted to belong to someone,' she said.

'You belong to me,' Imogen told her.

'Of course I do, but that's different. I wanted someone to share my life with.'

'But you would never have been able to share your life with Monsieur,' Imogen pointed out. 'He was married to

Madame. He belonged to her. And Charles and Oliver. So why did you think—'

'I wasn't thinking,' said Carol. 'I don't know what came over me.'

'You thought you loved Monsieur and now you think you love Kevin.'

'I *do* love Kevin,' said Carol. 'He's kind and generous and he loves both of us too.'

'Does he? Really?'

'Yes.'

'This isn't a choice, is it?' Imogen asked. 'You're telling me, not asking me.'

'Kevin will be a good husband and a good father to you.'

'Kevin isn't my father,' said Imogen. 'So he can't be a good one to me.'

'It's true he's not your dad,' agreed Carol. 'But he *is* a father. He has Cheyenne. He loves her and he'll love you too.'

'I don't need him to love me,' said Imogen. 'I have you and you have me. Why do you want someone else?'

'You and I will always love each other,' Carol said. 'But one day you'll leave home and find someone of your own to love.'

'So you're planning for the future?'

'I guess so,' agreed Carol.

'What if I don't find someone?' asked Imogen.

'You will.' Carol was certain. 'You'll find someone and you'll want to be with him all the time and you won't give me a second thought, because that's what loving a man is like.'

'Is that how you felt about Monsieur? You didn't give a second thought to anything then, did you?'

'I had loads of second thoughts,' Carol said. 'I ignored them. Which was the stupid thing.'

Imogen sat in silence as she weighed up everything her mother had said.

'I'm not sure I want to find someone like that,' she said eventually.

'You'll find him,' Carol said. 'Or he'll find you. And you'll be happy, Imogen, I promise. One of my favourite philosophers says that "being deeply loved gives you strength, and loving someone deeply gives you courage", and I think he's right.'

'Is that how you feel with Kevin? Strong and courageous?'

'Yes.'

'That's a good thing, I suppose.'

Carol nodded. 'Yes, it is.'

'OK,' said Imogen. 'In that case, you should marry him. But . . .' she looked at Carol, 'would it be OK if I stayed with Agnes and Berthe afterwards?'

'No!' Her mother was aghast. 'When Kevin and I get married, it'll be a whole new family. Me and him and you and Cheyenne, all together.'

'It's just . . . I'm not sure I want to be another family,' said Imogen. 'When I was very small, we were part of Berthe's. And then the Delissandes'. And then Agnes and Berthe again. Now you want it to be with Kevin and Cheyenne. It's exhausting. It would be simpler for me to stay with Agnes and Berthe because we can still be a family and they won't look for a man to love. They love each other instead.'

'This is the last time, I promise,' said Carol. 'And you'll like having Cheyenne as a sister.'

Imogen made a face. 'She thinks she's *trop* cool.'

'She's a nice girl and you'll have fun together,' insisted Carol. 'Besides, you know quite well that Agnes and Berthe are going back to America at the end of the year, and you can't go with them.'

'Why not?'

'Do you really want to move somewhere else?' asked Carol. 'Do you honestly want to leave me?'

Imogen shook her head. She and Carol were a partnership. They belonged together. But she was afraid that with Kevin permanently in the picture, her relationship with her mother would change. His feelings, and Cheyenne's too, would have to be taken into consideration. And Imogen was pretty sure that they wouldn't want to go back to Hendaye some day like Carol had promised. Although the memories of her time at the Villa Martine were beginning to fade, she still felt as though she had unfinished business there. She still hadn't said goodbye. It seemed to her now that she never would.

The two girls were bridesmaids at the wedding. Imogen had to admit that it had been exciting to get dressed up for the day. It had been fun to giggle with her soon-to-be stepsister and have glamorous photographs taken, although – unlike Cheyenne – she eventually got bored with the interminable posing. But the day itself had been better than she'd expected and there was no doubt that Carol seemed to be very happy.

It might turn out OK, she confided to Berthe later that evening. There were probably worse people in the world than Kevin. And Cheyenne made her laugh, especially when she made cheeky comments about other people's looks. But from

Imogen's point of view, living with them wasn't going to be the same as living with Berthe and Agnes.

'Of course it won't,' said Berthe. 'You'll be a family together.'

'Oh, I know,' said Imogen. 'Mum keeps telling me that.'

She didn't say that she'd once said the same about the Delissandes.

Berthe hugged her and told her that she'd be very happy with her mum and Kevin and Cheyenne. And she might have been, Imogen thought, if six months after their marriage Carol hadn't gone to the doctor looking for a tonic for the exhaustion that had taken hold of her, and ended up being treated for a cancer from which there had been no recovery. Imogen was shocked and disbelieving when Carol told her. She went to the nearby shopping centre and bought a dreamcatcher, hoping that it would trap the awfulness of Carol's illness, but it made no difference. She wondered if it was because, unlike Madame Delissandes, she didn't really believe in the dreamcatcher.

Agnes and Berthe came back for Carol's funeral. Imogen, grief-stricken and tearful, wanted to return to the States with them, but Kevin was adamant that he was her guardian and that she should finish her education in Ireland.

'Your stepfather is right,' Agnes told her gently. 'It would definitely be better for you to stay with him and Cheyenne. Besides, he loves you dearly. And he was wonderful to your mum, you said so yourself.'

'I know. But now she's gone and I'm not important.'

'You most certainly are,' said Agnes. 'Kevin cares about you, you know he does.'

'You mean you and Berthe don't care about me enough.'

'That's not true.'

'Feels like it.'

The truth, however, was that Agnes and Berthe had had long discussions with Kevin about Imogen's future, and they agreed with him. Nothing would be gained by uprooting her again. She was better off in Dublin. And so after a couple of weeks they kissed her goodbye and left her behind.

Nobody could have been kinder or more patient with her than Kevin. Even Cheyenne dropped the slightly patronising air she sometimes adopted towards her stepsister. But the next twelve months were difficult, and Imogen struggled with missing Carol, missing Agnes and Berthe and feeling like the interloper in Kevin and Cheyenne's lives.

Every night she tried to do what Carol had always told her to do and count her blessings. But even though she listed Kevin being nice and having redecorated her bedroom as one of them, and Cheyenne's gifts of eyeshadow and mascara as another, she still couldn't help finding a greater number of things to be worried and upset about. What bothered her most was the feeling that Carol had received a cosmic punishment for her indiscretion. Carol (and Madame) had often spoken about karma, good and bad. Her indiscretion with Monsieur had been really bad karma. So it stood to reason, if she believed in it, that her punishment would be really bad too. Imogen rationalised that this couldn't be completely true, yet she felt that if she herself could have gone back to Hendaye and apologised to Madame Delissandes for what Carol had done, everything would have been all right. She worried that her mother's illness had been caused by the anger that Lucie had felt. She worried that Lucie was angry with her too. Even worse, she worried about Oliver and

Charles's feelings towards her. Each time she had a headache or felt a little unwell, she was afraid that bad karma was out to get her.

It took her nearly a year to put things into perspective. During that time she hadn't been stricken by a deadly disease, which was yet another blessing. She couldn't honestly say she was happy, but nor did she feel as lost as she had before. Her life was quieter and calmer, and she felt calmer inside too.

But she should have known it would be a temporary situation, she told herself one night, because nothing ever stayed the same for her. This time the disruption was that Kevin met Paula Curtis, a PR consultant from Birmingham who was in Dublin doing some media work for the company where he worked. Suddenly Paula was coming over to Dublin every second weekend and sleeping in the bedroom with Kevin, something that gave Imogen a knot in her stomach and made Cheyenne grit her teeth.

'What do you think is going to happen?' Cheyenne asked her one night.

'I think it's another indiscretion,' Imogen said.

'Huh?'

'A big mistake.'

But no matter what she and Cheyenne thought, Kevin felt differently. And a little over two years after Carol's death, he announced that he and Paula were going to get married.

'Three wives,' Imogen muttered to Cheyenne one evening. 'This is ridiculous.'

'He's my dad, but he's a bozo,' Cheyenne said. 'Plus, last night I heard him talking to Paula about moving to Birmingham.'

'Birmingham!' Imogen was horrified. 'But that's England. I don't want to go to England.'

'I was a bit shocked when I heard it first,' said Cheyenne. 'It might be fun, though. There's a lot more going on in England than here.'

Imogen felt like closing her eyes, putting her fingers in her ears and pretending that nothing was happening around her. Then Kevin called both of the girls together to confirm the move.

'But you'll be uprooting me,' Imogen pointed out. 'You wouldn't let Agnes and Berthe uproot me to go to the States. I clearly remember you saying that.'

'You're older now,' said Kevin. 'You can cope better.'

'What about our education?' she asked.

'We won't go until after you've both completed your Transition Year,' said Kevin. 'And then you can do A levels in Birmingham. Paula has already checked up on good schools in the area.'

'But everything will be different!' cried Imogen.

'A smart girl like you won't have any problems,' Kevin assured her. 'Aren't you already a straight-A student, for heaven's sake?'

Imogen did well at school because she liked the time on her own that studying allowed her. Sitting in a quiet room, reading her textbooks, was soothing. But despite her grades, she wouldn't have called herself a straight-A student. She wasn't academically gifted. She just worked hard. If they moved to England, she'd have to start again. Why did adults think it was OK for her to have to do it over and over?

Kevin brought them to the city for a visit, which changed Cheyenne's mind completely about the move.

'I liked it,' she told Imogen when they got home. 'And what about that brilliant new shopping centre that's opening soon? It'll be way better than anything we've got.'

'I don't care about shopping centres!'

'Well I like the idea that we'll be close to some really good clothes shops at last.' Cheyenne flicked her hair out of her eyes.

'I promise you, it'll be great,' said Kevin. 'And you can come back to Dublin for college if that's what you want, Imogen. When the sale of this house goes through, I'm going to buy an apartment so there'll always be a place for us here.'

Imogen was mollified slightly by the thought, but she still didn't want to go. The decision was made, however, and once again she packed her case. Even though this time she had Cheyenne as support, she couldn't help thinking that her life was all about being pulled in directions she didn't want to go by people who didn't care how much it upset her. And she was tired of counting her blessings and looking on the bright side and trying to make the best of it. None of Carol's clichés were working for her. She wanted a life of her own and a place to call home. She didn't care if she never found anyone to love. It seemed to her that love messed up everything. She was better off without it.

The way she looked at it afterwards was that she got through the Birmingham years. She tried not to feel as though she didn't belong, but it was difficult. In Ireland she'd felt French and in Birmingham she felt Irish. She couldn't remember how she'd felt in France. It had never been something she'd had to think about.

Cheyenne loved Birmingham. She embraced their life there

and made lots of new friends. Imogen, on the other hand, was always thinking about where she'd go next. She did well in her exams and had offers from a number of universities, and although she briefly thought about the Sorbonne in Paris, she decided that she'd return to Dublin and do her European studies there. The decision was partly to do with economics – it would have been prohibitively expensive to go to Paris when in Dublin Kevin's apartment was available to her for free.

She moved in during the summer, unpacking her things before placing the framed photo of her and Carol taken on the beach at Hendaye on a shelf. The photo captured the eggshell blue of the sky and the azure of the sea, as well as the golden beach and – most importantly – the beaming smiles of her and her mother. Every time Imogen looked at it she felt safe and secure and at home. And every time she looked at it she promised herself that she'd have a home of her own one day, where she would live by herself and there'd be no chance of any indiscretions to ruin it all.

Over the following months, like a dry fern unfurling after a shower of rain, Imogen began to open up. She remembered how to count her blessings because suddenly she felt that she had some again. She was young, free and single with an apartment of her own, which made her very popular in her student group. Although she'd been self-contained at school, she found herself drawn into the social life of the college and she threw her apartment open to an eclectic mix of friends. On the occasions when they got rowdier than she'd anticipated, she placated the neighbours by bringing them trays of the thin French biscuits that Lucie Delissandes had taught her to bake. She grew more comfortable with the friendships she forged and enjoyed being part of the student community.

But she shied away from romantic relationships. She scoffed at her mother's favourite philosopher and his views about love. As far as Imogen was concerned, falling in love was a sure-fire way of getting hurt. She began to understand the nature of the affair between Carol and Denis Delissandes. She was disappointed in her mother and sad that she felt that way about her. The way she saw it, Carol had betrayed Lucie and thrown everything away for the sake of a few hours of passion. She swore that she wasn't going to allow that to ever happen to her. That she would never have an affair went without saying, but even more, she wanted to be a hundred per cent sure before she committed to anyone. She certainly wasn't in a rush. She was happy with her life the way it was now. She didn't want to change anything. She'd long dismissed her childhood need to return to the Villa Martine to say goodbye to the Delissandes and apologise for her mother's behaviour. She was pretty sure they'd all forgotten her by now, and even if they hadn't, they wouldn't want to set eyes on her. So although she kept the photo on the shelf, she stopped daydreaming about her childhood years in France.

Nevertheless, she spent a couple of semesters studying in Paris, and even went to Provence for a fortnight with a group of the other students. They spent a few nights in Cannes before moving on to a house in Marseille. There, Imogen wandered through the twisting streets and drank pastis at the old port without it sparking any memories for her. In fact she found it hard to recall anything of her life in Provence, and a lot less of her life in Hendaye too.

She was glad about that. It was good to think that her present was more important than her past, and that her future would be more important still. After she graduated, she threw herself with enthusiasm into her work with a European history professor who said he was writing the definitive book on the French Revolution; he in turn recommended her to another colleague, whom she was happy to assist in his research project on the Austro-Hungarian Empire. She felt as though she'd entered a new phase in her life. One in which she was the person in control. Where she was the one to say where she went and what she did. Although she kept in touch with Agnes and Berthe, she stopped calling them every week. Her contact with her stepfather and stepsister petered out, especially since Kevin and Paula now had a son of their own, Boris. Cheyenne was working as a freelance make-up artist in London. None of them mattered any more, thought Imogen. Other people messed up your life. Better to be alone. And it was better too, she decided, to confine her relationships with men to occasional dates that never went much further than a goodnight kiss. That way she'd never make the same mistakes as Carol. That way she'd never get hurt.

But then she met Vince, who understood exactly how she felt because he'd gone through the same things himself. She finally appreciated what Carol had meant about finding the right person. With Vince in her life, she felt stronger. It was as though he could read her mind and see the things in there that had hurt her the most, because they reflected what had hurt him too, and in talking to her about them, he made them seem less painful.

'I never got to know my father, but my stepfather always

thought about himself before he thought about me,' he told her on one of their nights out together. 'I had to fight to do the things I wanted. I was a brilliant footballer, but when he married my mother, we moved house and I had to move club and the new one wasn't as good. And then, when I was doing well at that club, they bought another house and it was too far away for me to get to training on time. So I stopped playing. OK, I was never going to be a professional, but I had talent and they didn't care about it.'

She nodded. It had been the same for her, being bounced from France to Ireland and from Ireland to the UK. It was the first time she'd met someone who truly understood how hard that had been. Who didn't say that it must have been fabulous to live in other countries and she should be grateful for the opportunities. Vince knew what it was like to want to stay somewhere but be told you had to be somewhere else. He promised her that life with him would never be like that. He told her that he'd be a rock of stability. He said that he liked an ordered life. She said that she did too.

When she allowed her defences to crumble and slept with him, he was kind and loving. He liked her inexperience. She liked that he didn't compare her to anyone else. She liked the feeling that she was the only person in his life.

That was why she fell in love with him.

And that was why she married him.

Which wasn't an indiscretion. But it was very definitely a mistake.

The first surprise came almost as soon as they'd stepped inside the front door of Bellwood Park after their week-long honeymoon in Sardinia. Imogen slung her jacket over the newel post at the end of the banisters and went upstairs with her hand luggage.

'Hey,' Vince called. 'Your jacket!'

'It's fine,' she shouted back. 'I'll get it later.'

'There's a place for jackets,' he said as he came up the stairs after her, the offending garment in his hand. 'And cluttering up the hallway isn't it.'

'I would have moved it eventually.'

'Would have? Eventually?' He stood at the doorway of the bathroom, where she was washing her hands. 'Would have is no use. You should put it where it's meant to be first time.'

'I had my case. I couldn't manage everything.' She grinned at him. 'I'm not Superwoman.'

'I'm not asking you to be Superwoman,' he said. 'I'm asking you to put things in their proper place.'

'And I said I would.'

'You shouldn't have taken it off when you came in,' he told her. 'That way you'd have brought the jacket upstairs at the same time as your case. It's simple time and motion, Imogen. It's being efficient.'

She stared at him, uncertain if he was joking or not.

'But I'll forgive you,' he said. 'Because you're my wife and I love you.'

He kissed her, and she laughed inside at how she'd almost believed that he was annoyed at her.

The following weeks, however, were more and more unsettling. She hadn't noticed when they were going out together and spending time in each other's homes that Vince had a million different rules, which he insisted were essential for the smooth running of their lives. She supposed they'd evolved over his time living alone, and at first she teased him about them, but his annoyed reaction made her realise that he was perfectly serious when he insisted that dishes were to be taken out of the dishwasher as soon as the cycle was complete. Newspapers had to be placed in the green bin immediately they were read. The only food bags to be used were the ones with the little zip to close them. The sink had to be bleached every day. She was to remove her hair from the plughole of the shower each time she used it. Biscuits were to be kept in the yellow-topped container, cake in the pink-topped one. Mugs were to be used in sequence. Red, then blue, then black. If she broke one of the rules (and she did nearly every day, because no matter how many she followed, there seemed to be a dozen more as backup), Vince would ask her if she was really so hopeless that she couldn't remember a simple sequence like red, blue, black.

'You need to chill out,' she told him on the day she'd accidentally put biscuits in the pink-topped container. 'Our lives won't implode if I don't put biscuits in a specific plastic box, Vince. Besides, all these rules and regulations are bordering on OCD. That might have been OK when you were living by yourself, but I can't keep every one of them and I can't bear it when you give me grief for getting something wrong.'

'They aren't rules,' he said. 'They're guidelines for successfully living together. All of them make perfect sense. I don't mind if you make mistakes, but I do mind when you wilfully disobey me.'

'Disobey?' She stared at him. 'Wilfully? Obeying wasn't in our marriage vows.'

'Perhaps I've used the wrong word,' he conceded. 'What

I'm trying to say is that sometimes I feel you do things I'd rather you didn't simply to test me.'

'Of course I don't!' she said. 'Look, Vince, everyone has to make adjustments when they get married. I need to be less slapdash. You need to be more flexible.'

He agreed. He didn't say anything on the days when she brought him the wrong-coloured mug. Or when she bought a brand of cheese that she knew wasn't a favourite of his. But the expression on his face was enough for her to know that he was annoyed, and his coolness towards her for the rest of the day was unbearable. In the end, it was easier to follow the rules and get it right than to put up with the consequences of being wrong. The trouble was, the more she got right, the more new things seemed to preoccupy him. Including Imogen herself, starting with her appearance.

'You're not working in academic circles now,' he told her one day. 'You're in an office. And appropriate office wear is skirts and blouses, not jeans and T-shirts. Proper shoes with high heels. And Imogen, you need to wear more make-up too. It all helps to make you look the part. Suit. Shoes. Face.'

'Chandon Leclerc isn't really the place for snazzy suits and shoes,' she said. 'It's in an industrial estate, not the city centre, the offices are pretty crummy, and it's perfectly OK to wear jeans. Anyhow, I kind of like my style. I thought you did too.'

If she were to define her look, Imogen would have called it boho-chic. She favoured loose floral dresses with pastel cardigans, or faded jeans and pretty jackets over plain T-shirts, along with comfortable wedges, which were her favourite footwear and, she thought, perfectly appropriate for her work environment too.

'It doesn't matter what your office is like,' he said. 'You should still dress the part. You should make an effort no matter where you are. Also,' he added, 'I don't like that shorter hairdo on you. I'd prefer it if you let it grow again.'

She said nothing.

'Did you hear me?' he asked.

'I heard you, but—'

'Please don't defy me on this, Imogen. I'm the one who's keeping it all together in this relationship. I'm a senior executive who earns considerably more than you and I know what I'm talking about. It was perfectly fine to wear scruffy clothes when you were faffing around with dusty professors, but it's different in an office situation. You don't understand it. You're hopeless at commerce. You need my advice.'

She wished he'd stop telling her that he was the main breadwinner. Her mother's money had helped to buy the house, after all. And she was tired of him telling her that she was hopeless, too. But perhaps he had a point about the difference between commerce and academia. So she bought the suits and the blouses, the shoes and the make-up. And after that, she never went anywhere, even the supermarket, without doing her face and wearing high heels.

He wanted to know where she was all the time. He told her to text him when she was leaving the office, or the shops, or the gym, which she'd joined with his approval. After all, he said, it was important for her to take exercise and maintain her slim figure. He hated the way some women let themselves go after they got married. He listed a number of the women in the housing estate whom he put in that category, including their next-door neighbour, Sadie. Hefty hippos, he said. Can't be bothered.

He approved of Shona because she always looked fit and healthy and because she dressed well when she wasn't in her workout gear. He was tolerant of Imogen's friendship with her, while letting her know that he wasn't so keen on some of her other friends. They often met at the gym where Imogen liked spending time on the treadmill, listening to a music mix that effectively stopped her thoughts from wandering in directions she didn't want them to go. Sometimes Vince would give Shona a lift home with them and they would happily share boxer dog stories during the journey. Imogen wondered how it was that he could appear so relaxed with other people when he was like a coiled spring with her. Was it something she was doing? Was it all her fault?

When she got it right, he was the Vince she'd fallen in love with. When she got it wrong, he retreated into sullen silences and dark looks. Yet if she stayed out of the house to give him space, he'd text her to find out where she was. He insisted on having the Find My Friends app on her phone activated, so that he could track her.

'You're making me feel like a caged bird,' she said one evening.

He shook his head and told her that he'd made a promise to take care of her and that was all he was doing. There were dangerous people in the world, and she was so pretty and so desirable that he wanted to protect her from them. She insisted that she was able to take care of herself, but one day after work her bag was snatched as she was standing alone at the bus stop. She was knocked to the ground and bumped her head. She was shaken by the event and relieved when Vince arrived to pick her up.

'Drink this,' he said, handing her a glass of brandy when they got home. 'You need it for shock. Now do you understand how important it is that you do what I tell you?'

He brought her to Paris for their first wedding anniversary. He said that he knew how much she'd loved living in France, even though she rarely talked about it these days, and he wanted to share the experience with her. It was a wonderfully romantic break, away from the house and its routines and close to Vince all the time so he didn't have to constantly text her to check where she was. When they got home, she was determined to be a better wife. So what if routines made him feel comfortable? she said to herself. It wasn't the end of the world, even if he was a little over-the-top about them. And the bag-snatching incident made his concern for her all the more understandable. All it would take for him to be the perfect husband was for her to go along with some of his fixations. When she did, when she put things away, kept in touch with him, cooked what he expected, he brought her flowers and chocolates, perfume and jewellery. He was kind and generous and told her how much he loved her. He made her feel special and wanted.

And yet she knew that she was taking the line of least resistance over almost everything because it was easier to give in over something trivial than risk days of silent brooding. She tried to tell herself it didn't matter. She wanted to believe that it was nothing more than give and take. Although she had to admit that she was giving in on more things than him. And it was beginning to wear her down.

'I expect you to know what I like by now,' he said when she brought home salmon instead of the steak they usually had on Wednesdays. 'I don't want this.'

'But it was on special offer,' she protested.

'Not a special offer when one of us doesn't eat it,' he said, and retreated into a grim silence that he didn't break until the weekend.

When she looked back on it, it seemed that the changes had happened at the flick of a switch, but she knew they'd been gradual. If it had been as simple as clicking a switch on or off, she might have done something about it sooner. But at the time, she didn't notice that she never did anything without getting her husband's approval first. That she didn't give her opinion on anything any more. That she hadn't spoken in months to any of the friends she'd known before him. That contact with her family was less than it had ever been. That she tiptoed around him, always trying to anticipate the things that would annoy him so that she could avoid them or deflect them. That her whole day was devoted to making sure he was in a good mood.

And that when he wasn't, she felt as though she'd failed.

And that it was all her fault.

Chapter 19

She'd lost contact so effectively with most of the people in her life that she was almost surprised to receive an invitation to Cheyenne's wedding. Vince, though, didn't want to make the trip to Birmingham, where it was taking place.

'We have to go,' Imogen said. 'She's my sister.'

'Stepsister, and you hardly ever speak to her.'

'That's true, but we spent a lot of our teenage years together.'

'Thankfully you've left that part of your life behind.'

'It'll hurt her feelings if we don't accept,' said Imogen. 'I can't do that, Vince.'

'Of course it won't hurt her feelings. Does she care about yours?'

'She came to *our* wedding,' Imogen reminded him.

'Oh, that's such a girl thing.' Vince snorted. 'You come to my house, I come to yours. You invite me to your wedding, I invite you to mine.'

'Maybe so,' she conceded. 'But it's all about being sociable.'

'It's insane,' said Vince. 'Women do a billion things they don't want to do because they're afraid of hurting someone's feelings. When you'd be much better off forgetting about it.'

'You might be right about that,' conceded Imogen. 'But I can't say no to Cheyenne. I can't. All the same, Vince, if you really don't want to go . . . well, I guess I could always go on my own.'

He stared at her.

'On your own?'

'I understand that the idea of a family wedding bores you to tears,' she said, the idea beginning to appeal to her even more. 'But I feel obliged to go myself.'

He exhaled slowly.

'I'd only be away overnight,' she added.

'You're a sweet girl, Imogen,' he told her. 'I know you mess things up sometimes, and you can be beyond hopeless at others, but you're kind-hearted and thoughtful and I worry that people trample all over you. I especially worry that your so-called family would take advantage.'

She said nothing.

'If you want to go to Birmingham, I suppose you can.'

Her face brightened.

'But I'm not letting you go on your own,' he added. 'What would people say? No, I'll come with you. And we'll show them what a strong marriage really looks like.'

'Great,' she said.

She was shocked at how disappointed she suddenly felt.

Vince booked the flights and the room at the hotel, which was also the wedding venue.

'It looks lovely,' Imogen observed as she peered over his shoulder at the website. 'What a fantastic place to get married.'

'Better than ours?'

'Of course not.'

She'd been perfectly happy with their registry office ceremony and low-key reception afterwards. Neither of them had wanted to make a big deal of things, especially given their family circumstances, although Imogen was afraid that the day had been a bit of a let-down for Agnes and Berthe, who'd travelled all the way from their new home in Palm Springs to be there.

'It's not the trappings, it's knowing that you're happy,' Agnes said to her when she voiced her concerns. 'You *are* happy, Imogen, aren't you?'

'I couldn't be happier,' she told her aunt. And she meant it then. She loved Vince. Their wedding ceremony had been perfect. She wasn't a person who liked fuss. She was comfortable with understated.

But Cheyenne didn't know the meaning of the word. She had always liked extravagance and bling, and that was what she brought to her own wedding. The ceremony took place in a gazebo decorated with masses of white roses and ribbons. A harpist played during the ceremony itself, a string quartet during the meal, and Cheyenne had said that there was to be a band for livelier music later.

'A desperate waste of money,' murmured Vince as they tucked in to the dinner. 'They could've plugged in an iPod for the music, and those flowers will be thrown out tomorrow.'

'Oh, but the string quartet is lovely,' protested Imogen. 'And I bet people will take the table flower arrangements home. I would, if we didn't have to catch a flight.'

'We could nab one anyway,' he said.

'I don't think it would fit in the overhead bin.' Imogen giggled and Vince shot her an irritated look.

He seemed to be irritated with her for much of the day.

She wished he hadn't come. It was ages since she'd been at a big do, and it was lovely to dress up and have fun, but she kept looking around and checking to see where Vince was and who he was talking to in case something or someone upset him. At the same time she was doing her best to enjoy the party. Even though she'd been out of touch with Kevin, Paula and Cheyenne for so long (as well as having only seen Boris a couple of times), she felt connected to them now in a way that she hadn't before. She posed for photos with her young stepbrother, got up and danced when the band started to play and chatted happily to people she hardly knew. She'd forgotten how good she was at casual conversation with perfect strangers; that her ability to get on with everyone had been nurtured in Provence, where she'd charmed the guests of the Maison Lavande with her sunny nature and wide baby smile.

Later in the evening she sat with Cheyenne and her new husband, Richard, and told them what a great day it had been.

'Thanks,' said Cheyenne. 'I always wanted a big do. I suppose you think I'm crazy, what with your small and intimate wedding.'

'It's not my thing,' conceded Imogen. 'But each to their own. We both got the day we wanted.'

'As long as we get the happy-ever-after, that's all that matters.' Cheyenne smiled at her. 'Remember when we were kids and we talked about our requirements for our future husbands? Of course you started off with not wanting anyone at all, but when you caved in, you went the traditional route – tall, dark and handsome. I was the one who wanted someone blond and hunky.' She put her arm around Richard's shoulder. 'And in the end I went for tall, dark and handsome anyway.'

'And I went for Vince.' Imogen hadn't meant her words to sound rueful, but even to her own ears they did. She saw Cheyenne's eyes widen a little in surprise.

'I haven't really spoken to Vince yet.' Richard stepped into the uncomfortable silence. 'Let's get him over here.' He raised his arm and waved at Imogen's husband, who was standing at the bar. Vince saw him and came over, a pint of lager in one hand and a sparkling water in the other.

'I got you this.' He put the water down in front of Imogen. 'You shouldn't be drinking alcohol in your condition.'

'Condition!' Cheyenne stared at Imogen. 'Are you . . . are congratulations in order?'

'No, no,' said Imogen hastily. 'I think Vince means I've had enough to drink.'

'Oh.' Cheyenne gave Vince a puzzled glance. 'I thought for a moment . . . Never mind.' She raised her own glass of wine. 'Anyhow, cheers, everyone. I'm so glad you came, Imogen.'

'Not that it was easy,' Vince said. 'Having a wedding on a Thursday is pretty inconvenient.'

'Vince.' Imogen frowned.

'Well it is,' he said. 'It's two days off work for most people. And of course we had the additional expense of travelling.'

'But we had lots of time to plan around it,' said Imogen. 'And it was great to get away. We wouldn't have missed it for the world, Cheyenne. I love the hotel.'

'Not one I would have chosen myself,' Vince said. 'A bit brash. But not bad.'

'It had everything we wanted,' said Richard. 'And I'm

sorry about the Thursday and the travelling. Most people didn't seem to mind.'

'Nobody would say anything, of course,' said Vince.

'Except you.' Cheyenne's tone was dry.

'I tell it like it is.'

'Vince, we're all having a lovely time,' said Imogen. 'You like the hotel, you said so earlier. There's no need to be snippy about it now.'

Vince looked at her. 'You agreed with me that it was expensive.'

'I . . .'

'It's time for us to dance.' Cheyenne stood up. 'Nice talking to you, Vince.'

She led Richard away, leaving Imogen and Vince sitting on their own.

'You embarrassed me in front of them,' hissed Imogen. 'That was a horrible thing to say.'

'It's the truth, isn't it? We both thought it was expensive. We both agreed that Thursday was awkward. So stop pretending, Imogen.'

'I'm not—'

'You've been doing nothing but pretend ever since we got here. Pretending that you give a shit for any of them when you know you don't. When you know that the one person who matters here today is me.'

He went to the bar and she sat by herself, watching Cheyenne and Richard laughing as they danced together.

This was why she'd wanted to come on her own, she realised. She'd known that Vince would eventually pass some kind of remark that would offend someone. He always managed to do that. She was sure he didn't really mean to give offence. He just said what was in his head and left everyone with a terrible impression. Yet she knew he could be warm and kind and generous. Unfortunately he often kept that side of himself hidden. Even from her.

'I'm taking this to the room.' Vince returned to the table, a beer in his hand. 'Are you coming?'

'We can't leave yet.' She looked aghast. 'Cheyenne hasn't thrown her bouquet or anything.'

'You don't need to catch it,' he said. 'You've got me.'

'It doesn't matter. It's too soon to leave,' she said.

'I don't care how soon it is, I've had enough of these people.'

'I can't go yet, Vince. I really can't.'

He regarded her thoughtfully.

'You can stay for another hour,' he told her. 'Then I want you upstairs.'

'OK.' She didn't want to argue.

He left the function room and Imogen exhaled sharply. She realised she was shaking. Had she blatantly defied him? Would he be furious with her when she went back to the room? Would it be better to go now anyway? But just as she was thinking that she should leave, Kevin and Paula pulled out the chairs at the table and sat down beside her.

'Having a good time?' asked her stepfather.

'It's . . . it's wonderful.' It took her a moment to gather herself, and then she smiled. 'Exactly as I imagined Cheyenne's wedding would be.'

'You know we would have organised something like this for you and Vince if that was what you'd wanted,' said Kevin.

'We didn't,' Imogen said. 'But thank you for saying so.'

'It's nice to see you again,' said Kevin. 'It seems such a

long time since your own wedding. We've hardly spoken since then.'

'We're all so busy these days,' Imogen said.

'Everything going OK for you?' His eyes searched her face.

'Fine,' she assured him.

'He treats you all right?'

'Vince? Of course. Why would you even ask?' Her tone was wary.

'When I first met him I thought he was a decent enough guy. But today . . . well, he seems very abrupt,' said Kevin. 'Bordering on rude, to be honest. I guess I wanted to be sure that he wasn't that way with you.'

'Thanks for your concern, but it's his manner, that's all. He means nothing by it.' Imogen was conscious that her entire body was as stiff as a board. She didn't want her family criticising Vince. She didn't want them saying the things she was thinking. 'He's not always like this,' she added. 'He's just a bit uncomfortable in certain situations.'

'He should be comfortable with us,' said Paula. 'We're your family, after all. And we've known you a lot longer than him. So he should be a bit more respectful and less of a twat.'

'I'll go and see how the twat is doing.' Imogen got up.

'Imogen, please sit down.' Kevin put his hand on her arm. 'Paula didn't mean to offend you.'

'Calling my husband a twat isn't offensive?'

'I'm sorry,' said Paula. 'I was trying to be light-hearted about my . . . my concerns, but it misfired.'

'Your concerns?'

'Look, sweetheart, we're both a little worried about you,' said Kevin. 'We—'

'Well it's a bit late for you to be worried about me now,'

said Imogen. 'You certainly weren't worried when you hauled me and Cheyenne from Dublin to Birmingham when we would've been better off staying where we were.'

'Imogen! That's not true. We had long discussions—'

'About how it would work,' Imogen said. 'Not about if we wanted to go.'

'Cheyenne was happy to move,' he said. 'I thought you were too.'

'I'd already moved from France. I didn't want to move from Ireland too,' said Imogen. 'I told you that a thousand times. But you didn't leave me with any choice.'

'I know it must have been hard,' Paula said. 'But we had a lovely home together. You were happy. You know you were.'

'Oh, please.' Imogen sighed. 'You knew what you wanted and you got it. Which isn't a criticism, Paula. But don't try to make out that everything was for my own good, because it wasn't. It was what you and Kevin wanted, and let's face it, I'm not your daughter and I'm not Kevin's daughter. So what mattered to me didn't matter to either of you.'

'You know I've always treated you exactly the same as Cheyenne,' said Kevin.

Imogen remained silent.

'Don't let's fight,' he said. 'Listen, the important thing is that we're all here celebrating with Cheyenne and Richard. And if we've misread your situation, Imogen, we apologise. The most important thing is that you're happy now. I'm going to go and get us all some champagne.'

He left the two women alone together.

'I'm sorry you blame me,' said Paula.

'I don't.' Imogen was already regretting the harsh words.

'It was a difficult time for me back then, but I know you did your best. I've been fine ever since. I'm adaptable.'

'Kevin always says that about you,' Paula told her.

'He does?'

'Yes. He told me he'd never met anyone like you before. He said that no matter what life threw at you, you coped with it. You'd start murmuring about always looking on the bright side and counting your blessings and moving onwards and upwards.'

'That's what I was taught to do.'

'He loves you,' said Paula. 'We both do. And you don't have to count those blessings on your own. We're here to help.'

Quite suddenly, Imogen felt a lump in her throat. For the first time in her life she believed that they did care about her, not just about themselves. She felt horribly guilty that perhaps she'd misjudged them.

'Thank you,' she said.

'We should be in touch more,' said Paula.

'Sure.'

'More than just Christmas and birthdays,' said Paula. 'Or weddings. We're part of each other's lives. We always will be.'

Imogen twirled her wedding ring around on her finger.

She'd always told Vince that she didn't feel connected to her stepfamily, and he'd agreed with her. You're not related, he'd say. Not to any of them. It's a connection that doesn't matter any more. They're nothing to you. They're not really your family, Imogen. I am. Only me.

He was wrong. They did mean something. She hadn't realised it until now.

'Kevin was very hurt when Vince told him not to call any more,' said Paula.

'Vince told him that?' Imogen was shocked. 'When?'

'Oh, ages ago,' replied Paula. 'One evening when he phoned . . . Vince said his calls upset you.'

'He . . .' Imogen was confused. 'Are you sure? Vince wouldn't say that, Paula. I was never upset by Kevin.'

Paula shrugged.

'This is nonsense.' Imogen got up. 'I've got to . . . I'll see you later, OK?'

She left just as her stepfather returned with a bottle of champagne.

But she didn't stop. She was thinking of how hurt she'd felt when Kevin's occasional calls had stopped altogether. How unimportant she obviously was to him. How forgotten. She hadn't called him. The way she'd looked at it, he'd moved on and so had she.

She was on her way back to Vince when one of the male guests who'd had too much to drink caught her by the arm and dragged her on to the dance floor. She allowed him to shuffle her around for a couple of minutes before disentangling herself and walking away.

When she let herself into the bedroom, it was empty. She was struck by a sudden fear that Vince had left without her, but when she checked the wardrobe, his clothes were still there. She released the breath she'd been holding, then sat in the armchair in the corner of the room. He returned fifteen minutes later.

'So you've stopped allowing men you don't know to grope you on the dance floor,' he said.

'What are you talking about?'

'I saw you,' he said. 'You and that old lech.'

'He's Cheyenne's godfather. I couldn't stop him.'

'Of course you could,' said Vince. 'If you'd really wanted to.'

'Vince, please . . . I don't want to argue.'

'Because you're in the wrong and you know it.'

'I was certainly wrong about coming to the wedding,' agreed Imogen. 'You haven't enjoyed it and neither have I.'

'I told you you wouldn't.'

'I might have had more fun if you'd put in some effort.'

'So you're blaming me?'

'No. But we could have made it fun, Vince. That's all I'm saying.'

'Nothing is fun about these people,' he said. 'Nothing at all.'

'Is that why you told Kevin not to phone me any more?' She hadn't meant to blurt it out, but she couldn't stop herself.

'What?'

'Paula told me that you asked Kevin not to phone me because his calls upset me.'

'Paula said that?'

'Yes. Is it true?'

'She's twisting it, like she always does. What I told him was that you'd found it difficult when he married your mother. And that sometimes you got upset after he talked to you, which was perfectly true. That's all.'

'And you didn't warn him off?'

'Why would I do that?'

Imogen sank back down into the chair.

'I don't know what to think,' she said.

'What you should be thinking is that this crowd of people mean nothing to you any more,' said Vince. 'They messed up your life and they'll manipulate you whatever way they like.'

'Maybe.'

'But I'm with you for the long haul. Better or worse, remember?'

She gave him a faint smile.

'And maybe the reason I've been a bit narky about it all is that I'm jealous.'

'Jealous?' She stared at him.

'They knew you when I didn't,' he said. 'They've had a head start.'

'Don't be silly.'

'It's true,' said Vince. 'Now, I'll tell you what. Since it matters so much to you that we have a good time tonight, let's go back downstairs together and join in the fun.'

'Really?'

'Yes.'

He led her from the room and back to the wedding party, where he danced with her and then Cheyenne and then Paula. She watched anxiously as he spun around the floor with them, but he was smiling all the time.

'Now,' he said when he came back to her. 'I've been nice to all of them.'

'So you have,' she said, although she wondered what he'd said to them. She hoped he'd been friendly.

'So it's your turn to be nice to me,' he said. 'Let's get out of here.'

Back in their room, she stood uncertainly in front of him.

'You're a beautiful woman,' he said. 'You don't need their approval.'

'I wasn't—'

'You were,' he said. 'You were wanting them to like us, but none of that matters, Imogen. What matters is the two of us together.'

She nodded.

'You look a million times better than the bride,' he said with satisfaction. 'A zillion times. But then I always knew you would. You're beautiful.'

Imogen was wearing an above-the-knee cocktail dress in pale coral, embroidered with sequins around the neck. It was high at the front, with a low-cut back, and she'd teamed it with a pair of sparkly nude shoes. Vince had been with her when she'd bought both the dress and the shoes.

'I suppose I was pissed off at you dancing with that old fart earlier because I allowed you to look gorgeous enough for him to want to dance with you. I was afraid he'd take advantage.'

'Don't be silly.'

'It's not silly to want to protect your precious things,' he said. 'And you're my precious thing.'

'I am?'

'Oh yes,' he said. 'Now let's get that dress off you . . .'

He began to slide the zip of her dress down, and suddenly he was kissing her in an almost frenzied way that was both exciting and a little bit unnerving. He pushed her on to the bed and lay on top of her, running his hands through her hair, which had fanned out across the duvet.

'You really are spectacularly lovely, you know that, don't you?'

'I . . . guess so.'

'And the other thing you know,' he said as he thrust into her, 'is that you're mine, Imogen. Nobody else's. Mine. For ever and ever. You belong to me.'

When he said the words, it was as though a blindfold had been ripped from her eyes. She lay where she was, unable to move. Fortunately Vince was too engrossed in his own satisfaction to notice. Afterwards, he rolled over on his side and closed his eyes. A few minutes later he was asleep. She stayed beside him, immobile, until he began to snore, and then she slid from the bed and walked slowly into the bathroom, where she sat on the edge of the bath. He was right. That was the thing. That was what had happened. She *did* belong to him, completely and utterly. It wasn't that he'd changed Imogen Weir into Imogen Naughton; he'd actually replaced her with someone he'd created. She wasn't simply different. She'd become another person. A person whose every word and action was dictated by him and his reactions.

She looked at herself in the mirror on the opposite wall and hardly recognised the woman reflected back at her. There was a tension in her eyes that had never been there before, and a wariness about her body that she hadn't noticed until then. Had she really changed that much? And was it all because of Vince? Was that what Kevin and Paula and Cheyenne thought? Were they all laughing at her? Feeling sorry for her?

Her jaw tightened. Vince was her husband. They'd built a life together. The kind of life that didn't need people poking around and making unkind remarks and passing judgement. They were a secure unit together. The two of them against the world. But maybe that's the problem, she thought suddenly. Maybe he's built this life around me like a tower, while I stand inside and hand him the bricks so that he can shut me up. So that I'm in a prison.

She shook her head. She wasn't really locked away like a present-day Rapunzel. She had plenty of freedom. She had her job. She went to the gym with Shona. She . . . well, there wasn't much else. But that was her choice. She'd made the decisions about what she did. Vince might influence them, but she made them. Didn't she?

But she always made decisions she knew he'd agree with. It was easier that way. Because she didn't want him to be angry with her and to shut her out. It had been a long time since she'd done something he didn't want her to do. Cheyenne's wedding was the closest she'd got to changing his mind. And maybe he'd been right about not coming, because if she hadn't, she wouldn't have spent the whole day like a coiled spring waiting for him to lose it over something. And she wouldn't have had to listen to Kevin and Paula expressing their doubts about her marriage and looking at her with ill-disguised sympathy in their eyes. Because she recognised that expression. It was the one that Agnes and Berthe had both worn the day that she and Carol had come back from France after her mother's indiscretion. Her big mistake.

Dammit, she thought. It's my life. I didn't make a mistake. And I don't belong to him. I don't belong to anyone. We love each other. We want what's right for each other, that's all.

But even as she said it, she wasn't sure she believed it any more.

She pressed her fingers to her forehead.

What's happened to me? she asked herself.

Who am I?

Why am I so afraid?

It was a long time before she realised that her fear was that Imogen Weir had been lost for ever. She knew that the only way to get her back was to leave, but she was concerned it was already too late. She'd become so dependent on him and his approval that she was afraid all he'd have to do was click his fingers and she'd come running back. She needed to be as far away from him as possible. So that she couldn't hear the clicking.

And so she came up with the Plan. It was a long time before she was able to carry it out. And she still didn't know if it had really worked. She didn't know what would happen if she heard the click again.

Chapter 20

Later in the afternoon, Imogen went to the beach. She brought a sun umbrella she'd found in the apartment and which she stuck, rather unsteadily, into the sand. She'd downloaded some free music to her smartphone, so she stretched out on a towel and listened to someone she'd never heard of before sing about unrequited love as the holidaymakers around her swam and sunbathed and chatted happily among themselves.

She was done thinking about her past, but she needed to think about her future. The Plan had been hazy about that. She'd been lucky in getting the apartment and the cleaning job, but it was clear that once the summer ended, Bastarache Immobilier wouldn't need extra cleaners. Despite the contracts with permanent residents, the bulk of the business was from the rental apartments. René seemed to like her and was prepared to accept the word of his partner that her work was good, but that didn't mean there'd be anything for her to do in the autumn or winter. Nor did she know what she was going to do about somewhere to live, or even if she'd stay in Hendaye. Regardless of where she ended up, her savings wouldn't cover the difference between what she earned and what she paid in rental for very long. She was going to have to look for some other kind of work, but she had no idea what. Perhaps I should have followed in Cheyenne's footsteps and become a beautician, she thought, as she watched two elegantly made-up women in well-cut bathing suits strolling along the beach. There always seemed to be work for people who could do faces and nails and hair.

Apart from her concerns about work and somewhere to live, the longer-term problem of being married to Vince still remained. At some point she would have to deal with it. But there was no way she could go back to Ireland yet. She was feeling much stronger and more independent now, but she was worried that as soon as she saw him, Vince would somehow manage to convince her that her flight had been some kind of mental breakdown. It didn't matter that she knew it wasn't true. His ability to get inside her head meant that she wasn't at all confident she could resist him. There had been countless times before when she'd tried to argue with him, but he'd always managed to tie her up in knots so that she would end up apologising for having brought up whatever topic it was in the first place.

I'm not ready to face him, she told herself. But perhaps I'm ready to talk to Shona. And that way I can find out what he's thinking. What he's saying about me. And, more importantly, what his plans are.

She sat up on the towel and gazed out over the water as she considered phoning her friend. If she ensured that caller ID was switched off first, it would be safe enough, wouldn't it? She wasn't going to tell Shona where she was, so there would be nothing Vince could worm out of her, other than the fact that she'd called. Even as she grew excited at the idea of talking to her friend again, she reminded herself that getting in touch with people wasn't part of the Plan. That had concentrated on getting away and staying away and not talking to anyone. But she couldn't stay cut off for ever. Vince had tried to make that happen before, and he'd nearly succeeded. If she did it to herself, if she never spoke to anyone she knew again, he'd still be in control of her. And she'd run away so that he wasn't. She'd make the call. Even though she wasn't entirely convinced it was the right thing to do.

She stayed at the beach until late in the evening, and by the time she got home again, she had convinced herself that calling Shona was a good idea. Nevertheless, as she sat at the window, her phone in her hand, she could feel the beat of her heart at the base of her throat, and her mouth was so dry that she had to take continuous sips from the small bottle of water by her side.

'In a minute,' she muttered to herself. 'First things first . . .'

She opened her email app on the phone.

There were plenty of new promotional emails from her usual sites, and two new personal ones. She felt her stomach clench as she saw Vince's most recent one, telling her all he wanted was to sort out whatever was wrong between them.

She read it a few times, noticing how different it was in tone to the first ones he'd sent. Maybe he really was beginning to understand how she felt. Maybe he could see why she'd done what she'd done. Maybe he was realising that his behaviour had been completely over the top. Did he want to fix it? If she went back and talked to him, would it be different? The way it was at the start, when he'd loved her and wanted nothing but the best for her? After all, he was a good person when you got to know him . . . She closed her eyes. She didn't know if he was a good person or not. She couldn't be objective about that any more. But he wasn't good for her, she'd learned that much over the past five years. So she shouldn't, couldn't allow herself to think any different. Because this was what had happened so many times before. She'd be unhappy and he'd say something, one thing, to make her feel as though it was all her own fault, and the next thing she knew she was apologising and trying to make it up to him and wondering how it was she always got it so wrong. And all she wanted to do was make it better.

But she never could.

She opened her eyes and read the second email.

From: Cheyenne@firstmail.com
To: Imozhen@gmail.com
Subject: Where are you?
Hi Imogen. This isn't an email I thought I'd be sending. I've been talking to Vince. He says you've disappeared and is trying to imply you're mentally unstable. I think you've left him. Fair play to you if you have – it's probably the least mentally unstable thing you've ever done! I know you're not supposed to say horrible things about anyone's ex in case they get back together, but truly, after you met him it was like all the light had gone from inside you. Talking to you was like talking to a shell. Anyway, I thought you should know that he's looking for you. He wanted to know places you've lived. I told him I couldn't remember. Which I can't really, France is France, *n'est-ce pas?* I also thought you should know that he got in touch with me through Facebook.

> Are there other people he'll contact? I noticed your account has been deleted or deactivated or whatever. So this is the only way I can get in touch with you. If you want to call me, please do. By the way, he also wanted to talk to Dad, but he's on a cruise with Paula so I said he was uncontactable.
>
> Take care.
>
> Cheyenne x

Imogen read and re-read the email and then began to pace around the apartment as her anxiety levels shot up. It had never occurred to her that Vince would be able to find Cheyenne on Facebook. That was why she hadn't bothered to get in touch with her or Kevin after she'd left. She knew she hadn't left any phone numbers or emails for them at home because Vince had practically ordered her never to talk to them again after Cheyenne's wedding. And although the wedding had opened her eyes to the fact that she was unhappy with Vince, she hadn't had the strength to defy him. In some ways she'd been relieved not to be in touch with her step-family. Not having to talk to them meant that she didn't have to talk about Vince either. She didn't have to justify being with him or make excuses for him.

She looked at the email again. Cheyenne said he was trying to find out the places she'd lived. But she couldn't see how he'd manage that. If Cheyenne wasn't telling him anything, if he couldn't contact Kevin, and with Berthe on the alert to say nothing, there was no way for him to get information. Yet even if nobody said a word, Imogen was beginning to feel as though Vince was uncomfortably close to her. It was a feeling that plunged her into despair. What if she never got away from him? What if he turned up in Hendaye and made her come home? It was easy for people to tell her that he couldn't force her, but they didn't know Vince. Somehow he'd manage it, and he'd be so angry with her, her life would be a total misery. It would be awful.

She was shaking. And as she realised that she was also crying, she couldn't help feeling that she was utterly hopeless. Just as Vince always said she was.

She didn't phone Shona.

She couldn't.

She was too afraid again.

Chapter 21

The problem with tracking down Imogen himself, Vince thought, was not having any decent leads. He knew that his wife had disappeared in Paris, but nothing more than that. He had no idea where she'd gone after leaving the hotel and he was afraid it would be difficult to trace her movements. Disappearing in Paris had been a smart idea, he had to acknowledge that. But no matter how smart Imogen thought she was, he knew he was smarter. If he went to Paris with her photo and showed it at the hotel, someone – the concierge, a receptionist, a duty manager – would surely remember her. And they might remember her saying where she planned to go. Even if they did, though, how far would it get him? What he really needed was something tangible to start from.

He was quietly confident that he'd find it. As his company's top salesman, his expertise was seeking out leads, persuading people to see him and talk to him, extracting information from them. This was a bigger, more difficult task. But Imogen had underestimated him if she thought he wasn't up to it.

Every evening, after he got home from work, he spent time going through the filing cabinet they kept in the utility room, searching among the old papers, bills and invoices for clues that might point him in the right direction. Irritatingly, his own desire for neatness and order were working against him, because he insisted on shredding documents more than a couple of years old. He'd nearly given it up as a bad job when he suddenly unearthed a single photograph caught between two old electricity bills. It was of a small girl and a woman he didn't recognise, and on the back it said: *Imogen and Madame Fournier on the beach*. He'd never heard of Madame Fournier, but at least it was a name of a real person he could track down. The photograph, with blue sea and even bluer skies, must have been taken when Imogen had lived in Provence. Vince was pretty sure that that was where she would have gone now. People were always drawn back to places they knew. It was human nature.

All the same, he decided that his first port of call would still be Paris and the hotel. Even if she'd gone to Provence, she might have left some clue in the capital city. Vince knew that he was good at his job because he was thorough. He would bring that same thoroughness to finding Imogen.

He spent the next day at his desk in the office drawing up a list of the people Imogen knew and how they might help her hide from him. He came to the same conclusion as Imogen herself: that he had successfully shrunk her group of friends so that there were very few people she could depend on. The mad aunts in California were out of the picture. She'd hardly flee there when one of them was in a home for the bewildered and the other one had one step over the threshold. But Cheyenne Scott, her stepsister, might prove more fruitful. Following Cheyenne's wedding, Imogen had more or less brushed her out of her life, but the email that Cheyenne had sent her after he'd spoken to her had been surprisingly sympathetic. Vince felt sure she had useful background information that might help him. What had she written? Fair play to Imogen for leaving him? He snorted. He was right about her. She was a bitch. But he would try to talk to her all the same. As for Kevin . . . Vince had always liked the fact that Imogen's feelings towards her stepfather were mixed at best. He knew she believed that he'd loved her mother and was grateful to him for the care he'd taken of her when she was ill. At the same time, she resented the way he'd dragged her from Dublin to Birmingham after he'd married Paula. Vince had surmised that she hadn't been very happy with him marrying Paula in the first place. He himself didn't like the other man at all, and he knew the feeling was mutual. Kevin would be unlikely to help him, regardless of how concerned he might be about Imogen's whereabouts.

He had to find her, and find her soon. It was all very well for Shona to talk about her needing space, but she was his wife and what she needed was to be back home. Even if Shona was right and she returned of her own accord, he wasn't prepared to wait. Nobody ever got what they wanted by waiting. And he wasn't the waiting sort.

He called Imogen's ex-boss, Conor Foley. Annoying though Vince found him, he was the last person to have seen Imogen and could well have vital information that until now he'd either forgotten or not shared. Conor hadn't wanted to see him, but Vince used all of his persuasive powers to make him agree. Their subsequent conversation, however, was less than satisfactory. Conor reminded Vince of Kevin – too damn self-confident for his own good, and not respectful enough towards him. He'd repeated that he had no idea where Imogen had gone after the exhibition, and had told Vince that the best thing he could do was wait until she herself got in touch. The single piece of satisfaction that Vince got from the meeting was confirmation that Imogen had stayed at the hotel she'd said she was staying in. He'd had a nagging feeling that she'd lied about that too.

'I do hope she returns safely, if that's what she wants,' Conor had said, signalling that the meeting was at an end. 'But sometimes people feel the need to move on.'

'I'd hardly call walking out on the one person who ever loved her moving on,' Vince said. 'If you hear anything at all from her, I expect you to let me know.'

'If she gives her permission,' said Conor. 'But I doubt she'll call me.'

'She still hasn't called me either,' Shona told him later that evening. 'But I wish she bloody well would.'

Vince had phoned her and asked her to meet him. They were now in an alcove in the local lounge bar, where, despite it being early in the week, quite a few people from the housing estate were sitting down to the burger-and-beer special. Vince had ordered the special for himself, but Shona had contented herself with a glass of wine and a packet of peanuts.

Vince outlined his plan to go to France as soon as possible.

'I can't afford a PI,' he said. 'I've arranged to take some time off work and find her myself. It can't be that hard. Everyone says it's impossible to disappear these days.'

'Maybe if the government is tracking you it is,' agreed Shona. 'But you're going as a private individual with no access to any sources of information. How on earth will you manage?'

'By being methodical,' said Vince. 'By knowing when I've unearthed useful information. Something always comes up, and when it does, I'll find her and bring her home.'

'What if she doesn't want to come?' asked Shona.

'She does,' said Vince. 'She just doesn't know it yet.'

'And what happens then?'

He looked at her pensively. 'What d'you mean, what happens?'

'Well she obviously had her reasons for leaving you.'

'I told you, she was upset. The baby and everything. You know.'

'It must be more than that,' said Shona. 'Disappearing without a word is an over-the-top reaction to not being pregnant. Something else must have caused it.'

'You know Imogen.' Vince gave a dismissive shrug. 'She's impulsive. She does stupid things.'

'I wouldn't call Imogen impulsive at all,' said Shona. 'She always seems very thoughtful to me.'

'You only see one side of her,' Vince said. 'She was a mess before she married me. She'll be a mess again without me.'

Shona ran her finger around the rim of her wine glass without speaking. She wasn't quite sure what to say.

'I promise you,' said Vince. 'By the time I catch up with her, she'll want to come home.'

'Listen to me, Vince.' Shona pushed the glass of wine away. 'Imogen left because she was unhappy. I'm not blaming you, but you must have contributed to it in some way.'

Vince's eyes sparked with anger. 'I did nothing to cause this! Nothing at all! You know that, Shona. I've never been anything but loving and caring to Imogen. I've tried to be the best husband possible. Why do women always blame men when there's a problem?'

'I'm not blaming you as a man,' said Shona. 'But . . . you were the one in the relationship with her.'

'I thought you were on my side,' said Vince.

'I'm not on anyone's side,' said Shona. 'All I want is for her to be OK.'

'And that's all I want too.' Vince stood up. 'I'm going home. I need to make arrangements for my trip.'

'OK,' said Shona. 'I'll stay here a little longer. I need to finish my drink.'

'Ring me.' Vince turned before he walked out the door. 'She calls you – you ring me. Clear?'

'Of course.' Shona nodded. She knew Vince was upset. She understood that. But there was a part of her that was beginning to see why Imogen might have left. And she wondered if her coming back would be such a good idea after all.

Vince made a list. He was good at lists. They were the mainstay of his working life and they were a big part of his personal life too. He wrote down everything he remembered Imogen telling him about her time in France. There hadn't been much, because she'd still been a kid when she left. He wrote down what she'd told him about her college years, and afterwards when she'd worked for two professors before getting the job at Chandon Leclerc. He recalled her talking about the research she'd done, but it was hard to remember anything very specific, as he hadn't listened very closely. It had been boring stuff. He did remember her saying that she felt ashamed that the professor she was working for had known more about the country where she'd spent her early years than she did herself.

He got up and checked the bookshelf. Although the books were arranged in alphabetical order, he couldn't remember the man's name, so it took a while before he saw one written by a Professor J. M. Julien. He opened it and read the acknowledgement that Professor Julien had made to Imogen, thanking her for her hard work. According to the biography of the author, he currently lectured at Trinity College. Vince looked up the number and called him.

He was surprised when he was put through to an extension that was answered straight away.

'Professor Julien?' asked Vince.

'Yes. How can I help you?'

'My name is Vince Naughton. My wife, Imogen, was a research assistant to you a few years ago.'

'Imogen . . . Imogen . . .'

'She would have been Imogen Weir back then.'

'Oh yes, Imogen. I remember her well. Lovely girl. Great worker. Very intelligent.'

'Indeed she is. Um, Professor, I'm ringing to ask if you could tell me exactly where Imogen lived when she was in France. I know it was Provence, but could you narrow it down for me?'

'How on earth should I know?' The professor sounded tetchy. 'Can't you ask her yourself?

'Yes, but that would spoil the surprise,' said Vince. 'I'm organising a trip for our wedding anniversary.'

'The last of the great romantics, eh?' This time his tone was more jovial.

'Something like that,' said Vince. 'I wanted to bring her back to where she was brought up as a kid. Trouble is, I'm not sure where it actually was. I'm contacting some of her friends to see if they can help.'

'I wish I could,' said Professor Julien. 'But it was a good few years ago and it's not something I even remember her telling me.'

'If you could try, that'd be great.'

There was a silence at the other end of the line. Then Professor Julien spoke, although his tone was doubtful.

'Near Marseille, I think,' he said. 'She talked about the soap, how it was supposed to be very good for you, and that her mother used to buy it even in Dublin. But I'm quite sure that no matter where in Provence you go, she'd enjoy herself. It's a lovely part of the country.'

'I'm sure she would. I'm just trying to be precise.'

'Isn't there someone else who could be more helpful? Imogen's mother, perhaps? Oh, but she died, didn't she?'

'Yes,' said Vince.

'And her father was killed before she was born, I remember now. A tragic situation. But Imogen was a positive girl. Very helpful, very enthusiastic.'

'She's had it tough,' agreed Vince. 'That's why I want to do something nice for her. It would be lovely to be able to surprise her by staying near her childhood home.'

'I'm sorry I can't help you,' said Professor Julien. 'Although . . .'

'Yes?'

'Didn't she live in a guest house? I think I recall her telling me that.'

'Do you remember the name of it?'

'That's something I'm sure you can find out from her without her guessing what you're up to,' said Professor Julien.

Vince gritted his teeth. 'You're right. Thank you. You've been very helpful.'

'Not really,' said the professor. 'Well, good luck with your— Oh.'

'Oh?'

'The guest house was called the Maison Lavande,' said Professor Julien triumphantly. 'I've just remembered because it's the same name as a bar in Lyon that was a centre of resistance during the Second World War. It's not far from Montluc prison, where Jean Moulin was incarcerated. Lots of interesting history there, and—'

Vince wasn't interested in the history of a French prison, and he interrupted the professor before he could say any more. 'This bar – Lyon isn't in Provence, is it?'

'No, no, but the guest house is, or was, I presume. It's the coincidence of them having the same name that reminded me. The bar was accidentally bombed by the Allies in 1944. But they've rebuilt it since. Worth a visit if you're in Lyon.'

'I won't be in Lyon,' said Vince.

'You should go,' the professor told him. 'When you and Imogen visit Marseille. She'll love it, I promise you. It's only an hour and a half or so by train. Imogen was very interested in the Resistance and the stories of people overcoming adversity. Not that the war was mere adversity, of course. But the individual stories, that's what she liked. I remember—'

'You've been very helpful, Professor.' Vince interrupted him again. 'I'm sure I can incorporate the bar into our trip. You said "when you and Imogen visit Marseille". Can you recall if she lived in the town itself?'

'Well, no,' said the professor. 'But I think . . . not far outside, I'm sure.'

'Thank you,' said Vince. 'That's very helpful.'

'Surely you've talked to her about this before?'

'Not that much.' Vince wasn't going to admit that he hadn't even known that Imogen had lived close to Marseille in the first place. 'She might have told me at some point but I'd forgotten, and it doesn't do to tell your wife you've forgotten anything.'

'I'm sure she'll be delighted with whatever you arrange,' said Professor Julien. 'Do please tell her I said hello, and pass on my best wishes.'

'Will do,' said Vince, and ended the call.

Then he opened his laptop and began a search.

Chapter 22

'Do you want to come to a boules tournament on Thursday evening?' asked René when Imogen arrived at the agency after the weekend. Simply walking into the office had made her feel better after her sudden bout of vulnerability following Vince and Cheyenne's emails, but she tensed up again at René's question.

'I'm flattered you've asked me, but I told you before that it's not a good idea for me to go out with you,' she said.

'No, no.' René held up his hands. 'I have totally accepted your harsh rejection of me. This is completely different. It's not a date.'

'What is it, then?' asked Imogen with relief.

'It's a charity event,' said René. 'A number of local businesses, including us, are taking part. I thought you might like to be on our team.'

'I wouldn't have a clue,' said Imogen, although she'd played the game before, on the beach with the Delissandes, with a set of brightly coloured plastic boules.

'It's a little like English bowls, except we throw the balls instead of rolling them,' explained René. 'See.' He reached beneath his desk and took out a small carrying case in which nestled six silver-coloured balls each the size of an orange.

'I wouldn't be any good at it.' Which was the truth, she thought. She'd never won a game against the boys. 'I'd let you all down.'

'Nonsense,' said René. 'It's throwing at a target. It's easy. Lots of people come out to support the evening by betting on us, and all the money goes to very deserving local charities.'

'Stop playing the charity card!' cried Imogen. 'Honestly, René, I'd be a liability.'

'Of course you wouldn't,' said René. 'None of us is an expert. The team so far is me, Angelique and Raoul. We need one more.'

Raoul was the sales manager. He was an affable married man from Bayonne whom Imogen had met a couple of times in the office.

'I'll think about it,' she said.

She'd absolutely no intention of competing in the tournament, charitable or not, but that evening, when she was having her noisette at the café, Céline asked her to be on a team too.

'Oh, I can't,' she said, in surprise. 'René's asked me already.'

'He has?' Céline shook her head and the curls of her topknot bounced. '*Merde*. I should've asked you sooner myself.'

'You're not losing out on anything,' said Imogen. 'I won't be taking part, Céline. I'm terrible at throwing things. You're better off without me.'

'Nobody's any good,' she said. 'That's half the fun.'

'That's what René tried to tell me. But he has his own

set of boules! And he said that people bet on you and everything.'

'Everyone around here has their own set,' said Céline. 'And as for the betting, it's just for fun. For the charity.'

Imogen looked doubtful.

'It's a great day,' Céline said. 'Honestly it is. And I agree that you can't play for me as René has asked you first, but you'd enjoy it.'

'Well . . .'

'You'll enjoy it,' repeated Céline. 'I promise.'

'OK. OK.' Imogen held up her hands in good-natured surrender. 'You've convinced me. It's for fun and for charity. I won't take it too seriously. I'll tell René the bad news tomorrow.'

René was delighted when she said she'd play, and offered to give her a little advance training.

'Training!' she cried, a note of panic in her voice. 'You said it would be easy. And both you and Céline promised it was for fun. Training doesn't sound like fun.'

'It's most definitely fun,' he assured her. 'But a little practice wouldn't go amiss.'

'I'll take my chances,' she said, and he shrugged and told her that the competition would start at eight on Thursday evening. It was taking place in the boules area of the Jazkiel camping site.

'I'll be there.' Despite herself, Imogen was starting to get a little excited at the idea of a night out. With the exception of the evening she'd spent with Gerry and Samantha, she'd been on her own every night since she'd left Vince, and although she enjoyed the peace and serenity, it was sometimes lonely. Besides, going to the tournament would be like picking up the threads of her life again. A life that didn't have to be only about work and sitting on the balcony by herself, watching the sun go down.

She arrived at the campsite exactly on time, wearing a plain white top, pink shorts and a pair of floral espadrilles that she'd bought at a shop near the seafront.

'You look *très chic*,' said Céline when she saw her.

'Chic? Compared to you, I don't think so,' said Imogen. 'How *do* French women always manage to look so . . . together?'

Céline grinned. 'I'm wearing an old T-shirt and capri pants. It's hardly the height of sophistication.'

'And yet you look fantastic in them.' Imogen shook her head. 'It's genetic, isn't it? You're all born with it.'

'If you say so,' said Céline. 'But that doesn't take away from the fact that I've never seen you looking better, Imogen.'

Perhaps it was because she was feeling good, thought Imogen. Maybe it was showing in her face.

Coloured lights had been erected around the sandy area designated for the tournament, and painted wooden kiosks were selling soft drinks, ice cream and food. A brass band was playing, and in front of them a group of giggling children marched back and forwards, swinging their arms in time with the beat. There was a bar at one end of the arena, where a cluster of people, including René, were gathered.

'I should check in with my team manager,' Imogen told Céline when René spotted her and waved.

'Indeed. From this moment we are bitter rivals.' Céline tried to look competitive, but the merriment shone from her eyes. 'I will see you later.'

'See you later.' Imogen walked towards the bar and was suddenly assailed by a memory of another time and another place where boules had been played. The image was of Agnes and Berthe roaring with laughter as they threw the silver balls on a court marked out on the beach. She remembered Carol laughing too. It must have been the beach close to the Maison Lavande. Her memory was vague – of biscuit-coloured sand and azure water and the clink of metal on metal as the boules collided.

A stronger memory came to her when René offered her a shot of pastis. The aniseed-flavoured drink had been a favourite at the Maison Lavande. Berthe's mother had kept a decanter full on the table in the hallway and had offered it to guests for free. Imogen had believed it was lemonade until the day Madame Fournier had allowed her the tiniest sip. She'd made a face at the sickly-sweet smell and gasped as the fiery liquid burned her throat. Carol had been annoyed at the older woman for giving alcohol to a four-year-old, but Madame Fournier had sniffed and said it was important that Imogen knew the drink wasn't lemonade, and that she'd given her nothing more than a taste.

It was the smell she recalled now as she took a tentative sip.

'Ugh.' She made a face and put the shot glass back on the table.

'This should be like home to you, Madame Provençal,' he teased. 'Pétanque and pastis – or boules and booze if you prefer! Everything you need to make you feel like you're in the south of France again.'

'I was a small child when I left.' She took another sip of the pastis and wrinkled her nose. 'I certainly didn't play boules or drink this stuff.'

'You'll get a taste for it,' René assured her.

'I'm kind of hoping not.' She drained the shot glass and asked for a sparkling water.

René gave her a good-natured smile, then stood up as two people approached them.

'Angie,' he said as he embraced them in turn. 'Raoul.'

It was the first time Imogen had met René's business partner, who wasn't at all how she'd imagined her. Instead of a formidable and chillingly beautiful entrepreneur, Angelique was a short, plump woman of about forty, with curly black hair and dark eyes. She gave Imogen a brief kiss on the cheek, told her that she was delighted to finally meet her, then handed her a bright yellow bib with the words 'Team Bastarache' printed on it.

'There is an extra two hundred and fifty euros for the charity of the winning team,' she said. 'We are supporting homeless children and I want us to win.'

'No pressure then,' muttered Imogen.

'None at all,' agreed Raoul, his voice filled with confidence. 'The rest of them are useless.'

'*Mesdames et messieurs!*' A voice boomed over the PA system. 'The fifth annual Jazkiel Boules for Benefits tournament is about to commence. Can all the teams please register at the desk.'

'*Alors!*' René patted Imogen on the back. 'Let's go and kick ass.'

Imogen laughed and followed him to the desk. Céline and an older couple were also waiting there, along with a tall, lanky man with sandy hair and grey eyes whose left arm was in a sling. Céline introduced the couple as her parents and the lanky man as Artemis. It was clear from her voice and the way she looked at him that they were in a relationship. He gave Imogen a polite kiss on the cheek, while Céline's parents greeted her cheerfully.

'I believe you ate in my restaurant some time ago,' said her father. 'What did you think?'

'It was wonderful,' replied Imogen. 'Who's looking after it tonight?'

'Adrien,' said Céline. 'My brother. Almost as good a chef as Dad.'

Her father gave her a jaundiced look before turning to his former son-in-law and nodding briefly at him. 'René.'

'Bernard.' René returned the nod. Then he kissed Céline's mother politely on the cheek. 'Florence.' Finally he turned to the lanky man. 'Art, *mon ami*. I hope you're not going to blame your broken wrist for your ultimate defeat. It is your left hand after all.'

'I'm sure we'll manage to crush you anyhow,' Art told him, and René patted him on the back.

It was all very civilised, thought Imogen. She tried to imagine the scene if, after a more conventional separation, she'd turned up to an event with a male friend and seen Vince there. She was pretty sure it would be significantly more awkward than this. She shivered in the warm evening air. She didn't want to think about Vince. Not tonight.

'There are six teams in the competition,' said the referee. 'Each team will play the others. The top two teams will play each other in the final. Is that clear?'

All the team members nodded.

'Meanwhile, Mademoiselle Mazarine and her helpers will take the bets of the spectators!' He looked around as a group of pretty blondes made their way through the crowd with betting slips. 'Bet early and often to raise money for our charities tonight.'

There was a buzz of chatter among the spectators.

'*Allez Team Le Bleu!*' cried someone.

'*Allez Team Chi-chi!*' called someone else.

Team Chi-chi, comprised of three beauty therapists all impeccably made up and wearing jewelled false eyelashes, waved at their supporters.

There were competing cries from the crowd as the teams took up their positions.

'Don't be nervous,' René said to Imogen. 'We're playing Chi-chi first. We'll beat them easily.'

'You think?'

'For sure.' René gave her a reassuring hug and then got ready to throw the wooden cochonnet that would become the target for their game.

'You get a point for each boule closest to it,' he told her. 'But you only score if one of yours is the nearest to start with. Come on, Angie. You're up first.'

She stood in the marked circle and threw her boule. It landed within half a metre of the cochonnet. Her next two were even closer.

'Excellent!' cried Raoul. 'Well done.'

The first member of Team Chi-chi stepped up for her turn. Her boule landed outside Angie's.

'*Bon,*' said René. 'We are holding the point. They must throw again.'

But although the Chi-chis threw all of their boules, none of them got inside Angie's.

'A winning position for us,' said René as he stood up to

take his throws. They were wide of the mark, but Raoul was more successful, leaving two of his boules close.

'We are already ahead,' said René. 'So there is no pressure on you, Imogen.'

'Just as well,' she muttered as she stood in the circle to throw. She reminded herself that it was supposed to be fun, but she couldn't believe how nervous she was as she weighed the boule in her hand before gently lobbing it forward.

It landed right beside the cochonnet.

'*Fantastique!*' cried Angie and Raoul in unison.

'Lucky,' said Imogen.

'Are you sure it's luck?' demanded René when her next two boules landed either side of the first. 'That was brilliant.'

Imogen knew it was chance, but she was pleased with herself. The rules were that the teams played three sets against each other. In each of the other two, her boules landed closest to the cochonnet.

'We have a natural here.' René beamed with delight. 'And they are all betting on you, Imogen.'

'Oh God,' she said, suddenly panicked. 'They shouldn't. It was a fluke.'

'No, no,' said Angelique. 'It is because you are from Provence. Pétanque is in your blood.'

Imogen shook her head. 'You can't really consider me a Provençal,' she said. 'After all, I lived . . .' Just in time she stopped herself saying that she'd lived in Hendaye for as long as she'd lived in Provence. That was something she didn't want broadcast yet. If ever. '. . . in Ireland for much longer,' she finished.

Her throwing wasn't quite as accurate in the next game, but they were still doing well. Then they played Céline's

Team Le Bleu. Almost at once, Imogen was aware of a different level to the rivalry. René and Céline might be civilised about their break-up, but there was a definite competition between them, egged on by Bernard on Céline's side and Angie on René's.

Nerves got to Imogen this time, and only one of her boules scored, but René was more accurate and they won the match by a point. When the referee added up all the scores, Team Bastarache and Team Le Bleu were in the final.

'I hate competing against René,' Céline told Imogen when the announcement was made. 'He always has to be the best. When we were married, every time I took up something new, he had to do it as well, so that he could beat me. I grew tired of it.'

'I'm sure it was difficult.'

'What was difficult was deciding to call time on it,' said Céline. 'But if I hadn't . . . well, he was stifling me. He didn't mean to, but he was.'

It sounded so familiar, thought Imogen. Yet René and Céline were not at all like her and Vince. At least not on the surface.

'I still care about him,' Céline added. 'But living with him was too damn difficult. He always wanted his own way.'

'Men are like that,' agreed Imogen.

Céline shot her a glance. There had been an undertone to Imogen's words that surprised her. But Imogen had turned away and was watching the brass band, which had tuned up again and was blasting out some rousing music.

René called his team together. 'It is important that we are focused on the final match. Not just because we want to beat

Team Le Bleu, but also because we want the extra money for our charity. OK?'

'OK,' said Angie. 'We don't have to worry, though. We're better. Especially as Imogen has turned out to be a star performer.'

'Please don't say that,' implored Imogen. 'I could crumble at any minute. I probably will.'

'Nonsense,' said Raoul. 'We haven't lost yet; we're not going to now.'

The music stopped and they lined up again.

'The final of the competition,' announced the referee. 'The best of three games. Team Bastarache versus Team Le Bleu. Team Le Bleu will throw first.'

Bernard stood up and threw the cochonnet, which landed quite a distance away.

'He prefers to throw long,' said René. 'He thinks he will beat us that way.'

'And he might have a chance,' murmured Angie after Bernard threw the first boule and it landed close.

'Huh. We'll see.'

But when it was his turn, none of René's boules landed inside Bernard's, and his ex-father-in-law gave him a self-satisfied smile.

'You go next, Imogen,' said René. 'You'll get one inside.'

She looked anxiously at the target as she took aim, but her boules too landed short, and Team Le Bleu won the game.

'One more for the win,' said Bernard.

'*Il ne faut pas vendre la peau de l'ours avant de l'avoir tué*, Bernard. Don't count your chickens . . .' René shrugged expressively, while Angie and Imogen exchanged anxious glances. They were both beginning to feel the pressure, although Raoul was very relaxed, and Art, who was clearly hampered by his wrist, didn't seem too bothered either. However, Céline and her mother both wore slightly hunted expressions.

'It's only a game,' said Florence.

Her husband snorted. 'Let's go.'

But this time Team Bastarache managed to score the points to take it to a decider.

'You'd swear we were playing in the World Cup,' muttered Céline to Imogen. 'Or the French Open tennis.'

'Let's agree that we're friends no matter what,' said Imogen, and Céline laughed.

'Of course,' she said.

Almost inevitably, the game was close, with the opportunities to throw going back and forth between the two teams. The crowd had completely got into the spirit of things and was cheering on first one side and then the other. Betting on the outcome was brisk.

'I don't believe it,' said Imogen when Florence got her final throw to rest right beside the cochonnet and put Team Le Bleu into the lead, causing Bernard to almost crush her in an excited hug.

'It's all up to you,' René told her. 'You need to get closer.'

'There isn't any closer than touching it,' Imogen told him.

'You need to move her boule and leave yours beside it instead,' Raoul said.

'The chances of that are practically zero,' said Imogen.

'You can do it.'

No you can't. You're hopeless, Imogen.

She whirled around, truly expecting to see Vince standing

behind her, because she could have sworn the words had been spoken out loud. But there was nobody there.

You're trying to ingratiate yourself with these people. But they don't care about you. Only I do.

She thought she was going to faint. She closed her eyes for a moment.

'Imogen?' There was concern in René's voice. 'Are you OK?'

'I . . .' She couldn't do this. Vince was right. She was pretending to be involved. Pretending to be part of something when the truth was she was an outsider.

'Come on, Imogen!' Céline was calling to her. Imogen opened her eyes again. The café owner gave her an encouraging smile. 'Noisettes for a week on me if you win. But,' she added with a wicked grin, 'I don't think you will.'

Imogen smiled faintly. She looked down at the boule in her hand and then stepped into the throwing circle.

'Come on, Imogen!' cried René. 'Come on, Team Bastarache!' He began a slow handclap, which was taken up by the crowd.

For Imogen, it wasn't about getting the boule close to the cochonnet. It was about letting go of it in the first place. She felt her head begin to spin and was afraid that she might pass out. Her fingers tightened around the silver ball.

'*Allez!*' chanted the crowd.

'Let's go, Imogen!' yelled Angie.

The boule felt like a ball of fire in her hands. She had to get rid of it. She exhaled sharply, then threw it.

It was an awful shot.

'Never mind.' René comforted her by patting her on the back, even though it had been so short that she knew he must have been horrified. 'Next one.'

She swallowed hard and, without waiting, threw the boule. This time it landed a yard past the cochonnet. A mixture of catcalls and cheers erupted from the crowd.

'Not to put the pressure on,' said René, 'but . . .'

'I'm doing my best,' she said tightly. 'I really am. I told you I was hopeless. I'm sorry.'

'No, no, *I'm* sorry.' René sounded genuinely contrite. 'I get carried away sometimes. Don't worry, Imogen. Just throw it and let *le bon Dieu* do the rest.' He squeezed her shoulders. 'And if he decides that it is not our turn for glory, I can live with that.'

Imogen turned towards him. His blue eyes twinkled and he gave her an approving nod. She realised she'd expected him to look like Vince, hard and angry with her for not living up to his expectations. She could still hear him saying it over and over again: *You're hopeless, Imogen. Hopeless.* But René wasn't saying anything at all. He was giving her a reassuring look.

She took a deep breath, hefted the boule in her hand and lobbed it at the cochonnet. It struck it cleanly, moving it away from Florence's boule and towards the ones both she and René had thrown earlier. Behind her, she heard him cry out in triumph, and then Angie was patting her on the back, congratulating her.

'We won! We won!' she cried. 'Wonderful shot! Well done, Imogen.'

Imogen was stunned. She couldn't tell them that she hadn't thought about the shot before throwing. She couldn't say that it was yet another fluke. She had to bask in their joy at winning while sending an apologetic glance in Céline's direction. But the café owner was smiling, not at all upset by the defeat.

'It doesn't matter to me,' she told Imogen later when they were drinking a glass of wine at one of the outdoor tables. 'It was for the charity, after all. But my father always wants to beat René. Even when we were married, there was this feeling between them.'

'I'm sure that didn't help your marriage either.'

'It was nothing to do with my father,' said Céline. 'The competition for top dog was always between me and René.'

'He tried to control you?'

Céline shook her head. '*Ah, non,*' she said. 'As I told you, he likes to be the best. He was always giving me advice that I didn't need. I wouldn't listen to him. I am my own woman, after all. However . . .' she gave Imogen a knowing look, 'it might be different between you and him.'

'What?' Imogen shook her head vigorously. 'There's nothing between René and me. I don't know what would make you think otherwise.'

'Sorry, sorry!' Céline held up her hands. 'I didn't mean to upset you. But it seems to me that there's a spark between you.'

'Not that sort of spark,' Imogen assured her.

'If you say so,' said Céline. 'But perhaps, given time?'

'I doubt I'll be here long enough to give it time,' said Imogen.

'You will leave us?'

'Not yet. But . . .' Imogen shrugged. 'I'll have to find a proper job at some stage. It's not that cleaning isn't a proper job,' she added quickly in case Céline thought she wasn't being thorough enough, 'it's just that I don't see myself doing it for ever.'

'What would you like to do?' asked Céline.

'I don't know,' admitted Imogen.

'What did you do before?'

Imogen told her about her time with the professors and afterwards at Chandon Leclerc, which made Céline look at her in surprise.

'And yet you're here, cleaning houses?'

'There's not much relevant work for people with European history degrees,' said Imogen. 'And I have to earn a living, so here I am.'

'We all have to earn a living,' agreed Céline. 'Maybe one day you can write a book about the history of Hendaye.'

Imogen made a face. 'I doubt that somehow.'

'Here you are, *chérie*.' Art arrived and sat down beside Céline. He put his good arm around her and drew her closer. 'I was wondering where you'd got to. I didn't think you'd be hobnobbing with your rival.'

Céline laughed. 'Once the game is over, we're friends.'

'I should probably go.' Imogen stood up. 'I've had too much to drink and I have to get home.'

'Are you crazy?' demanded Céline. 'There will be dancing!'

'It's Thursday night. I have to be at the agency in the morning.'

'No you don't,' said Céline. 'I know how it works. They don't send the cleaners to the apartments too early in case you get the holidaymakers out of bed.'

Imogen smiled. 'That's true. But I'm doing houses now, and—'

'Sit down.' Céline poured some more wine into Imogen's glass. 'We're all friends here. Have some fun.'

Imogen was trying to remember the last time she'd been in a group like this. The last time she'd been out on her own and not had to worry about getting a text from Vince wondering what time she'd be home. It had to have been before she met him. After their marriage she stopped going out by herself, unless she was with Shona. And she had to text him every hour to tell him where she was.

But tonight she didn't have to answer to anybody. And it was liberating.

She continued to chat to Céline and Art, until René told her it was time to dance. Wooden decking had been put over the boules surface and the brass band had been replaced by a DJ, who was encouraging the crowd to get up and move to the music. Which many of them were.

'I'm a hopeless dancer,' said Imogen.

'Nobody is a hopeless dancer,' René told her. 'They just haven't found the right partner.' He pulled her to her feet and led her to the improvised dance floor. '*Et voilà!*' he cried as he twirled her around. 'Not hopeless at all.'

Angie and Raoul joined them, along with Céline and Art, and some other people Imogen didn't know. The music was hard and fast and so was the dancing, but everyone kept going until René finally said that he needed a rest.

'You young people might have all the energy in the world. But us older folk . . .'

They laughed but joined him at the table again, where more wine was drunk. Then there was more dancing. And then water to rehydrate.

'I really have to go home,' said Imogen. 'I'm falling asleep.'

'We are that boring?' complained René.

'No,' she said. 'I'm exhausted, that's all.'

'You're working her too hard,' said Céline. 'And she's worried about being in on time in the morning.'

'Everything will be happening an hour later tomorrow,' said René.

'Not for me,' Céline said. 'I will be in the café as usual.'

'You always had that work ethic.' René stretched his legs out in front of him. 'It wore me out.'

'I know,' said Céline.

There was a sudden taut silence between them. Then René sat up straight again.

'Do you really wish to go home?' he asked Imogen.

She nodded.

'I'll walk with you,' he said.

'That's not really necessary,' she told him. 'It's less than twenty minutes. I can manage.'

'I'm sure you can. But I'll walk with you nonetheless.'

'Please let him,' said Céline. 'This is a nice town, but you're a woman on your own and you've had a few drinks.'

'Why should that be a problem?' Imogen asked. 'Why should I have to worry?'

'You shouldn't,' agreed Angie. 'But unfortunately in this world we have to worry about too many things.'

'Come on,' said René. 'Let's go.'

Imogen stood up and René took her by the arm.

'I'm fine,' she said.

'I know,' said René. 'I want to keep it that way.'

They walked in silence back to her apartment. The night air was still warm, and heavy with the scent of oleander and hibiscus. René opened the gate that led to the block and walked up the path with her.

'Thank you very much for taking care of me,' said Imogen as she took out her key. 'You're a lovely man, René.'

'But not your type?' He grinned at her.

'Nobody's my type right now,' she said.

'That's OK.' He gave her the lightest of kisses on the cheek. 'It's good to have a professional relationship with a woman.'

'You have lots of them,' Imogen pointed out. 'Céline, Angie, me.'

'Céline will never be entirely professional,' admitted René. 'I care about her even though we are no longer together.'

'Are you still in love with her?' asked Imogen.

René shook his head. 'That is past. Our marriage failed. But you have to move on, don't you?'

'That's what I keep telling myself.'

'You're doing great,' he said. 'Whatever you're moving on from, you're doing great.'

Imogen felt the tears well up in her eyes. It was lovely to be told she was doing well. What have I become, she asked herself, if a simple compliment from a stranger has me feeling weepy? She swallowed hard.

'Goodnight, René.' She kissed him, just as lightly. 'I'll see you tomorrow.'

'*Beaux rêves,*' said René. Then he turned and walked away.

She felt good. She felt happy. And although she was tired, she was also suddenly wide awake. For the first time since leaving home, she really believed she might get it right. She was making friends and becoming part of the community, and although she didn't know if she'd stay, she knew that she'd managed to find a place where she felt comfortable. And it was a place she'd come to on her own, not somewhere she'd been forced to be by somebody else.

But the problem with being on her own was that there

was nobody to share her happiness with. And she wanted to share it. She wanted to let people in her life, the people that she'd kept her location a secret from, know that she was all right. They deserved to know that, didn't they?

She was subliminally aware that texting or emailing after a few drinks wasn't a good idea, but she was going to do it anyway.

She took a deep breath, opened her new email account and clicked on 'compose'.

From: Vanished@mymail.com
To: Cheyenne@firstmail.com
Subject: It's me
Hi Cheyenne, thanks so much for your email. As you can see, this is a new address. It's the one to get me on these days. I'm not using the old one any more, because even though I can't be sure, I have a feeling that Vince is able to access it. Does that make me sound paranoid? It's probably because I am. He's made me that way.

You're right, I've left him. There are too many reasons to talk about, but it was the right thing to do. I didn't get in touch with anyone because it was something I had to decide for myself. Besides, we've all got our own stuff going on these days and I'm not sure what you could have added to the mix. I knew I had to leave. And I knew I had to hide away for a while. I'm sure he's not happy about what I've done. Well, who would be!

I'm fine and safe and getting myself back together. Please, please don't talk to Vince (not that you would) and don't let Kevin talk to him when he comes back from the cruise (because he might, if only to swear at him).

It would be good to meet up again soon. I'll be in touch again.

Hope everything is going well for you.

Love, Imogen

It was a bit factual, she thought as she pressed 'send'. It didn't say anything about how awful things had been and about how much better she was feeling. But at least she'd been in touch.

She started another email, but as she began to type Shona's address, she changed her mind. She'd chickened out of phoning her friend before, but she didn't feel as anxious about it now. Maybe it's the alcohol, she thought, as her finger hovered over the keypad. Maybe it's affecting my judgement. But it can't do any harm to phone her, it really can't. Not if I don't tell her anything she doesn't need to know.

She took a deep breath, then tapped out her friend's number. It took a while before the phone was answered and she heard Shona's voice ask sleepily, 'Who's that?'

'It's me,' she replied.

'Imogen!' Shona was fully awake. 'Oh my God, how are you? Where are you?'

'I'm fine,' replied Imogen. 'Doing well.'

'Where are you?' repeated Shona.

'I can't tell you that right now.'

'What's going on?' asked Shona. 'Why did you leave like that? Why didn't you tell me?'

'I left because I couldn't take it any more. I know Vince seemed to be perfect for me, but he wasn't.'

'He said you were upset because you weren't pregnant,' said Shona. 'Is that it, Imogen? Do you need counselling?'

'Why would I want to get pregnant when I was planning to leave him?' asked Imogen. 'That's nonsense.'

'I guess so,' said Shona. 'What I'm struggling with, though, is that you just vanished. You scared us all, Imogen. Vince included.'

'Nothing scares Vince.' Imogen was feeling completely sober again now. 'Except thinking that he's not in control of things. Me in particular.'

'He certainly hasn't been in control of anything over the last few weeks,' said Shona. 'He's devastated.'

'Really?'

'Yes. And he wants to find you. He's planning to go to France.'

Imogen's heart somersaulted and she felt sick.

'Why?'

'Because that's where you disappeared,' said Shona. 'Is that where you are?'

'I can't say.'

'It's me you're talking to. You can tell me anything. We're friends. Are you OK?'

'Of course I'm OK. I wouldn't be ringing if I wasn't OK. But I'm not telling you where I am because you might tell him.'

There was a silence at the other end of the phone.

'Don't you trust me?' Shona sounded hurt.

'Yes. But I don't trust him.'

'You're scaring me a little, Imogen. Did he hurt you?'

'Not physically.'

'I can see . . .' Shona picked her words carefully. 'I can see how he might be a bit overwhelming at times. But you can't simply disappear for ever. You need to deal with stuff.'

'Not yet I don't.'

'When you're ready,' agreed Shona. 'And I'm here for you. How are you managing?'

'Not bad.' Imogen smiled to herself. 'I have a job.'

'Doing what?'

'I'm not telling you that either.'

'Why did you ring me if you won't confide in me?' asked Shona.

'I rang to apologise for what I did,' answered Imogen. 'And to let you know that I'm fine. And happy. That's it really. I wanted to tell you I'm happy. I wanted to share it.'

'Have you found someone else?' asked Shona. 'Is that it?'

Imogen thought about René and his invitation to dinner. About the boules tournament. And how he'd smiled at her.

'No,' she said.

'Are you ever going to come back?'

'When I'm ready.'

'When will that be?'

'I don't know.'

Shona sighed. 'I'm glad you're all right,' she said. 'I've been so worried about you.'

'There's no need,' Imogen assured her. 'I can cope on my own. But I do miss you.'

'I guess that's something,' said Shona. 'I felt as though you'd cut me out of your life.'

'I needed a break,' Imogen said.

'That's what I told Vince.'

'He's the wrong man for me,' said Imogen.

'Fair enough.'

'Please don't tell him I called.'

'It would reassure him.'

'I don't want him reassured.' Imogen's voice was sharp.

'He deserves to know you're not dead,' Shona told her. 'That was something we were both afraid of.'

'But I called the Missing Family line,' said Imogen. 'You knew I was all right.'

'It's not the same as hearing from you directly. Maybe if you told him that . . .'

'No.'

'OK, OK. I understand. But you need to know that he's quite determined to find you, Imogen. He was looking at hiring PIs and everything.'

'And has he?' Imogen's heart somersaulted again.

'No. He's going to do it himself.'

'Email me if he leaves Ireland,' said Imogen.

'Are you in France?' asked Shona again.

Imogen didn't reply.

'He thinks France. Alternatively England, with your step-sister. Or, at a push, the States, with your aunts.'

'I'm not with my aunts.' Imogen didn't want Vince going to Palm Springs and upsetting Berthe and Agnes. 'That's the truth, Shona.'

'Do you want me to tell him that?'

'I don't want you to tell him anything at all,' said Imogen. 'But if he starts talking about going to the States . . . well, let me know.'

'OK,' said Shona. 'I want to help, that's all.'

'Thank you,' said Imogen. 'You're a good friend, Shona. I'm sorry I gave you a fright.'

'It's OK. The most important thing is you're all right.'

'I am,' said Imogen. 'I really am.'

'Well look, keep in touch with me,' said Shona. 'Call me any time. Or email.'

'I have a new email address,' said Imogen. 'I think he can access my old one. You'll keep it secret, won't you?'

'If you want.'

'Please.'

'Of course,' said Shona. 'What is it?'

Imogen gave it to her and once again stressed that she didn't want Vince to know it.

'I promise,' said Shona. 'Take care of yourself, Imogen.'

'I will.'

'You're sure there's nothing I can do to help?'

'Not right now. But if that changes, I'll let you know.'

'In that case . . . I'm glad you called.'

'I am too,' said Imogen.

After she'd ended the call, she went to bed. She lay on her back and stared into the darkness. It had been nice to talk to her friend again. But she hoped it hadn't been a different sort of indiscretion.

Chapter 23

She woke up at seven the next morning with the nagging sense of something being wrong. As she poured herself a glass of water, she remembered her conversation with Shona. She'd made the phone call in a haze of alcohol and happiness, and to assuage the guilt she'd felt for leaving without a word. But now, in the light of day, it seemed like a bad idea. Vince might worm it out of Shona that they'd spoken. And although Imogen knew she'd been careful not to give any clues about her whereabouts, she reminded herself that the Plan hadn't allowed for conversations with people back in Dublin. It had been a mistake. She wasn't going to do it again. Ever.

She finished the water and decided to go for a swim in the pool to clear her head. The man she'd seen the first day, an athletic-looking guy with a shock of inky-black hair, arrived when she'd finished her paltry length and was sitting with her feet dangling over the edge. He nodded at her, dived in and swam ten lengths before he stopped and introduced himself as Max Gasquet.

'I live in apartment number one,' he said. 'I've seen you here before.'

'I'm renting for the summer,' she explained.

'I'm the one long-term let in the place. If there's anything you need, let me know. I do a lot of DIY stuff for the students.'

'Are you a student too?' she asked.

'An intern at the hospital,' he replied. 'So I'm good at fixing bodies as well as putting up shelves.'

'Useful to know.'

'Seriously,' he said. 'If you want anything, just ask.'

'I will.' She picked up her towel and wrapped it around her. 'Thank you.'

'Hey, I hope I haven't frightened you off!'

'It would take more than that,' she said with a smile. 'Sadly I've got to go to work.'

'See you around,' he said as she slipped her flip-flops on to her feet.

'See you.'

She was still smiling as she let herself into her apartment. Fair enough, she'd slipped up last night, but she hadn't made a critical error. And it was lovely to be able to speak to people here – especially men – knowing that Vince wasn't looking over her shoulder, ready to get angry or jealous. Not that there had ever been the slightest reason for him to be jealous. She hadn't even looked at another man after she'd married him. Certainly not with any kind of sexual interest. She was afraid of men other than Vince. Afraid of what they provoked in him.

She had a shower and dried her hair. After three full weeks, the shorter style was already beginning to grow out. Imogen wasn't sure if she'd let it grow completely again, or whether she preferred the slightly more severe cut. My choice, she thought as she brushed it. Mine alone.

After a slice of toast and a cup of coffee, she hopped on to the bike and cycled to the estate agency. Even though she was early, the halogen lights were already shining over the pictures of the houses in the window, and when she tried the door, it was open. René was sitting behind his desk and looked up in surprise when she walked in.

'I thought you weren't going to be here till later,' he said.

'I woke up early.'

'How are you feeling?'

'Great,' she said.

'And so you should be.' He beamed at her. 'As the person who won us the boules tournament, you are our superstar. I hope you can come along when we make the presentation to the charity.'

'I'd like that,' she said.

'Good. Now, do you want a coffee before you start?'

'I had one before I left,' she told him.

'I didn't. And I'd love a croissant.'

Vince used to do this. Ask her if she wanted something, and when she indicated that she didn't, he'd say that he did. And she'd feel forced into joining him. She felt a sudden surge of panic.

'But if you're already high on caffeine, that's OK.' René reached into the desk drawer and took out some keys. 'Here's today's list. Oh, and I've got the clean laundry for the Villa Martine. Can you pick it up and drop it to the house when you've finished for the day?'

'Of course . . . René?'

'Yes?'

'How many other cleaners do you have working for you?'

'Why do you ask?'

'I was the only one at the boules tournament. I can't help feeling you're treating me differently.'

'We don't have any other cleaner who's also a client, so perhaps I do,' he conceded. 'Lana and Danielle both have families, so in this case it seemed better to ask you. Besides, you're also the only one who's friends with my ex-wife.'

'And that matters because . . . ?'

'It doesn't, I guess.' He shrugged. 'I feel that we get on, and I enjoy being in your company. We needed someone for the tournament, and so I asked you.'

'Who played last year?'

'Viktoria. But as you're her replacement in the agency, it's even more appropriate that I asked you, so you don't need to turn it into a conspiracy theory.'

'I may have a habit of looking for conspiracies when there aren't any,' she admitted. 'And as you're right and I'm here too early to start, I'd be delighted to join you for a coffee and croissant.'

They went to the café, where Céline raised her eyebrows when she saw them.

'I didn't think anyone else would be up so early,' she said. 'But the two of you . . .'

'Not up early together!' cried Imogen, seeing the expression in the other woman's eyes.

'It doesn't matter to me if—'

'It matters to me,' Imogen interrupted her.

'And to me,' said René. 'I would never bring a woman I slept with to the café directly afterwards, Céline. You should know that.'

'I should,' she acknowledged. 'And of course you're entitled to have other women. You can even bring them here.'

'But I wouldn't,' said René.

'Ever the gentleman,' Céline said. 'Why on earth did I divorce you?'

Because he's a control freak, thought Imogen. Like Vince. Although not like Vince, because René didn't try to make people do things they didn't want to. Unless you included getting them to play in boules tournaments, of course.

Céline brought the coffee and croissants, then bustled away to deal with her other clients. Imogen and René ate without speaking, but it was a companionable silence, and Imogen didn't mind that René's thoughts seemed to be miles away. Hers were too.

Eventually she got up and said that she'd make a start on the day. René went back to the office while she set off up the Rue de Lilas to her first stop, feeling more light-hearted than she had done in years. I've been lucky ever since I began to execute the Plan, she thought as she hopped off the bike and leaned it against the wall of the house. Maybe it's true that you make your own luck. And maybe I should have realised that sooner.

She worked her way steadily through her schedule, and freewheeled back to the estate agency to leave the keys with René. The late night and the alcohol were beginning to catch up with her, and she was looking forward to getting back to her apartment. She'd forgotten, until he brought the bag of washing out to her, that she'd promised to drop it off at the Villa Martine.

'You needn't bother coming back with the keys tonight,' he said as she stifled a yawn. 'Go directly home and relax.'

'Are you sure?'

'Just keep them secure,' he said.

'Of course,' said Imogen as she hefted the bag into the basket at the front of the bike. 'See you tomorrow.'

Cycling with the laundry in front of her was a little more precarious than she would have liked, but she made it to the Villa Martine without any problem. She tapped in the gate code and pushed the bike up the path, then let herself into the house. She left her bright green tote bag in the hallway and went upstairs with the sheets and towels.

She was dividing them into neat piles and arranging them on a shelf in the main bedroom when she heard the front door bang and footsteps on the tiled floor below. Then the cheerful sound of someone whistling the theme to *The Great Escape* wafted up the stairs.

She stood frozen, unable to move as she listened to the owner of the footsteps walk through the hallway towards the back of the house. Her heart was thumping like a hammer on an anvil, and the thought going through her head was that Vince was whistling his favourite tune because he'd tracked her down. But how the hell had he done it? Had she let something slip to Shona after all? Had her best friend betrayed her? Or had she herself made a mistake and overlooked something that had given her away?

The whistling stopped and she heard the sound of the kitchen door being opened. Her legs were shaking so much that she could hardly stand.

She had to get out before he came up the stairs and discovered her cowering in the corner. And then she had to cycle away as quickly as possible and go . . . where? She couldn't return to the apartment, that was certain. He might already have been there. And there was nowhere else. Except, of course, Bastarache Immobilier, although René had probably left for the day. But the café was still open. Céline would help her, she was sure of that. René too, if he was able. And it struck her that in a place where she'd stayed for only a few weeks, she'd managed to find people she could trust. Somehow in Dublin, because everyone she knew also knew Vince, she'd been afraid to trust anyone at all.

There was total silence from downstairs. She opened the bedroom door a little wider, tiptoed to the top of the stairs and peered down. There was nothing to see. Except her bag, neatly placed alongside the wall. Had he spotted it? It was new but would he guess it was hers? Did he know for sure she was here? And how had he got in? Had he persuaded René to give him the keys? In which case, she couldn't depend on René to help her after all.

She waited another few seconds while she tried to control her pounding heart, and then, hearing nothing more from downstairs, began to descend the staircase as quietly as possible. She was about halfway down when the sound of footsteps on the kitchen floor reached her again. She waited, petrified, until they stopped. Then she hurried down the remaining stairs and grabbed her bag. Her hand was trembling and she struggled to undo the latch. She heard the rattle of the kitchen door as she turned the knob and hauled the front door open frantically, but just as she tried to leave the house, she felt a hand grab her by the arm. She squirmed and pulled away, but his grip was firm.

'Who the hell are you, and what are you doing in my house?' he demanded.

It took her a couple of seconds to realise that the question had been asked in French.

* * *

Vince didn't speak French. In his view, other languages were unnecessary, as everyone who mattered spoke English anyway. So it couldn't be Vince who was holding on to her and talking rapidly about calling the police.

'I'm sorry, I'm sorry,' she gasped eventually. 'I didn't realise anyone was coming today. I'm supposed to be here. I'm the cleaner.'

His grip on her arm loosened but he didn't let go. He pulled gently at her so that she was facing him. His dark hair was swept back from a tanned face. His eyes were blue-grey. He was wearing Bermuda shorts and a navy crew-neck T-shirt, and he was looking at her with an angry expression that was somehow shockingly familiar. She'd seen that expression before, on the face of Denis Delissandes the first day she and Carol had arrived at the Villa Martine, when the boys had kicked a football in front of the car. She'd seen it a number of times over the following years too, usually when his sons had done something to annoy him.

'Oliver?' she said. 'Charles?'

He looked at her in surprise. 'I'm Giles. Do you know my brothers? Am I supposed to know you too?'

'I . . . Not exactly, no . . .'

Suspicion flickered in his eyes. 'You know their names, you say you're the cleaner, but you run away when you think one of them might arrive?'

'I thought you were an intruder,' said Imogen, while she processed the fact that there was another Delissandes boy. One who must have been born after she and Carol had left. 'Please let go of my arm,' she added.

'An intruder who opens the door with his own key?' he asked, nevertheless doing as she asked.

'I thought that perhaps I hadn't closed it properly,' she admitted.

'Well that was careless of you, wasn't it? What if I'd been a real burglar?'

'But I had and you weren't.' Imogen rubbed her arm. 'Why didn't you give the company notice you were coming?'

'Because there was nothing that needed to be done in advance of our arrival.' The sharpness had left his voice and he was looking at her with exasperation rather than anger. 'The house was cleaned after my mother left.'

'I know,' she said. 'I'm the one who cleaned it. I'm not here to clean again. I simply came to replace the bedlinen. It's been laundered.'

'Oh,' he said. 'Well, if you don't mind, I'm going to call Bastarache Immobilier to check that you're supposed to be here.'

She watched him as he dialled the number and wondered when he'd been born. The fact that Denis and Lucie had had another child was a good sign, she thought. It meant that the indiscretion (the affair, she told herself; she'd have to get over calling it by that stupid word) must have been forgiven. So at least Carol hadn't been responsible for breaking up the family. A wave of relief washed over her. She'd worried about that for years.

'And your name?' he asked, while he waited for the phone to be answered.

'Imogen. Imogen Weir.'

'Well, that's fine,' he said when René had vouched for her. 'I'm sorry I frightened you, but you scared the hell out of me too.'

'Apologies on both sides in that case.' She was recovering

her equilibrium but was still shaken by the sudden encounter with the unknown Delissandes boy.

'Would you like a drink?' he asked. 'To steady your nerves.'

'My nerves are perfectly steady,' she assured him, although her heart was still beating like a piston and her hands were shaking. 'But thank you.'

'Can I say that Monsieur Bastarache has certainly upped the stakes with his cleaners,' said Giles. 'Have you worked for us before? I don't remember you, and I always remember a pretty face, but you've obviously met my brothers.'

She had to confess. It would lead to all sorts of complications if she didn't.

'I lived here when I was younger,' she told him.

'And you knew them how?'

'I knew all of your family,' she said. 'When I said I lived here, that's exactly what I meant. I lived *here*.'

'Here? In this house?' He looked at her in disbelief. 'That's not possible. It's been in our family for generations. Nobody else lived here.'

'My mother was the housekeeper.'

'We didn't have a housekeeper.' He sounded suspicious again.

'It was before you were born obviously,' she said. 'My mother and I lived in this house. With Madame and Monsieur Delissandes and Oliver and Charles. She did the housework and I spoke English to them.'

'They've never mentioned you,' he said.

'Why should they?' She smiled even though inside she was in turmoil. 'We were . . . we were staff, you know. And then we left.'

'Nobody in my family ever spoke a word about you or

your mother,' said Giles. 'If what you're saying is true, surely they would have mentioned you at least once.'

'It was a long time ago.' She shrugged.

'You need to tell me your story,' he said. 'It seems a little too coincidental to me that a cleaner I've never seen before is skulking around the house where she says she used to live. There's a stalker element to it that I'm not very keen on.'

'I'm not a stalker and there's no story,' said Imogen. 'My mother worked for yours for a while, that's all. We left before you were born, so maybe that's why . . . Oh.' It had suddenly occurred to her that Lucie could have been pregnant when Denis and Carol had been having their affair. She felt queasy at the thought.

'Oh?' he repeated.

'Nothing.' She shook her head.

'How old were you then?'

'I was four when we came here first. Nearly nine when we left.'

'You were here for all that time and yet I've never even heard of you!' He was incredulous.

'I guess the family forgot about us,' she said.

'Where did you sleep?' He put the question to her abruptly.

'In the garden bedroom,' she replied. 'It was divided into two then.'

'What were the names of our dogs?'

'When I was here?' She screwed up her face as she recalled them. 'Mimi and Loulou. They were puppies when I came.'

He believed her now. She could see it in his face.

'Mimi was ten when she was put to sleep,' he said. 'Loulou was nearly fifteen.'

'I'm sorry,' she said. 'I liked those dogs. But I'm glad they had long lives.'

'And I remember my father renovating the garden bedroom. I remember him taking down the dividing wall.'

'So, you see.' She smiled at him. 'All true. No big deal. Now can I go? I only came to leave the laundry after all.'

'You will be coming back to clean?' he asked.

'I don't know,' she answered. 'It depends on Monsieur Bastarache.'

'Imo-zhen.' He said it slowly and deliberately. 'You're not from around here, though, are you? You moved away from Hendaye?'

She nodded. 'We returned to Dublin. It's where my mum was from.'

'And she's still living there?'

'She died,' said Imogen quietly.

'I'm sorry.' His voice was a good deal softer.

'That was a long time ago too,' said Imogen.

'Nevertheless . . .'

'Nevertheless, I've taken up too much of your time,' she said. 'And I'm truly sorry about . . . about the mix-up.'

'I'm not.' He grinned. 'It's made my day a lot more interesting. Or at least it would have done if you'd actually been a masked intruder raiding the house. I've always fancied myself as being able to stand up to a trespasser. I never expected one as lovely as you, though.'

'I have to go,' said Imogen.

'Indeed. But I hope to see you again.'

'I'll be back next week.'

'And my apologies if I hurt you in any way.'

'You didn't,' she said.

'I thought you were a burglar. I doubt I was gentle.'

'I'm fine.' She flexed her wrist.

'I didn't bruise you, did I?'

'No, no.'

He reached out and took her hand in his, then looked at her arm.

'I think it's OK,' he said.

'As I said, I'm fine.'

'In that case, *au revoir*.'

'*Au revoir*,' she said, and walked out of the door.

He closed it firmly behind her.

She stood on the step for a moment, gathering herself and her thoughts and trying to get her ragged breathing under control, before beginning to wheel her bicycle down the driveway. She hadn't gone more than a couple of metres when the electric gates opened to admit a white Range Rover Evoque. The driver tooted the horn, and behind her, Giles opened the front door again. Imogen moved to one side as the car passed her. This time the driver slowed down and she saw him glance at her. It was probably because she'd already met Giles and had an idea of how the Delissandes boys looked in adulthood that she recognised him instantly. It was Oliver, the eldest. Oliver, who'd teased her mercilessly when she'd been smaller and on whom she'd exacted her revenge by putting ants in his bed. And now he was driving an expensive car and undoubtedly wondering what on earth a woman pushing a pink bicycle was doing in his garden.

The gates had glided shut again, but she stayed where she was, mesmerised, as the car came to a stop in front of the house and Oliver got out, followed by his brother Charles and a tall blonde woman with a baby in her arms.

'*Bienvenue, bienvenue!* You've arrived much quicker than I thought!' Giles's voice wafted towards her. 'I only got here a short time ago myself.'

'We didn't stop except to change drivers,' said Oliver. 'And there were no roadworks.'

'*Bonjour*, Giles.' The blonde woman kissed him and then Charles embraced him, but Oliver was looking back down the driveway with a puzzled expression to where Imogen was standing watching them.

'And she is?'

'Imogen!' called Giles. '*S'il vous plaît.* Come here.'

She hesitated before pushing the bike back towards the house. The three Delissandes brothers were standing side by side looking at her curiously. They were very alike, she thought, although Charles, in the middle, was lighter-haired than the other two. He was the one who spoke first.

'Imogen?' he said. '*The* Imogen?'

'*Our* Imogen?' said Oliver. 'Really?'

'Yes,' she said.

'So it's definitely true,' said Giles. 'We once had a housekeeper with a pretty daughter living in our house. I didn't know we were that sort of family.'

'We're not,' said Oliver, who was looking at her with a shocked expression.

It was Charles who stepped forward and embraced her, kissing her quickly on each cheek and saying that it was good, if surprising, to see her again. She didn't return the hug because she was still holding the bike upright.

'Are you visiting?' he asked. 'Did you come looking for us? Are you staying in Hendaye?'

'She's the cleaner,' Giles said. 'She came with the laundry.'

'What?' Charles looked surprised. 'Have we changed from Bastarache?'

'She works for Bastarache,' said Giles.

'You came back here to work for René?' It was Oliver who spoke now, and he pushed his slightly too-long hair from his eyes as he looked at her. 'Why?'

Imogen said nothing and Oliver continued to stare at her, a puzzled look in his navy-blue eyes.

'But we don't want her to clean for us,' he said to Giles. 'And I can't believe . . .'

'I think she's a competent cleaner,' said Giles. 'The house is in perfect order.'

'That's not what I mean,' said Oliver. 'Imogen doesn't . . . This is . . . Why are you here?' He spoke directly to her.

'You can tell him, Giles.' Imogen tightened her grip on the bike. 'I've already explained.'

The blonde woman spoke. 'You are a friend of the family?' she asked. 'Or a friend of Charles and Oliver?'

'I'm not a friend of anyone,' said Imogen. 'Like Giles said, I'm just the cleaner.' She turned away and began to push the bike down the driveway again.

Nobody stopped her.

When she reached the gate, she keyed in the code. She didn't look to see if they were watching her as she left.

It wasn't until she was back in her apartment and making herself a cup of tea that her heartbeat finally slowed down.

But her hands were still trembling as she sipped the tea and looked out over the garden. It was dusk now, and she wondered if the Delissandes were having a barbecue around their pool like they'd done in the past, when Denis had lit the coals under the grille before going off to get juicy steaks from the charcuterie. She and Carol usually joined the family for barbecue nights, even though on other evenings they would eat by themselves in the kitchen after Carol had helped Lucie prepare something for the family's evening meal. The dividing line between employer and employee had been blurred in Imogen's mind. She'd known that she and Carol only lived at the Villa Martine because they worked for the Delissandes. Yet Lucie had made them a part of almost everything they did. Perhaps that was why Carol had entered into the indiscretion with Denis. Perhaps she'd felt entitled.

And for a moment today, Imogen had felt entitled too. When she'd opened the door of the house and stepped inside, it had been homely and familiar. Even though it couldn't have been, because, as she reminded herself for the umpteenth time, she'd only lived there for four bloody years and she couldn't possibly say that those years were better or more important or more memorable than the subsequent ones with Agnes and Berthe or Keith and Cheyenne and Paula. Yet there had been something defining about her time there, and the manner in which they'd left. Nevertheless, she had to remember what her mother had forgotten. That it hadn't been home. That it never would have been. That the Delissandes lived a different sort of life to the one she and Carol lived. That they were nothing to her and she was nothing to them. After today, perhaps, not even their cleaner!

On the plus side of the day's terror, though, was that despite her fear that Vince might have found her, he hadn't. She'd left no clues behind. Nor had she accidentally betrayed herself to Shona. As for Cheyenne, she was confident that her stepsister would never help him find her. Which meant that she was safe in Hendaye and could stay here for as long as she wanted without looking over her shoulder.

After that . . . well, she'd have to think of something. But at least that something wouldn't involve Vince Naughton. Or the Delissandes. It would be her. Alone. Which was the way she wanted it to be from now on.

Chapter 24

It took Vince longer than he'd expected to organise the time off for his trip, but by the end of the following week, he was on a flight to Paris. He had a checklist of things he intended to do to find Imogen, starting with the hotel where she'd stayed and where (despite the expense) he'd booked a room too. However, he was pretty certain that any success at the hotel would simply point him in the right direction, which he believed was Provence. Unless he learned anything to the contrary, he planned to journey from Paris to Marseille within a day or two.

There he would look for the Maison Lavande and anyone who remembered Agnes, Berthe or Carol. The difficulty was that despite an intensive search, he hadn't been able to find a website for the guest house, but it was entirely possible that it had been sold or changed its name over the past few years. He planned to try to track down anyone called Fournier in the area, in the hope that they'd know the history of the Maison Lavande and its owners. He knew it seemed like a long shot, but it wasn't entirely impossible. He was quietly confident of his ability to find Imogen.

He ran through his plans again sitting in the taxi from

the airport to the hotel while he watched the tourists who thronged the Parisian streets, camera phones snapping everything around them. He had to admit that there was an undoubted elegance to the French capital, a feeling that the buildings had been erected to enhance the city rather than for mere function. Imogen had said something similar when he'd brought her here for their romantic break. He'd been at a disadvantage in not understanding the language, but he hadn't let her deal with any of the people they met, and had insisted on talking to the hotel staff in English. Which hadn't been a problem because (as he'd expected) they all had perfectly adequate English, although they spoke in what he considered to be a condescendingly arrogant way. At least they did until Imogen suddenly burst into a torrent of French with lots of *s'il vous plaît*s and *merci*s. Even though her intervention had sorted out the minor problem with the room he'd been complaining about, he'd been annoyed with her and had told her not to undermine him that way again. She'd shrugged and said that it made sense for her to talk to them in French and he'd retorted that there was no need for them to be rude no matter what damn language they were speaking in.

He was right about the rudeness, he thought as he took his bag from the taxi driver outside the hotel. The man merely pointed at the meter to show him the fare and acknowledged the tip with a grunt before getting out of the cab and retrieving Vince's wheelie bag from the boot. Vince extended the handle of the bag and walked into the marble foyer of the hotel. He checked in, got his key and went up to the room (at no time requiring assistance from anyone who spoke French. Which, he reckoned, proved his point).

For a company on the verge of bankruptcy, Chandon Leclerc had looked after its employees pretty well, he thought as he surveyed the room. Enormous bed, modern fittings, bottled water, a Nespresso machine – and a half-bottle of red wine on the dresser too. The red wine wasn't complimentary, he realised on further inspection. Drinking it would add €30 to his bill. He wondered if Imogen had indulged in wine in her room before embarking on her ridiculous adventure. Being drunk might explain her behaviour. At least it might explain her thinking about it, though not her decision to actually do it.

He left the room and went downstairs to the hotel bar, where the prices were so extortionately high he decided to look elsewhere for a drink. Although he would have preferred to relax in a decent pub, he eventually sat down at a pavement café, where he ordered a Stella and allowed the cool beer to soothe his frayed temper. After he'd finished it and ordered another, he took out his phone and checked for text messages. He'd called around to Shona's house the previous day and told her of his plans, but she'd been less enthusiastic than he'd expected.

'Why don't you wait until she contacts you herself?' she asked. 'I'm sure she will sooner or later.'

'Because she's my wife,' said Vince.

'You won't find her if she doesn't want to be found.'

Something in her voice made him pause. When he spoke again, his own voice was harder.

'Do you know where she is?'

'No, of course not.'

'You'd tell me if you knew, wouldn't you?'

'I . . .'

'Has she been in touch with you?' demanded Vince. 'Has she?'

'No.' Shona looked Vince straight in the eye, hoping that her guilt wasn't written all over her face. 'But listen to me, Vince. You shouldn't go looking for her. She'll come home when she's ready.'

'Why are you suddenly on her side?' asked Vince. 'She abandoned you too, remember?'

'It's not that!' cried Shona. 'It's just . . . well . . . I don't think this is necessarily the best way to go about things.'

'Perhaps you should come with me,' said Vince. 'She might be more inclined to speak to you.'

'I can't,' said Shona.

'She hasn't been well,' he continued. 'I know you're sceptical, but she's been unstable for a while. This running-away lark isn't a lone event. It's part of a pattern. So if you do have any thoughts, any information, anything at all, you've got to tell me. You won't help her by keeping secrets.'

'What sort of a pattern?'

'Putting things away in the wrong place,' said Vince. 'Buying the wrong groceries. Not calling me when she says she will. It doesn't sound much, but it makes me worry about her.'

Shona exhaled slowly. 'If I hear from her, I'll let you know,' she said.

'It's for her own good,' Vince told her as he stood up. 'Everything I do for her is for her own good. You have my number. If she gets in touch with you at all, text me.'

She closed the door behind him and leaned her head against the wall. Not saying something about Imogen's phone call had been difficult, especially as Vince had sounded truly concerned about her. Maybe Imogen really was having a breakdown. Maybe she needed medical help. She'd sounded OK, Shona thought, but how could she be sure of that? So if Imogen rang again, she'd tell Vince. He was a responsible kind of guy, after all. She felt a sense of relief at having made a decision, even though she still wasn't sure it was the right one.

Later that evening, she sent an email to Imogen's new email address.

> . . . I didn't tell him we'd spoken and he doesn't know where you are. He's staying in the hotel in Paris where you stayed. He's going to look for you there but I think he feels that Provence is the place to go. Is that where you are? Oh Imogen, I don't know what's best. You sounded OK on the phone, but are you really? Should you be seeing a doctor? I've spent a lot of time talking to Vince over the last couple of weeks and he can be a bit overwhelming, but is it really as bad as you say? Can't you at least see him? Talk things through? He'll hardly drag you back kicking and screaming after all. It's not the eighteenth century. You know I'm a hundred per cent behind you, but are you going about this the wrong way? Call me.

Chapter 25

Imogen was still wary every time she opened her email account, but she smiled when she saw the one from Cheyenne.

From: Cheyenne@firstmail.com
To: Vanished@mymail.com
Subject: It's me
You don't sound paranoid at all. I always thought you were far too good for him! I'm glad you left though obviously sorry that you've gone through a hard time and feel you have to hide away. But I understand. And don't forget you can come and stay with me any time you want. If there's anything you need me to do, let me know that too. I could tell him you've gone to New Zealand or something!!! Send him off on the wrong track!!!! Whatever.

Take care of yourself. Keep in touch.

Cxx

It was an appealing idea to have Cheyenne call Vince and say she was living in Auckland, thought Imogen. But it was unlikely he'd fall for it.

She scrolled down to Shona's email and her chest tightened as beads of sweat broke out on her forehead. So he was definitely coming to France. Well, that wasn't such a surprise. She'd always thought he would. She'd expected him to go to Paris and check the hotel. She'd expected him to go to Provence too. But even if he found the Maison Lavande, there was nothing and nobody there to point him in her direction now. She was safe. There was no need to panic. France was a big country with a population of around sixty-six million people. He wouldn't find her. She repeated the number a few times times to convince herself. Sixty-six million. She was a needle in a haystack. She knew that she herself wouldn't have the faintest idea how to get in touch with some of the people she'd known when she was studying in Paris. So what chance had Vince, especially when he didn't speak the language?

Knowing that he'd come after her had been part of the Plan, Imogen reminded herself. She wasn't going to obsess about it. He wouldn't find her. She was safe. She had a job to do. She didn't have time to sit around like a frightened rabbit.

And today was a busy day of house cleaning, which included the Villa Martine. All through the week, as she'd cleaned and polished and brought order to the chaos of the other houses, she'd thought about having to go back there again. The Delissandes brothers hadn't been in touch with René to request a different cleaner as she'd feared they might. Although she was beginning to regret not having told her boss about her childhood years in Hendaye, she still hadn't put him in the picture. It wasn't anything to do with him, after all.

When she finally arrived at the house that afternoon, she hesitated before ringing the bell. There was no reply, so she input the code and pushed the bike through the pedestrian gate. It was clear that the family had gone out, and she was relieved and disappointed in equal measure.

It was strange, she thought, as she started off with the upstairs rooms, that a time that had seemed so special to her was totally trivial to them. The manner of her leaving had been a massive wrench in her life, but it meant nothing to Monsieur, Madame or the boys. They carried on regardless. They came back every year as they'd always done. They went to the beach, played their sports, did their own thing and never needed to think about Carol or Imogen. And now the boys were coming on their own, one of them at least with a wife or girlfriend and a child, making new memories, continually moving on. Which was how it should be.

The bedrooms were surprisingly tidy, and she was able to do them quickly before moving to the bathrooms. She was puzzled to see no personal items in the en suite apart from a squeezed tube of toothpaste sitting on the shelf above the sink. However, there were significantly more toiletries in the main bathroom, where bottles of shaving foam and expensive aftershave vied for space with a selection of men's moisturisers. She studied them with interest. Vince wasn't into the whole male metrosexual thing – he wouldn't dream of moisturising, and although he splashed his face with aftershave, he was ambivalent about the brand. But the Delissandes appeared to like their luxury. Two bottles of Guerlain's L'Instant were placed beside Dior Homme and a Thierry Mugler fragrance, while the moisturisers were Clinique and Moosehead.

She wondered whether it was Oliver or Charles who was married. It was hard to picture either of them as a married man with a child when all she could remember was them chasing her on the beach and playing football in the garden.

But I'm a married woman, she reminded herself, glancing at the bare finger on her left hand. And eventually I'll be a divorced woman. Which surely puts me into the properly grown-up category by now.

When she'd finished with the bathrooms, she moved downstairs again. She dealt with each room quickly and efficiently and was putting away her equipment when a sudden insistent beeping from the utility area caught her attention. She walked in and saw that the washing machine had completed a cycle. They'd obviously decided to start doing their own laundry now that they were here for a while, she thought, as she peered through the door. She supposed she could hang it up for them.

The wash load was mainly bedlinen and towels. Imogen piled it all into the plastic laundry basket beside the machine and then carried it outside. As she pegged the sheets to the line, a waft of lavender-scented conditioner hit her, and she was transported back to the time when she and Charles and Oliver had played at pirates, waving plastic cutlasses and shouting pirate cries at each other as they raced and dodged between the sheets, which they were pretending were the sails of their ships. And then they made me walk the plank, she recalled with a grin. The little shits!

'Hello.'

She spun around, dropping the peg she was about to use to secure the pillowcase in her hand.

'Oliver,' she said as the thudding in her heart at the sound of the English word abated.

'That's right.' He continued speaking in English.

'I hope everything's OK in the house and that you're having a lovely break.'

I sound horribly artificial, she thought, but I really don't know how I'm supposed to be. If we'd grown up in Ireland, there'd probably be a big hugging session, we'd be dying to talk about what's been going on since we last met and it'd be like no time had passed at all, but it's different here.

'It's always lovely to be in our second home,' he said.

'Of course it is.'

'But it's . . . odd to meet you again, Imogen. And like this.'

'Not at all odd,' she said briskly. 'I'm following in my mother's footsteps! Your weekly clean is scheduled for today. Is everyone back from wherever you've been? Did you have a good time?'

'It's just me right now,' he said. 'Charles and Justine went home this morning. Giles and a friend have gone to Bilbao for a few days.'

'So you're Billy no-mates,' said Imogen.

He looked puzzled.

'All alone,' she said. 'Sorry, your English is so good, I expect you to know everything.'

'Not as good as your French,' he said. 'But then after you left us, we didn't get the same practice as before.'

'I'm not sure I was much of an English teacher.' She turned away and continued to hang out the washing.

'Oh, I don't know. I remember lots of things you taught me. Like "get away out of that", which nobody I know really understands.'

She laughed. 'It's an Irish way of saying "you're joking".'

'Ah,' said Oliver. 'I've been using it incorrectly for twenty years! Now it finally makes sense.'

'And how have those twenty years been?' she asked. 'Good, I hope.'

'Up and down,' replied Oliver. 'Like life always is. What about you, Imogen? Have the years been good to you?'

'Up and down,' she repeated with a smile.

'And is it an up or a down that you've come back to Hendaye?' he asked. 'I have to say that I was completely taken aback to see you last week. Neither Charles nor I could believe our eyes. I'm not sure we were exactly polite.'

'It was a shock, I understand,' she said. 'It was a bit of a shock to me too. In my head, I'd begun to believe that you'd sold the house.'

'Giles has asked a million questions about your time with us,' said Oliver. 'He was totally astonished to learn that you lived here.'

'It seems a bit unreal now,' Imogen agreed. 'And yet while I was hanging up the sheets, I was remembering playing pirates with you.'

'Ah yes!' Oliver screwed up his face with the effort of recollection. 'Awash, me hearties!'

'"Avast" is the word, I think,' said Imogen. 'Not that I'm totally up to speed on pirate talk these days.'

'Pirates was fun,' said Oliver.

'Except when you and Charles caught me and insisted on making me walk the plank,' Imogen said.

'The plank . . .' He glanced across the garden to the small swimming pool, then turned back to her with a guilty smile. 'I remember.'

They'd rigged up a sheet of plywood to extend over the water and had made Imogen walk along it. The plywood had bent beneath her weight and she'd fallen in, fully dressed.

'My mother was very angry,' she reminded him. 'It was the third change of clothes for me that day.'

'I'm sorry if we got you into trouble,' he said, although his eyes danced with merriment. 'It's nice to remember those days. Would you like to share a drink with me on the terrace while we reminisce a little more?'

'Oh, I don't think so.' She picked up the laundry basket. 'That was then, this is now. Things have changed, Oliver. I have to get on with my work.'

'How have they changed so that you're back here working for René Bastarache?' he asked. 'And why did you leave us so suddenly in the first place?'

'Your parents didn't say anything to you?'

'Nothing much,' he replied. 'All I remember is that one day you were here and the next you were gone. I was terribly upset. So was Charles.'

Imogen blinked back the tears that had unexpectedly pricked her eyes. She hadn't thought of Oliver and Charles being upset at her disappearance. She'd always supposed they'd been annoyed at her for letting them down over the camp-out in the garden.

'I don't know why you'd be upset,' she said. 'After all, as you told me so many times, I was only a girl.'

'We were teasing you, you must know that!' exclaimed Oliver. 'We were devastated when you went. We'd had such good fun together.'

'We did, didn't we?'

'You were game for anything,' he said. 'Not every girl would have walked that plank, you know.'

'You didn't give me a choice.' But her voice bubbled with laughter.

'Have a drink with me,' said Oliver. 'Let's talk. Please?'

It seemed rude not to, although she was very conscious, as she sat on one of the cushioned chairs, that she had a different status in the house to him.

'So why *did* you leave so abruptly?' he asked, when he'd poured her a citron pressé from the fridge (he'd offered wine, but she told him she didn't want to be drunk in charge of a bicycle, at which he'd snorted and said that it was probably the best way to be in charge of a bicycle, and she'd said yes, someone who drives an Evoque would probably think that, which made him laugh).

'You really don't know?' she said. 'Nobody talked about it?'

He shook his head. '*Maman* said you had to go back to Ireland, that was all.'

'Oh, Oliver . . .' She said nothing for a moment. 'How are your parents?' she asked.

'My parents?' He was surprised at the question. 'They're OK.'

'Is your *maman* still working as an editor? Your dad in the bank?'

'You remember that much?' He raised an eyebrow. 'They're still in the same industries, although they've moved on. From each other as well,' he added.

'They're separated? Divorced?'

'Divorced. A few years after you and your mother left us.'

Imogen grimaced. Carol's affair with Denis had had an impact after all. Oh Mum, she thought. You should never have got involved with him.

'Giles would have been pretty young at the time,' she said.

'Four or five.' Oliver shrugged. 'But it was amicable.'

'Really?'

'They didn't love each other any more.'

'That was the only reason?'

'A pretty good reason, I'd've thought.'

'Yes, yes, of course it is,' she said. 'Have they remarried or anything?'

'*Maman* is in a relationship with a man she's known for the last four years.'

'Is she well?'

'Very,' said Oliver. 'The publishing company she worked with was bought by a larger company, and she's now an editorial director. She sits on the board.'

'Wow.' Imogen was surprised. 'I never would have thought that, to be honest. She always seemed so dreamy and creative to me. I can't imagine her in an office laying down the law.'

'She does it very well,' said Oliver. 'I should know. I work for the same company.'

'You do?'

'In a different division,' he said. 'I don't deal directly with her. But I hear the talk. Firm but fair is what they say.'

'I'm glad she's doing well. And your dad?'

'My dear *papa* is on his third marriage,' said Oliver, a note of exasperation in his voice. 'We hope this one might last, but we're not terribly confident.'

'Why?'

'My father has always taken the view that there is an inherent difference between a wife and a mistress, and that having one shouldn't impact on the other.' Oliver shrugged. 'He's a believer in the *cinq à sept*. You know this?'

'I've heard of it. The time after work when French men are supposed to have their extramarital trysts.'

'Yes,' said Oliver. 'A bit of a cliché, but sadly true as far as my father is concerned. Unfortunately neither my mother nor his second wife was too keen on the idea, although I think *Maman* was more accepting than Elodie.'

'Your father had a *cinq à sept* when he was married to your mother?'

'More than one, I suspect,' said Oliver.

Imogen moistened her lips with a sip of the lemon drink.

'And not just *cinq à sept*,' she said.

'In what way?'

'Oh, Oliver.' She put the glass on the table. 'I'm so, so sorry about it, but my mother and your father had an affair. That's why we left.'

He said nothing for a moment, then nodded slowly.

'I should've guessed. But I was only twelve at the time, and probably a young twelve at that. I didn't think . . . You don't, do you, when you're a kid? I wouldn't have even considered your mother and my father . . .'

'I didn't realise for a long while afterwards,' admitted Imogen. 'I always believed that my mother had been blamed for something that had happened in the house, and your dad had got off scot free. I thought it was horribly unfair.'

'Oh, Genie.' Oliver gave her a sympathetic look.

'I know it sounds daft,' she said. 'Whenever I thought about it, I didn't think of it as an affair, just as something for which Mum had been punished. All the same, she was in the wrong and I spent a lot of time wanting to come back and apologise.'

'You? Apologise? What for?'

'Causing trouble between your mum and your dad.'

'She wasn't the first, or the last.' Oliver's tone was dismissive.

'But your mother was devastated,' said Imogen.

'I'm sure she was angry,' agreed Oliver. 'Devastated . . . I don't know.'

'It was my fault she found out,' said Imogen. 'I told her that your dad had been rubbing my mum's feet. I realised later that that was what had given them away. She must have been so angry and hurt! I don't blame her in the slightest for throwing us out straight away. This was her home. It's not quite the same as having a secret assignation in a hotel.'

'True. But you and your mum suffered the consequences too. That must have been hard.'

'I was very upset,' she admitted. 'It took me a long time to settle in Ireland. For all that Mum kept calling it home, it wasn't home to me.'

'I understand,' said Oliver. 'But everything was OK in the end?'

Imogen told him about Kevin, about Carol's illness and about the eventual move to the UK.

'I'm so sorry,' he said. 'That must have been tough.'

'Losing Mum was hard. Moving was hard. But Kevin is . . . a decent guy.'

'You don't sound convinced.'

'I spent a while not liking him,' said Imogen. 'But for the wrong reasons.'

'And now?' he asked.

'Now I'm here.' She'd skipped over her marriage. She didn't want to talk about Vince.

'But you must have done something else between school and coming to Hendaye.'

'Stuff,' she said. 'Not worth mentioning. Anyway, it's been lovely talking to you, Oliver.' She finished the lemon. 'But I really have to go. I have to report back to René.'

'Can we meet again when you're not busy?' said Oliver. 'It would be great to talk a little more. You're like family, Genie.'

Hearing him use her childhood name so casually was both strange and familiar.

'I'm not family,' she told him. 'Not at all.'

'A distant cousin, perhaps.' His eyes crinkled. 'Someone we don't see any more. But also a person who was a part of our lives. It would be nice to catch up properly.'

She didn't think so. They were worlds apart now. They always had been. But she smiled warmly as she stood up.

'I'm sure we'll bump into each other again,' she said.

'I hope so.' He got up too and walked with her to the front of the house, where she'd propped the pink bicycle against the wall. 'Love the bike.'

She smiled and explained about it being Céline's.

'Is divorce really more civilised in France?' she asked as she got ready to cycle away. 'Or does everyone just think it is?'

'Thankfully I've yet to be divorced,' said Oliver. 'So I can't tell.'

'You're the married one?' she asked.

'Not me,' he said. 'Marriage and divorce are experiences that have been closed to me so far.'

'But girlfriends?' She didn't think he was gay, but it was always possible.

'Of course girlfriends!' He sounded slightly affronted. 'None right now, though, which suits me as I'm too busy for them.'

'At this publishing company with your mother?'

'I'm an editor,' he said. 'I came here for some peace and quiet while I work on a complicated novel. Also I'll be meeting a new author who lives in San Sebastian and who's written a brilliant book about life in the Basque country sixty years ago. It's going to be a massive seller. So better to be free of entanglements.' He grinned. 'Unless an opportunity presents itself to me. I'm my father's son after all.'

She looked slightly shocked. 'You'd have an affair?'

'I've only ever had one,' he told her. 'And it wasn't all it was cracked up to be. I prefer not to skulk around in the shadows. No, *ma petite*, I meant if while I was at the Villa Martine I met a beautiful girl, then I might be persuaded to put the work away for an afternoon.'

'There are plenty of beautiful girls on the beach,' she acknowledged as, with a quick *au revoir*, she swung herself on to the saddle and pedalled away.

She brought her schedule and the keys back to René, who glanced at the clock on the wall.

'You're late,' he said. 'Any problems?'

She shook her head. 'Oliver Delissandes delayed me. We were talking for a while.'

'He is happy with our service?'

'I think so,' said Imogen.

'I'm always anxious when we have a long-term client and they see that the cleaner is different from year to year,' said René. 'I don't want them to worry about the security of their homes.'

'Oliver . . . Monsieur Delissandes didn't say anything about being worried,' Imogen told him.

'Good.'

'I'll be off,' she said. 'Have a nice weekend.'

'Are you coming to the beach barbecue on Sunday?' he asked.

'I didn't know about it,' she said.

'It's part of the summer festival,' he said. 'Open to everyone, but you must buy a ticket for food. You can get one at any of the shops.'

'I'll think about it.' She put her bag over her shoulder. 'If not, I'll see you Monday.'

'*A bientôt,*' said René.

She left the bike at the office and strolled back to the apartment. There was a spring in her step and a lightness about her spirit that she hadn't known for a long time; she could feel it almost as if a physical weight had been lifted from her. Perhaps it was because she'd apologised to Oliver. It wasn't quite the scenario she'd imagined when she'd envisaged coming back with Carol, but it had been cathartic all the same. Yet she couldn't help thinking that over the years she'd built it into something far bigger than it actually was. 'Drama queen,' she murmured as she let herself into her apartment. Shona was probably right about that.

She changed into her swimsuit and did a few lengths of the pool before stretching out on one of the sun loungers. Max Gasquet, the young intern whom she'd spoken to previously but hadn't seen since, arrived a few minutes later and began doing lengths too.

'Are you going to the barbecue at the beach on Sunday?' he asked as he towelled dry afterwards.

'You're the second person who's mentioned it to me,' she said. 'Is it a big deal?'

'Lots of people go,' he replied. 'It's fun.'

'I like the idea of fun,' she said.

'Perhaps I'll see you there.' He gave her a brief smile and walked back to the apartment building.

She was ready to have fun, she thought. She'd already started on it by playing in the boules tournament. And by ignoring all the rules that had dominated her life over the past five years. With each passing day she was beginning to see how tightly they'd bound her, and she was becoming more and more horrified at how long she'd accepted them. She wished she understood how it was that Vince had managed to control her like that. It seemed extraordinary to her now that she hadn't seen it happening, hadn't reacted sooner. How following the line of least resistance had seemed normal.

'I'm so glad I made the Plan,' she said out loud. 'And even gladder that I followed it.'

She got up from the lounger and went inside. She poured herself a glass of wine and curled up on the small sofa. She felt at home. And after talking to Oliver Delissandes, she felt liberated too. Denis had been serially unfaithful, so his affair with Carol hadn't been the sole problem in a marriage that Imogen had always thought was idyllic. It hadn't helped, of course, but her mother wasn't totally to blame for later events.

Marriages, she thought, as she sipped the wine and stared into the distance. Far more complicated than anyone outside them would ever know. And maybe far more trouble than they were worth.

Chapter 26

When Vince returned to the hotel, he set about finding out if any of the staff remembered Imogen and knew where she'd planned to go after checking out. In the movies, it was a relatively simple task to accost a receptionist or bellboy and get information, but real life was different. Everyone refused to talk to him until finally the duty manager came to meet him.

'She's my wife,' Vince told the sceptical man, who towered over him. 'She's missing.'

'The police have not been here about a missing woman,' said the manager.

'It's not a police matter.' Vince wasn't going to go into explanations. 'Nevertheless, I need to find her.'

'I'm afraid I cannot help you.'

'Yes you damn well can.' Vince thrust his phone with Imogen's photo in front of him and told him the dates she'd stayed. 'All I want is to check your reservations and talk to your staff and see if she said anything about where she was going after she left.'

'There would be no record of her movements after she left the hotel.' Despite himself, the manager was looking at the photograph. 'She is very pretty, your wife.'

'I know.'

'Could it be . . .' the manager gave an imperceptible shrug, 'an affair of the heart?'

'No,' said Vince. 'It isn't. Now are you going to help me or not?'

The manager sighed and began tapping at one of the computer terminals.

'We do not have a reservation for Madame Naughton,' he said.

'Try her company,' suggested Vince. 'Chandon Leclerc.'

The manager tapped at the keyboard again.

'We have a Monsieur Foley and a Madame Weir,' he said.

'Of course she would have used her own name.' Vince nodded slowly. 'She hadn't changed it on her passport.'

'I am sorry,' said the manager. 'I have no further information for you other than that she checked out on the morning of her departure.'

'Did she come back here later that day?' asked Vince.

'There is no way for us to tell.'

'Are any of the staff who were there that day here now? They might remember.'

The manager looked around and his eyes stopped at the concierge. He waved him over and explained the situation to him.

'I remember her,' said the concierge. 'Hard to forget a face like that. Although I think she was wearing her hair differently.'

'Differently how?' demanded Vince.

'A little shorter.'

'And did she ask you for any information? About other hotels? Other cities?'

The concierge frowned at Vince's abrupt tone.

'I cannot say, Monsieur.'

'You can't say or you won't say?' asked Vince.

'There's no need to be aggressive with me,' said the concierge.

'I'm sorry.' Vince took a deep breath. 'I'm worried, that's all.'

The concierge looked at him intently.

'Madame took a bus,' he said after a moment. 'There is a stop nearby.'

'Where to?'

'There are a number of destinations,' said the concierge. 'But I believe she said something about Montpellier.'

'Montpellier? Where the hell is that?'

'It is in the Languedoc region,' said the manager.

'That means nothing to me,' said Vince. 'Is it near Marseille, by any chance?'

'A couple of hours along the coast,' replied the concierge.

'How long to get to Montpellier from here?' asked Vince.

'Driving or by train?'

'Train.'

The concierge took out an iPad and began searching.

'There is a train in half an hour,' he said. 'It leaves from the Gare de Lyon and takes approximately three and a half hours.'

'Where's the Gare de Lyon?'

'Not far. Ten minutes in the Métro. Or we can call a cab for you.'

'A cab,' said Vince. 'It seems I'll be spending enough time already on public transport. Did my wife mention anything about where she'd be in Montpellier?'

The concierge shook his head. 'I'm afraid not.'

'Well, thanks for your help.' Vince extended his hand and the concierge shook it. He walked outside with Vince and hailed him a cab. When it pulled away, he went back inside again.

'I'm not happy that we gave him that information,' said the manager. 'There's something about that man I don't like. I'm not sure Madame will be pleased to see her husband.'

'The information was accurate,' said the concierge. 'But I doubt very much that he'll find her in Montpellier.'

'Why?'

'Because although she asked me about it, I saw her heading in the opposite direction. And I'm pretty sure she had no intention of taking that bus at all.'

Vince was keeping a record of how much money he was spending in trying to find Imogen. He planned to present it to her when he eventually caught up with her. His initial plan had been to tell her that her housekeeping budget was being reduced in order to pay it all back, but of course that would affect him as much as her. Nevertheless, she would have to atone for her actions somehow. He gritted his teeth as he boarded the train. How many other husbands would put in so much time and effort trying to find their missing wife? he wondered. How many others would go through what he was going through to bring the woman they loved home again?

It was while the train was speeding through the French countryside that he considered his destination. He wished he'd listened more attentively on the occasions Imogen had spoken about France. The more he racked his brains, the more certain he was that she'd never mentioned Montpellier in all the time she'd lived with him. It had always been Provence. And . . . he frowned with the effort of remembering . . . a throwaway comment or two about the 'time after Provence'. But nothing specific. So Montpellier might have been 'after Provence'. Yet more and more he was beginning to feel that he'd been sent on a wild goose chase. And he didn't know if that was because of Imogen, or the concierge at the Paris hotel.

It was early evening when he finally arrived. He booked himself into a relatively inexpensive hotel near the station and his heart sank as he looked at the view from his fifth-floor window. He'd imagined that Montpellier would be small and charming, somewhere it would be easy enough to find someone. But even if the old town had character (and he hadn't had time to find that out yet), it was still a far bigger place than he'd expected, and he couldn't see how on earth he was going to find Imogen. At least in Paris he'd had somewhere to start. Here there was nothing. Looking at the information booklet in the room, he could see that there were lots of smaller towns along the coastline between Montpellier and Marseille. She could have gone to any of them. Or, as he'd originally thought, to Marseille to find her childhood home.

The more he thought about it, the more likely that option seemed. She'd deliberately mentioned Montpellier at the hotel to put him off the scent. He almost admired her for it. But she needn't think she could fool him. She wasn't that smart. And he wasn't that stupid.

Vince was annoyed at having been sidetracked to Montpellier, but he still didn't leave before checking with the local police.

They looked at him in astonishment when he asked about Imogen, but the only thing they were able to tell him was that his wife hadn't turned up as an unknown person. He gave them a perfunctory nod of thanks before turning his attention to the train timetable. He was pleased to discover that there was a train to Marseille in fifteen minutes, and was suddenly quite convinced that he would find Imogen there. Or some trace of her at least. She'd thought she could simply walk away from everything. But she couldn't. And he was going to make sure of it.

An hour after arriving in Marseille and checking in at the hotel he'd reserved on the train by phone, Vince was sitting in one of the multitude of cafés at the old port, watching the tourists walk by. He'd never been much for sightseeing himself – the way he looked at it, when you'd seen one old castle you'd seen them all – but the motley crew of tourists all seemed to be on their way somewhere or coming back from somewhere, and a babble of languages floated towards him as he drank his beer.

Even though he was perspiring beneath the canopy of the café he'd chosen, he was enjoying the atmosphere. The sky was clear and the water the deepest blue. Boats were bobbing at their moorings while owners tried to tempt the chattering tourists into trips to the Château d'If. It was noisy and colourful, and he had a sudden image of Imogen strolling along the pedestrian streets wearing the boho-chic clothes she'd always chosen before he'd met her. More appropriate for a Mediterranean location, he thought, than Dublin's greyer streets. He'd been right to change her. She should be grateful to him.

He pictured her sitting in the garden of one of the pretty whitewashed houses overlooking the sea, feeling secure in the knowledge that it was too difficult for him to track her down. But she hadn't counted on his determination, thought Vince as he began to study the brochures and leaflets he'd taken from the hotel. She hadn't counted on the fact that he was prepared to do whatever it took to find her. And that he was going to scour France until he did.

Chapter 27

It was the hottest day of the year, and even though it was early in the evening, the beach at Hendaye was thronged with people. Imogen didn't know how on earth she was going to find René or anyone else she knew among the crowds, but as she walked along the shore, she was spotted by Nellie and Becky, the Australian sisters from the apartment next door. She hadn't seen much of them over the last couple of weeks, and she'd half thought that they might have moved on.

'We're heading off soon,' said Becky. 'We would have been gone already except Nellie pulled a muscle in her back and couldn't get on her bike without screaming.'

'Are you OK now?' asked Imogen.

'Nearly,' said Nellie. 'Of course I've been helped by the hunky Dr Max from number one. He gave me some stonkingly good painkillers. Have you met him?'

Imogen nodded.

'I could almost stay here just for him,' said Nellie.

Imogen laughed and then gave an exclamation of surprise as, against the odds, she spotted René walking along the beach. She waved at him.

'Do you want to come to the kiosk to pick up your free soft drink?' he asked when he reached them. 'And did you buy your ticket for the barbecue?'

'No,' she said. 'I wasn't sure I'd be coming.'

'I'll get a ticket for you,' said René.

'There's no need . . .'

But he dismissed her objections and strode towards a beach hut with a little blue flag on it, after telling the girls to get their drinks and stake out a spot on the beach.

'I didn't realise you knew the rental agent so well,' said Becky.

'I've ended up working for him,' Imogen told her.

'Really? He's kinda cute,' Nellie said.

'Not my type,' Imogen assured her. 'Plus I work for his ex-wife too.'

'You haven't been here very long but you seem to know everyone already,' said Becky in admiration.

'Only them,' said Imogen. 'Do you want me to go and get those drinks?'

'Let me,' said Nellie. 'I need to keep moving so that my back doesn't seize up. You and Becky make yourselves comfortable. Our towels are over there.' She indicated a spot where two brightly coloured towels were laid beneath a wide beach umbrella. 'Flop down, save our space and I'll be back shortly.'

Becky and Imogen did as she said and were opening their bottles of juice when René joined them twenty minutes later.

'I was beginning to think you'd got lost,' said Imogen.

'There was a queue for tickets,' René said.

'I'm so sorry I didn't get one sooner,' said Imogen. 'How much do I owe you?'

'Nothing,' said René.

'Please let me pay for my own ticket.' She took her purse from her bag.

'Five euros, if you must,' he said.

'Is that all?'

He nodded and she handed him the money. As he put the note in his pocket, she saw Oliver Delissandes walking along the beach. He was wearing navy swimming shorts and a pair of Ray-Bans and had a pair of expensive-looking headphones over his ears.

'Wow,' said Becky, who had followed her glance. 'He's hot.'

'Who? Oh, him.' René caught sight of Oliver. 'He's a client. Nice guy.'

As if he'd heard them talking about him, Oliver glanced in their direction. René waved to attract his attention and Oliver trudged through the sand towards them, sliding the earphones from his head as he arrived.

René did the introductions in English, although when he got to Imogen, Oliver said that they'd already met at the house.

'Of course,' said René. 'I forgot.'

'I never thought I'd meet Imogen again,' Oliver said. 'It was a bit of a shock.'

'I don't think it's a shock to meet anyone on the beach today.' René gave him a puzzled look.

'No, I meant at the house.'

'You're talking at cross-purposes,' said Imogen.

'Cross-purposes?' This time it was Oliver who looked puzzled.

'About different things. Look, it's not important.' She spoke quickly, not wanting him and René to get into a discussion about her. 'Have the rest of the family returned to the Villa Martine yet?'

'Not yet,' he said. 'Although Giles is due back next Sunday. We don't have the same sort of family breaks as we did in the past.'

'But it's nice to have the house all the same.' Imogen didn't want him talking about the past either. 'Are you staying for the barbecue?'

'I hadn't really thought . . .'

'You need a ticket for the food,' said René. 'There's a twenty-minute queue.'

'That's not so bad,' said Oliver. 'Especially if . . . Will you queue with me, Imogen?'

'I—'

Nellie broke into a guffaw. 'That's a good one,' she chortled. 'René queues for Imogen but Imogen queues with the hot man.'

'Pardon?' Oliver looked at her enquiringly.

'Never mind,' said René. 'Go with him if you want, Imogen. I'll disport myself with the girls.'

Imogen looked at him for a moment.

'Go,' said René. 'You're cramping my style.' He winked at Becky, who laughed.

'You're incorrigible.' Imogen grinned, and followed Oliver towards the large tent where the tickets were being sold.

' I like Bastarache. He's a good man,' he remarked as they joined the end of the queue.

'He's been great to me. I love him to bits.'

Oliver raised an eyebrow.

'Not literally,' Imogen said. 'It's just an expression.'

His face cleared.

'How's the editing coming along?' she asked suddenly.

'Very well,' said Oliver. 'It's a pleasure to work on the book. I will give you a proof copy when it's ready.'

'But that won't be for ages, will it?'

'A couple of months,' said Oliver.

'I don't think I'll be here in a couple of months.'

'Why? Where do you plan to go?'

The two of them shuffled forward in the queue.

'I haven't made plans yet,' said Imogen. 'But I'm sure there won't be as much work for me in the winter.'

'Probably not,' agreed Oliver. 'Nevertheless, we have our home maintained all year round. I'm sure other people do too.'

'Well, yes. All the same, I don't know that I'll stay.'

'Will you stay in France or go back to Ireland?'

'I don't know that either,' she said.

'I hope you stay long enough to meet my mother again.'

'Oh no.' She shook her head. 'I don't think that would be a good idea.'

'Why?'

'Well . . . I don't think she would want to see me. Not after my mum betraying her with your dad.'

'Don't be absurd.' Oliver's tone was dismissive. 'She has a man in her life, remember?'

'Even so.' Imogen looked him straight in the eye. 'It was a horrible time for her. To find out that her husband and someone she trusted were shagging each other senseless in her house . . .'

'Shagging each other senseless?' He raised an eyebrow.

'You can guess what that means,' she said. 'Anyhow, it would be horrible for her to meet me.'

'Don't be silly,' said Oliver. 'She'd love to see you. She did speak a little of you after you left. She hoped that you – and your *maman* – were all right. Perhaps she regretted asking you to leave.'

'It was perfectly understandable that she threw us out,' said Imogen. 'If I discovered that my husband was bonking the hired help in my own house, he'd be out on his ear without a moment's thought.'

Oliver took a moment to process the sentence. 'I understand what you're saying – I think,' he said. 'But it was different for *Maman* and *Papa*. And you have to remember that there had been lots of *affaires*.'

'I don't care.' Imogen sounded mutinous. 'You don't shit on your own doorstep.'

'Ah, I know that one.'

'It wasn't me who taught it to you,' said Imogen.

'You're still angry with your *maman*, aren't you?'

'Yes,' admitted Imogen. 'If she hadn't been so stupid, we might have stayed here and she wouldn't have met Kevin and I wouldn't have been hauled off to Birmingham and I wouldn't have come home and everything would have been OK.'

'Are you trying to say that everything is not OK at the moment?'

They were almost at the head of the queue now.

'Only sometimes,' she told him with a sudden smile. 'Only if I forget to look on the bright side.'

When they returned with Oliver's ticket, they found that Max had joined Becky, Nellie and René and had brought a large cool bag of beer and soft drinks with him.

'Some of the people from the hospital will be along later,' he said. 'We can keep replenishing the bag.'

'Excellent idea,' said René.

Over the next hour, their group expanded with the arrival of a collection of nurses, doctors and administrators as well as Céline and Art. Imogen found herself chatting to people she'd never met before, while the Australian girls happily divided their attention between Max and René. Meanwhile Oliver was talking to one of the nurses, a flaming redhead wearing a cropped top and skimpy shorts, who seemed to be finding everything he said hilariously funny, as she was laughing a lot and squeezing his arm playfully.

'Reminds me of home,' Becky said to Imogen as she loaded a plate with chicken wings. 'Though we don't see these sunsets on the east coast.'

The sun was sliding slowly beneath the horizon, painting the sky and the sea in shades of pink and gold.

'It's spectacular,' agreed René. 'I never get tired of it.'

'Me neither,' said Céline. 'We're lucky to live here.'

'Absolutely.' Art's arm was no longer in a sling, and he slid it around Céline's waist. Imogen noticed René's expression harden and she wondered if he still cared for his ex-wife. But then he turned back to chat with Becky and Nellie and ignored Céline altogether.

By the early hours of the morning, Imogen was starting to feel tired. Although the party was still going strong, a number of people had drifted away, and she decided to go home too.

'We'll head back with you,' said Becky.

'I'll come too,' said René. 'To make sure you get home OK.'

'No need.' It was Max who spoke. 'I'll be with them, René. They'll be safe in my hands.'

'Maybe I was thinking that they needed to be safe *from* your hands,' he said.

'Everyone knows that my hands are perfectly safe,' Max joked as he stretched his arms out in front of him. 'They've held a scalpel without shaking.'

'Ugh,' said Becky as René made a face.

Imogen stood up and gave him a goodnight kiss on the cheek. She did the same for Céline and Art, then looked around for Oliver. He was deep in conversation with the red-headed nurse again. She wasn't sure if she should disturb them, but then he looked up and saw her.

'Going so soon?' he asked.

'Soon?' she laughed. 'It's after midnight.'

'The night is young.' He grinned at her.

'Not for me it isn't.'

'But we haven't had time to talk.'

'You've been otherwise occupied.' Imogen's glance slid towards the redhead, who was lying on a beach mat looking up at the starry sky.

'Virginie and I go back years,' he said.

'As far as us?' The words were out of her mouth before she could stop them.

'Nobody goes back that far,' he said in amusement.

'I've got to go.' She nodded towards Becky, Nellie and Max, who were waiting for her. 'I'll see you when I come to do your house.'

'OK,' he said. 'See you.'

She turned away and joined the others. But she wondered how long Oliver would stay at the party. And if Virginie would be with him when it ended.

Chapter 28

Vince was conscious that he was running out of time to find Imogen. He was due back at work at the end of the week and he was still no further forward in locating her. He'd begun to get so frustrated at his lack of success that he frequently asked himself if he wanted her back at all. But he wasn't going to give her the satisfaction of defeating him.

The concierge at his hotel in Marseille had never heard of of the Maison Lavande, but suggested going to the town hall, where someone might be able to give him information. They know everything about everybody at the town hall, he said, a little sourly.

Vince had walked past the elegant seventeenth-century building that housed the town hall a number of times already, although despite the French tricolour and the EU flag hanging outside, he hadn't realised what it was. Inside, it reminded him of every government building he'd ever been in, with its quietly bureaucratic air. An employee told him that he would have to make an appointment to see one of her colleagues, and when Vince suggested that he'd come back later that afternoon, she'd looked at him as though he was an alien with ten heads, and told him that the earliest he could see anybody was the following week. Vince snorted and insisted on speaking right now to someone with better English than her. After a wait of about forty minutes, a man of around Vince's own age appeared and told him in precise and faultless English that he would have to make an appointment.

'For crying out loud!' Vince exploded. 'All I want to know is if this damn B&B still exists, and if so, where it is. And if it's still being run by someone in the Fournier family. That's not too much to ask, is it?'

'We will have to check the records,' said the man smoothly. 'That takes time.'

'But not a bloody week!'

'We have other things to do,' the official said. 'It is the tourist season and we are busy. Also, people from the office are on vacation.'

'I'm trying to find my missing wife.' Vince waved the photo of Imogen and Madame Fournier in front of him. 'Doesn't that mean anything to you people?'

'If you are looking for a missing peson you should be talking to the police.'

Vince stared at him. 'Is it a case of money, is that how it works? Because I'll pay—'

'Are you trying to bribe me?'' The official looked startled.

'If that's what it takes. I want the information. There's no point in my going to the police. It's not like that.'

'You cannot bribe an official.' The man looked at him grimly.

'OK, maybe I was out of line there. But the thing is, my wife is missing and I need to find her.'

The official regarded him thoughtfully for a moment, then held out his hand for the photograph. He studied it intently then returned it to Vince.

'I cannot say for certain where that was taken,' he told him. 'It could be anywhere along the coast. Although it looks to me more like Toulon than Marseille.'

'How far away is Toulon?'

'Less than an hour by car,' replied the official.

'If I check it out, can you find out for me about the Maison Lavande and the owner, Madame Fournier, by this afternoon?'

The official looked at him in disbelief. 'We will be closed before you get back,' he said. 'Return on Thursday and ask for me. Marcel Royale. I will try to have some information for you.'

'Thursday!' exclaimed Vince. 'But that means hanging around here for a few days.'

'Where better to stay than our beautiful city! Or you can take a trip along the Côte d'Azur.'

'This is a bloody scam,' said Vince.

Marcel frowned. 'I'm sorry?'

'Oh, for God's sake! What time on Thursday?'

'Eleven am,' he replied. 'Hopefully I will be able to help you then.'

'Thanks,' said Vince.

He turned on his heel and walked out into the brilliant sunshine. He was seething. It was beyond doubt, he thought, that all they had to do in the town hall was click on a few records to find out about the bloody Maison Lavande, but they couldn't be arsed to do it. As for being busy – well, it hadn't looked busy to him. Government offices, no matter what the country, never did.

He went into a bar that offered free Wi-Fi and ordered a small beer while he took out his phone and searched for Toulon on Google Maps. According to the map, it was sixty-five kilometres from his current location, so he supposed it would be an easy enough job to check it out. He'd hire a car, he thought. He was fed up with trains, no matter how good they were. When he'd finished the beer, he turned back towards the town and went into a car hire agency that he'd noticed earlier near his hotel.

The selection was limited but he managed to obtain a Renault Mégane with sat nav, which he drove carefully along the Quai du Port before turning on to the motorway. It was a pleasant enough drive, he conceded, the French roads being as good as the French railway system. Fifty minutes after setting out, the disembodied female voice of the sat nav told him he had reached his destination, and he pulled into the first available parking space he could find.

He got out and made his way towards the seafront, holding the photograph in front of him and checking it against the houses he saw as he walked. But there was nothing even vaguely resembling the building in the photo, and Vince began to think that Marcel Royale had deliberately misled him. But he might as well be chasing shadows here as in Marseille, he thought. The damn house could be anywhere. And so could Imogen.

He didn't find any clues in Toulon, nor in the other small towns he visited along the coast over the next couple of days. His last stop was Cannes, where he remembered Imogen saying she'd stayed with a friend when she'd been a student in Paris. He had no idea where the friend had lived, but he held out a vague hope that he might simply bump into his errant wife walking along the Croisette.

The colourful streets were busy, but there was no sign of her. It looked like he was going to have to depend on Marcel Royale in the town hall in Marseille to come up with something to point him in the right direction. He couldn't believe Imogen was hiding herself so successfully. He refused to believe that she could evade him for ever.

He sat at yet another quayside bar, ordered a coffee and rang Shona. He thought his wife's friend sounded guarded.

'She's been in touch, hasn't she?' he said. 'I thought as much before.'

'Not at all.' But there was no conviction in Shona's voice.

'Has she sent you a text? An email? You know, Shona, you're not helping her by keeping stuff from me.'

'OK. OK. She phoned me to say she was safe and well,' admitted Shona.

'When?'

'A little while ago.'

'And you didn't tell me?'

'She asked me not to.'

Vince's grip tightened around his phone.

'Did she say where she was?'

'No.'

'Are you sure?'

'Yes.'

'What's her number, Shona?'

'I don't know. The caller ID was blocked.'

'What about her email address?'

'What about it?'

'She's changed it, hasn't she?'

'I don't . . . Why would you think that?'

'I just know.'

'I . . .'

'I've sent her emails. She hasn't replied.'

'It was the same with me until she phoned,' said Shona.

'Why did she phone?'

'I told you. To say she was all right.'

'How did she sound?'

'Fine,' said Shona. 'A bit . . . a bit reticent, I suppose.'

'Why didn't you tell me?'

'What good would it have done?' said Shona. 'I don't know where she is, Vince. Honestly.'

'Did you tell her I was in France?'

'Um . . .'

'You did, didn't you?'

'I had to,' said Shona.

'You realise you might have messed it all up for me?'

'We weren't talking for very long.'

'She must have given you some clue about where she is,' said Vince. 'Listen to me, Shona. I understand that you're on her side. Of course you are. You're friends and you want to believe her. But you're on my side too because you know that all I want is for Imogen to be OK. And when I find her, if she doesn't want to come home, that'll be fine. All I want is to be sure that nothing awful has happened to her.'

'She seemed happy enough to me.'

'She's good at putting up a front,' said Vince. 'You don't know her as well as I do, Shona. She has issues.'

'I rather got the impression that you were the issue,' Shona told him.

'I'm not going to deny there have been some bumps in

our relationship,' Vince said. 'But deep down she knows I love her. My main concern now is for her health and her happiness.'

'She didn't say a word about where she was. Honestly,' said Shona. 'But I promise faithfully I'll let you know if she rings again. I want to do what's best.'

'What's best for Imogen right now is to come home with me and get some help,' Vince said. 'I appreciate what you've said, Shona, and I promise you that I won't do anything to upset her.'

'OK,' said Shona.

'Keep in touch.'

Vince ended the call and looked out over the water as he tried to bring his anger under control. Bloody women, he thought. He'd known that eventually Imogen would cave in and ring Shona. If he'd been with her when she'd got the call, he could have sorted it there and then. Imogen wouldn't have been able to keep her location a secret from him. In fact, she would have been begging him to come and get her. As it was, he couldn't be entirely sure he'd managed to get Shona on side again, but at least she'd promised to phone if Imogen got in touch with her. It was a pity, really, that he hadn't brought Shona along with him. If she were sitting in front of him right now, he knew he'd be able to wheedle any information she had out of her, but it was considerably more difficult over the phone.

He waved at the proprietor and asked for a menu. At least the hoteliers and bar owners in this part of the country were less snooty than their Parisian counterparts, he thought, as he ordered a steak and a half-bottle of red wine. Which was one small mercy.

* * *

By the time he returned to Marseille and his appointment with the town hall official, he was fed up with France and everything French, even if he'd finally managed to persuade them that when he asked for well-done meat, that was exactly what he wanted. He wasn't in the mood to take any crap from Marcel Royale, who'd be looking at a damn scene if he didn't have any information for him.

At least it was promising that he'd only been kept waiting for ten minutes, he thought, before he was brought into a small, impersonal office where the civil servant was waiting for him.

'Mr Naughton,' he said, making a reasonable attempt at the pronunciation of Vince's name. 'It's good to see you again.'

'It is?' Vince's tone was sceptical.

'It's always good to have visitors in our beautiful city,' said Marcel. 'I hope you've enjoyed your stay and managed to see some of the other towns too.'

Had the whole come-back-on-Thursday thing been a ploy to keep him spending money in the south of France? Vince wondered. It wouldn't have surprised him.

'I have some information for you,' said Marcel. He picked up a sheet of paper and looked at it.

'The Maison Lavande was a chambre d'hôte residence on the Rue Florette, about ten kilometres outside the town,' he said. 'It was in the Fournier family for nearly fifty years, and then was sold to the Benoits. It remained as the Maison Lavande until it was sold again three years ago, this time to an English couple named Johnson. It is still run as a chambre d'hôte but is now called La Vie en Rose.' He smiled slightly. 'The English have romantic ideas about running businesses in this country, but it seems that it is doing quite well.' He pushed the paper towards Vince. 'I hope this helps you.'

Vince glanced at it, although as it was in French, all he understood were the names that Marcel had read out to him.

'This is the address?' He pointed to the words Rue Florette.

'Yes,' said Marcel. 'It's off the Avenue du Prado.'

'Thank you.' Vince stood up.

'I hope you find your wife,' said Marcel.

'So do I.'

'But sometimes . . .' He sighed. 'Sometimes the bird flies away, no? And we have to accept it.'

'My wife hasn't flown away,' said Vince. 'She wants to come home. She just doesn't know it.'

Marcel Royale looked at him thoughtfully and extended his hand.

'Good luck,' he said

'Thanks.' Vince shook the man's hand, then walked out of the office and the building.

The sat nav guided him effortlessly to the Rue Florette, a narrow tree-lined street with an air of faded gentility and detached houses behind tile-capped walls. It wasn't what he had been expecting. Whenever Imogen had spoken about the Maison Lavande, she'd talked about a big house with lots of open space. He'd visualised it as being out on its own, not in a residential area. But perhaps there was space behind the walls, Vince thought as he parked the car, although it was equally likely that his wife's memory was faulty.

He walked along the street, looking at the numbers of the houses and assuming there'd be something to identify the Maison Lavande, or La Vie en Rose as it now was. Bloody stupid name. Even the French official had thought so. He was halfway along when he saw it, a two-storey house with a terracotta tiled roof, set behind dark green double gates. A tiled plaque with the name painted on it in pink was attached to the pillar beside the gate, and a tumble of bougainvillea arched over the walls. A bronze bell hung from the pillar too, but there was also a modern intercom system and Vince pressed the button.

Nobody answered, but the gates slid open and he stepped inside. The garden was beautifully tended and the house itself had clearly been recently renovated. The shutters were painted dark green to match both the gates and the Juliet balconies outside the upstairs windows, while potted plants and the bougainvillea were vivid splashes of colour against the green and the sand-coloured walls.

The front door was made of glass and was propped open. Vince walked into the entrance hall, where a petite blonde woman stood behind a small desk.

'*Bonjour*,' she said, and immediately switched to English when he said hello in response. 'Can I help you?'

'Are you Mrs Belinda Johnson?' asked Vince.

'Yes.'

'Then you can. I'm trying to find out about the previous owners of this house.'

Belinda Johnson looked at him with a startled expression.

'My wife lived here as a kid,' said Vince. 'I'm trying to help her rediscover her past.'

'Oh.' Belinda peered past him.

'She's not here,' Vince said. 'I'm doing this to surprise her.'

'Oh,' said Belinda again.

'So what I want to know is what happened to Mrs Fournier who used to own the house.'

'I'm sorry,' said Belinda. 'You've caught me completely unawares. You are . . . ?'

'My name is Vince Naughton,' said Vince. 'My wife's name is Imogen. Imogen Weir.' He frowned as he said Imogen's maiden name. 'She lived here when she was younger.'

Belinda, who'd been looking at him with a degree of suspicion, suddenly smiled. 'Weir . . . Weir. I think I know the name,' she said. 'But can you give me a moment? I was dealing with a guest query when you rang the bell. Why don't you sit on the patio and I'll join you shortly.' She waved in the direction of the back of the house, and Vince, after a moment's hesitation, went outside.

The garden was beautiful. Slender trees and box shrubs, as well as still more potted plants, were set around a fountain, which shot a spray of water high into the air, making a rainbow of light in the noonday sun. Chairs and loungers, some occupied by guests, were arranged beneath green parasols. Vince sat beneath one himself and waited until Belinda Johnson came out of the house carrying a large ledger and a small photo album.

'Sorry about that,' she said. 'Now, tell me what you want to know.'

Vince repeated the story about wanting to find out about Imogen's past, a story that he'd decided would be perfect for the English owners of the guest house. And he was right, because Belinda was only too keen to help him.

'I did recognise the name but I don't have very much information, I'm afraid,' she said. 'We bought from a French couple a few years ago. The place needed a lot of upgrading, so we practically gutted it, although we tried to retain its original charm.' She paused, and it was only when she started speaking again that Vince realised he was supposed to have congratulated her on doing just that. 'Our guests are very happy,' she continued. 'We have a lot of repeat business.'

'I'm not surprised.' Better late than never to stroke her ego, he thought. 'You've done a great job. The house is lovely, and so are the gardens.'

She beamed at him. 'Thank you. The old garden was full of mismatched styles and overrun by lavender. We ripped out most of it and decided a change of name was in order.'

'Good idea,' said Vince.

'But in all the renovations, we did find this.' She handed him the ledger. 'It's a guest book from nearly thirty years ago. And here are some photos we found too.'

Vince opened the ledger. Some photographs had been pasted on the inside cover, with inscriptions underneath. The first was of an elderly woman with grey hair coiled in a plaited bun on her head. It was captioned *Jeanne Fournier, propriétaire, Maison Lavande*. Beneath were photos of Agnes and Berthe; although they were much younger, Vince recognised them from the day of his wedding to Imogen. Below their photos were two more. One of Carol Weir, smiling at the camera as she leaned on a broom handle, and another of Imogen as a baby, sitting on a rug in the garden clapping her hands.

'Isn't it lovely?' Belinda beamed. 'We keep it here for guests to look at because we have some people who come back year after year and their parents or grandparents visited the Maison Lavande in the past. Of course we don't have a guest book now – it's all website comments and TripAdvisor. But this is a lovely keepsake. Maybe the photo album will help you a little more.'

Vince turned the first page. Most of the photographs were of people he didn't know, but there were a few more of Agnes, Berthe and Carol, and half a dozen of Imogen as a toddler and a young child. It was a weird sensation looking at her doing handstands in the garden, unaware of her future.

'My wife would love these,' he said.

'Aren't you going to bring her here?' asked Belinda. 'We'd be delighted to have you both as our guests. Where is she now?'

'Visiting other friends,' said Vince. 'As I said, I'm doing this as a surprise for her. However, I was thinking about somewhere to stay for this evening, so if you're not fully booked . . .'

'Actually we're not.' Belinda beamed at him. 'We had an unexpected cancellation this morning, so I have a vacant room for two nights. If you and Imogen want to stay, you'd be more than welcome.'

'She's overnighting with her friends,' said Vince. 'But I'll take you up on the offer, for tonight at any rate. And I know she'll be very excited when I tell her about this. She didn't remember where the house was and she's lost touch with the other people . . .'

'It's such a shame when that happens,' said Belinda. 'I wish I could tell you where they are, but I'm afraid I've no idea.'

'Agnes and Berthe are in the States and unwell now, so I can't really talk to them,' said Vince. 'What I was trying to do was find out where my wife and her mother moved after the house was sold. Unfortunately Imogen's mother died and she herself doesn't remember.'

'Oh dear.' Belinda looked at him sympathetically. 'That's sad news. She looks such a vibrant woman in the photographs. I don't think I can help you with that, but there might be something in the albums or the ledger to give you a clue. You're welcome to keep them for this evening.'

'Thank you,' said Vince. 'I appreciate it.'

'I'd best be getting back to work,' said Belinda. 'Would you like the key to your room?'

'Great,' said Vince. He followed her indoors, where she registered him as a guest and gave him a big key on an old-fashioned fob.

'We did think about electronic keys,' she told him as she led him to the room on the ground floor. 'But the house is so charming that we thought it would be inappropriate.'

The room, when he went inside, was light and airy, with patio doors leading to the garden.

'You have everything you need,' said Belinda. 'There's tea- and coffee-making facilities, water and free Wi-Fi. We don't have a minibar in the room, I'm afraid.'

'This is perfect,' said Vince. 'I'll get my things from the car.'

'I'll leave you to it in that case,' said Belinda. She gave him the code to open the gates, which, she said, also opened the door to the guest house.

When he'd retrieved his bag, Vince put the kettle on and made himself a cup of tea. He sat in the small tub chair beside the window and went through the photos in the album. Some had clearly been taken at the guest house, but others were on the beach or in the town. Not that they could help really, he thought. After all, the album had been left at the guest house, so everything had been taken prior to them leaving.

But where they hell had they gone? Vince was absolutely certain that Imogen was somewhere she knew well. It made perfect sense. Paris was still a possibility, yet she'd never spoken with any great fondness of the capital city. He remembered her shrugging once and saying that Paris was Paris but it wasn't France. No, thought Vince, she wasn't in Paris. She'd come back to where she'd lived before. To where she'd gone after this place. All he had to do was figure out where that actually was.

And then he did.

It was purely by chance and he couldn't believe how fortuitously it happened. He'd been reading a review of La Vie en Rose on TripAdvisor and then clicked, as he often did, to see what other places the reviewer had been to. All over France seemed to be the answer, and Vince started to read the reviews because they were well written and sharply observed. He particularly liked the ones about French restaurants, especially the Parisian ones, where he agreed entirely with the reviewer's comments.

Sometimes it's better not to try your school French, SammieG had written. *Better to be dismissed as a stupid foreigner for not having a word of the language than be sneered at for pronouncing* l'addition *incorrectly.*

Vince found himself nodding in approval as he read, and then clicked on another SammieG review that had been posted a few weeks earlier. It was of a restaurant called Le Bleu, and it was the accompanying photograph that made him stop and stare. Because in the photo, captioned 'Gerry and Imogen enjoy Basque cooking with a twist', was his wife. Barely recognisable at first, with her beautiful hair hacked into a style that Vince found unattractively short, but it was her nonetheless. And the man named Gerry had his arm along the back of her seat as both of them looked straight at the camera.

Vince felt such a surge of anger and betrayal through his veins that his head felt as though it was going to explode. The sneaky bitch had left him for another man after all. And for this Gerry bloke, who was singularly unattractive, with his round face and slightly glazed eyes. Balding too, thought Vince as he enlarged the photo. He'd been spending the last few weeks worrying about her, while she'd been cheating on him with some other guy. She'd be sorry, he thought. She really would.

It was a while before his rage abated enough for him to check the location of the restaurant, and he frowned when he saw that it was in a town called Hendaye on the south-west coast. He'd never heard of it before and he was certain that Imogen had never mentioned it. Why had she chosen it? Because of Gerry? Was he someone from her past that she'd managed to hook up with again? Was he the one who'd lured her away, who'd planned her disappearance?

Vince got up from his chair and went outside. He looked at the house from the garden and tried to imagine his wife living here. It was easy, because the atmosphere of La Vie en Rose was exactly what she'd tried to recreate in her Dublin kitchen. Yet she hadn't come back here. She'd gone to this Hendaye place instead. Presumably because she didn't think he'd find her there. But she was wrong. She was always wrong.

He returned to his room and began looking for travel options. Annoyingly, they were limited. Much to his disgust, there wasn't a train, and there only seemed to be direct flights every second day. There were lots of connecting flights through Paris, which gave him more flexibility but would be almost as tiresome as driving. But he knew that there'd be an extra fee to pay for taking the car to the other side of the country and leaving it there when his contract was to return it to Marseille.

Imogen's disappearance was causing him nothing but trouble, he thought. But at least he knew where she was now. She couldn't hide from him any more. When he found her, he wouldn't let her know how very angry he was. He wasn't going to alienate her. He'd treat her with the compassion she clearly believed she deserved. As for Gerry . . . He gritted his teeth. He would deal with Gerry, whoever the hell he was. He would make him see that there was no future for him with Imogen. He would put an end to this nonsense once and for all.

He would bring her home.

And things would change for ever.

Chapter 29

Imogen arrived at the Villa Martine exactly on time for its scheduled clean that afternoon. Unlike previous occasions, her ring on the bell was answered by a male voice asking who was there.

'It's me, Imogen,' she replied. 'Here to clean.'

'Come on in.'

The gate swung open and she pushed her bike up the path. By the time she reached the house, Giles was standing on the doorstep.

'Hi,' he said.

'Hello.' She smiled at him. 'Back from your . . . well, I was going to say holiday, but obviously being here is a holiday for you already.'

He grinned at her. 'A few days with a friend. A few days here. And then back to Paris. But I'll be here again in August for a couple of weeks.'

'I do like the way French people take holidays,' she told him. 'At home, random days off can be seen as slacking.'

Giles made a face. 'You can't work all the time,' he said. 'You need to recharge the batteries. Your mind works better after a break.'

'I agree with you.' Imogen walked past him into the kitchen and then gave him a horrified look. 'What on earth was going on here?'

'I'm sorry,' said Giles. 'We had people to dinner last night and I cooked my special rabbit stew.'

'*Pauvre lapin,*' said Imogen as she looked at the blackened Le Creuset pot soaking in the sink. 'It seems to me that he was overcooked.'

'It was delicious,' Giles said. 'But we should have cleaned up.'

Imogen wanted to agree with him. Although the plates had been loaded into the dishwasher, the kitchen table was still littered with cups and wine glasses, which Giles began to pick up.

'Leave it,' she said. 'It's my job, after all.'

'Cleaning the house, not cleaning up after us,' said Giles. 'This was thoughtless. I forgot that you might be coming today.'

'It's not so bad.' They must have been drinking till all hours, thought Imogen, looking at the glasses.

'If you're sure . . .' said Giles. 'I was on my way out. Sorry again.'

'No problem.'

And it wasn't, not really. The dishwasher was a two-drawer affair, which meant that she could put all the glassware in the bottom and wash it on a different cycle to the crockery and cutlery in the top. When she'd programmed them and started the washing, she turned her attention to the pot, which wasn't as hard to clean as she'd first feared thanks to Le Creuset's forgiving nature towards burnt-on food. She wiped the table, then returned to her more usual system, which was to begin upstairs and make her way downwards.

She worked automatically, dusting, polishing and sweeping, comfortable in the rhythm that she set herself. She'd lost half a stone since she'd come to France and she was sure it was all down to the amount of physical work involved in cleaning houses. She wondered if she could incorporate her cleaning routine into a diet and exercise plan for the future. Maybe she could write a book, she thought, and it would become an instant best-seller, after which she could give up cleaning for ever and live off her royalties. Oliver's publishing house could publish it for her. It would be a win-win situation. She smiled to herself at the idea, and hummed beneath her breath as she worked, comfortable in what she was doing, untroubled by her thoughts. In the last few years, living with Vince, her free time had invariably been consumed with worry about the mood he might be in and what she needed to do to keep him happy. She'd always believed that if he was happy, she'd be happy too. Although that had become impossible. And she couldn't help feeling responsible for making him unhappy, and for being the author of her own misfortune whenever he took his unhappiness out on her.

But everything's OK now, she thought as she opened the door of the library. I'm making a new life. And with a bit of luck he will too.

'Oh.' She'd been so preoccupied with what was going on in her head that she hadn't realised there was anyone in the room. Now she saw that Oliver was sitting behind the rose-wood desk, a pile of paper in front of him. 'I'm sorry,' she said. 'I didn't mean to disturb you.'

Oliver blinked a few times as though trying to figure out who she was.

'It's OK.' He took off a pair of narrow-rimmed reading glasses and placed them on the desk. 'I was absorbed in what I was doing. I didn't know you were in the house. Did you let yourself in? I didn't hear the bell.'

'Giles did,' she said. 'He's gone out now.'

Oliver nodded. He stretched his arms over his head before standing up.

'You don't have to abandon your work because of me,' said Imogen. 'I can leave this room until later.'

'Are you nearly finished?' he asked.

'I still have the kitchen to do,' replied Imogen.

'The kitchen!' Oliver suddenly looked aghast. 'Giles had friends around last night. I told him to clean up after himself, but it was a mess this morning.'

'It's OK,' said Imogen. 'The dishwasher is doing most of the work.'

'Nevertheless . . .' Oliver shrugged. 'Do you need a break?'

'No, I'll get on with it,' said Imogen. 'René expects me back with the keys.'

'I was going to have a coffee break myself,' said Oliver. 'Are you sure you wouldn't like to join me?'

'If you insist.'

Something in her words made Oliver look at her curiously.

'I'm not insisting,' he said. 'I'm asking. And if you really don't want to join me, please don't feel you have to.'

It had happened with René too, remembered Imogen. He'd asked her to join him for coffee and she'd thought of it as a command, not an invitation. But Oliver, like René, hadn't been upset with her when she'd demurred. Both of them had been relaxed about it.

'I don't want coffee,' she said. 'But a glass of water would be nice.'

'And you can take five minutes out to have it with me?'

'Sure,' she said.

She followed him into the kitchen, where he took a bottle of Perrier from the fridge and filled a tall glass while he waited for the coffee machine to warm up. She brought the water outside and sat at the table, where he joined her a couple of minutes later.

'I guess it puts you in a difficult position,' said Oliver. 'I say I want a coffee and you feel obliged to have something too. I didn't think of that.'

'It's OK,' she said.

'It's because I don't see you as an employee,' he told her.

But she *was* an employee and she was never going to forget it. Not like Carol.

'So how's life going for you?' He took a sip of coffee and sighed appreciatively.

'Pretty well,' she said.

'Did you enjoy the barbecue?'

She nodded. 'It was good fun. Nice to meet different people. How much longer did you stay on the beach after I left?'

'Someone came with a guitar,' said Oliver. 'There was music. And more wine. A lot more wine.'

'Oops.'

'It could've been worse,' said Oliver. 'I got home before dawn.'

She wondered if Virginie had come home with him.

'How long are you going to stay working for Bastarache?' he asked when she didn't say anything.

'I don't know,' replied Imogen. 'The work is seasonal.'

'Do you plan to stay in town? If there isn't anything?'

'I haven't decided yet,' replied Imogen. 'My plans are flexible.'

She loved being able to say that. She loved thinking that her life wasn't mapped out for her any more.

'And are they flexible now?' asked Oliver.

'At this exact moment?'

'In general,' he clarified. 'There's something you might be able to help me out with.'

'Help you out? How?'

'I have a meeting with my author in San Sebastian tomorrow. I think I mentioned him to you before. The guy who wrote a book set in the Basque country. That's what I was reading when you came into the library earlier.'

'I don't see how I can help you,' Imogen said. 'I know nothing about writing or editing. Especially in French!'

'He's living with an Irish girl,' Oliver told her. 'She writes a great blog about being an Irishwoman abroad. I know it's very short notice, but I wondered if you might come with me and talk to her while I'm closeted with him. To break the ice socially, you know, one Irish girl to another.'

'You're right. It's very short notice. When did you come up with this particular idea?'

'While I was making coffee,' he said. 'I'd been thinking about the meeting earlier and how I was going to deal with him. Paul Urdien has a reputation for being a little difficult to deal with. Not in a horrible way, thankfully; it's simply that he's nervous and anxious about the process. I was hoping the girlfriend might be a way to reassure him.'

'She might not have the faintest desire either to reassure him or meet me,' said Imogen.

'I understand that, of course. But when I was talking to him on the phone, I got the distinct impression that she was very involved with him and his work, so . . .'

Imogen gave him a doubtful look.

'If it doesn't work out, you can do a bit of exploring on your own,' said Oliver. 'If you don't mind, that is. It was *Maman* who acquired Paul's book for the company, and she's the one who dealt with him and his girlfriend when they came to Paris for an initial talk. She thinks I would be a better fit for him editorially, but obviously it's entirely up to him. However, we both think that the girlfriend will be an influence.'

'I'm still not convinced that me befriending her will be much help.'

'Everything helps,' said Oliver.

'Maybe.' Imogen was still doubtful.

'You'll think about it?'

'I see where you're coming from,' she said. 'I don't know how good an idea it is, but if you'd like me to come along to your social evening, I will.'

'Thanks.' Oliver looked pleased. 'But it's not an evening. It's a morning meeting, followed by lunch.'

'In that case, I'm sorry,' said Imogen. 'I have to work during the day. I don't have time for lunch.'

'Even on a Saturday?' He sounded horrified.

'Afraid so,' she told him.

'I can't believe you have to work at weekends.'

'The weekends can be busy times for cleaners,' said Imogen. 'I don't usually have too much on, but I have a house to do in the morning.'

'How long will that take you?' asked Oliver.

'A couple of hours. It's not part of my work for René. The house belongs to his ex-wife, Céline Biendon.'

'I know Céline,' said Oliver. 'She was at the barbecue too, wasn't she? With a new man?'

'Yes, she was,' said Imogen. 'Anyway, I clean her house on Saturday mornings.'

'I'm not meeting Paul until noon,' said Oliver. 'Maybe Céline wouldn't mind you starting earlier than usual?' Then he shook his head. 'I'm sorry. I'm trying to pressurise you into doing something you might not want to do or have time for.'

'Well . . .' She was beginning to warm to the idea of a literary lunch with Oliver, his author and the author's girlfriend in the Spanish coastal city. It seemed a little glamorous to her, and she liked the idea of doing something different. 'I normally start early anyway, but I won't be finished until after eleven.'

'It's only a half-hour drive.'

'I'd have to get home and change first.'

'No problem,' said Oliver. 'I'll pick you up. Where do you live?'

She told him.

'So you'll do it?' he asked.

She thought about it again for a moment, then nodded. 'Why not? Besides, it'll be nice to talk to someone from Ireland again.'

'Her name's Blanaid O'Casey.'

'Not a bad effort,' she said as she corrected his pronunciation.

'This reminds me of when we were kids,' he said. 'You were so precise correcting us.'

'It was my job,' said Imogen.

He laughed.

'Seriously,' she said. 'When my mum was employed by yours, we were told that she was the housekeeper and I was to help you with your English. I took it very seriously.'

'That's true. I hated it, though.'

'Why?'

'You were so much younger than me. I didn't like being corrected by a baby. Although I had to revise my opinion of you after the ants-in-the-bed incident.'

'I'm sorry about that,' she said, although there was a bubble of amusement in her voice. 'But you'd really annoyed me that day. I can't remember why now. Anyway, I enjoyed correcting your English. It made me feel useful.'

'Oh, you had a lot more uses than that!' exclaimed Oliver. 'D'you remember when we played at magicians and you were my assistant?'

'You wanted to cut me in half,' she recalled. 'With your mother's Sabatier knife.'

'I wouldn't have actually done it,' he assured her.

'Somewhat madly, I trusted you.'

He grinned. 'God knows why.'

'Indeed.' She drained her glass and put it on the table. Then she stood up.

'Back to work?' asked Oliver. 'Already?'

'I've a lot to do today,' she said. 'So yes.'

Much to his annoyance, Vince hadn't been able to get the direct flight from Marseille to Biarritz on Friday morning because it was fully booked. He played around with the alternatives for a while before eventually deciding that it would be less stressful to drive himself. So he went back to the car hire people and asked about a rental that involved leaving the car on the west coast. After a lot of discussion, and a flurry of paperwork (Vince wondered what had happened to the concept of a paperless office), they said that he could leave the car at Biarritz once he'd paid a fee for a different drop-off point. The fee was nearly as much as the flight would have cost, but Vince preferred to think that he was spending his time heading in the right direction instead of flying back to Paris and then on to Biarritz.

The drive from Marseille was a little over seven hundred kilometres, which was a lot more than he'd normally do in a single day. Mainly on the motorway, it got tiresome after a while, and Vince found himself stopping at service stations more often than he'd originally anticipated simply to break the monotony. In the end, it took him over eight hours to reach his destination, and he was tired and tetchy by the time he turned in to the car park of the Hotel Pyrénées – having had to go around the block because he'd missed the narrow entrance the first time, thinking that it was the gateway to a large suburban villa.

After he'd parked the car and checked in to a room far more basic than the one at La Vie en Rose, he went down to the hotel bar, had two beers and then stepped outside. The hotel was about two kilometres from the beach, which was why, he decided, they'd had a free room. The walk, through what was mainly a residential area of private properties, was pleasant enough, but he couldn't see why on earth anyone would want to come to this place on holiday. He understood it a little better when he reached the beach, which was long and wide and reminded him of Irish beaches he'd been to see as a child. Despite the fact that it was after six, it was still busy, and flooded by the evening sun, which hung over the Atlantic and turned the water to liquid gold. He stared at the holidaymakers, wondering if Imogen was among them, but it was difficult to make out anyone's features in the sunlight. Had she come to this out-of-the-way spot to hang around on the beach? Or to meet the mysterious Gerry of the photograph? He took the printout he'd made of it from his pocket and looked at it again. He clenched his fist.

He began to make his way along the Boulevard de la Mer, looking at the street names as he passed them, until he came to the Rue Berbier. He walked along it until he was standing outside the Le Bleu restaurant. The wooden doors were closed and a notice in the window informed him that it opened at 7 p.m. He looked at his watch. It was almost seven now, so he waited outside until a young waiter in a black suit opened up.

'M'sieur?' He looked at Vince enquiringly. 'You have a reservation?'

'No.' Vince took the printout from his pocket and showed it to the waiter, asking if he knew any of the people in the picture. When the younger man shook his head, Vince asked to speak to anyone else in the restaurant who might be able to help.

'Not now.' The waiter was shocked. 'We are starting service. The chef is busy. The staff are busy.'

'You don't have any customers yet,' Vince pointed out, even as an elderly couple arrived and stood behind him. He waved them ahead, and the waiter escorted them inside and to a table near the wall. Vince followed them in. It was an upmarket restaurant, he thought as he noted the modern place settings and the contemporary art on the walls. Not really the kind he and Imogen normally went to.

'I'm sorry, M'sieur.' The waiter returned to him. 'I cannot help you with your question . . . Perhaps if you come back later someone else can talk to you. After ten. It will be quieter then.'

'It's bloody quiet now!' exclaimed Vince, although more diners were beginning to arrive and were queuing at the door.

'Later, M'sieur,' said the waiter.

Vince gave him an angry glare but went outside again. He walked back along the seafront and stopped at a pizzeria, where he ordered a calzone and a glass of beer. He showed the printed photo to the waitress who served him, but she shook her head and said she didn't recognise them.

Sooner or later somebody would, Vince thought, as he cut through the dough of the folded pizza. Somebody would look at that photo and nod in recognition and tell him where she was. The town wasn't all that big. She couldn't hide from him here. He was close to finding her. And when he did, and brought her home, she'd learn to live by his rules. New rules. No going out to work, for starters. No going to the gym with that lying bitch Shona. She'd find out that she couldn't mess with him. She'd be sorry she'd tried.

Imogen was excited about the trip to San Sebastian. It was nice to think that she was going somewhere different, and it would also give her the opportunity to take some more money out of her account. Given that Vince was in France (something that she was trying very hard to put out of her head), it felt even more important to lay whatever false trails she could, even if he wasn't really able to follow them.

She wondered where he was now. Her first attempt at misleading him had been in Paris, when she'd asked about transport to Montpellier. She'd acknowledged to herself that it was a feeble and probably futile stab at sending him on a wild goose chase, and even at the time she'd been resigned to the fact that it wouldn't stall him for long, and he would eventually make his way to Marseille. But she was utterly confident that he'd fail in his efforts to find her from there. Nevertheless, Vince never gave up. It was his greatest strength and his greatest weakness. If there was the faintest possibility of finding a connection, he would. But there wasn't the faintest possibility. None at all. She was safe. And as long as she didn't blurt out her location to Shona, nothing could go wrong.

She poured herself a glass of sparkling water, dropped a slice of lemon into it and sat at the window overlooking the pool, watching as Max, Nellie and Becky splashed about. The two girls were leaving on Sunday, something that had made Imogen realise that time was passing. It had made her think again about her own plans, though right now she was happy without any. Her life wasn't mapped out. Even though she currently had a routine with her job, every day was different. She loved that. She thrived on the unpredictability of it. So even though she knew that financially she needed to sort out her future, she was content to let things drift for the time being.

She took out her phone and saw another email from Shona.

From: Blondie@moonshine.com
To: Vanished@mymail.com
Subject: Vince
He's in Marseille. He's trying to find the place you used to live. He asked again if you were in touch and I'm sorry, Imogen, I had to tell him you were. He really wants to help you but I know he's angry too because I can hear it in his voice. I thought you should know. Call me if you need anything.
Sxx

She took a long drink of water. Marseille was all right. Marseille had been inevitable. And it was seven hundred kilometres away.

There was nothing to worry about.

Nothing at all.

At 10.30 that evening, Vince went back to the Le Bleu restaurant. Even at that relatively late hour, it was buzzing with people. He spotted the waiter he'd spoken to earlier carrying plates to a table near the window, and when he started to walk away again, he accosted him.

'So can I speak to someone now?' he demanded.

The waiter looked irritated. 'I really think—'

'I don't care what you think,' said Vince. 'I only care that you let me talk to someone else about the photograph.'

'I will ask Monsieur Biendon to talk to you,' said the waiter. 'He is the owner. Please wait a moment.'

Vince stood watching the diners while the waiter disappeared through a black door marked *Privée.* A few minutes later, a tall, burly man in a chef's apron walked out. There was a smattering of applause from the diners and the man raised his hand in acknowledgement before standing in front of Vince.

'I am Bernard Biendon,' he said in heavily accented English. 'What is it that you want?'

Vince took the photograph from his pocket again. 'This woman and this man ate in your restaurant,' he said. 'I want to know where I can find them.'

'Excuse me?'

'I want to find the people in this photograph,' said Vince. 'Do you know where they are?'

The chef waved his arm to encompass the restaurant.

'You see all these customers,' he said. 'Every night this many and more in my restaurant. You want me to tell you about two of them? I cannot.'

'Look at them again,' said Vince, thrusting the printout in front of him. 'All I want to know is if you know who they are and where they might be.'

'What am I?' asked Bernard. 'A telephone directory?'

'Just look,' said Vince.

Bernard sighed and took the piece of paper from him.

'Him, I do not know,' he said dismissively. 'Her . . .' He frowned. 'She is familiar, but I cannot remember . . .'

'Try,' said Vince.

'Why do you want to know?' asked Bernard.

'The woman is my wife,' said Vince.

'And he is her lover?' Bernard gave him a knowing look.

'It's possible.'

'*Merde*,' said Bernard. 'I am sorry if there is a personal problem for you, *mon ami*, but—'

'Don't give me any of your French free-love crap or whatever it is,' said Vince. 'Tell me if you know where she is.'

'I truly cannot remem— Oh!' Bernard tapped his forehead. 'I *do* remember. Not her visit here with this man. That, I do not. But she was at a charity boules match a few weeks ago.'

'Here? In the town?'

'Where else?' asked Bernard.

'Did you talk to her?'

'Well that's the thing.' Bernard was looking at the photograph more intently. 'I remember her at the tournament because she was with my daughter's ex-husband.'

'This man is your son-in-law?' Vince was incredulous.

'This man is clearly English.' Bernard was dismissive. 'René is from the town.'

'She's with a man from here?' Vince was bemused. The list of people that Imogen could have been having an affair with had got longer again. Conor Foley. The man in the photograph. And now the chef's ex-son-in-law. Rage with his wife balled up inside him.

'So where does he live, this René?'

'I'm not going to give you his address so that you can rush to his house and have a quarrel,' said Bernard. 'That is not the way to do things.'

'I'm sure I can find him myself,' said Vince. 'And I don't want to fight with him. I want to talk to him. My wife isn't a well person.'

'She is sick?'

'In the head.' Vince tapped his temple.

'I do not remember her well, but I would not say she was sick in the head.'

'You don't know her,' said Vince. 'Now, are you going to give me this man's address or not?'

Bernard hesitated. Then he walked over to the small bar, took a card from it and scribbled on the back.

'Rue Gorosuretta?' Vince stumbled over the name.

'It's at the northern end of the town,' said Bernard. 'Wait.' He took a tourist map from behind the bar and opened it. 'We're here.' He circled an area of the map. 'Rue Gorosuretta is here. It's about a fifteen-minute walk.'

'Thank you,' said Vince.

'You're welcome.'

Vince nodded briefly and walked out of the door.

Bernard stared after him until he disappeared from view. Then he picked up his phone and dialled a number.

Chapter 30

René heard his phone ringing, but when he saw the caller ID, he didn't bother answering. He wasn't going to talk to Bernard while he was sitting in his ex-wife's house, sharing a bottle of wine with her. His unexpected arrival, bottle in hand, had been motivated by the concern he'd felt when he'd seen her at the beach barbecue with Art Barthoullet. It was the proprietorial way that Art had put his arm around Céline's waist that had bothered him. He told himself that he didn't mind her seeing someone else; he knew she'd had a couple of short-lived romances since their divorce, but Art definitely wasn't good enough for her. He had no ambition. Céline was an ambitious woman herself. She needed someone with some get-up-and-go. Not a man like Art who was nothing more than a functionary for the train company.

But he didn't say any of this to her while they sat opposite each other in her cosy living room. It had been a long time since René had been in the house they'd once shared, and his first impression was that his ex-wife had suddenly embraced her inner domestic goddess. Everything was in its place and yet nothing looked too studied or artificial. Céline had turned the house into a welcoming home, and René couldn't help thinking that it was much more inviting than when he'd lived there. It compared favourably to his own rather stark apartment too. He wondered why she'd never bothered before, and whether it was all for Art's benefit. Then he remembered that Imogen was doing her cleaning. He suddenly realised why his clients praised his employee so much. She wasn't just a cleaner. She was a home-maker. And as such, a true domestic goddess At least as far as turning an untidy, unattractive room into a warm and welcoming space went.

Maybe I should have turned up at Imogen's with the wine, thought René, as Céline kept their conversation strictly on topics related to their businesses. Even though Imogen seemed closed off and distant as far as relationships were concerned, he wondered if he could be the man to change all that. The one to make her melt. And then Céline looked at him with her dark eyes, tilted her head to one side and asked him what the real reason for him coming to her house on a Friday night was. And he forgot about Imogen.

'I came because I'm concerned about you and Art Barthoullet,' he admitted.

'What?' Céline looked at him in astonishment. 'Why on earth would you be concerned? And what gives you the right to be?'

'Nothing,' said René. 'It's simply—'

'When we were married, you were always trying to run my life,' said Céline. 'And now we're divorced, you're still trying.'

'That's not true.' René gave her an injured look. 'I never interfere.'

She snorted.

'I don't,' he said. 'I never advise you any more.'

'You know better.'

'All I wanted was to help,' he said.

'You interfered,' Céline told him. 'You drove me nuts.'

'I interfered because I cared.'

'For heaven's sake, René. I can live my own life.'

'Without me.'

'Without anyone.' She gave him a half-smile. 'I don't need you and I don't need Art either.'

'I don't want you to make a mistake, that's all.'

'If I make a second mistake, it's my own to make,' said Céline.

'I'm an idiot,' he said ruefully. 'I was back then and I still am.'

'That's true.'

'An idiot with good intentions.'

'Really?' She raised an eyebrow.

'Absolutely.'

'I still care for you, René Bastarache,' said Céline. 'But I won't be influenced by you.'

'*Bien sûr.*'

'Have another one.' She picked up the bottle of ruby-red merlot. 'Let's talk about old times.'

'Old times,' said René, and clinked his glass against hers.

Vince stood outside the address Bernard Biendon had given him. It was a three-storey apartment block, more modern than most of the buildings around it, set back from the road and surrounded by a small garden. He had rung the bell a number of times, but there had been no reply, and after working out which apartment might be René's, he could see that it was in darkness. His lip curled. Was the fucker with his wife? he wondered. Was he doing things to her that only Vince had a right to do? He felt the blood boil in his veins and his head pound with fury.

He sat on the low wall outside the apartment block for about twenty minutes, but nobody came or went, although one or two passers-by looked at him curiously. Vince realised that he was making himself noticeable, and after looking at his watch and realising how late it had become, he decided to go back to his hotel for the night. The man wasn't going anywhere and would come back to his apartment sooner or later. He could talk to him tomorrow. There was nothing to be gained by waiting for him now.

He stood up. As he walked, tiredness began to overtake him. He'd been up early that morning, and the drive from Marseille had been a long one. He needed to sleep. He yawned as he crossed the road, and then stumbled over an uneven part of the pavement, pitching forward so that he nearly fell.

'*Faites attention!*' A young man hurried to help him, catching his arm and steadying him.

'I'm all right,' said Vince irritably.

'English?' said the man.

Vince nodded. He couldn't be bothered to say that he was Irish but spoke English as Imogen always did when she met someone from a different country.

'Take care on the street,' said the man.

'I'm not drunk,' said Vince, feeling that he was being stereotyped.

'I didn't think you were,' said the man. 'Goodnight.'

'Goodnight.' Vince strode swiftly away.

* * *

Max Gasquet turned the corner and walked up the pathway to the apartment block. He forgot about the encounter immediately as he put his key in the lock and went into the hallway where Imogen was standing.

'Hello,' he said. 'Are you on your way out?'

'No, no,' said Imogen. 'I've just put my laundry in the machine.'

'At this hour?'

'I meant to do it before I went out this morning,' she said. 'But I forgot. That's the trouble with doing housework for other people. You neglect your own. And I'm going to be busy tomorrow, so I thought I should put a wash on now.'

'You will leave the machine all night?'

She grinned. 'You're being safety-conscious, aren't you? No, I'm putting on a quick wash now, then I'll wait for it to finish, put the clothes in my basket and peg them out in the morning. Is that OK?'

'I'm sorry, I'm sorry.' Max held up his hands. 'I didn't mean to interfere.'

'You're not,' she said. 'It's sort of sweet that you worry.'

'I don't worry,' protested Max. 'But . . .' He looked a little shamefaced. 'When I was a kid, a neighbour left the dishwasher on while they went to work. Something happened to the timer and it didn't stop. It actually went on fire and the house was destroyed.'

'Not really!' exclaimed Imogen. 'I've heard of that happening but always thought it was an . . . an old wives' tale,' she added in English.

'A what?'

'I'm not sure of the right expression. Something that

you've heard and that might be true but you can't really believe it is.'

'Ah.' Max nodded. '*Une histoire à dormir debout.*'

'More or less.' She smiled at him. 'I'll be awake until the cycle has finished, so you don't have to worry about the apartment burning down.'

'Great,' he said. 'Would you like to have a drink with me while you wait?'

She looked at him in surprise.

'I don't sleep when I've been working late,' said Max. 'It takes me time to unwind. Would you like to unwind with me?'

This time her expression was startled.

'I don't mean . . . not . . . Just a drink. As neighbours,' he said.

'OK,' she agreed. 'Why not.'

The forty-five minutes she spent with Max were pleasant and relaxed. He chatted about his work at the hospital, about his family and his hopes for the future. She listened, adding a remark from time to time but happy to let him talk. It was weird, she thought after she'd said goodnight to him, retrieved her washing and got into bed, how many men she was talking to these days. And it was equally weird (to her if maybe not to other people) how many men were perfectly straightforward and nice and didn't read deep and dark hidden meanings into casual remarks. Vince had done that all the time. No matter what she said, he always found a way to take another meaning from it. One that inevitably seemed to disrespect him in some way. Imogen had got out of the habit of having light-hearted conversations with men without having to second-guess what they might be thinking.

I thought it was all about me, she told herself as she slid beneath the single sheet on her bed. I thought it was my fault, that I said the wrong things all the time. But I didn't. I really didn't. I wasn't a bad person. I'm not a bad person. And from now on, I'm going to be my own person. Which is definitely a good thing.

She was smiling when she fell asleep.

The following morning she arrived at Céline's a little ahead of schedule, having first put her washing out to dry. Céline was rushing around, putting down her bag and forgetting where she'd left it, looking for the keys to the café and generally dithering in a way that was totally unlike her.

'Everything OK?' asked Imogen.

'Yes, yes, fine,' said Céline. 'But wondering why on earth I open the café so early on a Saturday.'

'I've wondered that myself,' confessed Imogen. 'But I suppose there are a lot of people wanting breakfast.'

'Those who swim in the morning, or walk on the beach, and those whose businesses are open all want coffee and croissants,' agreed Céline. 'But nobody ever has a cup of coffee ready for me.'

Imogen paused, duster in hand. 'Are you sure you're OK? You seem distracted this morning.'

'Yes, I'm distracted.' Céline made a face. 'I've been a total idiot.'

'Why? What's happened?'

'René came here last night,' she said. 'He brought a bottle of wine. We drank it. One thing led to another, and—'

'No!' exclaimed Imogen. 'You didn't sleep with him, did you?'

'Of course I slept with him, the *salaud*!'

'Oh dear.'

'Now he thinks I'm crazy in love with him all over again.'

'Are you?'

'It didn't work out the first time,' said Céline. 'We haven't changed. It wouldn't work out a second time either.'

'Because he's too bossy?'

'Exactly! He always thinks he knows best. He was forever giving me unwanted advice.'

'Did you take any of it?'

'Some,' admitted Céline. 'But that doesn't mean any of it was good.' She sighed. 'If he thinks he can walk back into my life, he has another think coming.'

'I thought you were going out with Art.'

'So did I.' Céline sighed. 'I am an imbecile.'

'We all make mistakes,' said Imogen. 'But maybe . . . maybe you and René aren't a mistake.'

'Don't say that!' Céline spoke sharply. 'Look, the sex with him was always great. And it was great last night too. But I divorced him for a reason, and that hasn't changed. Now he's left here like a cat with the cream and I know he's thinking that I melted back into his heart. But I didn't.'

'Actually I'm quite pleased to see you upset about it,' said Imogen. 'I always thought you two were amazingly polite and friendly and so cool about your divorce. I'm glad that you can get emotional about each other too. And that sleeping with him was a bit of a big deal after all and not a forgettable French affair.'

This time Céline laughed. 'Of course you would have your English way about it, wouldn't you?'

'Sometimes it's the right way.' Imogen made a face. 'Revenge and anger and bitterness have their place.'

'Oh well, I guess I'll get over it, and René will learn that a one-night stand with me was just that.'

'Perhaps that's all he wanted.' Imogen folded some clothes.

'Actually, I think he wants me as a standby for when his other *affaires* aren't working out.' Céline made a face. 'He doesn't seem to have a woman in his life at the moment. So I'm his fallback.'

'Don't be cynical,' said Imogen.

'Years of experience. I must go.' Céline, who'd finally found her bag and her keys, bustled towards the door. 'Please don't tell him you know he was here.'

'Absolutely not,' Imogen assured her.

Left alone with her cleaning, Imogen couldn't help wondering if there was the possibility of a second chance for René and Céline. The café owner had a point when she said that people didn't change. Imogen believed that essentially that was true. But their behaviour could change. Would René's? And would Céline give him a second chance if it did?

Would I? she asked herself. If Vince turned up and told me that there would be no more rules, that he was never going to track me on Find My Friends again, that everything in our lives would change – would I be prepared to give it another go? If I really and truly believed him? If he promised?

She shivered. That was exactly what he would do, she thought. He'd tell her that he'd changed. He'd promise her that things would be better. He'd try to make her believe that she'd made a terrible mistake by leaving him. And her job was to remember that she couldn't afford to trust him. She had to trust herself instead.

She glanced at the clock and tut-tutted in annoyance. She needed to stop obsessing about her damn marriage and speed up with her cleaning so that she'd be finished in time for the trip to San Sebastian. Which was a much better use of her time than trying to second-guess her own emotions.

Even though she'd been sceptical at first, she was looking forward to the outing as a welcome change in the routine she'd set for herself. She hurried through the house, pausing in the bedroom to notice that although Céline had straightened the summer duvet on the bed, the sheets below were still a tangled mess. She hesitated, then took off the duvet and made the bed, trying not to think of René and Céline entwined on it the night before.

She sped through the rest of the cleaning, then locked up the house before getting on her bike and cycling as fast as she could up the hill. She turned in to the gateway to her building and hopped off the bike almost in a single movement when she saw Oliver already waiting for her.

'Am I late?' She looked at her watch in dismay.

'No. No. Don't worry. I was ready and I thought I'd see if you were too. If so, we could have had a coffee or something in San Sebastian before meeting Paul.'

'I'm sorry,' she said. 'I have to shower and change. But it'll only take me ten minutes.'

'There's no rush, take your time.'

'Do you want to wait in the apartment?' She made the offer without thinking.

'*Bien sûr.*'

He followed her into the building and praised the compact neatness of her home.

'It's a shoebox,' she said, going into the bathroom. 'But it *my* shoebox.'

It took her twenty minutes to get ready. She didn't need to wash her hair, which was now gently curling closer to her shoulders, but she changed from her shorts and T-shirt into a pretty carmine-red dress that hugged her waist and skimmed her hips. She wore red espadrilles on her feet.

'*Très jolie*,' said Oliver.

'Thanks,' she said. 'I don't really have any dressy-up clothes in my wardrobe. I don't need them.'

'Good clothes are an art form,' said Oliver. 'At least that's what my mother believes. But sometimes it's the person wearing them who is the art form.'

'Oliver!' Imogen blushed. 'That's a very chic compliment. Thank you.'

'You're welcome,' he said. 'Now, let's go.'

They went outside and Oliver opened the door to the Range Rover.

'It's very high up.' Imogen hauled herself into the passenger seat. 'And totally extravagant.'

'That's the joy of it,' he told her as he got in beside her. '*Allons-y*.' He put the automatic into drive and they glided away from the apartment block. Imogen sat back in the leather seat, enjoying the comfort and smoothness of the car. They made a left turn at the Hotel Pyrénées, but because she'd leaned forward to adjust the passenger climate control, she didn't see Vince standing in the doorway, his map in his hand.

* * *

Vince glanced up when he heard the Range Rover approaching. He saw the driver and then, as she sat up again, the passenger. It wasn't until after the vehicle had disappeared down the street that it registered with him that the girl in the red dress had been Imogen. At least he was pretty sure it was his wife, although with the new hairstyle it was hard to tell. But there had been a definite something in the way she'd moved her head that had triggered a mental picture of Imogen.

He ran to the bottom of the road but the car had already disappeared. He was annoyed but not despondent. In fact, he was somewhat elated. Despite the 66 million to 1 odds, he'd found her. Just as he'd believed he would. She was definitely here and sooner or later he'd come face to face with her and tell her she was coming home with him. He'd demand an explanation too about how she'd come to be cavorting with someone who owned a damn flashy car. She'd changed her tune about that, hadn't she? She'd always sneered at 4x4s before. So was the driver the ex-son-in-law of the restaurateur? René? Or was it Gerry, the moon-faced man in the photograph that had put him on the right track?

He reconsidered his plan for the day. He'd been on his way to René's apartment when he'd seen the car. Now it seemed that Imogen had gone somewhere with him. It was always possible, of course, that it wasn't René behind the wheel of the Range Rover. In which case he wasn't sure what to think about her behaviour. If she was running around France with multiple partners, he didn't want anything more to do with her. Nevertheless, she was his wife and he deserved an explanation. Being honest, he didn't think she was having affairs with all and sundry. But even if she was, she still belonged to him and she still had to answer to him.

He returned to the hotel lobby and mulled over his options. He took out his phone and looked at it. There had been a text message earlier, from Shona:

Hi Vince – any luck in the search for Imogen? Sx

He hadn't been sure how to answer it. He didn't trust Imogen's friend any longer and wasn't going to give her any information she might pass on to his wife.

So he simply replied: *No joy so far. Maybe I've made a mistake coming here. Will keep in touch.*

Chapter 31

The motorway to San Sebastian snaked through the mountains, enchanting Imogen, who exclaimed with delight at the spectacular scenery.

'We're on the edge of the Pyrenees here,' Oliver remarked as they climbed a steep hill, leaving some wheezing trucks in their wake. 'This is easy stuff. It's more dramatic on the other side of San Sebastian. Reminds me of scenes from *Lord of the Rings*.'

'I never saw that movie.' Imogen gazed towards a forest that swept the mountainside. 'And it's a long time since I read the book. But I remember mixing up my Orcs and my Elves and whatnot.'

Oliver laughed. 'Don't you think there could be Orcs and Elves here?'

'Very probably,' agreed Imogen. 'Did we visit San Sebastian as kids? Do you remember?'

'Charles and I came with Dad a few times,' replied Oliver. 'I'm not sure if you were with us. It's very pretty. Though not as pretty as Hendaye, obviously.'

'I feel sure I would have remembered this drive, but childhood memories can be faulty. Things get mixed up in your head.'

'Mine are a mixture,' he admitted. 'Of the lovely summers when my parents were together and then the more difficult ones when they split up.'

'I really wish—'

'Don't start blaming your mum again,' he said. 'I told you already. There were plenty of *affaires*.'

'When did you realise?'

'After Giles was born,' said Oliver. 'I was a bit older by then and I could see that everything wasn't right. *Maman* and *Papa* were very polite to each other – that was probably part of the problem. They were skating their way around the difficulties between them. And then it all blew up and *Maman* threw him out. We were in Paris at the time.'

'It must have been horrible.'

'To be honest, it was more horrible before,' he admitted. 'The atmosphere in the house was terrible. In the end, it was a relief when he left.'

'Did you divide your time between your parents?'

He snorted. 'Are you kidding? My dad embarked on a very bachelor lifestyle. He moved into a fashionable apartment and kept a steady stream of women friends. I thought it was a glamorous life at first. Later it seemed a bit sad.'

'How about your mother?'

'You know *Maman*. She's a formidable woman. She sat us down and explained what was going on and then told us we were the men in her life. There may have been boyfriends, but none I knew about until Giles was at least fifteen. Now she has Armand. They keep separate apartments but they're together a lot of the time.'

'And the Villa Martine? Who owns that?'

'The option had been to sell it as part of the divorce

settlement. But neither of them wanted to do that. My father spends a lot of time there in the cooler months. He enjoys sailing and skiing, so it suits him better.'

'Another remarkably civilised-sounding arrangement,' said Imogen, thinking of René and Céline.

'It's better to be civilised if you can,' said Oliver.

'Hmm.' Her thoughts turned to Vince. Whatever happened between them in the future, she couldn't imagine it being civilised.

'And you?' she asked after a moment's silence. 'What about your life?'

'I told you,' he said. 'I work with the publishing company.'

'I was thinking of your personal life,' she said. 'Virginie and the others on your list.'

He laughed. 'Civilised every one.'

'I wouldn't have expected anything less.'

'How about you?'

'A bit messier,' she said.

He glanced at her, but she'd turned her head so that she was looking at the scenery. They were on the downslope of the mountain now, and the town of San Sebastian was spread out in front of them, a cluster of red roofs in the distance.

'Tell me more about your author.' Imogen turned to him and changed the subject. 'Is he really difficult?'

'I don't think he means to be difficult,' said Oliver. 'He's very passionate about his work and he's reluctant to let anyone interfere with it. But the truth is, Genie, everything can be improved.'

'Do you think you can make the book better than it already is?' she asked.

'It's my job to make it better,' said Oliver. 'Does that make me sound pompous?'

'No,' answered Imogen. 'Just confident. But I guess all of the Delissandes are confident.'

'Why would you say that?'

She shrugged. 'You're a successful family. You're used to having money. You're comfortable with your lives and that makes you confident.'

Oliver was taken aback. 'You see us as a family of fat cats, do you? Treading all over the little people in a condescending way?'

'Of course not,' she said. 'All I'm saying is that you've never had to struggle.'

'And you have?'

'Not like some people,' said Imogen. 'We've never starved. Things haven't always been easy, that's all.'

'And they have for us?'

She could hear the defensive tone in Oliver's voice and she turned to him.

'Nobody has it easy all the time,' she said. 'I suppose . . . Oh, don't mind me, Oliver. I'm tying myself up in knots here. And you've never been condescending towards me even though I'm the hired help.'

'OK, now you're making me feel worse,' said Oliver. 'You already know I'm not a hundred per cent comfortable with the fact that you're cleaning our house.'

'You were comfortable enough with my mum doing it,' Imogen pointed out.

'That was then,' said Oliver. 'Times change.'

'Not really,' she said. 'There are always people who need someone else to look after them. It's life. And there are people who are good at doing the looking after. I need the job with René Bastarache and I'm perfectly prepared to clean up after anyone he wants me to. I didn't realise before that I was good at it, but I am.'

'Why didn't you go to college after school?' asked Oliver. 'You're obviously smart; why have you settled for looking after other people's messes?'

'First of all, there's nothing wrong with looking after other people, and you really are being condescending if that's what you think,' said Imogen. 'It makes no difference whether it's taking care of them or their houses, there's still a skill to doing it properly. And secondly, I did go to college, but the opportunities for people with a degree in European history are limited.'

'You have a history degree?' He glanced at her in astonishment.

'For all the good it's done me.'

He was silent as he approached the outskirts of the city and took the exit from the motorway. His gaze flicked between the tree-lined road, which followed the line of the river, and his sat nav, which was warning him that he would have to turn soon towards the centre of the town.

'Oh my goodness!' exclaimed Imogen when he made the turn and stopped, not in the middle of a busy city centre as she'd expected, but close to a picturesque bay. 'How amazing.'

'It's the Playa de la Concha,' said Oliver. '*Concha* means shell. It's beautiful, isn't it?'

Imogen nodded. It was the perfect name for the bay. Its golden sand was surrounded by low hills, the silver-blue water forming the shape of a clamshell.

'Paul's place is close by and he said there was a private

car park just after . . . Oh, there it is!' Oliver put the Range Rover into drive again and made for the underground car park, which was guarded by a steel door. He leaned out of the window and punched a code into the keypad on the wall. The door opened slowly upwards, and as soon as his eyes had adjusted to the gloom, he drove to the allocated space. Once he had parked and locked the car, he and Imogen walked up the stairs of the stiflingly hot garage to street level again.

'Where does he live exactly?' Imogen blinked in the sunlight and looked around her. A wide promenade separated the bay from the apartment buildings that overlooked it. Some were modern, but others, with elegant facades and wrought-iron balconies, had clearly been built closer to the turn of the last century.

'He's renting an apartment in that one there.' Oliver pointed to an old building with turrets at the sides and intricate carvings above the doors and windows. It looked directly over the bay, and Imogen couldn't think of a more beautiful place to live. Oliver pressed the brass button beside the door, and after a moment a gruff voice asked in English who was there.

'It's Oliver Delissandes, Paul.' Oliver winked at Imogen, who made a face in return. The voice she'd heard through the speaker sounded as though it belonged to a much older man, and she immediately imagined the author as a Hemingway character, bearded and weather-beaten, a pipe hanging out of the side of his mouth.

'Come up.' The command sounded equally gruff and reaffirmed Imogen's imagined picture of him, so that when the apartment door was opened by a clean-shaven man in his thirties, with jet-black hair and vivid blue eyes and wearing a navy T-shirt, she was sure he was the author's assistant. But Oliver held out his hand and greeted him before introducing them to each other as 'the soon-to-be-famous novelist Paul Urdien', and 'Imogen Weir, a noted Irish historian'.

She shot him a startled look at that, but he winked again as they followed Paul into an airy living room decorated, once more contrary to Imogen's expectations, with bright colours and modern furniture. Glancing upwards, she saw a mezzanine level with a neat and tidy glass desk. Then a door opened and a red-headed girl of around Imogen's age walked in.

'I'm Blanaid,' she said. 'It's good to finally meet you, Oliver. And you are . . . ?' She looked enquiringly at Imogen.

'Imogen. I'm an old friend of Oliver's. He asked me along because he thought that it would be cute to double-date.' Imogen spoke quickly so that Oliver couldn't introduce her as a historian again. 'But if you and Paul want to talk to him and lunch with him on your own, that's perfectly fine by me. I've never been to San Sebastian before, so I'm sure I can find plenty to occupy me.'

'You're Irish.' Blanaid smiled.

'Currently spending some time in France,' replied Imogen.

'Whereabouts are you from?' It was the question that all Irish people asked when they met another Irish person abroad.

'I lived in Cabra when I was younger, but more recently Glasnevin.'

'Really? I'm from Mobhi Road myself.'

'I had a house in the new estate they built around the corner,' said Imogen. 'Bellwood.'

'I know it well. We're practically neighbours, for God's sake! How long have you been in France?'

'I lived there for a while when I was younger,' said Imogen. 'But I only returned recently. What about you?'

'I've lived in San Sebastian since I met Paul, a couple of years ago. Listen, d'you want to go and get a coffee or a juice or something at the beach and leave these two to talk shop? We planned to have something at one of the cafés at lunchtime, so they can join us there when they're finished.'

'Well, sure, if that suits you and everyone else.'

The men nodded. Blanaid swung an embroidered bag over her shoulder and the two women left the apartment, crossing the main road to reach the promenade. Blanaid led her to one of the shaded tables at a beachfront café, where both of them ordered orange juice.

Blanaid settled back in her chair. 'So did you come back to France to work with Oliver in Paris?' she asked Imogen.

'Oh no.' Imogen shook her head and explained about working in Hendaye for the summer.

'Pretty place,' said Blanaid. 'We went there once. I get confused when they start talking to me in a different language as soon as we cross the border. I realise it's commonplace in mainland Europe for that to happen, but it seems bizarre to me.'

'Me too,' said Imogen. 'Still, it's great that Paul's book is going to be published in French, even if you'd have expected it to be in Spanish first.'

'Paul doesn't care what language it's in. All he wants is for it to be published.'

'Oliver's very excited about publishing it,' said Imogen.

'He's nice,' said Blanaid. 'Paul was really worried about who his editor was going to be. Then Oliver rang him and was totally supportive and friendly and said he'd come to meet him here, which Paul really appreciated.'

'Hopefully it'll be a massive seller. What do *you* do when you're not writing your blog? It's great, by the way. Really funny and insightful.'

'Thank you,' replied Blanaid. 'Obviously I'm not in Paul's league as a writer, but I enjoy it. The rest of the time I work for a tour company. It's OK; this is a nice part of the country and there are lots of things to promote. Is that what you're doing in Hendaye? Cultural stuff? I heard Oliver say you were a historian. Is that why you got involved with him and the publishing house?'

'I'm not involved with it at all,' said Imogen. 'Like I said, we're old friends and we met up recently, that's all.'

'Because the way he looked at you, I thought there was something more to it than that.' Blanaid gave her a knowing smile. 'I was thinking office romance at first.'

Imogen was taken aback. 'There's nothing there,' she assured Blanaid. 'Nothing at all.'

'You say that very fervently.'

'I've just come out of a rocky relationship,' Imogen said. 'I'm not getting into another one. Least of all with Oliver Delissandes. That would be too unsettling for words.'

'I'd disentangled myself from something rocky shortly before meeting Paul,' said Blanaid. 'But as soon as I saw him, everything changed.'

'I'm not good with men,' said Imogen.

Blanaid snorted. 'Don't give me that crap, woman.'

'Truly.' But Imogen laughed. 'Please don't try to set me up with Oliver. My mother had an affair with his father. I'd be in therapy for years.'

'No!'

'Oh yes. Unfortunately.'

'Was it an affair with a bad ending?'

'Pretty much.'

'I suppose there aren't many that end well.' Blanaid raised her arm and ordered another couple of juices.

'None that I know of,' agreed Imogen. 'Tell me, what are the touristy things to do around here?'

Blanaid gave her a potted history of San Sebastian and then started talking about her upbringing in Dublin. As they were of a similar age, she and Imogen had often frequented the same bars and clubs and they were well into their orgy of reminiscences when Blanaid's phone rang and Paul told her that the men were on their way to join them. When they did, about five minutes later, they immediately ordered food, because Paul told them he was hungry.

'A very productive time,' he said in a noticeably less gruff voice while they waited for the order to arrive. 'I can definitely work with Oliver. He understands me and what I'm trying to do.'

'And Paul understands the process,' said Oliver. 'Which hopefully will end up with a best-selling book for him and for our publishing company.'

'Cheers to that,' said Imogen. They raised their glasses and toasted the success of the venture, then tucked into the plates of calamari and salad that the waiter placed in front of them.

Imogen didn't know how it happened, but the next time she looked at her watch, it was nearly five o'clock. Paul and Blanaid had been easy company, and the atmosphere of the beach bar had relaxed her so much that she hadn't noticed time passing. It was Blanaid who reminded Paul that they were supposed to be meeting up with some friends later and that she needed time to make herself presentable.

'You must come and see us again,' she said to Imogen when they'd all walked back to the apartment building. 'It was such fun talking to you and it's always nice to hear another Dublin accent.'

'I'd like that a lot,' said Imogen.

'I'll be in touch by phone and email,' Oliver told Paul. 'You can contact me any time.'

'Thanks.' Paul grasped his hand. 'I'm looking forward to working with you.'

He opened the door to the building and he and Blanaid went inside, while Oliver and Imogen walked to the pedestrian entrance to the car park.

'Do you want to return to Hendaye now?' asked Oliver. 'We can if you like, of course, but it seems a pity to be here and not have a wander around.'

'You've had a busy day,' said Imogen. 'I'm sure you'd rather get home.'

'Not really,' Oliver told her. 'I'm quite happy to stretch my legs for a while.'

'If you're sure,' said Imogen. 'It would be a shame for me not to see a little more of the city while I'm here.'

'We could do a speed visit to the Catedral del Buen Pastor,' suggested Oliver. 'So that we can say we did a cultural thing. Then, if you're up to it, there are fantastic views from the top of Monte Urgull.'

'There are fantastic views right here,' said Imogen. 'But I'm game.'

They turned away from the car park and followed the

signpost that led to the cathedral, although Oliver knew exactly where he was going.

'Impressive,' said Imogen when they were standing outside. 'Is it still used as a cathedral?'

'Oh yes,' said Oliver. 'Not that I've ever attended any services here. D'you want to go inside?'

'Let's have a peek,' said Imogen. 'Mainly to get out of the sun.'

'I'm sure God won't mind,' said Oliver.

They spent fifteen minutes cooling off inside, although Imogen also lit a candle at one of the shrines. She thought about her mother as she stood in front of the flickering electronic flame and prayed that her spirit was content.

'It's not that I believe in an afterlife,' she admitted to Oliver. 'It just seems the right thing to do.'

'I know what you mean,' he said as they emerged into the bright sunshine. 'Unlikely though it may be, you'd like to think there's a place where everything works out in the end.' He smiled at her. 'It's still quite warm. Are you OK to walk up to the top of the mountain?'

'If it was a huge mountain, I'd say no,' said Imogen. 'But it's more of a big hill, isn't it? I'm surprised they didn't build the cathedral at the top, towering over everything and everybody.'

'That's because the military got there first with its barracks,' said Oliver.

'War and Peace.' Imogen smiled at him as they started to walk.

After a short distance, Oliver stopped outside a gift shop and bought Imogen a baseball cap emblazoned with *España* on the front to shade her face.

'Thank you,' she said, arranging it on her head. 'How do I look?'

'Charming,' he told her.

'Liar. I'm hopeless at hats and caps. Though it's easier to keep on with this hairstyle.'

'It's a new look for you?' asked Oliver.

'I used to wear my hair longer. This is more practical.'

Imogen adjusted the cap so that the peak was shielding her face, and they continued up the stepped paths that led to the summit of the hill, where other tourists were taking photographs of the battlements and the stunning views of the city.

'I wish I'd brought my phone to take photos!' she exclaimed as she turned towards the town. 'This is spectacular.'

'You don't have a phone with you?' Oliver's was already in his hand as he prepared to take a photograph. 'Who doesn't bring their phone with them these days?'

She grinned. 'I don't get many emergency cleaner calls. And I'm not much of a photographer.'

'In that case, stand over there and let me.'

Oliver framed her in his phone's camera and showed her the result. It was a good photo, although the baseball cap still hid a lot of her face.

'Take it off,' he said, 'and let me do another.'

'I'm not good at having my photo taken,' she said. 'It's fine, really.'

'Don't be silly. Tell you what, let's do a selfie.' He stood beside her and held the phone at arm's length. 'Smile, Imogen!'

She leaned towards him and he took the photo.

'Not bad,' he said as he showed it to her. 'Although you look as though I'm about to chop your head off.'

'Sorry.'

'Never mind.' He gave her a quick hug. 'It's nice to have it.'

They wandered around the top of the hill for another twenty minutes before beginning their descent to the town again. By the time they reached the bottom, Imogen's feet were sore.

'Let's have a quick drink before we head back,' said Oliver, stopping outside a pavement café. 'All that walking around is thirsty work.'

'Great idea.' She sat down thankfully.

'Why don't you have a glass of wine?' he suggested after the waiter had brought them water and some olives. 'There's something very civilised about sitting in the sun sipping wine and eating olives, don't you think?'

'I couldn't possibly have wine when you're drinking water,' she said. 'I'd feel guilty.'

'Why?' He looked astonished. 'You don't have to have it if you don't want, of course, but they have some nice ones on this list.'

Vince had never allowed her to drink alcohol if he wasn't having it himself. It was one of his rules, and when she'd questioned it, he'd retreated into an icy silence. Afterwards he'd told her it was about respect. He'd banged the respect drum a lot, she remembered, using it as the definitive closing argument even when it didn't make sense.

'Maybe one glass,' she conceded.

Oliver ordered, and when the chilled white was in front of her, she took an appreciative sip.

'Thanks for today,' she said. 'I really enjoyed myself. It was good to meet different people.'

'Don't you meet many in Hendaye?' he asked.

'Quite a few,' she replied. 'But not socially. I like it like that, though.'

'Have you decided how long you're going to stay there as a cleaner?'

She shook her head. 'It depends on René too,' she said.

'Imogen, I don't want to interfere, but—'

'People always say that but go ahead and give unasked-for advice anyhow,' she interrupted him. 'Please don't try to mess with my life, Oliver. It's fine. I'm fine.'

'You're right,' he said. 'I apologise.'

'I'm sorry too,' she said after a moment's silence. 'It's simply that I want to live my own way. Things are working out for me at the moment.'

'They didn't always?'

'Whose life works out all the time?' She looked him in the eye. 'I've had my ups and downs, but they don't matter any more.'

'Of course. And I didn't mean to pry. It's simply . . . Well, I'm so pleased to see you again, and I wanted to know everything about you. Like I did when we were kids.'

'You didn't know everything about me then either.'

'I knew that you were utterly fearless,' said Oliver. 'The amount of times you climbed things or jumped off things or ran into the water even when the waves were high – I've never met a girl like you before or since.'

She laughed. 'I wasn't fearless at all. I was terrified of you boys! Terrified that you and Charles would make fun of me.'

'We never did.'

'Huh! Of course you did. A million times. You were boys, after all; what else could I expect?'

'I didn't realise . . .'

'It was good for me,' she said. 'It toughened me up a bit, and I needed toughness.'

'Why?'

'Because I've moved around so much and there have been so many different people in my life, I never know if I'm French or Irish or even a little bit English. No matter which country I'm in, I feel like the foreigner. And you have to be tough when you're always the outsider.'

He looked at her, his expression serious. 'I understand. So why did you choose to come back to Hendaye?'

'Because I felt most at home there when I was younger,' she replied. 'I loved living in your house and I loved your family and I wanted to, oh, recapture that, I suppose. Which is daft, because you can't go back, can you? And being honest with you, I'm not a small-town girl any more. Dublin has a population of over a million people. Hendaye only has about sixty thousand. I know you can't exactly say that everyone knows everyone else, but it's still the sort of community where you know what's going on pretty much all of the time.'

'So you won't stay?'

'I don't think so,' she said. 'Even being here in San Sebastian is making me nostalgic for a big city.' She gave him a rueful smile. 'I think I'm condemned to keep wandering around, never settling down, trying to find my place.'

'I'm sorry you feel that way.' He reached out and put his hand on hers. 'You deserve to belong somewhere. And to someone.'

She pulled her hand away. 'I don't belong to anyone. I don't want to. I'm not a possession.'

'I never thought you were.' Oliver looked at her with

concern. 'I meant . . . well, it's nice to feel that you're part of something, that's all.'

'Don't mind me, Oliver,' she said. 'I'm being weird, that's all. I didn't mean to snap at you.'

'Imogen Weird,' he said slowly. 'We used to call you that sometimes.'

'So you did, you wretches! I'd forgotten.'

In their laughter, Imogen's words were put to one side. But as they walked back to the car park nearly an hour later, she knew that they weren't forgotten at all.

Chapter 32

'When will you meet up with Paul again?' Imogen asked when they arrived at the car park and got into the Range Rover.

'Not for a while,' said Oliver. 'We've gone through his ideas for the second draft and I want to let him run with them. But I told him to call me any time. Day or night.'

'Literally?'

'He does a lot of work at night,' said Oliver. 'I need to be there for him.'

'Like a doctor on call.'

'Something like.' Oliver grinned as he started the car.

'You sound like you don't mind. As though it's fun.'

'Publishing *is* fun,' said Oliver as they waited for the garage door to open. 'At least, it can be. There are always horror stories.'

'Have you had horrible people to deal with?' asked Imogen.

'I'd tell you but I'd have to kill you,' said Oliver. 'What on earth is keeping this door? Ah!'

It began to open slowly, and then stopped about a foot off the ground.

'Do you need to press a button?' asked Imogen. 'Or put in another code?'

'I didn't think so. I asked Paul earlier and he said it was an electronic beam.' Oliver looked around but he couldn't see anything that looked anything like an exit button. 'Let's give it a second.'

But the door remained obstinately still.

'I'll get out and look,' said Imogen.

She clambered down from the Range Rover and walked up to the door. There was a small box low on the wall, and beneath it, on either side of the door, were the inserts for the beam. She waved her hand in front of them. The door juddered for a moment but stayed where it was. There was no separate button she could see to activate it. She stood in front of the car and raised her hands helplessly.

Oliver got out and did the exact same things as she had. Why do men always have to do that? she wondered. Doesn't he trust me to have broken the damn beam?

'I know you did it yourself,' Oliver told her, as though reading her thoughts. 'But I still had to try.'

Suddenly they heard the purr of another car's engine on the ramp outside. The door moved up a centimetre before stopping again. They heard the door of the other car open and close, then saw a pair of trousered legs approaching the gap.

'It's stuck!' Oliver called out in French.

'*Qué?*'

'It won't open.' He spoke in English this time.

'There is a way to open it.' The owner of the legs bent down so that Oliver and Imogen could see his face. He was a middle-aged man in a suit. 'Near the ground. A yellow box.' His English was highly accented but perfectly understandable.

'I see it.' Imogen bent down to look at it more closely. 'But it needs a key.'

'The key should be in the lock of the box.'

'Well it's not,' said Imogen while she scanned the immediate vicinity for any other place the key could be concealed.

'*Joder*.' The man swore, then straightened up and walked away from the door. Imogen and Oliver heard him getting into his car and the sound of the engine revving up.

'You don't think he's going to ram the door, do you?' asked Imogen in alarm.

'Of course not.' But Oliver ushered her away from it all the same.

The engine revved more loudly and then faded.

'He's bloody well driven off!' Oliver was outraged.

'Maybe he's gone for help.'

'I'll put the car back in the space and give Paul a buzz from outside. He might have a number for the maintenance people.'

Imogen waited for Oliver to return the Range Rover to its original position and the two of them went up the stairs again. Outside, she gave a squeak of dismay as she spotted a large oil stain on the hem of her red dress. It must have happened when she'd hunkered down to look at the yellow box.

'I'm sure it'll come out,' said Oliver, but Imogen was doubtful. She was about to speak but realised that Oliver was pointing to a couple of cars parked directly in front of the ramp to the car park, both drivers speaking urgently on their phones.

'Calling the cavalry, I presume,' said Oliver. 'Maybe I won't have to bother Paul after all.' He walked over to the middle-aged driver who'd first tried to come into the garage, the man recognisable by his shiny shoes. He told Oliver he'd phoned the maintenance company and that somebody would be there shortly.

'Shortly?'

'Within the hour,' said the man.

Imogen and Oliver exchanged glances.

'I guess we may as well go back to the beach till then,' said Oliver. 'I can't walk another step.'

'Me neither. But nor can I eat or drink any more.'

'Let's sit on the sand,' Oliver said. 'We can watch the sunset.'

'I hope they manage to open it before then!' exclaimed Imogen. 'I wasn't planning to be here all night.'

'Have you something you need to get back for?' asked Oliver. 'Am I messing up your day?'

'Well, no,' she admitted. 'I've enjoyed myself immensely.'

'Let's eke out a little bit of extra enjoyment before we have to go back,' said Oliver.

They crossed the road and went down the steps to the beach, which, in the long summer evening, was still crowded with locals and holidaymakers alike.

'D'you want to sit here?' he asked, stopping at a shaded spot. 'Would you like a sun lounger or anything?'

'Don't be silly, this is fine. It's like the barbecue at Hendaye.'

'That was a fun night,' agreed Oliver.

'Did you know many of our group already?'

Oliver shook his head. 'Bastarache, of course,' he said. 'I see him occasionally because I call in to the office at least once a year to chat about the house maintenance. And I know his former wife, although not well. I think she worked with him for a while.'

'She has a café in town now,' said Imogen.

'And of course Virginie,' he said. 'I dated her when we were younger.'

'Ah.'

'I lost my virginity to her.' His tone was matter-of-fact.

'Oliver!'

'What?'

'Too much information.'

'It's true, though. She was way more experienced than me.'

As Imogen shook her head, he leaned towards her. She jolted backwards, but he reached out and wiped her cheek with his thumb.

'More oil,' he explained.

She said nothing, but she was suddenly conscious that she was sitting closer to him than was strictly necessary.

'We'll give them a bit more time to sort out that garage door.' His tone was light, as though he hadn't talked about sex with Virginie and hadn't wiped her face with the gentlest of touches. 'Hopefully it won't take much longer.'

'It's OK,' she said steadily. 'Like I said, I had nothing else planned.'

'How would you normally spend a Saturday afternoon?' he asked.

'That depends. In the garden – there's a nice one at my apartment. On the beach. Reading usually.'

'Not exploring?'

'I can't really do much of that,' she said. 'I don't have a car, and although the buses and trains are great . . . well, I prefer to stay away from them at the moment.'

He gave her a curious look but made no comment.

'You could always come to the Villa Martine,' he said. 'Use the pool if you'd like.'

'That's kind of you,' she said. 'We already have a pool at the apartment. Thanks for the offer, though.'

'And if you want to see some places – Bayonne, Biarritz – I'll happily take you there.'

'That's even kinder,' she told him. 'But I'm sure you've other things to do. Work on Paul's book, for example.'

'That's for the week,' he said. 'Never on the weekend.'

'I thought you said that you were there for him day and night.'

'Hopefully he won't call at midnight on a Saturday,' said Oliver. 'But if he does, I'll be there for him.'

'You like what you do, don't you?'

'Of course. We live one life. It's good to enjoy both your work and your leisure time.'

'I love your attitude. If only it was that simple.'

'I'm lucky,' Oliver admitted. 'Also that I can work whenever and wherever I chose. It's great to be able to come to the Villa Martine when I need solitude. But there won't be much this time of the year because we're all there. Back and forward between Hendaye and Paris. Me, my brothers, my mother – and my father too, of course.'

'But your dad doesn't come in the summer, isn't that what you said?'

'Occasionally he does,' said Oliver. 'It depends on who

has free time. We check in advance so that there isn't a bloodbath.'

'Is your mother planning to come any time soon?'

'Oh, *Maman* always turns up when we least expect it,' said Oliver. When he noticed the expression on Imogen's face, he added, 'Does it bother you that she could be here?'

'A little,' confessed Imogen. 'After what happened.'

'Get over it,' advised Oliver. 'If you meet *Maman* again some day, I hope you will say hello to her and not feel embarrassed.'

'Possibly . . .'

'However, I really do think you should be coming to the Villa Martine as a guest and not a cleaner,' said Oliver.

'Would you stop with all that nonsense?' she demanded. 'I'm proud of the work I do. And I'm happy to be able to do it in your house as much as any other.'

He said nothing, but stood up and brushed the sand from his body.

'I'll go and see if they've had any success with the garage door yet. You can wait here if you like.'

Imogen stood up too. 'It's OK. My bum is getting sore. I'll go with you.'

The area around the car park was devoid of people and cars, which they both took as a positive sign. Oliver punched the code into the keypad.

'*Et voilà!*' he cried as the door opened. 'Thank God for that.'

Thank God indeed, thought Imogen, as they walked down the ramp to the Range Rover. The day in San Sebastian had been interesting and fun. But she couldn't help feeling that it had brought her a little too close to Oliver Delissandes. And that wasn't a good idea, for a thousand different reasons.

Chapter 33

It was after eleven by the time René Bastarache woke up for the second time that morning. His eyes were gritty from too much wine and too little sleep. He stretched his arm out to pull Céline closer to him, before remembering that she'd turfed him out of her bed more than four hours previously, muttering that Imogen would be coming to clean the house and saying that she didn't want her to find him there. René had accused her of bourgeois sentimentality and Céline had snorted and told him that it had nothing to do with bourgeois anything, it was simply polite for him to leave before his employee – and hers, she added – turned up for work. There was no need to embarrass Imogen, she said, and undoubtedly the girl would be embarrassed to find them cavorting beneath the sheets.

'We have time for some more cavorting first,' René had said, but Céline wasn't having any of it and had told him in no uncertain terms to get dressed and leave. René had kissed her on the head and told her he'd call her and she'd said not to bother. But she hadn't meant it, he thought as he stretched in the bed. She'd enjoyed the night as much as he had. They'd always been good in bed together. That wasn't what had driven them apart.

The shrill sound of the doorbell startled him, and he realised that that was what had woken him in the first place. He got out of bed, pulling on a T-shirt and a pair of shorts, before pressing the button on the intercom.

'*Oui*,' he said.

'René Bastarache?'

'*Oui*.'

'My name is Vince Naughton. I want to talk to you.'

René yawned. He didn't know any Vince Naughton and he didn't feel like talking to anyone. Especially an English-speaking someone who'd jolted him out of bed when he'd been having pleasurable dreams about his ex-wife.

'What do you want to talk to me about?'

'My wife,' said Vince.

For a split second, René wondered who the hell he'd slept with recently, but there had been no one in the last few weeks, and he was pretty sure that Céline hadn't got herself married to anyone in secret. Besides, surely Art would have been at the head of the queue if that was the case. Not that she'd thought much about him last night one way or another. René smiled to himself with quiet satisfaction.

'I'm sorry, *mon ami*,' he said. 'You've got the wrong man.'

'I don't think so,' said Vince. 'Your name was given to me by . . .' There was a pause, and then he spoke again. 'Bernard Biendon, the owner of Le Bleu restaurant.'

'What!' René was confused again. What the hell was Céline's father up to? Did he know he'd spent the night with his daughter? Was he trying to land him in some sort of trouble?

'I spoke to Mr Biendon yesterday. He gave me your name.

I called around last night but you weren't here. I'm hoping you weren't with my wife, but I can't be sure that you didn't spend the night with her.'

'Look, I'm sorry, Mr Naughton,' said René, stumbling slightly over the unfamiliar surname, 'but I don't know you and I don't know your wife. You've clearly mixed me up with someone else.'

'According to Mr Biendon, you *do* know my wife,' said Vince. 'Her name is Imogen.'

'Imogen!' René didn't know what to say. 'Imogen.'

'Ah, so I've finally jogged your memory,' said Vince. 'Now can I come up?'

'Hold on,' said René. 'I'm coming down to you.'

Whatever this was about, he didn't want a man he didn't know, a man who was clearly angry, coming up to his apartment. He glanced at his reflection in the wall mirror, ran his fingers through his hair, slipped on a pair of deck shoes and walked downstairs.

Vince was standing at the entrance to the apartment block.

'Hello,' said René.

'Hello.' Vince's tone was curt.

'So what can I do for you exactly?' René asked.

'You can tell me where my wife is,' said Vince. 'I don't care about your relationship with her. I just want her back.'

'I'm sorry, but I don't know you or anything about you,' said René. 'And I'm not talking to you about Imogen until I know more.'

Vince put his hand in his pocket and took out his mobile phone. He opened the photo album and handed it to René.

'This is my wife,' he said. 'This is Imogen. Now tell me where she is!'

René flicked through the photos. They were of Imogen alone, Imogen with Vince, Imogen with another girl. She was even more lovely with longer hair cascading around her face, he thought. But although she was smiling in all the photos, her eyes remained serious. Watchful even.

'Certainly I know the woman,' he said, handing the phone back to Vince. 'She has lived in the town.'

'She's still living in the town,' said Vince. 'I saw her this morning, being driven by someone in a white Range Rover Evoque. I thought it might be you. But since it's not, there must be another man in Imogen's life. Given that the car is expensive and possibly even exclusive here in France, I don't imagine there are many of them around. So perhaps you know who she was with. Perhaps you'd like to meet that man yourself.'

René had no idea who Vince was talking about, for which he was profoundly grateful.

'I'm sorry,' he said. 'I don't know. I don't know Imogen very well.'

'Don't you?' Vince frowned. 'Mr Biendon said that she was at a boules match with you.'

Damn Bernard, thought René. Couldn't he tell this guy was trouble?

'Not with me,' he said. 'With my company. She's done a little work for us.'

'What sort of work?'

'Cleaning.'

'Cleaning! My wife is working as a bloody cleaner!' Vince was outraged. 'And you let her?'

'It's not up to me to tell people what they can and can't do,' said René. 'She asked for work, I gave it to her. And now, Monsieur, I have things that will occupy me today, and as I cannot help you any further—'

'Of course you can help me further,' said Vince. 'If you employed her, you must have an address for her.'

'No,' lied René. 'I don't. She has done casual work for me. That's all.'

'Is she still working for you?'

'Like I said,' René spoke nonchalantly, 'she came looking for something. But she's not a permanent employee.' He didn't want to tell too many direct lies. He didn't want to get Imogen into trouble.

'Where is she now?' asked Vince.

'I have no idea.'

Vince's eyes narrowed.

'You're lying to me,' he said.

'I most certainly am not,' said René. 'I don't know where Imogen is and I don't know if I'll even see her again.'

'What cleaning work did she do for you?' asked Vince.

René gave him an exaggerated shrug. 'The occasional holiday rental. Nothing more.'

'I want addresses.'

'I can't give you addresses,' said René. 'Reasons of client confidentiality, you understand.'

'I'll find her with or without you,' said Vince. 'It would be a lot easier for her if you made it easier for me.'

'Are you threatening me?' asked René. 'Or her?'

'Not at all,' said Vince. 'What you don't understand, Mr Bastarache, is that Imogen has been unwell. She lost a baby. She's a little unstable mentally. She needs help.'

'I'm sorry to hear that.' René kept his voice steady with difficulty.

'You must be able to contact her,' Vince said. 'If she works for you, you must have a number.'

René said nothing.

'Call her,' said Vince. 'Tell her to come here.'

'I cannot.'

'Oh for heaven's sake.' Vince looked at him angrily. 'Imogen is my wife and she's unwell and I need to see her.'

'Imogen said nothing about being married.'

'I told you, she's upset and confused right now.'

'She seemed fine to me.'

'That's the problem with people like her,' said Vince. 'They seem fine but they're not. And she's not. So I need to talk to her.'

René looked at him for a moment, then nodded slowly.

'OK,' he said. 'I'll call her. And then we'll see her together.'

He took his phone out of his pocket. The missed call from Bernard Biendon was the last one he'd received. Obviously his ex-father-in-law had made it after Vince had found him. Dammit, thought René, I should have answered. He dialled Imogen's number, but the call went directly to her voicemail, which still had an automated message from the carrier rather than a personal one from Imogen herself.

'There's no reply.' He ended the call without saying anything.

'Give me her number,' said Vince.

'No,' said René. 'I'll try her again later, and if she wants to see you, I'll meet her with you.'

'I thought you said you didn't know where she lived.'

'I said I'd meet her with you. Not that I'd bring you to her apartment.'

'You know she lives in an apartment?'

'Apartment, house! It's all the same,' said René.

Vince looked at him thoughtfully.

'In that case, give me your number,' he said.

René called it out to him and Vince added it to his phone. Then he rang it. René's mobile shrilled loudly.

'Just checking,' said Vince. 'I'll keep calling. So you'd better tell me when you contact her.'

'I will,' said René.

He turned away and went back inside his apartment. He phoned Bernard Biendon immediately.

'Why on earth did you give that man my address?' he demanded after he'd told him about Vince.

'I wanted him out of my restaurant,' admitted Bernard.

'Well he's lurking outside waiting for me to either phone or call around to Imogen.'

'And that's a problem because?'

'There's obviously something wrong between the pair of them,' said René. 'That's why she's here. She ran away from him.'

'*Je n'y suis pour rien.* It's none of my business. Not yours either.'

'You did it on purpose, didn't you?' demanded René. 'Because you thought there was something between the two of us. Because you are still angry about me and your daughter. I saw the way you looked at me at the boules tournament. You're a fool, Bernard Biendon, has anyone ever told you that?'

'I'm not listening to this.'

'You've messed up that poor girl's life by telling her shit of a husband that she's in the town,' said René. 'I honestly think—'

But he was speaking to thin air. His ex-father-in-law had already hung up.

René had a shower and then changed into a clean T-shirt and shorts. He tried Imogen's phone again, but there was still no answer. Then he called Céline.

'Look, last night was—' she began, but he interrupted her and told her about Vince's arrival.

'Oh!' exclaimed Céline. 'So that's it. I knew there was something. *Pauvre* Imogen.'

'This guy is a dick,' said René. 'I'm not surprised she left him. He says she's mentally unstable. And that she lost a baby. I'm not sure the two are related.'

'Imogen unstable! That's rubbish. And if she is, it's because of him. But she isn't. I'm not even going to think that. As for the baby . . .' Her voice softened. 'If that's true, I'm very sorry for her. But, *chéri*, I don't think losing a baby would make her come here. Not at all.'

'I agree.' René noted that she'd used a term of endearment towards him. Another time he might have made something of it. But not now.

'What are we going to do?' asked Céline.

'I don't know. She's not answering her phone. Did she say anything to you this morning about her plans for the day?'

'Not a word,' said Céline. 'Actually this morning she was brighter than usual. Cheerful and smiling and in very good form.'

'He said he saw her with a man in a car. Do you have any idea who that might be?'

Céline shook her head. 'None at all.'

'Could you go to her apartment?' he asked. 'See if she's there now and warn her? This Vince *salaud* is still outside, and I'm afraid he'll follow me if I leave.'

'You're joking!'

'I wish I were.'

'Then of course I will go to her place.'

'You're a good woman, Céline Biendon.'

'I know,' she said, and took off her apron.

She told Arlene, the waitress, to take care of things for a while, then drove immediately to Imogen's, but there was no answer when she rang the bell. As she turned away, Max Gasquet walked up the path and she asked him if he'd seen Imogen that day.

'Is something wrong?' he asked.

Céline shook her head. 'I need to talk to her, that's all. But it's urgent.'

'I was with her last night,' said Max, and when Céline raised an enquiring eyebrow, he laughed. 'Not in that way, of course. She had some laundry to do and we had a glass of wine together while she waited for it to be finished. Actually . . .' he frowned, 'I think she said something about going to San Sebastian.'

'San Sebastian! Why on earth would she go there? And with whom?'

'I don't know,' replied Max. 'It came up casually in conversation.'

'I really need to contact her before she gets home.'

'Why?'

Céline took a deep breath. She knew and trusted Max, who often came into the café for an espresso after a shift at the hospital. She knew his parents, too. Monsieur

Gasquet was a lawyer and his wife a teacher in the local school.

'There's someone looking for her and I don't think she wants to see him,' replied Céline.

'A lover?' Max looked interested.

'An ex-husband,' said Céline.

'Oh.'

'He seems to be a bit of a . . . type,' said Céline. 'And we – René and I – don't think she should be surprised by him.'

'I understand,' said Max. 'Unfortunately I don't know who she might have gone to San Sebastian with, or even if that's where she is.'

'She always said that she doesn't know anyone here and doesn't do anything very much,' said Céline. 'She told me she likes it that way, which is understandable if she's getting over a bad relationship. But it must be someone she knows.'

'What sort of car was she in?' asked Max.

'René didn't say. I'll ask him.' She dialled René's number.

'You've found her?' he said when he answered.

'No. I'm at the apartment with Max Gasquet. You know, the doctor who works—'

'Yes, yes, I know Max,' said René. 'There isn't anything between them, is there? Would she have confided in him?'

'No, but she spoke to him last night and said something about going to San Sebastian this morning. Do you know what sort of car she was in?'

'A Range Rover Evoque,' said René. 'White. But San Sebastian? Why?'

'I don't know,' replied Céline. 'And neither does Max. Hold on.' She put the phone on speaker.

'I've seen a white Range Rover recently,' Max said. 'Near the seafront. An expensive model.'

'And relatively new,' added René. 'I don't think they made that marque before 2011.'

'I'm sorry,' said Max. 'I can't think of who might own one, but if I come up with something, I'll let you know.'

'I'll ring her again,' said René. 'I'll use the office mobile. Hang on.'

But there was still no reply from Imogen.

'She can't have gone far,' said Max. 'I'm around until later this afternoon. I'll keep an eye out for her. If I see her, I'll warn her.'

'Thank you.'

'No problem. I'm sure everything will be OK.'

'I hope so.'

Céline got back into her car and drove to the café. She was worried about Imogen. The fact that the other girl had kept her status as a married woman a secret concerned her. Not that she felt she had to know anything about Imogen's private life, but she'd always suspected that she was harbouring a hidden sadness. Losing a baby would explain it. But if she'd left her husband because she was stressed over it, and if she really did have mental health issues, perhaps she and René and Max might make things worse by butting in where they weren't needed.

Yet Céline trusted René and his judgement. Even when they'd been married and he'd been giving her unwanted advice, she'd had to admit that he knew what he was talking about. She didn't know this husband of Imogen's, so she was ready to support Imogen in whatever way was needed. After all, the girl was part of the community now. And it was a community where everyone looked after everyone else. Even people from a different country.

After almost an hour of standing outside René's apartment, Vince decided that he needed to buy a bottle of water as he was dehydrating in the heat of the sun. He wasn't too concerned about leaving. Now that he knew about René, he'd be able to keep on top of things.

René happened to glance out of the window at the exact moment Vince walked away. He raced down the stairs on to the street where his car was parked, and drove to the office, where he picked up the spare set of keys to Imogen's apartment. Then he drove to her building and parked outside.

The first thing he saw when he let himself into the apartment was Imogen's phone lying on the table. Maybe there really was something wrong with her, he thought with irritation. Who went out and left their phone behind these days?

He looked around for a pen and paper, but the best he could find was a brown paper bag and a black marker.

Your husband is in town and looking for you, he wrote in big capitals on the bag. *Call me if you need help. Call me anyway.*

There was nothing more he could do. Perhaps he was overreacting anyway. Just because he didn't like Vince Naughton didn't mean that Imogen wouldn't want to talk to him. Although, René reminded himself, she'd obviously left him, which had to mean something. He phoned Céline and told her what he'd done, and said the same to Max Gasquet, who'd seen him arrive at the apartment and come to check on what was happening.

'I told Céline I'd watch out for her,' said Max. 'Don't worry.'

'Fair enough.' René clapped him on the back. 'Call me if you need anything.' He gave Max his number and then got into his car. But he didn't want to go home, sure that at some point Vince would turn up again. Instead he went to the café, which was full of customers.

'I don't have time to talk,' said Céline when he sat down at the only available table. 'And if you're going to occupy that space, you'll have to order something.'

'Iced tea,' said René. 'Sit down when you get a moment.'

It was nearly fifteen minutes later before Céline sat opposite him.

'There's nothing more we can do,' she said. 'And I worry that we're interfering.'

'It's not interfering to tell her he's looking for her.'

'What about the baby?' asked Céline.

'I don't believe in this baby,' said René. 'Something about the way he said it . . .' He shrugged. 'I don't trust him.'

'Me neither,' said Céline. 'Though I suppose it could be true. And yet she seems so well and happy now. I hate to think she's going to come back to this worry when she's obviously off having a nice time today.'

'Indeed. I'm intrigued as to who she's with.'

Céline looked at him. 'Are you jealous?'

'Don't be absurd.'

'You are.' Her eyes opened wider. 'You really are.'

'I'm not jealous.' René looked embarrassed. 'It's just that she's pretty and vulnerable and—'

'You idiot,' said Céline.

'OK, OK, so I'm a sucker for an attractive woman,' said

René. 'It's why I keep coming back to you, like a moth to the flame.'

'You don't keep coming back,' said Céline. 'You came back once. Last night. And you left again.'

'Because you threw me out,' he reminded her. 'Yet I'm always at the events you run here. You have a special coffee day next week. I said I'd come to that.'

'Because you are a business owner like me,' Céline reminded him. 'And we all support each other. Did I not bring macarons for your open night in the agency last month?'

'Yes.'

'So that's it. Mutual support.'

'Don't you think—'

'René, you bossed me around when we were married. You can't boss me around any more.'

'Did I?' he asked.

'Yes.'

'And that's why you wanted a divorce?'

'You know it is.'

'Not because I'm, generally speaking, a *con*?'

'That too.' Her mouth twitched.

'Céline . . .'

'I don't want to talk about it.' She stood up. 'I have a business to run. And that's what I'm going to do. Would you like another iced tea?'

René shook his head. He got up, left five euros on the table, and walked out.

Chapter 34

The sun was close to setting as Oliver and Imogen arrived back in Hendaye. He stopped the car at the seafront for a moment so that they could watch the ever-changing pink and gold light filter over the bay, then he turned back towards the town.

'I know it's been a long day,' he said. 'But would you care for a nightcap at the Villa Martine?'

Imogen was tired, but she didn't have to get up early in the morning, and for the first time since arriving in France, she didn't want to be on her own either. It wasn't that she was afraid of solitude; rather that she'd enjoyed sharing her entire day with other people. And Oliver, despite that sudden frisson she'd felt when he'd wiped the oil from her face, had been such an easy person to spend time with. He talked with her and not at her. He made her feel as though her opinion was important to him. There was something tremendously comforting about being with him. And so despite her reservations at getting too close to him, she agreed to a drink at the Villa Martine.

'Giles must be here,' he said as the gates slid open and they saw that there were lights on in the house. 'He said he'd be back for a few days. Hopefully he hasn't turned the kitchen into a drinking den again!'

But when they got out of the car and walked around to the back of the house, it wasn't Giles who was sitting on the terrace surrounded by lemon-scented candles. The person who got up from the cushioned wicker chair to greet them was Lucie Delissandes.

'*Maman.*' Oliver kissed her on the cheek. 'Such a surprise! But lovely to see you.'

'I was fed up at the office and decided to take the mid-morning train,' she said. 'There's no better way to travel. How did it go for you with Paul Urdien today?'

'Don't say you came all the way from Paris to check up on me?'

'Of course not,' she said. 'I don't have any meetings until next week so I thought it would be nice to visit for a few days.'

'I was teasing,' said Oliver. 'It went well with Paul.'

'I'm glad to hear that. I thought you'd be home a lot sooner.'

'We were delayed.'

'Indeed.' Lucie glanced at Imogen and then back to her son.

'*Maman*, this is Imogen.' Oliver put his hand at the small of Imogen's back and gave her a gentle nudge forward. 'Imogen Weir.'

'Imogen! *La petite Imogen?* Here in Hendaye. I don't believe it!' Lucie looked at her in astonishment. 'Oh my dear, how I've wondered about you over the years.'

'Hello, Madame,' said Imogen.

'Don't Madame me!' cried Lucie. She stood up and held

out her arms to embrace the younger woman. 'Come here. Say hello properly.'

Imogen took a step closer, and Lucie put her arms around her, hugging her tightly and murmuring over and over again that it was good to see her.

'So have you come back to visit us? Is that it?' In the soft light of the candles, Lucie's eyes glowed. 'I'm so glad you did. Oliver, why didn't you tell me she was here? Where are you staying, Imogen? You must come to us. I insist.'

Imogen slowly disentangled herself from Lucie's embrace and checked that her stained dress hadn't in turn marked the elegant ivory skirt that the older woman was wearing.

'It's good to see you too, Madame . . . I'm sorry, I think of you as Madame.'

'You must call me Lucie, otherwise you'll make me feel like a Parisian matron,' insisted Lucie. 'Come here. Sit down. Tell me everything. How have you been keeping? And how is your *maman*?'

'I'll get some glasses and a bottle,' said Oliver.

'Yes, please do. We must toast Imogen's return.' Lucie beamed at him and waved Imogen towards a chair. 'So, *ma p'tite*. What has happened in your life?'

Imogen waited until Oliver returned before telling the story of her and Carol's return to Ireland, Carol's subsequent marriage and her terminal illness.

'Oh no.' There was genuine sadness in Lucie's eyes. 'I'm so sorry to hear that.'

'I'm sorry too.' The opportunity that Imogen had always wanted had now presented itself. 'What my mother did to you was very wrong, and I feel ashamed that she betrayed your trust.'

Lucie looked at her over the rim of the glass she'd just raised to her lips.

'You think your mother betrayed me?'

'Of course. She was your employee. You'd been amazing to us. And yet she and Monsieur Delissandes had an indiscretion.' The word was out of her mouth before she could stop it.

Lucie laughed. 'An indiscretion!'

'That's what I heard one of my aunts call it,' said Imogen in embarrassment. 'It's how I always think of it.'

'Well, your aunt was right, it was certainly indiscreet,' said Lucie. 'But it wasn't *your* fault, Imogen.'

'So I keep telling her,' said Oliver. 'But I don't think she believes me.'

Imogen glanced at him and then looked at Lucie again. 'I know it wasn't my fault. Nevertheless, she was my mother, and—'

'And you certainly weren't responsible for her actions,' finished Lucie. 'Naturally I was furious with her. But more furious with Denis. He should have known better than to create a mess on his own doorstep.'

'All the same . . .'

'And it did seem to me afterwards that I'd sent the wrong person away,' said Lucie. 'I was stuck with serially unfaithful Denis and I lost the best housekeeper I ever had.'

'We had three housekeepers after your mum,' said Oliver. 'None of them lasted for more than a couple of months.'

'Nobody could ever match up,' said Lucie.

'I'm sure you would have found somebody perfectly suitable eventually,' said Imogen.

'But not as *sympathique*. And not with a child who fitted

into our household. Sometimes I think Denis and I had Giles to make up for losing you. He was meant to keep us together, but in the end I couldn't take it any more. Denis was incapable of fidelity. When it was with women my own age, I was more accepting of it. But you know how it is with men. They want younger and younger models. Idiots.'

'I'm sorry,' said Imogen again.

'There is nothing for you to be sorry about. I'm so glad to be able to tell you that. It seems to me you've been carrying your mother's guilt as a burden, Imogen.'

'Perhaps a little.'

'Well, please forget it. And please tell me you can stay with us here for a few days.'

'That's very sweet of you, but I have a place of my own.'

'Of your own? You mean you've come back to live in Hendaye?' Lucie looked surprised.

'Only for a short time,' said Imogen.

'Imogen is working as a cleaner,' Oliver said. 'She cleans our house, *Maman*.'

'*C'est pas vrai*.' Lucie was even more surprised. 'You are joking me, Imogen, no?'

'Like mother like daughter.' Imogen smiled faintly.

'I should have told you before, *Maman*,' Oliver said. 'After all, I met Imogen a couple of weeks ago. But we were busy with stuff in the office and it slipped my mind. Giles and Charles also met her. They didn't say anything to you?'

Lucie shook her head. 'And this is your chosen career?' she asked Imogen. 'A housekeeper like your *maman*?'

'No, she's a historian,' said Oliver. 'But without a suitable job.'

'Please stop answering for me, Oliver,' said Imogen. 'I'm perfectly capable of speaking for myself.'

'Of course.' Oliver looked at her apologetically.

Imogen explained to Lucie that she'd decided to get away from it all in Hendaye for a few months, and that she'd taken up cleaning to earn some money while she stayed in the town.

'And then you go back to Ireland? Do you have a job there?'

'I was working for a French company. I'm sure I'll get something.'

'Though not in the field of history,' said Oliver. 'Imogen has struggled with that.'

'It's somewhat specialised unless you pursue an academic career,' agreed Lucie.

'Anyhow, I'm fine and enjoying Hendaye for the moment,' said Imogen. 'It's been absolutely wonderful to see you again, Mad— Lucie.'

'And you. I've never been more surprised. Or, I have to say, delighted.'

Imogen drained her glass. 'I'd better go. It's getting late.'

'Not that late,' said Oliver.

'Late enough.' She stood up. 'Thank you for a lovely day, Oliver. And I'm delighted to have met you again too, Lucie.'

'I'll drive you back to your apartment,' Oliver said.

'No you won't,' said Imogen. 'You've had a large glass of wine. It's not that far. I'll be fine.'

'You're right. I shouldn't drive. But I'll walk with you.'

'There's really no need—'

'Yes he will.' Lucie interrupted her. 'I'm not having you wander the streets on your own at night, no matter that this is a very safe area.'

'But—'

'No buts, Imogen,' said Lucie. 'Let Oliver go with you.'

'Well, if you're sure . . .' She looked at him helplessly.

'Sure I'm sure,' said Oliver. 'It's a nice evening for a walk.'

'We were walking half the day,' Imogen reminded him.

'Why? Did Paul insist on showing you around?' asked Lucie.

'No, Imogen and I went exploring afterwards,' replied Oliver. 'We climbed Monte Urgull.'

'Goodness, in this heat?'

'I think I burnt my nose,' said Imogen.

'You couldn't have!' Oliver protested. 'I bought you a baseball cap to protect it.'

Lucie looked from one to the other. 'I'm glad you both seem to have had a good day.'

'We did,' said Imogen. 'It was nice of Oliver to invite me. Paul's girlfriend is lovely and we're definitely going to keep in touch.'

'That's why I asked Imogen along,' Oliver told his mother. 'She has been working for Flèche Publishing all day as an entertainment consultant. Because Paul's girlfriend is from Ireland I thought it would be nice for the two of them to meet.'

'Good idea,' agreed his mother. 'We must use your talents in other directions as well sometime, Imogen.'

'Unfortunately I can't commute between Hendaye and Paris to clean houses,' Imogen said lightly. 'Anyway, now I really must go.'

'*A bientôt*,' said Lucie, and kissed her on the cheek.

'See you later, *Maman*,' said Oliver, and he and Imogen walked down the driveway together.

* * *

Vince lived by the mantra that everything comes to he who waits. He also believed in seizing the moment. So when he checked the rear-view mirror of his car and saw René Bastarache leave the apartment building, he immediately forgot about his thirst and began to follow him. As he did, he mused that he should think about changing careers himself. Over the last fortnight, he'd arrived in France, a country about eight times the size of Ireland and more than ten times the population, and without any major leads managed to track down his errant wife to this small town on the west coast. He'd done it without incurring the kind of expenses that the PIs he'd spoken to had quoted to him, and he'd done it with an impressive level of efficiency. Now, as he hung back and watched René turn left at a junction, he might be being brought directly to Imogen's doorstep.

He felt comfortable allowing a reasonable gap to open up between himself and René, not wanting to alert the other man in any way. After all, if René was heading to talk to Imogen, he'd be looking out for Vince too, wouldn't he? At least he should be. But then perhaps René was underestimating him. As everyone did, Imogen included.

A hundred metres ahead of him, René parked the car. Vince dampened down a desire to get out and follow him immediately, and was rewarded when he saw the man cross the road and walk into one of the many whitewashed buildings. A few minutes later, he came out alone, got back into his car and drove off again. Vince debated with himself for a moment, then got out of his car and walked up the road. Two young women were strolling towards him, and as they turned in towards the building, he slowed down until they caught up with him at the gate.

'Hi,' he said. 'Do you speak English?'

'Yes,' said the taller of the two. 'Can we help you?'

'I'm looking for a friend who told me she's living around here somewhere. But I'm not sure I have the right address.'

'Oh? Who is she?'

'Imogen Nau— Imogen Weir.' He knew she'd be using her maiden name.

'Imogen! You're in luck. She lives here.' The girl gave him a bright smile. 'Next door to us in fact.'

'How fortunate is that.' Vince beamed at her in return. 'I guess I'll follow you lovely ladies, in that case.'

He walked with them and waited as they unlocked the front door.

'Which number is she?' he asked.

'Number six. Top of the stairs and the first door to your left. We're the second.'

'That's brilliant,' said Vince. 'Thanks so much.'

'You're from Ireland too?'

He nodded.

'She might have mentioned us. Becky and Nellie.'

'She sure did.' Vince beamed at them again. 'She said she couldn't have asked for better neighbours.'

'Neither could we,' said Becky. 'Imogen's lovely. She really is. That's her apartment.'

'Thanks.' Vince rapped on the door while Becky and Nellie walked to their apartment a little further up the corridor.

'Isn't she in?' asked Nellie, seeing that the door hadn't been opened.

'I'm probably early,' Vince said. 'I don't think she was expecting me yet.'

'Oh. Well you could wait for her in the garden,' suggested Becky. 'I'm sure she won't be long. She's never out late.'

'It might be better if I come back a bit later. Is there anywhere around here to get something to drink?'

'There's a bar at the end of the road,' Becky told him. 'You can get coffee there too.'

'Perfect, thank you.'

'Hopefully she'll be home soon,' said Nellie.

'Hopefully,' said Vince, and walked out of the apartment building again.

'Your mother looks amazing,' said Imogen when she and Oliver had left the Villa Martine. 'She hasn't changed at all. Well,' she added before he could say anything, 'she's become glossier.'

'Glossier?'

'More sophisticated. Not that she wasn't always grown-up and sophisticated to me, but back then she was sort of hippy-chic, and today . . . glossy.'

He smiled in the darkness. 'I'm sure she'll be delighted to hear that.'

'Don't tease me.'

'I'm not,' he said. 'I meant it. *Maman* would be delighted to think she looks well. All women want to look well.'

Imogen gave a rueful look at her stained dress. 'She was lovely to me, but she was probably thinking that I'm still the same messy kid as I was before.'

'You're certainly not a messy kid,' said Oliver. 'You're a beautiful woman.'

She felt herself blush. 'Not in comparison to most French women,' she told him. 'They're always stunning.'

'Nonsense.'

'I bet all your girlfriends are gorgeous. And glossy.'

He grinned. 'I could certainly list them by the amount of products they use to try to be that way.'

'Please don't,' said Imogen. 'I'm sure it's a long list.'

'And why would you be so sure of that?' he asked.

'Why wouldn't it be?' she asked. 'You're a single man in your thirties. Don't tell me you haven't made a list.'

'I might have,' he admitted.

'Starting with Virginie whatever-her-name-was.'

'Oh no.' Oliver shook his head. 'Starting way before that. Just because Virginie was the first one I slept with doesn't mean there weren't women before.'

'Oliver!' she cried.

'What?'

'Oh, nothing.' She looked at him in amusement. 'You and René can be so very . . . *French* sometimes!'

He grinned. 'What about you?' he asked. 'My not-glossy-but-very-beautiful Imogen. Who's on your list?'

'Nobody worth talking about.' She knew that she sounded abrupt, and from the corner of her eye she saw Oliver's expression tighten. 'We're like teenagers asking about boyfriends and girlfriends,' she said hurriedly. 'Silly stuff. Much more interesting to talk about our achievements.'

'And yours is to have a degree in European history yet work as a cleaner,' he remarked.

'Oliver Delissandes.' She stopped in the middle of the pavement and turned to him. 'There's no need to be such a damn snob. But of course that's to be expected, because you come from a family with two houses who flit between Paris and Hendaye at the drop of a hat. And because you drive a top-of-the-range car with leather seats and all sorts of gadgets. And because you have a cushy job in a company where your mother is a director. And because you can afford to have a cleaner in the first place!'

She tossed her head and began walking up the street ahead of him. He followed a few steps behind.

'Imogen!' he cried as she crossed the road and turned the corner. 'Stop.'

But she kept walking. And then she was at the gate to her building.

'Imogen.' He caught up with her. 'That's not how it is.'

'I know,' she said as she turned to him. 'I'm sorry. But sometimes . . .'

'Sometimes what?'

'When I was small, I felt part of it,' she confessed. 'Part of how you lived. Especially in the summers, when we spent hours on the beach and your dad took us out in his boat and we played pirates in the garden. In the winter, when Mum and I were alone there together, the Villa Martine felt like our own house. But of course it wasn't and we weren't really part of the family. It was an illusion. Which is perfectly right, Oliver. I'm nothing. Nobody. Tonight, though . . . it all came rushing back, and I couldn't help envying how you all seem to have it mapped out. Even your parents' divorce doesn't seem to have caused a change in your lifestyle. Every one of you is someone *bien dans sa peau.* Comfortable with who you are. I contrast it with how utterly, utterly messed up my own life is and I wonder why it is that some people get it right while others . . . don't. You're right about another thing too – I should have pursued some kind of academic career, and I might have, only . . .'

'Only what?'

'I messed that up as well,' she said. 'I made poor choices. I'm trying to get over them. But today – tonight – reminded me of how damn silly they were and how stupid I am too.'

'You're not stupid, and everyone makes a silly choice at some time,' said Oliver. 'The thing is not to let it ruin your life. As your *maman* used to say to me: always look on the bright side. Count your blessings.'

Hearing him repeat Carol's words, exactly the way she used to say them, brought a rush of tears to Imogen's eyes.

'I'm sorry, I'm sorry,' said Oliver. 'I shouldn't have . . . Don't cry, Genie, please. Look, something's obviously gone wrong for you and naturally you're upset. Maybe I can help. Is there anything I can do?'

'No. No. I'm fine,' she said, brushing her tears away as he looked at her in concern. 'I'm being incredibly silly, Oliver.'

'No you're not.'

'I totally am.' She spoke firmly. 'Please forget I said anything.'

'Genie . . .'

'Thank you for a lovely day. Goodnight, Oliver.'

'It'd be nice to do it again.' He spoke gently. 'But for pleasure next time. Without me using you as our free entertainment consultant! We could go a little further. Bilbao perhaps, that would be nice. Or maybe Biarritz for a day – do you remember we went there with Mum and Dad when we were kids? It'd be fun. What d'you think?'

'I think you were very kind to bring me today,' said Imogen. 'But I don't need you to make up jobs you consider suitable for me out of some misguided sense of sympathy. I can look after myself.'

'Imogen . . .'

'Goodnight, Oliver,' she said.

He looked at her intently for a moment, then gave her an easy smile. 'Goodnight, Genie.'

She walked up the pathway and unlocked the door of the building.

She didn't look back.

Chapter 35

She hurried up the stairs and fumbled with the lock on the apartment door. She was close to tears again, and angry with herself because of it. She wished fervently that she hadn't gone anywhere with Oliver Delissandes today and that she hadn't met his mother either. She wished she didn't feel so lost all of a sudden, as though the Plan was unravelling around her.

She opened the door and walked into the living room. She blinked in surprise as she realised that the standard lamp in the corner was illuminated. And then she stood perfectly still, transfixed by the shock of seeing him there.

'Sweetheart.' Vince got up from the chair he'd been sitting in. 'I'm so glad I've found you at last.'

She couldn't speak. Even as he stood in front of her, she doubted the evidence of her own eyes. He'd found her. Against the odds. Despite the Plan.

'Well,' he said. 'Nothing to say to me?'

She remained silent.

'No apology for all the stress you've caused me? For the time I've had to spend looking for you?'

She stared at him.

'Not even a "pleased to see you"?'

'How . . .' She cleared her throat and formed the words with difficulty. 'How did you get into my apartment?'

'Your apartment?' he looked around. 'Yours, Imogen?'

'I live here.' Her voice was strangled.

'You live with me in Dublin,' he said. 'And I've come to take you home.'

'How did you get in?' she repeated.

'Your neighbours,' he told her. 'The two girls next door let me in.'

Imogen closed her eyes for a moment and remembered the day, just after she'd first moved in, when the twins had been locked out of their apartment. She'd allowed them in to hers, and then Nellie had climbed precariously from her balcony to theirs and got in through the open patio door. Imogen had been so traumatised by the potential for the young Australian to plunge to her death that she'd immediately insisted on keeping a spare key. They'd done the same for her. It had seemed a good idea at the time.

'They were delighted to discover that I was your boyfriend,' said Vince.

'Boyfriend?'

'Well, they might not have let me in if I'd said husband,' Vince told her, his voice calm and reasoned. 'In case you'd spun them some kind of story about leaving a man who didn't understand you. When the truth is I understand you only too well. Anyway, I told them I'd arrived as a surprise, and when you still hadn't come back after I'd gone for coffee, they were happy to let me in. I showed them photos of the two of us on my phone to prove that I was one of the good guys.'

Imogen heard his words but wasn't truly listening. She was asking herself what she'd done wrong. How he'd discovered she was in Hendaye in the first place.

'You led me on a merry dance around France,' he said, as though she'd asked the question out loud. 'Paris. Montpellier – a good one that, Imogen – Marseille. Here.'

'How?' she asked him finally. 'How did you find me?'

He took the printed photo of her and Gerry out of his pocket and handed it to her.

She stared at it in disbelief.

'Where did you see this?' she asked.

'TripAdvisor,' he said.

She felt sick. She hadn't wanted Samantha to take the damn photo in the first place, but she'd comforted herself with the fact that she couldn't be tagged in it and that Sam was a random stranger. But there were no random strangers on social media. Everyone was fair game.

'So who is he?' Vince's voice hardened.

'Nobody,' she said. 'The husband of the woman who took the photo. They were on holiday.'

'And you forced yourself into their company.'

'They asked me,' she said.

'They probably felt sorry for you,' said Vince. 'Thinking that you didn't have a man in your life.'

She said nothing.

'Despite the trouble and expense and heartache you've put me through, I forgive you,' Vince told her. 'Now get your stuff. We're going home.'

'No,' she said.

'Don't mess with me,' he said. 'I'm giving you another chance.'

'I don't want another chance from you,' she said. 'I came here to get away from you. I'm not coming back.'

'Of course you're coming back,' said Vince. 'You're my wife and you belong by my side.'

'No,' she said again.

'Don't try my patience,' said Vince. Then his voice suddenly softened. 'Look, I know you've been upset lately. I know you hoped you might be pregnant . . .'

'That's utter nonsense,' she said. 'Even though you say it to people all the time. I don't want a baby, Vince. And neither do you.'

'Let me be the judge of what I want,' he said.

'I know exactly what you want,' she said. 'You want me in your life and following your rules. You want someone to order around. You want to control me, Vince, but that's not going to happen any more. You don't love me and I don't love you. And I'm certainly not coming anywhere with you.'

'How can you say that?' asked Vince. 'When I've spent the last two weeks searching for you.'

'Wanting me back isn't the same as loving me,' she said.

'Of course I love you,' said Vince. 'You know I do. And I know you love me too, no matter what you're saying now. So sit down and let's talk about this like grown-ups.'

She shook her head.

'I'm not sitting down,' she said. 'And you have to leave.'

'Listen to me, darling,' said Vince. 'I accept that something I've said or done has upset you. And I'm upset too. I admit that I was very angry with you. Furious, in fact. I'm still a bit angry, there's no point in denying it. I still can't believe you'd walk out without talking to me first. But no matter who's right and who's wrong in this scenario, we're husband and wife and we do love each other. This is a blip.'

'I tried,' she said. 'I tried to do everything you wanted the way you wanted, but it was never enough. You kept changing the goalposts. I was always in the wrong.'

'That's not true,' said Vince. 'I agree I might have been a little bit compulsive about some things. I accept that. But I didn't blame you for everything.'

'You *always* blamed me!'

'If it seemed like that, I'm sorry,' said Vince. 'Maybe I need to look at myself a bit more.'

'A lot more,' said Imogen.

'You see.' He smiled at her, the smile that had once beguiled her, gentle and understanding. 'It's all about adapting and making it work.'

'I made it work,' she said. 'I'm the one who followed the rules. Who made sure that everything was where it should be. Who cooked the right meal on the right night. I'm the one who had to adapt all the time.'

'It's unfortunate if you feel that's the case,' said Vince. 'I didn't realise it was bothering you so much. You should have said something.'

'I did!' cried Imogen. 'But every time I opened my mouth, you made me feel as though I was being ridiculous. You told me that we needed the rules. You told me it was for my own good. You told me how you wanted me to dress. You messed up my relationship with my family.'

'Your family?' He raised an eyebrow. 'You used to say that I was all the family you needed. You called the others the peripherals. And when we met, you hadn't spoken to them in months.'

She looked shamefaced. 'That's true. Though I never meant Agnes and Berthe when I said that. But you're right about Kevin and Paula and Cheyenne. Boris too. I said some horrible things about them and I was wrong. They were the closest thing I had to family, after all.'

'Until I came along,' said Vince.

'And you stopped me from talking to them.'

'You're exaggerating,' said Vince. 'I never stopped you from talking to anyone. You told me that you were glad you didn't have to interact with Cheyenne and your stepfather any more. You were happy to walk away from them.'

'At the time I was,' she admitted. 'But that was my problem, not theirs.'

'Look.' Vince walked across the room and put his arm around her shoulders. 'We've made mistakes, both of us. We got it wrong. We need to make it right. And we can do that together. Because we belong together, Imogen. You belong to me. You know you do.'

She closed her eyes. She remembered when she'd first met him, when he'd persuaded her to have a coffee that she'd never really wanted, when he'd walked her to the bus stop even though she'd said she was fine on her own, when he'd given her his umbrella to protect her from the rain. She'd thought he was pushy and not really her type, but in the end she'd fallen for him because she was sure that everything he did was out of caring for her so much. And she had to accept some of the blame too. She was used to doing what other people wanted. At the start, Vince had treated her like a princess. A piece of fragile china. He asked her opinion on everything and it took her a long time to realise that what she thought was irrelevant. And in the end he chipped away at her self-confidence by constantly pointing out the mistakes she'd made and the rules she'd broken so that she began to believe that she truly would be hopeless without him.

It was only after Cheyenne's wedding that she realised she had to escape before she lost herself completely. So she'd begun working on her escape route. And she'd succeeded.

She'd got here and she'd got a job and she'd made friends and she was living a happy life. She thought about René, and how he treated her as a rational, sensible woman. And Max, who was always helpful. She thought about Céline, who'd become a good friend. And Oliver, with whom she'd spent such a lovely day, even if she'd messed up at the end. But she didn't feel hopeless about that. Just annoyed with herself for being silly. She thought about Lucie Delissandes, too, who hadn't looked at her with disgust as the daughter of the woman who'd wrecked her marriage, but had treated her with kindness and affection.

She thought about the life she'd built and the life she'd left behind.

Who was she, really? Imogen or Genie? The girl who'd married to feel secure and who'd followed the rules to stay that way? Or the one who'd run carefree along the beach not caring what the next day would bring?

Everyone wanted to be the person running on the beach, she said to herself, but whose life was really like that? Perhaps it was for the Delissandes, with all their privilege. But for Imogen and everyone else she knew, it was harder than that. It was about dealing with complicated situations. Like the accident that killed her dad. Like her mother's indiscretion. Like having to move every time she thought she'd found somewhere to stay. Like Agnes's Alzheimer's. None of it was simple. None of it was carefree. It was crazy to think otherwise.

'Stop faffing about, Imogen.' Vince whispered into her ear. 'It's time to leave all this behind. We're going home. And we're going now.'

She went into the bedroom. She stood in front of the mirror and looked at her clothes hanging on the rail. New clothes, bought since she'd arrived in Hendaye. Summer dresses. Shorts. Tops. And her navy suit, in the corner. It seemed a lifetime since she'd put it on for the trade exhibition.

'We're going to my hotel tonight,' Vince called to her. 'There's a direct flight to Dublin in the morning and I've booked us on it.'

Had he been so sure he'd find her? she wondered. But then, he was always sure. Always self-confident. And he was right to be. Because he'd succeeded. He was in her apartment. Despite all her precautions.

A sudden insistent knock at the door startled her and made her heart race.

'Imogen!'

It was René's voice, loud and urgent.

'Imogen! Are you OK? Open the door.'

She stepped out of the bedroom. Vince was standing beside the door. He put his finger to his lips.

'No need to answer it,' he murmured. 'Let them go away.'

'Imogen!' This time it was Oliver. 'Can we come in?'

'What are they saying?' asked Vince quietly.

'They want to come in,' she said.

He shook his head and put his finger to his lips again.

'Imogen!' Two voices together. Nellie and Becky, speaking

English. 'What's going on? Please open the door. If not . . .' There was a mumbled conversation on the other side, and then Nellie continued, 'If not, we'll climb over the balcony again.'

Imogen looked at Vince.

'I'm opening the door,' she said.

'No.'

'I'm not having them climbing into the apartment.'

'Let them try,' said Vince.

'Don't be so stupid.' She pushed past him and turned the handle. The door was locked. She hadn't locked it after her. So he must have, when she was in the bedroom.

'Imogen!' Both René and Oliver this time. 'Is that you in there?'

'For God's sake!' Imogen gasped as Vince pulled her away from the door before she could unlock it. 'Let them in.'

'Them? Them? Who are they?' he demanded.

'Friends.'

'Friends? Male friends, Imogen. You're married to me but you've made male friends?'

'And female friends,' she pointed out. 'They're people who live here.'

Before Vince could stop her, Imogen spun away from him and turned the key. At the sound of the click, the door was pushed open from the other side.

René, Oliver, Becky, Nellie and Céline spilled into the room.

'Imogen.' Oliver hesitated for a second as he saw Vince behind her. 'Are you OK?'

'I'm fine,' she said. 'Really. It's all . . . it's a misunderstanding. There's nothing to worry about.'

'Are you sure?' asked Céline. 'Because, *chérie*, you don't sound fine. And your dress . . .'

'That happened earlier.' Imogen glanced at the oil stain that had attracted Céline's attention.

'Is this your husband?' demanded René.

Becky glared at Vince, who put his arm around Imogen's shoulder again. 'He said he was your boyfriend.'

'Look, I don't understand half of what's being said here,' said Vince. 'But my wife has told you that she's fine. Now can you all get the hell out and leave us. Thank you.'

'Imogen, do you need help?' Oliver's dark eyes were fixed on hers. 'Tell me what you want and I will do it.'

'No French,' said Vince. 'If you have something to say, say it in English.'

'We are friends of Imogen.' It was René who spoke. 'We are concerned for her.'

'I'm Imogen's husband,' said Vince. 'And as you can see, there's nothing to be concerned about. She's packing. She's coming home with me.'

'You're leaving?' Oliver's eyes grew even darker as they shifted from Vince to Imogen.

'Of course she's leaving,' said Vince. 'She doesn't belong here.'

'Do you really want to do this, *chérie*?' asked Céline in her heavily accented English. 'Because if you don't . . .'

'I've asked once, politely, but I won't ask again,' said Vince. 'I want all you people to get out. Now.'

'If Imogen is leaving of her own free will, of course we will go,' said Oliver. He continued to keep his eyes fixed on her face. 'But, *ma p'tite*, if you want to stay, you only have to say the word.'

'She doesn't want to stay,' said Vince. 'She was packing when you started banging the door down.'

'Imogen?' Oliver spoke gently. 'What do you want to do?'

She couldn't believe that they were all here. Not knowing the situation, but clearly concerned. Looking out for her. Wanting to be sure she was OK. It was good of them to worry about her, but she was able to take care of herself. Besides, there was no threat to her physical safety from Vince. That wasn't how it worked. It wasn't how *he* worked.

'You get on with your packing,' Vince said to her. 'I'll get rid of this mob.'

'It's your choice, Imogen,' said Céline.

'I know.' Her voice was steady and determined. 'Thank you all for coming. I really appreciate it. It was good of you. But everything's all right.'

'You heard her,' said Vince. 'Now get the hell out, all of you. You're trespassing.'

They exchanged worried looks.

Then Imogen took a sideways step, so that Vince's arm was no longer around her shoulder. She looked at her friends and gave them a small smile before turning towards him.

'Everything's fine, but I'm not coming with you,' she said. 'I'm staying here.'

He stared at her in shock for a moment, then grabbed her by the wrist so that she gasped in surprise.

'You're doing no such thing,' he said. 'Leave your stuff behind. We're going right now.'

'No,' said Imogen. 'I'm not going anywhere with you, Vince. I've left you for good.'

'You damn well haven't!' Vince jerked her wrist as she tried to twist away.

Which was when Oliver punched him.

* * *

There was a stunned silence in the apartment as Vince sank to the floor with a grunt.

'*Trouduc!*' Oliver rubbed the knuckles of his fist against the palm of his other hand as he spat out the insult.

'Well done, whoever you are,' said Becky. 'He deserved it.'

'*Bien joué.*' Céline patted Oliver on the back.

'Shit,' said Vince, who was half lying, half sitting on the floor, holding his bloody nose. 'You maniac. I'll have you for this!'

'What the hell is going on here?' Max Gasquet, who'd just arrived home and had heard the disturbance, walked into the apartment. 'Here, let me.' He knelt down beside Vince and helped him to sit up. Then he pinched the bridge of his nose to staunch the flow of blood.

'Call the police.' Vince's voice was muffled. 'That man assaulted me.'

'What man?' asked Max.

'Me,' said Oliver.

'You hit him?' Max was incredulous.

'He was acting in defence.' There was a note of admiration in René's voice as he switched to French again.

Max looked at him enquiringly.

'Defence of Imogen,' explained René. 'This man is Imogen's husband.'

'Ah!' Max nodded to René. 'I'm sorry. I had to leave earlier to an emergency call. Otherwise I might have seen him before he got this far.'

He turned to Imogen. 'Has he hurt you?'

She shook her head.

'I told you before.' Vince's voice was still muffled. 'No French.'

Max continued to hold Vince's nose while the others watched. When the bleeding had finally stopped, he helped the other man to his feet.

'Why are you people still here?' asked Vince. 'I told you to leave.' He turned to Imogen. 'Give me your phone. I'm calling the police. I'm going to have them arrested for trespass and assault.'

'If you wish to call the police, that is up to you,' said Oliver. 'But please remember that Imogen opened the door and let us in. So we are not trespassing. We are concerned citizens.'

'Also,' added René, 'you should know that my cousin is a police officer.'

'Is he?' Imogen looked at René.

'Yes.'

'So if you wish to make a report to the police, Monsieur, I will take you myself.'

'Of course I'm going to make a complaint,' said Vince. 'But I'm certainly not going anywhere with you.' He looked at Imogen. 'You're going to come with me to report this disgraceful assault, and then we're going to the hotel. And I can assure you that this is the last night either of us will ever spend in France again.'

'Oh, Vince . . .'

'This is your chance,' he said. 'Your chance to prove that you love me. That all this was a cry for attention on your part. That you're not as stupid as you're appearing right now.'

'Don't call Imogen stupid!' It was Céline who spoke this time. 'She's a wonderful, intelligent person.'

'Get your stuff.' Vince ignored Céline. 'I've had enough of this bloody French farce.'

'I told you already,' said Imogen. 'I'm not going.'

'You heard that?' said Oliver. 'She's not going anywhere with you. So you're the one who'd better leave. Right now. Or I'll call the police myself and tell them you attacked her.'

'She's my goddam wife and I can do with her as I please,' said Vince.

There was a shocked silence.

'I didn't mean it like that.' He knew he'd made a mistake. 'I'd never hurt her. Tell them.' He turned to Imogen. 'Tell them,' he repeated.

'He wouldn't,' she assured them. 'Really he wouldn't. Not like that. But it doesn't matter. I'm not going anywhere with him. I'm going to divorce him.'

'Imogen!' He made to move towards her, but both Max and René held him back.

'I'm sorry,' she said. 'When I married you, I loved you. I really did. But it was a mistake, Vince. You know it and I know it. There's no point in pretending.'

'You'll be sorry,' Vince told her. 'You really will.'

'I don't think so,' she said.

'Right.' René looked at Vince. 'You're out of here. And I'm going to make sure of it by bringing you back to your hotel myself.'

'It's a hospital I need to go to,' said Vince as he touched his nose gingerly.

'You'll be fine.' René was unsympathetic. 'Now come on. Let's go.'

He hustled Vince out of the apartment. As soon as they'd gone, Imogen flopped into a chair. Céline sat beside her and took her by the hand.

'Are you OK?' she asked.

Imogen nodded.

'You need a brandy,' said Oliver, who began looking in her cupboards.

'I don't have brandy in the house,' said Imogen. 'I hate brandy.'

'Some tea, then,' said Céline. 'For shock. All my English friends tell me that, although I agree with Oliver. A brandy would be better.'

Oliver filled the kettle and found the tea. Meanwhile Max knelt in front of Imogen and checked her pulse.

'You seem fine,' he said.

'I *am* fine. Really. It's true what I said earlier. He wouldn't have hurt me.'

'He grabbed you by the arm,' said Oliver. 'He was going to drag you from your home.'

'I'm not sure you needed to hit him, though.' Her voice was stronger now.

'It's only the second time in my life I've ever swung a punch,' said Oliver. 'I know it was wrong and I know it was dangerous. But I was worried for you, Genie.'

'We all were,' said Becky.

'And I really appreciate your concern,' said Imogen. 'It was good of you to come to my rescue.'

'It was the least we could do after letting him into your apartment.' Nellie was contrite. 'But he seemed so nice . . .'

'That's the problem,' said Imogen. 'He can be very charming when he wants to be.'

'And you're sure he's never hurt you before?' Max asked as he finished his quick examination.

Imogen released a slow breath. Although she didn't really want to talk about Vince, her friends deserved some kind of explanation. So while Oliver handed around cups of tea, she told them a little of their life together and explained about the Plan.

'That's so cool,' said Becky when she'd finished. 'Setting up a secret bank account. Slipping away like that. Amazing.'

'And brave!' Céline clapped her hands together. 'You're a marvel, Imogen.'

'I'm not so sure about that.'

'Céline is right,' Oliver said. 'But then I always knew you were brave.'

'Always?' Céline glanced at him, a puzzled expression on her face.

'That's for another time,' said Imogen.

'I agree,' said Max. 'And now I think you should get some rest, Imogen. If you need anything at all, you know where I am.'

'Perhaps it would be better if you stayed with me tonight,' said Céline. 'You'd be very welcome.'

'That's sweet of you,' said Imogen. 'But I'm OK. Honestly. I'll stay here.'

'You have my phone number,' Céline said. 'Call if you need me.'

'Or us,' said Nellie. 'Bang on the wall. We'll come in straight away.'

'You've all been wonderful.' Imogen finished her tea. 'Thank you very much.'

They got up to leave.

'I'll wait,' said Oliver. 'Until I've heard from Bastarache that everything's OK.'

'You're sure you don't want to come to me?' Céline asked Imogen again.

'This is my home,' she replied. 'But thank you for the offer, Céline. I appreciate it.'

'OK then. I'll leave too.' She dropped a quick kiss on Imogen's cheek.

'*Au revoir.*' Max did the same.

'See you tomorrow,' said Becky as she and Nellie left.

Oliver closed the door behind them.

Chapter 36

'Well,' he said as he sat down again. 'That was an unexpected end to the day.'

'What on earth made you come to the apartment?' asked Imogen.

Oliver explained about Vince having accosted René earlier in the day. And told her that he'd been walking down the street after leaving her apartment when he'd seen René and Céline walking towards it.

'Céline suddenly remembered that I drove a Range Rover,' said Oliver. 'So she asked if I'd been with you. When I said that I'd just left you, they got very agitated and told me that your husband was looking for you and that they were worried about you. So we all came back to the apartment. Céline was distraught that it was her father who betrayed you.'

'Her father? How?'

Oliver explained how Bernard Biendon had given René's name to Vince.

'I never wanted Samantha to take that photo,' said Imogen. 'I had a horror of it appearing somewhere and Vince seeing it, although I never truly believed it would happen. I'd closed all my social media stuff so I thought I was safe enough.

Vince spotting it on TripAdvisor was the million-to-one shot that gave me away, not Bernard. He was asked a question and he answered it. I'm sure Vince would have found me with or without his input.'

'Nevertheless,' Oliver said, 'Céline reckons he should have known better. Men with photos asking about women – never a good thing in her view.'

'Oh well.' Imogen smiled. 'All's well that ends well, I guess.'

'Fortunately,' said Oliver. 'However, I agree with the others, Imogen. I don't think you should stay here tonight.'

'I doubt Vince will come back,' she assured him. 'Not after his bloody nose.'

Oliver took out his phone and dialled René's number. They spoke quickly to each other and Oliver nodded as he ended the call.

'Vince is at the hotel and René is going to bring him to the airport tomorrow. I said I'd go too. René is going to keep an eye on him overnight. But I'd still feel better if you weren't alone.'

'I'm not going to impose on Céline,' protested Imogen. 'She's supposed to be a client, after all.'

'I'm a client too,' he said, 'but I'd be a lot happier if you came to the Villa Martine.'

'Oh, Oliver, it's kind of you, but I'm not going to impose on you and your *maman* either.'

'It's not imposing.' Oliver spoke impatiently. 'It's being sensible. Staying with us would be a sensible thing to do, really it would.' Seeing the hesitation in her eyes, he added, 'If you want to stay here, that's your decision. But if you do, I'm going to sleep outside the door.'

She laughed.

'I'm serious,' he said. 'I don't care what you say about that guy; he grabbed you by the arm and he was going to hustle you away, and that's assault in my eyes.'

'Less of an assault than punching someone on the nose,' Imogen pointed out.

'*Touché*.' Oliver gave her a rueful grin.

'He won't come back,' she repeated. 'You've embarrassed him and he hates to feel embarrassed.' She hesitated for a moment and then gave him a faint smile. 'However, if it makes you feel better, I'll come with you. Mainly because I can't bear to think of you stretched out on the floor.'

'Good decision.' He smiled. 'Do you want to get some things before we go?'

She went back into the bedroom. Her clothes were still hanging neatly on the rail in the wardrobe. She hadn't packed any of them while she'd been alone with Vince. She'd never intended to. She'd been quite determined on that point. Even though the arrival of the others at her door had changed how things had developed, the bottom line was that Vince hadn't persuaded her that she should come back to Ireland with him. He hadn't managed to get inside her head as he'd done so many times before. She'd broken free of him. And now, no matter how difficult things were in the future, she knew she'd always be free of him.

She took her small case from the wardrobe and put a few things inside. Then she walked back to the living room.

She smiled at Oliver.

Her heart was light.

She felt good about life.

* * *

Lucie Delissandes was still sitting on the terrace when they returned. Her surprise at seeing Imogen turned to shock when Oliver gave her a distilled version of the evening's events.

'*Ma pauvre*,' she exclaimed, getting up and wrapping her arms around Imogen's shoulders. 'What a horrible thing. Are you all right now? You must have a brandy!'

'Everyone seems determined to get me drunk,' observed Imogen as Lucie hurried to the kitchen.

'It's restorative,' Lucie told her when she returned and handed her a glass.

'It's firewater,' gasped Imogen after she'd taken a sip. But even as she spluttered, she felt the golden liquid spread a warm glow through her body and she almost visibly relaxed.

'I will make sure that the guest room is tidy,' said Lucie.

'It is,' Imogen told her. 'I know, I cleaned it.'

'It seems somewhat *déclassé* that you had to do it for yourself,' said Lucie. 'However, I will take your word for it. Do you wish to go to bed now?'

At the mention of bed, Imogen was suddenly overwhelmed by tiredness, and she yawned involuntarily.

'I think that would be a good idea,' said Oliver. 'But not until you finish your brandy.'

It took her ten minutes, during which time Lucie went to check on the room anyway, and returned saying that it was indeed perfect.

'I will say goodnight myself,' she told Imogen, kissing her on both cheeks. 'Sleep well.'

'Thank you,' said Imogen.

She waited while Oliver locked the house, then followed him up the stairs.

'I have to say that this is weird,' she remarked as they stood outside the bedroom door.

'Somewhat,' he agreed. 'I hope you do sleep well tonight, Genie. It's been an eventful day.'

It seemed like a lifetime since he'd picked her up that morning to take her to San Sebastian. A lifetime in which she'd come face to face with her worst fear – that Vince would somehow be able to persuade her to come home again. And she'd overcome it. In that one day, she knew she'd changed for ever. She'd found her inner strength again and she was never going to lose it.

'Goodnight, Oliver,' she said as she opened the bedroom door.

'Goodnight,' he said.

Then, like his mother, he kissed her on the cheek.

She was so tired she thought she'd fall asleep straight away, but even as she drifted off, she told herself that she had to get in touch with Berthe and with Cheyenne and Shona to tell them what had happened. In their individual ways they'd given her strength over the past weeks, despite the fact that she'd been unwilling to open up to them completely. She should have said something before now, she acknowledged, instead of trying to pretend to herself and to everyone else that she and Vince were happy, and that he hadn't turned her into a shadow of the woman she used to be. She'd wasted five years of her life with him and she hadn't needed to.

Or perhaps she had, she thought, as she rolled over in the comfortable queen-sized bed. Perhaps she'd needed to go through all of it to be able to put things into perspective. Because she'd done that now. The past, the present and the future. Nothing as perfect as she'd wanted. None of it as scary as she'd thought. Maybe it was time she started to believe in her mother's clichés. Like always looking on the bright side and counting her blessings. Because there *was* a bright side, and one of her blessings was that there were people she could turn to. People who cared.

Mind you, she added, as she threw off the light coverlet because the night was warm, Mum was wrong about one thing. Running away actually did solve something. I'm glad about that. She smiled to herself. Then she closed her eyes and fell into a deep, dreamless sleep.

Vince didn't sleep. His nose was swollen and sore and one of his teeth was loose from where Oliver's punch had connected. He'd thought about going to the police station after René Bastarache dropped him at the hotel, but the estate agent hadn't left him alone there, instead telling him to get his things together, that they were going to stay in the twenty-four-hour coffee dock until dawn. At which point, he said, they'd be going to the airport together. He was going to put Vince on a flight out of France. Any flight. Vince was about to argue with him, but the other man was taller and stronger and suddenly it didn't seem worth the effort.

At around six thirty, after numerous coffees, he saw the man who'd punched him stride into the coffee bar and announce that he was there to bring them to the airport. The two Frenchmen bundled him into the Range Rover and drove for ninety minutes to Biarritz. Vince muttered about the car hire and René told him not to worry about it, that his cousin would sort everything out.

'If I'm stuck with extra charges because of this, I'll sue you,' Vince said. René laughed.

He almost allowed them to buy him a full-price ticket to another destination, but he'd checked both himself and Imogen in for the Ryanair flight to Dublin while he'd been waiting in her apartment. They walked with him as far as the departure gate.

'I don't want to see you back here. Ever,' said Oliver.

'I've no intention of returning to this hellhole,' said Vince. 'And you know what . . .' he looked from one man to the other, 'whichever of you is banging her, you're welcome to her. She's not that good anyway.'

For a moment he thought Oliver was going to punch him again, and he took an involuntary step backwards. But René put his hand on the other man's shoulder and Oliver relaxed.

'Know that Imogen has friends here,' said René. 'And that she will always be a treasured part of our lives. Whatever she might have to do to end her relationship with you, we will support and help her.'

'She's not worth it, you know,' said Vince. 'You'll find that out for yourselves. She was hopeless when I met her and she'll be hopeless again. She never deserved me. I'll be happy never to see her again.'

Then he walked through the departure gate and out of sight.

'What a pig,' said René as he and Oliver left the airport after watching Vince's flight take off. 'I can't believe she got involved with him.'

'She said last night that he was charming,' Oliver said. 'And kind to her at the start.'

'Women can be such fools over men.' René got into the car beside Oliver. 'But she will be happy here with us, don't you think?'

'I hope so.'

'And I hope you treat her better than he did.' René glanced at the man beside him.

'Don't talk nonsense,' said Oliver. 'Besides, Imogen isn't ready for anything like that.'

'I think Imogen is ready for anything she wants,' said René as he fastened his seat belt. 'And I would never bet against her.'

It was much later before Imogen herself woke up. She gasped in horror as she squinted at her watch and hurried into the bathroom for a quick shower before getting dressed. Then she brushed her hair, dabbed some moisturiser on to her face and hurried downstairs.

Lucie was sitting on the terrace, reading the newspaper.

'How are you, *ma p'tite*?' she asked. 'You look a lot better.'

'I feel fine,' said Imogen. 'Thank you for letting me stay.'

'You're more than welcome,' Lucie said. 'And you'll stay until Oliver returns from the airport, no?'

'So they've run him out of town?' The corners of Imogen's mouth twitched.

'Something like that,' agreed Lucie. 'Oh, Genie, I'm so sorry that this happened to you.'

'It's not your fault,' said Imogen. 'I was the one who made crappy choices. Truth is, I wanted to be in love with Vince more than I actually loved him. I told myself that it was good to have someone who cared so much that he wanted to make sure every aspect of my life was looked after.'

'Didn't you feel that anyone else cared?' asked Lucie.

'I felt . . .' Imogen paused as she gathered her thoughts. 'I felt as though I was always second choice. That whatever I wanted came after whatever anyone else wanted. Vince made me feel I came first. At least at the start. Obviously I'm a terrible judge of character.'

'We all make mistakes,' said Lucie. 'Don't beat yourself up about making one with a man. That's almost inevitable. I did it myself, after all. But why did you come back here to Hendaye? Why not anywhere else in the world? Oliver told me that your aunts are in America. Why didn't you go to them?'

'They have troubles enough of their own,' said Imogen. 'Berthe certainly didn't need me landing on her. Besides, I always felt that here was where I was happiest. Sure, Mum and I were living in your house, but we had total freedom. Nobody bothered us. I wanted to recapture that feeling.'

Lucie nodded. 'And the cleaning job?'

Imogen explained about renting the apartment from René and asking him for a trial as a cleaner.

'And it worked out perfectly,' she said. 'Obviously I was a little taken aback to have to clean the Villa Martine, but I thought it was serendipity really.'

'It is,' said Lucie. 'It's truly lovely to see you again. I often wondered about you, you know. You and your *maman*.'

'All she wanted was security for me,' Imogen said. 'She said that she loved Kevin and I believed her, but the truth was that she thought marrying him was a safe bet. And in a way it was, because after she died, he did his best. It wasn't his fault that his best wasn't what I thought I wanted. Which reminds me,' she added. 'I really must make some phone calls.'

'Use the telephone in the library if you want some privacy,' said Lucie.

'It's OK. I have my mobile. But I'll use the library to make the calls,' said Imogen.

She walked into the house and let herself into the room that had been Denis Delissandes' domain and which Oliver now used. There was an indefinable masculine scent in here, and she could recall Denis sitting behind the rosewood desk, reading glasses perched on his head or sliding off the tip of his nose.

She sat in the leather armchair and dialled Cheyenne's number. Her stepsister answered on the first ring.

'Oh, Imogen! It's so good to actually hear your voice. I've been worried about you.'

As Imogen told her what had been going on, culminating in the events of the previous night, Cheyenne exclaimed over and over that she should have called sooner, or come to England, or asked for some help.

'I was too embarrassed,' said Imogen. 'I know that sounds ridiculous, but I thought you'd all laugh at me.'

'Why on earth would we do that?' demanded Cheyenne.

'Because I was a snotty little cow when I was younger,' said Imogen. 'And I thought you might believe I deserved everything I got.'

'That's absurd,' said Cheyenne. 'You're my sister. Why would I think that?'

'I sometimes felt like the cuckoo in the nest,' admitted Imogen. 'Mum and I barged into your lives and then Mum died and I was left and I was in the way. And instead of being grateful that you and your dad were there for me, I resented it.'

'You could be a bit of a pain,' agreed Cheyenne. 'But then so could I. We were teenagers after all. We had fun together when we ganged up on Dad, though. We made his life a misery over Paula, remember.'

'I guess.'

'You've blown things up out of all proportion,' said Cheyenne. 'You need to visit. Get it all into perspective again.'

'I'd like that.'

'So would I,' said Cheyenne.

'Soon,' Imogen promised. 'When I get myself together. I'm sorry I didn't confide in you. It might have been a better option.'

'Oh well,' said Cheyenne cheerfully. 'I'm glad it's turned out OK. And I'm doubly glad you've left him. He was a . . . I won't say it, Imogen. In case you ever get back with him and hate me for ever for making snide remarks about him.'

'That's never going to happen,' Imogen assured her. 'I've broken away from him, and it's for good.'

'I'm truly delighted,' said Cheyenne. 'And I look forward to seeing you soon.'

'Me too,' said Imogen. 'Tell Kevin I was asking after him. Paula too.'

'OK,' said Cheyenne. 'Take care, Imogen.'

Her next call was to Shona, who sighed with relief at the sound of her voice.

'I didn't know what to do!' she wailed. 'Part of me hated you for walking away without a word to anyone. Part of me felt so sorry for Vince. And yet when he went to France to find you, I was scared of what might happen if he did.'

'He got punched in the face,' said Imogen.

'You actually *punched* him?' Shona's voice was full of disbelief.

'Of course I didn't.'

'Who then?'

'A friend. Anyway, as my mum used to say, all's well, et cetera, et cetera.'

'What are you going to do now?' asked Shona, who wanted to know more about the punching but could tell that Imogen wasn't going to be forthcoming, at least for now.

'Take some time to think about things,' Imogen said. 'I'll be in touch, though.'

'I wonder will Vince call me.' Shona sounded anxious.

'Most likely he'll cut you out of his life,' said Imogen. 'That's what he does to people who annoy him.'

'You should have told me,' said Shona. 'I'd've helped, you know I would.'

'I know that now,' she said. 'Back then . . . back then, he had me believing that the only person I could really talk to was him. I know it might sound bizarre. I'm not a stupid browbeaten woman. I can stand up for myself. But not against Vince. There's something about him . . .'

'Yes, there is,' agreed Shona. 'I felt it too whenever he was with me. And when he told me about you and the baby—'

'There was no baby,' said Imogen. 'There was never going to be a baby with him. He didn't want one either, but he used the idea to manipulate people's thoughts.'

'He certainly had me in a total mess,' agreed Shona. 'But the important thing is that you're OK. Please keep in touch with me, Imogen. Let me know what's happening.'

'I will,' said Imogen. 'I promise.'

It was too early to make a call to Berthe, so she put her phone in the pocket of her shorts and went outside again.

She was surprised to see Giles Delissandes on the terrace with his mother.

'Imogen.' He smiled at her. '*Maman* has been telling me. You've been through an ordeal.'

'It all sounds worse than it was,' said Imogen. 'And everyone's been so wonderful to me that I can't really claim to have had much of an ordeal at all.'

'It *was* an ordeal,' said Lucie firmly. 'Would you like coffee, Imogen?'

'That would be lovely,' she said.

Lucie made coffee for the three of them, and they were drinking it and nibbling at croissants when Oliver returned.

'He's gone,' he said. 'We waited until the flight took off before we left.'

'You and René both?' asked Imogen.

'For sure,' said Oliver. 'We didn't want him coming back and hassling you.'

She released her breath slowly.

'I still can't quite believe it happened. He came, he found me, he's gone.'

'With a sore nose and a black eye and his tail between his legs.'

'Black eye? Oh, Oliver.' Lucie's attempt to look stern failed as much as Oliver's effort to appear repentant.

'It gave me great satisfaction to give it to him,' he said.

'You hit him?' Giles looked surprised. 'I didn't think you were that kind of man, Oliver. Fighting over a woman, no less. Bravo.'

'They weren't fighting over me,' said Imogen hastily.

The brothers laughed and Lucie sighed.

'I tried to bring them up properly,' she said. 'But I failed miserably.'

'You did a great job, Madame,' said Imogen. 'Now, I'd better go. Given that I know I'm definitely not going to be accosted in my apartment, I'll leave you in peace. Thank you so much for your hospitality.'

'You're very welcome,' said Lucie. 'And I do hope you'll visit us again. Not as a cleaner,' she added. 'We cannot have you cleaning for us, Imogen. It won't do. You're a friend. Part of the family.'

'I'm really—'

'I've spoken to René about it already,' said Oliver. 'He's reassigning you.'

'One of the things that drove me crazy with Vince was the fact that he liked to arrange things on my behalf,' said Imogen. 'I can look after myself. Really I can.'

'It's not for your comfort, it's for ours,' said Oliver. 'I can't bear to think of you cleaning up after me. That's all. Now come on, Imogen. I'll drive you home.'

She was going to say that she could walk, but it was already hot and so she simply nodded and thanked him before embracing Lucie and Giles and getting into the Range Rover.

They didn't speak on the short drive to her apartment, but as they drew near, Oliver pointed out the spot where he'd met Céline and René the previous night.

'I do appreciate how you all rushed in to save me,' said Imogen when they pulled up outside the building.

'Any time,' Oliver said. 'It was great for my ego to rescue a damsel in distress.'

'I was going to say that I wasn't in distress and I had everything sorted,' Imogen told him. 'But the truth is, I don't know what would have happened. I'd made up my mind, you see, that I wasn't going with him. I'd never actually defied him before.'

'Was it really awful, living with him?' asked Oliver as they both got out of the car.

'In retrospect,' said Imogen. 'Well – I ran away. That tells its own story. But the thing is, it was slow. It started off with his housekeeping rules, which I thought were a bit daft but also sort of cute. Then it was my clothes. And my hair. Things I said. Him always answering the phone and opening the post. I didn't quite realise how much they were all adding up at first. And when I did, it was too late. I couldn't talk to him. The only thing I was able to do was run.'

Oliver hugged her, and she let him. Then they walked up the path to the apartment together.

'I didn't realise there was blood on your floor,' said Oliver when she let them in.

'It'll come off.' Imogen left her bag inside the door and fetched some kitchen towel, which she used to clean the floor. Then she flushed it down the toilet.

'A bit daft, I know,' she said. 'But I don't want anything of him in my home.'

'Naturally,' said Oliver.

They stood silently for a moment.

'Would you like to meet me a little later?' asked Oliver. 'A drink, something to eat perhaps . . .'

She said nothing.

'I'm not trying to muscle in,' he added. 'Realising there's a vacancy for a man in your life and all that. Or maybe I am. I don't know. I just . . . I enjoyed being with you yesterday. I'd like to see you again. I realise this might not be the right time and that it's possibly a little strange, having known you so long ago. Like meeting a childhood sweetheart again.'

She'd told Céline she hadn't had a childhood sweetheart. That was true. Oliver hadn't been one. They hadn't cared about each other except as people to tease and irritate and play pirate games with. He'd actually been quite annoying as a boy.

Not now.

'It's nice of you to ask,' she said. 'But I think I need some time on my own. To reflect. To think about the future.'

'Of course.'

'Another time, perhaps?' she suggested.

'Another time.' He kissed her once on each cheek. And then, so gently that it hardly seemed to have happened at all, a fleeting brush of his lips over hers before he let himself out of the apartment.

Chapter 37

The dinner two weeks later was Céline's idea. Everyone who had been at Imogen's apartment on the night of her show-down with Vince was invited: Becky and Nellie (who'd delayed their return to Australia), René, Max and Oliver. When they all accepted, Céline suggested that it might be nice if all of the Delissandes came too.

'And your sister and brother-in-law if they're still here,' she said. 'Let's make it a fun night.'

Cheyenne and Richard had turned up the day after Imogen had called to tell her what had happened.

'Someone punched Vince on the nose?' said Cheyenne, as they sipped wine in the garden outside Imogen's apartment. 'I'd like to meet him!'

'You will if you stay for the dinner,' said Imogen. 'I'm not sure why Céline wants to do it, to be honest.'

'It's a wonderful idea,' Cheyenne told her. 'And we'd be delighted to stay. We haven't been away at all this year and the Hotel Atlantique is great. I'm sure Dad and Paula would love to visit some time.'

'I'll call him soon,' Imogen told her.

'He'd like that,' said Cheyenne.

'I wish I could be with you too,' said Berthe the following day, when Imogen phoned. 'But obviously I can't leave Agnes. I hope you have a lovely night, Imogen.'

'I'm sure it'll be fun,' said Imogen. 'And I'll try to visit you both before the end of the year.'

'That would be wonderful,' said Berthe. 'I miss you.'

'I miss you too. I promise I'll get to you when I can.'

It would be fun to visit her aunts in the States, she thought as she ended the call. They'd been invited before, but Vince had never wanted to go. Now she was free to do as she pleased. It was exhilarating.

She arrived at the restaurant exactly on time, and Bernard himself greeted her, then immediately began to apologise for giving Vince the information that had led to him tracking her down. Imogen waved away his apologies and told him that he would have found her anyway. Besides, she said, it had been a good thing that he had showed up.

'It was time for me to meet him,' she assured Bernard. 'I couldn't keep hiding for ever.'

Bernard gave her a gruff kiss and told her that she was a gem of a girl and that some man would be lucky to have her. At which Imogen said that no man was ever going to have her in the way that Vince had wanted – ownership of her and everything to do with her. The next time I meet a man, she said, it will be a partnership. Fifty-fifty.

'You might be waiting a long time in that case.' Bernard winked at her.

'As long as it takes,' Imogen said.

He brought her to the dining room, where the other guests had already assembled.

Céline had done place settings with names in front of them, and Imogen found herself between Oliver and Cheyenne, with René directly opposite her. She noted with interest that Céline had placed herself between her ex-husband and Max Gasquet. She also noticed that Céline hadn't invited Art, and that she was allowing René to monopolise her conversation.

The meal was as good as any that Bernard had ever served, with starters of onion squash, red tuna and goat's cheese, followed by delicately cooked filet mignon, seafood risotto and spiced chicken. Céline's mother, Florence, had made lemon tarts and strawberries dipped in dark chocolate for dessert, and by the time they got to coffee, Imogen was grateful that she'd worn a floaty summer dress in yellow and purple that allowed its wearer to overindulge at the table.

'That was the best meal of my life and I can't eat another thing,' she told Oliver.

'Indeed it was,' agreed Oliver. 'A toast to the chef!'

They all raised their glasses, while Bernard and Florence beamed with delight.

'It's just as well I'm not living here,' Cheyenne murmured. 'I'd find it very hard to stick to my diet.'

'What diet?' Imogen gave her a sceptical glance. 'You look fantastic, Chey.'

'Because of my current diet,' retorted Cheyenne. 'I could still do with losing a few pounds. But then I'm always trying to lose a few pounds, with very limited success.'

Imogen grinned. 'Remember the beetroot diet? And the green-foods-only one? You were bonkers back then.'

'Oh yes.' Cheyenne nodded. 'And the water-and-lemon one too. I try to be a bit more sensible these days, but I'll never find one that'll make me look like Céline. Or Lucie – what a fab body she has for her age.'

'They both seem to eat like horses, so it's probably down to genes,' said Imogen.

'I hate that it might be true that French women don't get fat,' Cheyenne said. 'Although if it is, staying here might be a good idea.'

'I doubt I'll stay for ever.' Imogen smiled. 'But maybe long enough to develop really good eating habits again. Although if I come here too often, I can't see it having the desired results!'

'Your *papa* excelled himself tonight,' murmured René to Céline while Imogen and Cheyenne were chatting. 'I swear to God he gets better every year.'

'Maturing with age,' Céline said. 'Like a good wine.'

'Or a bad husband,' said René.

She glanced at him. His expression was serious.

'You admit you were a bad husband?' She raised a delicately shaped eyebrow.

'I was a shit husband,' he said. 'And I don't know why, because I was a good boyfriend.'

'That happens,' said Céline. 'Imogen thought Vince would be good for her, but he wasn't.'

'You're not comparing me to that *salaud*, I hope.'

'Of course not. With you, René Bastarache, there was always something to love. With him – there was nothing about him I could like. Nothing at all.'

'And is there still something in me you could love?' he asked.

'We got divorced for a reason,' Céline told him. 'That reason hasn't changed.'

'I hope I'm a better man than when I married you,' said René. 'I'd like to think I've learned a lot since then. I don't know if I'd ever be good enough for you, Céline Biendon. Nevertheless, we could . . .' He shrugged. 'We could try a little moment or two again.'

'If you're trying to get back into my bed, you've another think coming,' she said.

'Not back into your bed,' said René. 'Back into your heart.'

'Honeyed words, René.'

'But true ones.'

She stared at him.

'I mean it,' he said. 'I used to think you should be grateful for me. Grateful that I chose you. That I offered my advice. When the truth is that I'm the one who should have been grateful to you. I'm a fool, and I'm more like Imogen's husband than I thought.'

'You're nothing like him,' said Céline.

'Nevertheless, he made me see . . . well, I have things still to learn. I'm not expecting you to jump at the chance. I'd like it if you'd think about it, though.'

His hand met hers beneath the table. He squeezed it.

'No promises,' she said.

'No pressure,' said René.

Becky and Nellie were talking about their return to Australia, telling Giles Delissandes that they'd be sorry to leave France but quite glad to get back to Sydney.

'You should visit,' Becky said to him. 'You'd like it.'

'I'm sure I would.'

'Definitely.' Nellie nodded. 'Think of the open spaces, and lots of surfing . . .'

'Like Hendaye,' he said.

'The same. But different.' Nellie grinned at him and flicked her blond hair over her shoulder.

'My God,' said Giles. 'You're flirting with me.'

'You've only noticed that now! I must be losing my touch.'

'What's it like with twins?' asked Giles. 'Does one of you get annoyed if the other . . . you know . . . has somebody?'

'We share.' Becky spoke with a straight face.

'You . . . Wow.'

The two girls burst out laughing. And although Giles laughed too, he couldn't help feeling slightly disappointed at the fact that they were joking.

Lucie had got up from the table and was talking to Florence.

'Do you ever stop worrying about your children?' she mused as she looked at Oliver, Charles and Giles laughing and joking and not giving her the slightest thing to worry about at all.

'I don't think so,' said Florence. 'I'm worrying about Céline now, seeing her head so close to René's, knowing that he's doing his best to seduce her. Again.'

'How long were they married?' asked Lucie.

'Two years.'

'Maybe they gave up on it too soon.'

'Maybe. Or maybe she saw sense in time. As for poor Imogen! Five years, and half of it planning to get away from him.' Florence shook her head. 'I feel so sorry for her.'

'She's got a strong core,' Lucie said, as Imogen laughed at something Oliver had said. 'She always did. I remember her as a little one, toughing it out with my sons, going head to head with them all the time. She put ants in Oliver's bed once to teach him a lesson. She's brave, that one. A survivor.'

'Strange, then, that she let him manipulate her so much.'

'I suppose we all have times when our defences are down,' said Lucie. 'That's when we make mistakes. Realising it is the key thing. Not making them again is the result of learning. Genie is a quick learner.'

'She seems very close to your eldest,' remarked Florence.

'Which is a little disconcerting, I have to admit,' admitted Lucie. 'And yet . . .' She looked again; this time Imogen was shaking her head at Oliver. 'They go well together, don't they?'

'I rather think they do,' said Florence as Imogen said something that made Oliver put his arm around her and give her an enormous hug.

'Stop it!' Imogen said, although she was laughing. 'You're giving your *maman* ideas.'

'Good,' he said.

'It would do her head in,' Imogen said. 'The idea of you and me.'

'It doesn't do my head in,' said Oliver.

'You're being terribly nice to me and you've done wonders for my self-confidence,' said Imogen. 'But we're just friends.'

'*Zut.*' Oliver's tone was light-hearted. 'And there was me thinking we could be so much more.'

He was smiling as he took his arm from her shoulders. But his smile faded when Imogen got up from the table and went to talk to Max Gasquet, who was sitting back in his chair and allowing the conversation to flow around him.

* * *

They walked along the moonlit beach afterwards, in groups of two and three, revelling in the warm night air. It was Charles who suggested a race.

'Me and Oliver against Genie,' he said. 'Like the old days.'

'I can't possibly run,' protested Imogen. 'Not after all that food.'

'We're all equally handicapped,' Charles pointed out. 'Everyone ate far more than was good for them.'

'Come on, Genie.' Oliver smiled at her. 'For old times' sake.'

'You used to tell me about those races,' Cheyenne said to her. 'You always insisted you'd win one day.'

'Now's your chance,' said Charles.

'But you don't stand a chance,' Oliver teased.

'Is that a challenge?' She took off her wedge sandals. 'I could never turn down one of your challenges, Oliver Delissandes. Though I'm not sure about running in this dress. It'll get in the way.'

'When you were small, you used to tuck your dress into your knickers,' Lucie told her.

'I'm certainly not doing that now!' Imogen looked horrified. 'Where do we start, and how far?'

'At this rock here,' suggested Charles. 'As far as the beach hut?'

'That's miles!' wailed Imogen as she took up her position. 'I'll collapse before I ever get there.'

'You and me both,' muttered Oliver.

'Ready. Steady. Go!' cried Lucie.

They started to run to the cheers of the others. It came back to Imogen then. The sand beneath her feet. The sound of the waves breaking on the shore. The feeling of exhilaration as she abandoned herself to the sheer joy of moving as fast as she could. Her mind and her body as one. And because she'd spent so much of the last few years on the treadmill with Shona pushing her hard, she was a stronger runner than she'd been before. Fitter too. Fitter than Oliver and Charles. Fitter and faster. So that for the first time ever, she crossed the finish line ahead of them.

She stood panting as they caught up with her, and then shrieked as Oliver picked her up and swung her into the air.

'I never thought you'd beat me,' he said as he planted a kiss full on her lips. 'Well done, Genie.'

'Better late than never.'

It was another of her mother's favourite clichés. And as she kissed Oliver in return, Imogen suddenly realised that it could apply to more than just the race.